Truth & Dare

Truth & Dare

20 Tales of Heartbreak and Happiness

Edited by Liz Miles

RP|TEENS
PHILADELPHIA · LONDON

Constable & Robinson Ltd
3 The Lanchesters
162 Fulham Palace Road
London W6 9ER
www.constablerobinson.com

First published in the UK by Robinson,
an imprint of Constable & Robinson, 2011

A copy of the British Library Cataloguing in Publication
Data is available from the British Library

UK ISBN 978-1-84901-586-8

1 3 5 7 9 10 8 6 4 2

Printed in the United States

First published in the United States in 2011 by Running Press Book Publishers

9 8 7 6 5 4 3 2 1
Digit on the right indicates the number of this printing

Library of Congress Control Number: 2010941312
US ISBN 978-0-7624-4104-4

Published by Running Press Teens
an imprint of Running Press Book Publishers
2300 Chestnut Street
Philadelphia, PA 19103-4371

Visit us on the web!
www.runningpress.com

Contents

Introduction

You know those intriguing warnings you get before the start of a suspect TV show or movie, such as: "This show contains scenes that some viewers may find disturbing" or "This program contains strong language?" Or those little letter-symbols that pop up in the corner of the TV screen, such as TV-PG-S (parental guidance suggested, due to possible sexual situations)? Well, as a "responsible editor" I wondered—should we slap one or two of those on the front of the book? But then I thought . . . No, the title *Truth & Dare* does the job. It entices—just as those TV warnings focus rather than diminish our attention—and it kind of warns, too (I mean, truth-seekers and their daring lives aren't all sweetness and light, are they?).

In fact *Truth & Dare* pretty much says it all, and gives a feel for all the glorious colors that you can expect to find in this anthology: from thrilling red to edgy black (not forgetting lots of banana-yellow laughs). So re-read the title, then it's up to you—do you dare to read on?

When I was asked to gather some stories for an anthology called *Truth & Dare* I was jumping around like crazy. Because right away I wanted to do something really daring so I could write a story about it and put it in myself. But time was too short to achieve a shockingly daring incident (deadlines), so instead I imagined, then I excitedly phoned, tweeted, emailed and searched under the bed for the utterly skilled authors who *really* know about/feel "this kind of thing." I wanted the best: the biggest dares, the funniest dares, and I wanted truths—or at least an inkling of a few. Plus confessions—how teens feel as they search around looking for those Love, Sex, Work, How-Do-I-Look?, Friendship, and Who-Am-I? answers.

And I got all of it. I think so anyway. So many laughs along the way, too. After reading through the stories now—the whole anthology—I realize that, perhaps, the whole of life is like one big game of "Truth or Dare." I wonder if you'll agree?

Liz Miles

Girl Jesus on the Inbound Subway

BY MATTHUE ROTH

THE SAVIOR OF the universe is a girl in a trench coat, a hoodie, and twenty-pound headphones, and more than anything I want her to kiss me.

Not to talk to me—because I'd try to pay attention, and then I'd get hung up on her intentions, and the sound of the words, and to whatever it is that she'd be saying to me in the first place—and I don't want her to listen to me, either, since I doubt anything would get through those manhole-sized earmuffs anyway. And I definitely don't want to kiss *her*, because there's no way I could do justice to those thin, unwavering, Mona Lisa pencil-sharp lips of hers. Also, there'd be all these expectations. What would we do next? Whose move did it count as, since it was my stare but her kiss? And both of us wondering: what does it *mean*?

No. What I want right now is for her to smile at me like she knows that I need it, share a deep, eye-sex look that says she knows exactly what I'm thinking and she doesn't want to talk about it either, in Russian, or English, or any other language that either of us might speak, and then I want her to make out with me.

I don't mean kissing, in that soft, understanding, grace-and-stuffed-bunny-rabbits way. I mean grabby, desperate,

3

forget-everything-else-because-all-we-have-is-each-other Hooking Up.

And that's why I say she's my savior. Because she has the kind of eyes you can get lost in, and the kind of face you can believe in. Because—and I realize that looks don't really matter, but I *need* something to believe in, something to trust—she looks like the kind of person who I'd want to be my friend.

The subway comes. It's an answer to our prayers. It's also a huge interruption to a conversation that we haven't actually started having yet. By now, though, I know her so well that I can sit down right next to her and ask her why she's not in school and tell her the reason I'm not there either—except that, again, there's this whole thing of us not having spoken yet. It's the most deserted hour of the subway day, past lunch and not yet rush hour, so we have a whole car to ourselves.

I climb in first and sit near the empty conductor's booth, staring in through the one-way glass. She enters and, though the car's completely empty, she sits down right across from me. *Victory!* my mind screams at me, which only compounds when, upon sitting in the next row over—in one of the backwards seats that's actually facing me, no less—she offers me a smile.

And we sit.

And we sit.

We sit in silence as the subway rolls out of the station into open air, then disappears beneath the city's steel belly. We ride through Margaret & Orthodox Station, then Church, Tioga, and on, halfway across the city, eyes focused severely on each other and not saying a word. At Girard Avenue, for a quarter of a block, the subway rises above the wall-to-wall row of houses brushing up against each other, stops running along Frankford Avenue and starts to soar above it, hovering over the afternoon traffic (On its way to an early concert festival on the waterfront, racing to catch the first opening band? Leaving work early to make an Atlantic City casino run?) and you can see the Ben Franklin Bridge, a dreamlike periwinkle blue against the flatter and more mundane blue of the river.

As soon as the subway hits open air, she jumps out of her seat and throws both arms in the air, spreading out her glove-encased fingers wide, like an orchestra conductor at the grand apex of the final encore of the night. And I hear that very same orchestra in my head, every violin broiling like an electric guitar, and I think to myself, *This is it. Now's the time.*

If we are going to kiss, make it now, and give it everything you've got.

The moment goes.

She sits down, offers me a brief but comradely conspiratorial grin, and literally collapses back into her seat. "Sorry," she says to me. "Just needed to get that out."

Da, I am about to tell her, *I understand more than you would know.*

I am astounded. I am captivated. But I can't do it myself. From here on out, it would only seem like an imitation.

The lights flicker. We are back underground.

We reach my stop. It occurs to me that the name has never sounded more appropriate: *stop.* Doors slide open, the exit beckons, and I feel like saying goodbye. The train station is looking its most splendid shade of desolate, as if, somewhere in Heaven, there is an angel whose job it is to run down this specific subway station. Half of it is boarded up, a man with bubbly cartoon eyes sits monitoring the other half, perched atop a fence, slurping up God knows what from inside a brown paper bag, and I regret ever coming here, and I wish I didn't have to. I actually wish that I was back in school. For the past half hour, the train car has become my own personal haven, sanctified almost, and I don't want to give it up.

I especially don't want to give *her* up.

I almost do say goodbye to her—my courage, though small, nonetheless exists—except that, while I'm doing my getting-off-the-train rite of checking the seat to see if I've forgotten the book that I forgot to bring in the first place, and sliding over to the nearest pole to lift myself up—I notice that she's not sitting there any more, she's already gone.

I jump up, breeze out the doors at the last possible moment, just as that voice is finishing announcing the name of the next stop. Why do they wait until after the doors close to tell you the stop's name? So you can be absolutely sure you've missed your station? Everyone is against me. Everyone.

And, in that split second when the doors are shutting and most (but not all) of my body is through the door but I *know* I'm gonna get my leg or my shirt sleeve or my backpack caught—that thing has more subway door-torn strings than a rat's ass—I realize, Jesus Girl's already gotten off.

• • •

I am not imagining her. I repeat this in my head like I'm trying to convince myself. Do I sound desperate? Yes, I've sounded like that since I started sounding like anything. Well, dreams are for desperate people. And people have always said I'm a dreamer.

The street yanks on the cuff of my dreams and smashes me into the cement of reality. Harsh daylight, screaming horns, and street vendors trying desperately to sell the passerby absolutely anything—bootleg CDs, AAA batteries, knitted pom-pom hats, even though it's warm enough for shorts. This morning, the aluminum walls of my bedroom in our sorry white-trash excuse for a house were burning up. The outside exacerbated the effect, rendering the place all but completely uninhabitable after 8 a.m.

I went into the kitchen and stuck my head in the freezer. My dad snored loudly, his head on the table where a bowl of cereal ought to be. Next to him, in place of the milk, stood an empty glass bottle. His phlegmy snores sounded eerily distended, warped by the wood polymer of the table.

"You want to buy that?"

The vendor's cold voice cuts through my acrid daydream. I almost want to hand him a twenty and tell him, *Keep the change*, just to thank him for getting me out of there.

I take a final look at the film I'm holding. "Fifteen bucks for *Godfather*, man?" I spit, tossing it messily back on to the pile. "I could steal it from my grandfather for free."

I'm lying, and he knows it. Poor Russian kid, doesn't even have the money to spend on shoes that aren't from Payless— this is a guy who makes his living reading people, and he knows that I sure ain't in the market for new DVDs. "Right," he snorts at me. "You gonna go to Siberia to do it?"

Everyone is laughing, even the other vendors. The people on the street. I move on, feeling like I did it again, tripped over my tongue and landed in a puddle of mud. I want to grow a shell, duck inside it, and twist myself into the turtle equivalent of the fetal position.

This is what they don't know, what they can't read in my face: I've got enough in my pocket to buy the whole table. The other tables, too. The idea that it's right there in my pocket makes me suddenly nervous for the first time since getting on that bus, as if people could smell the scent of it on me. I take one last suspicious glance at the crowd—as if anyone's going to be wielding a ski mask and a Saturday night special—and, two tables down, kneeling over a used book bin, is the girl from the train.

As if doing weird synchronous exercises, she throws down the book she's reading the inside front cover of and jumps into a heady walk, moving as though she's on a tight deadline. I have to remind myself, I'm on a deadline too—and I follow up her briskness with my own.

It feels pretty amazing to walk in the city. Some days, the skyscrapers reduce you to a maggot-sized nothing. Others, they reflect the sun so bright that you feel like you own them. It's impossible to predict what kind of day you'll have until you're in the middle of it. Today, in spite of everything, was turning out to be a Number Two kind of day.

To get to the office, I didn't have to make any turns or deviations—just follow Girard Avenue all the way down. I'd heard my dad talk about the walk countless times, from when he'd gone there to pay the rent before. The managers for the landlord company were all-right people. Have the check in the mail by the first of every month, and you were square in their books—but miss that deadline, and you were straight out of luck: straight to their office in North Philadelphia, with cash only (no personal checks accepted) in a plain white envelope, due by 3 p.m. on the fourth of the month, or else.

Usually my parents made the mail deadline. Sometimes they forgot about it till school let out, and they'd send me running to the post office, a twenty-minute walk away from our house, fifteen minutes before it closed. Other times there'd be something—a payout they were waiting for, a check that wouldn't clear for another day or two—and then my dad would go to the bank, withdraw our entire fifteen-hundred-dollar rent in cash, and brave the Philadelphia subway for a morning full of fun.

And usually he wasn't too drunk to.

He's a good man, my father. Funny, clever, good humored and well read, always ready to jump into a conversation or take a friend's good news with as much joy as he would his own. There were men in Little Russia who beat their children, or their wives, or who always veered on doing so. My father has never so much as raised his voice at either one of us. But life is hard, and things are expensive, and I can feel the strain in his voice when I ask for a bus fare, or when bills come in, or when I say I don't feel like running errands for them.

He's completely imperfect, and within that, he's kind of perfect at being that way. And I feel guilty for feeling this way, but I know that I hate him for it.

And now you see why I don't like to talk about it. And why having someone to ride the train with, in complete and utter silence, and not having to start a conversation or talk about what was on our respective minds, was just fine with me.

• • •

For a moment I fear losing her, but I cross the street and she's right there, halfway down the block, like a promise of a better day.

The buildings are starting to thin out, skyscrapers giving way to fast-food restaurants and blocks of once-mighty Victorian homes in Ozymandian condition. It's sad how everything crumbles, but that's what it's supposed to do, as my father would say. Only he'd say it all cheerful, like death is a part of life and it's one more thing to look forward to. It's living that's no walk in the park.

Park! I pass a sign with the name of the street I'm supposed to turn onto, a street that couldn't look less like a park if it really put its mind to the task. Slabs of concrete, a computer-monitor shade of gray, alternate with rusting shacks that should be condemned and probably have been, except no one had bothered to knock them down. At the far corner of the street sits one house, similarly crumbling, but newly painted and with people milling about. Its stairs are freshly swept, and the sign outside is in a healthy, not-cracked state, with red block letters that look as though they might be indicating a government office. It announces, as if everything else about it didn't, that this is my destination.

I sigh. I cram my hand in my pocket once more, checking for the thousandth time that the envelope is still where I left it. It is. The sky clouds over. I turn the cheap new doorknob, which feels like plastic, and enter.

The room is small and bare and crowded, just like my father said. There is one generic art print on the wall, probably bolted there, of a cabin in the woods. A window is cut into one wall, like a bank teller's, small and cased in glass. A huge line starts here and spirals around the office. Everyone in the line is pressed close together but it's cold, so at least that part isn't awful.

It *is* still disgusting, though. These people are vagrants, unemployed, on drugs. How they have the money to pay a few hundred dollars' worth of rent each month, I have no idea. I get a wave of revulsion, and then I feel revolted at being revolted because I start to think of my father, unconscious in the kitchen, and I remind myself: I am one of these people.

I dip my head, stick hands in pockets and mope all the way to the end of the line. I'm so distracted—not by anything, just by the loud and rapid sucking of life—that it takes me a full five minutes before I realize I'm standing directly behind my Jesus girl.

And then, a curious thing happens.

It doesn't bother me that she's here.

I expect immediately to be turned off. I stand there, growing fascinated by the way her hair meets the back of her neck. Her hair is a soft, girlish blonde, cut like a bell curve, and beneath it the soft, girlish fur of her skin. This is broken

10

up by the triple layer of the collar of her jacket, her hood, and the band of her headphones. It was iconic, her own private insignia. I drew a letterbox around it in my mind.

The line seems to go on forever, but now I don't mind. She spots me when we reach the first turn in the line, and she shoots me a look. In that look, she clearly recognizes me from the subway car. There is a certain amount of guardedness in her look, as if she isn't quite sure that I'm not stalking her, but, after all, why would anyone come to this place if they didn't have to? Suddenly, as if she's just thought of this, the corners of her lips turn upward, the hint of a grin. This, of course, would be the appropriate time to drop a casual friendly remark about how cold the weather's been, or what kind of a shoddy power structure exists in this country to keep this kind of place in business. I, of course, don't.

Finally, we are two people away (well, she's two away, I'm three) and each person is taking for ever, and she turns around and remarks, as nonchalantly as if we'd been talking this whole time: "Waiting sucks, doesn't it?"

I swallow. The person at the window leaves, and the man in front of her steps up to the glass. I have no illusions—I'm not going to wow her into being my best friend for ever, much less a game of, what did Vadim call it, tonsil hockey?—but I might at least be able to get her to walk back to the subway with me.

"It does," I say to her, praying to God that my throat doesn't spontaneously dry out or close up. "Worst part is, there is no reward at the end—you don't, like, buy a CD or ride a roller coaster. All there *is* is more waiting."

She smiles—a real one this time, and it lasts. "You do this often?"

I shake my head, and hope it doesn't look too fake. Too many times, or too few. "Usually, my father. But he could not, today."

Her eyelids flicker. "So you're the man of the house, then?"

I shrug, not sure if she is teasing me. "If I was rich and owned a place like this, I would just let everyone keep their houses, none of this."

"You wouldn't be rich for long."

This should be the part where I make my move. Let loose some line: *That's just the kind of guy I am* or *For you, it would be worth it.* I have this one friend, he would know exactly what to say and be up against the wall with this girl by the end of the line, limbs writhing on top of each other, going crazy. Another friend, he would fantasize about this moment constantly and never get far enough to actually open his mouth and say something to her. I am neither of those, too embarrassed to either manipulate the situation to my advantage or let my real feelings be known. I guess that's the kind of guy I am. But I wish I could be one of the others.

The whir of the money-counting machine dies down. The man at the window, dismissed, moves quickly to the door.

"Here goes, I guess," she says, offering me the most generous and pretty of her smiles yet.

"Hey, do you want me to take . . ." I start, but she is already at the window, perching her purse on the ledge, rifling through it. She pulls out a gun.

The cashier screams.

It takes everyone a moment to realize what's going on, but once they do, they react. I am slow. It's still early for me. A gnarled, heavy hand wraps itself around my arm, yanks it down hard, and I find myself being lowered to the ground by a grandmother half my size.

The cashier, whose face I can see over the shoulder of Jesus Girl, is only a few years older than us, maybe eighteen or twenty, a bored and lost-looking girl with her hair in long spirally braids. She seems remarkably composed, although everyone in the room is pulsing with fear. The gun is pressed right between her eyes, which have grown wide in astonishment, if not in fear.

My girl is composed, alert, on guard. "Don't hit the alarm," she says. Her voice is calm, meditative even, wary and collected. "And don't think this glass is really bulletproof. It's not. I can tell."

"How—how can you tell?" asks the cashier, whose hands are in the air, but who is still exuding a calm that I wish I could manage.

"Bulletproof glass is a special kind; you can't see your reflection in it. But I know no glass is bulletproof when you shoot from this close."

She jams the pistol forward. Its mouth bangs against the glass. The sound is as loud as a gunshot. Everyone jumps. Bodies pull closer to the ground.

Her voice comes, calm and low and reassuring, as certain as a promise.

"Just pack up the money," she says. "All of it. And I won't hurt anybody."

The cashier's face disappears.

From behind the wall, sounds of frantic packing. The whole time, Jesus Girl keeps a vigilant, obsessive watch over the proceedings through the window.

Finally, the cashier reappears. "We've got it," she tells the entire waiting room. "It's in a sack. We're going to open the door and pass it through."

Jesus Girl considers her lack of other options. "Fine," she agrees. "You stay at the window."

"Me?"

She nods. The gun stays pointed at the glass.

This whole time, I'm thinking about her. I can't not be. There are other things going on, too, in the back of my mind—what schoolwork I missed. If anyone's going to believe me about this. Whether I'm going to die. These questions flash before me every time I run through a red light or step too close to the subway ledge. Now, though, with a gun in the room—my first real, live gun experience—it feels so tremendously realer.

But, for real, I just feel stupid. Spending all my time falling slowly in love with her while she spent the whole time plotting this. Humans use less than 10 percent of their brains, and I use 95 percent of that part thinking about girls. If I hadn't, I could've discovered the cure for cancer by now.

But, more than that, I feel ridiculous. In another few minutes, we are all going to lose our money. One month's rent, gone just like that. It's one-twelfth of what my parents make in a year. Barely. Counting the costs of food and clothes and birthday presents, they are totally in debt. And they are in debt instead of doing something productive like this—yes, robbing people is stupid and malicious, but at least it pays. Getting smashed on rent day—now, that was 100 percent stupid. And it didn't take any thinking at all.

I was so pissed off at her I could scream. I hated her more than our landlord. If I had a cell phone, I would have called the cops right then and there.

The door slides open. A grocery-store-sized bag is pushed out, hesitantly but quickly. She tips it into her purse—which is, by the way, huge—a massive retro thing, vintage 1950s, which swallows all the stacks of bills easily. In the distance is the irritated squeal of a cop's siren, and I don't know how but I do know, as does everyone else, that they are on their way here.

It doesn't matter. She'll be out the door, vanished, in another few moments. Real life will have kick-started itself back into existence, and she will have left us far behind. She is already halfway out the door, the siren still sounds semi-far

14

away, and the woman who first pulled me down is struggling, haggardly, to her feet.

Jesus Girl turns around, almost out the door.

"Hey, cute boy," she says.

It takes me a while to realize she means me. "Da?" I say, too surprised to remember to speak English. Or maybe I said *duh*.

"How much is your rent?"

"Fifteen hundred dollars?" I say without thinking.

She reaches into her newly full bag and counts out money with her thumb. "Damn," she says. "You people have some seriously trashy cash."

Reaching for what I can only assume is fifteen hundred, she tosses it through the narrow slit of the cashier's window. "That's for him," she tells them. "What's your name?"

"J-Jupiter Glazer," I say, still not totally convinced that she is speaking to me.

"Address?"

I tell her.

"Account number? Can I tell you, I hate it when they interrogate you like this? Name, rank, serial number. It makes you feel like a prisoner. God, I've always wanted to say that right to their dumb-ass, glass-protected faces." Behind the window, the cashier, though thoroughly startled, is writing down my information. When she says that bit about prisoners, the cashier winces. You know she's thought it, too.

"You got that down? All right, then," she says, turning the doorknob. "I'm sorry to inconvenience you folks. I hated every second of this, but we all gotta eat."

Another flash of the smile, cheeky and egotistical and so incredibly hot, and she's gone.

Not two minutes later, the police are crashing through the door, guns drawn, demanding to know What's Going On? and Is There A Hostage Situation? and the like. Nobody tells them anything. According to witnesses, the perpetrator is either one man, three men, or an entire soccer team of middle-aged women, white, black, or something in the middle, extremely tall or extremely short, but not average height. "This happens to us all the time," one of the cops confesses to me. "People are stunned. They don't expect to be attacked where they feel most secure."

The cops leave, and the line recommences, shakily, where we left off. Two people have moved in front of me, an old man and a young mother, but I'm not bothered. When I do step up to the booth, ready to hand over my family's hard-earned cash, the cashier looks me in the eye and says, with a soft feeling of kindness, "You're already paid for."

I have a vision of returning home, thick envelope in hand, of going straight to the kitchen where my father is still asleep. He'll shoot right up in his chair the moment I walk in, a big goofy smile on his face, his drunkenness fading like a bad dream. "What'd I miss?" he'll ask, forever wacky, a true American sitcom father.

And I will toss the money on the table, and tell him and my mother about my unexpected day. And we will all laugh together, knowing the story has a happy ending because all stories do. My dad will say, "Why didn't you just leave it there? We could've been early for next month's rent!" and my mom will say, "Thank God you're safe, that's the important part," and we'll all sigh warmly, because we'll remember what really is important.

The Young Stalker's Handbook

BY SARAH REES BRENNAN

"JUST BECAUSE HE'S wearing skin-tight gold trousers doesn't necessarily mean he's a homosexual."

I was in a music store with my friend Rachel when I said these words. In a way, I feel like that sentence summed up my personality completely. Anyone who overheard us would have known immediately that I was optimistic, a dreamer, and utterly clueless about men.

"No," said Rachel doubtfully. "But it does make you wonder."

She bent and picked up the CD we were both transfixed by. A strand of her hair came loose over her blue jacket, a circle of pale gold in the store's fluorescent lights.

Rachel was my best friend. She was also ice blonde, beautiful, funny and clever—you know, the friend who always makes you look a bit of a mess when she stands next to you, but is so generally awesome that most of the time you don't care.

She was also very sensible, which right now was making me sad.

"Don't put him in a box," I said sternly. "We all have the right to wear what we want without anyone drawing unwarranted conclusions about our sexuality. This is a free country and a new millennium. I hope we're open-minded enough to give him the benefit of the doubt."

"I think I might be kind of close-minded," Rachel said, apologetically. "Whenever I tilt the CD case, his ass gleams. And every time his ass gleams, I doubt his heterosexuality. Look—there it goes again. Gleam, doubt. Gleam, doubt. Gleam . . ."

I whipped the CD out of her hand and restored it to its rightful place, where the lead singer's ass could gleam benevolently down on us both.

"Anyway, it is his music that counts," I said firmly. "I, for one, could not care less about his orientation or, indeed, his superficial good looks. He's an artiste."

Rachel had many talents. One of which was that she could raise a truly excellent skeptical eyebrow.

"What about the guy over by the posters you keep sneaking looks at?"

Damn. I'd thought she hadn't spotted me doing that. I was going to have to learn to be sly about stealing looks. I'd be like the cat burglar of looks from now on, I promised myself. Quick as a cat. Nobody would ever catch me.

"Be fair, Rachel," I said with dignity. "I don't know if he's an artiste or not. Sadly, all I have to judge him on are his superficial good looks."

"Yeah," Rachel murmured. "That is a tragedy."

She glanced casually over her shoulder, and then away. She was a true master; perhaps I should be asking her for look-burglary lessons.

"Right," she said. "I think he looks okay. At least his ass isn't gleaming."

"It certainly is not," I said, but I kept an eye on it just to be sure.

"You should go talk to him."

I looked at Rachel with complete disbelief.

"You've got to be less shy, Sam," she said. "Men need to be

18

chased. Think of yourself as a leopard bringing down an antelope."

That was easy for her to say. Rachel always went for guys who were about as smart as antelopes—gorgeous guys who looked like knights who had wandered out of fairy tales and were really confused about the real world. I called the latest Sir Colin the Dimwit.

"What would I say?"

Rachel made a dismissive gesture. "Whatever comes to mind."

"Oh yes," I said. "Splendid idea. You were there at the party last week, weren't you?"

Sadly, a lot of people had been at the party last week.

"It wasn't that bad," said Rachel, a loyal friend and a terrible liar.

"Our tale begins on a warm summer evening, full of wine coolers, women and song." I made a grand gesture, as if I was a bard of old, and kind of hit a dad-aged guy in the belly. "Sorry, sir. So, our heroine was standing in her usual glamorous position by the hummus, and then her gallant suitor, known only as Twizzler for some reason we don't know and prefer not to inquire into, sidles up and says the magical words, 'You look great, Sam.'"

I wasn't actually being as facetious as I was trying to sound. At the time, I had been pretty thrilled he'd come over. Despite the name, he was tall and he seemed nice, and it wasn't like boys were forming an orderly line behind the hummus to talk to me.

"And what did I say then, Ray?"

Rachel closed her eyes, apparently overcome with being the best friend of the party fool.

"I said, 'Ha! Thanks!' I was afraid that my lipstick made me look like I was eating crayons again.'"

19

"You were six when you ate crayons the last time!"

"I know that, Ray. You know that. Sadly, Twizzler does not know that."

Rachel crossed her arms over her chest.

"Well, I don't see why Twizzler had to make that face. Anyway, he should be into the creative use of arts and craft supplies. I heard he sniffs glue."

"The moral of the story is that I am never allowed to attempt any dangerous solo missions like talking to members of the opposite sex. It never ends well."

My voice had got a bit loud while I'd been telling the Twizzler story. I glanced nervously at the guy perusing the posters, but he seemed absorbed by a picture of a girl in leather who looked like an anorexic vampire. Another time I might have been upset by the blatant objectification of women, but since I was busy objectifying him I gave him a pass on that.

"He's much better looking than Twizzler."

"And with any luck, he isn't called Twizzler," I said. "A good name is a much more important feature in a man than people think. I mean, think about calling out some names in the throes of passion. 'Oh, Adrian, you're an animal.' 'Rock me like a hurricane, Nigel.'"

I stole another glance at poster boy. He had excellent shoulders, and the kind of brown hair that was especially nice— soft-looking and falling in a natural drift over his forehead. I thought longingly that he looked like a Chris.

"So you're going to go and talk to him?" Rachel asked eagerly.

I looked at him again. Possibly he was a Dave; he had the strong chin of a Dave. "Yeah," I said uncertainly, and then with more conviction, "Yeah, okay."

Rachel, a woman of action, seized both my shoulders and

spun me around. Then she gave me a solid push between the shoulder blades.

"Remember," she said firmly, "you're awesome! You're beautiful. And you haven't eaten crayons in years."

She pushed me again. I bit my tongue a little.

"Right," I mumbled through the pain.

I shuffled forward, mostly because I was afraid of Rachel. I recited her mantra under my breath.

"You haven't eaten crayons in years. You haven't eaten crayons in years."

A man browsing through the jazz section gave me a very startled look. I found that extremely unfair—he wouldn't have wanted to hear me say I *had* been eating crayons recently.

I stared at my feet so I wouldn't get unnerved by the handsomeness I was approaching. I took one step, then another, and another.

I looked up. There was no sign of excellent shoulders or a strong chin.

He was gone.

I felt robbed.

"Oh my God," I said and stomped over to Rachel. "Can you believe that? It'll take me months to work up the courage to approach another guy. You know what would solve this problem? Radar. If humans were like bats and we all had a way of sending some kind of getting-hit-on radar. That would solve everyone's problems."

"Okay," Rachel said. "If we ever meet Batman, I understand that you have dibs. Failing that, Colin has a friend who he thinks you might get on with. What do you say we go down to GTI's and grab a coffee?"

"After him!"

I don't know why I said it. I don't know why I grabbed Rachel and towed her behind me. I guess I was just all keyed

21

up; the adrenaline I'd worked up bracing myself to talk to the guy was just floating around in my system doing nothing.

I saw the excellent shoulders and the drift of nice hair out of the corner of my eye. I saw Possibly Dave heading out the door and out of my life.

I had an adrenaline-related burst of insanity. It could have happened to anyone.

• • •

I followed him, dragging Rachel in my wake, and kept his gorgeous back in sight until it stopped. I pressed Rachel against the side of a garage and prayed we hadn't been spotted.

No, he was just going into a shop.

I stopped squashing Rachel and went after him. Given a chance to draw breath, she had some objections.

"Please tell me we're not really doing this!"

"If you think about it, this makes complete sense," I told her. "We're practicing a skill we could have a lot of uses for in the future. Think about it—what if we grew up to be spies? Or snipers? Or dogcatchers? We've got to learn how to track down our prey."

"I'm not growing up to be a dogcatcher," Rachel said flatly.

"What about a spy?" I saw a trace of weakness in her eyes. "A glamorous spy in a red evening gown. Carrying a concealed weapon in her thigh holster. She's the only one Her Majesty can trust to track down the robot the Russians have sent into the country—a machine constructed to look like a gorgeous human boy, but with a heart of clockwork and ray guns built into his fingers. Rachel, the fate of England rests in your hands."

"Sam, you are crazy," Rachel said, but I heard the click of her shoes coming after me.

When we reached the front of the shop Possibly Dave had gone into, both Rachel and I stopped short in dismay.

"Aw, Claire's?" Rachel said. "Honey, I think we might have another gleaming ass on our hands."

A woman passing on the street gave Rachel a funny look. Passersby were always judging us.

"You don't know that!" I told her and marched in. I heard her sigh behind me.

Unfortunately, Possibly Dave was standing pretty close to the entrance, talking to the lady who worked there. I was prepared to hate her on sight, but she was about twenty years older than me and reminded me of my old drama teacher, so I decided to absolve her of the intention of stealing away the boy I'd never actually spoken to and whom had no idea I existed.

"I'm looking for something for my sister," he said. "She loves penguins, so I was thinking—little penguin earrings? Or something?"

Rachel and I were cowering behind a stand decorated with hairbands and hair ribbons. I couldn't stop myself digging her in the stomach with a triumphant elbow.

"Well, that's what any guy would say," Rachel said in an unacceptably loud voice. "That's what I'd say, if I was a guy. No boy is going to admit he wants tiny penguin earrings because he thinks they'll look cute on him."

"Once more your judgmental nature leaves me simply appalled, Rachel," I informed her and peered through the peacock feathers on a headband at our quarry.

He had a lovely voice, actually. He sounded American. Maybe his name was Brad.

"Those would suit Jessica," said Potentially Brad.

"See?" I whispered. "She has a name. Nobody names an imaginary sister! That would be crazy."

"I bow to your greater experience in crazy," Rachel said.

Once Could-Very-Well-Be-Brad had purchased the earrings for his definitely not imaginary sister and walked out, Rachel and I were poised to follow him when the shop lady said, "Excuse me."

Oh, God. We'd been seen. I turned around and prepared for the inevitable, "Excuse me—but are you aware stalking is a criminal offense?"

"Excuse me, are you Samantha Armstrong?"

Oh, no, wait, even better! This was going to be, "Excuse me—but are you aware stalking is a criminal offense? Because I'm going to report your behavior to the police and your parents."

I toyed with the idea of going, "No—oh my God, do I have a really law-abiding double?"

"Yes," I admitted.

"It was all her idea!" said Rachel.

That quisling!

"Don't you remember me?" said the shop lady. "I used to teach your drama class."

"Oh," I said. "Oh, right! Hi, Mrs. Nelson! Good to see you again."

The relief was overwhelming. I did not give in to the temptation to cling to the headband stand and hyperventilate.

"Good to see you, Sam." Mrs. Nelson regarded me fondly, which was very gratifying. "You look just the same," she added, which was less so.

She'd known me when I was eight. When I was eight, I'd had a bowl haircut and tucked the ends of my tracksuit bottoms into my socks.

"Just the same except, you know, all elegant and grown-up," I grinned.

Mrs. Nelson laughed a bit more than I would have

preferred. "Do you remember how you used to wear your socks over your tracksuit bottoms?"

"No," I said with great conviction. "No, I do not remember that at all."

Mrs. Nelson laughed again. "The other kids used to call you Socks!"

If Mrs. Nelson only knew that Socks had grown up to be a dedicated stalker and menace to society. Speaking of which, all this hanging around chatting meant that my future husband Dave-or-Brad was getting away!

"You must be thinking of someone else. Um, wow, it was great to see you, Mrs. Nelson, but Rachel and I kind of have to be going. I'll drop by again!"

I grabbed Rachel's hand and ran. When we were outside the shop I shielded my eyes with my hand and scanned the streets. There was no sign of him.

"There, he's going into McDonald's," Rachel said, pointing.

I knew she'd been sucked into the thrill of the chase. I was, too. And even if I had gone crazy and was chasing a total stranger around the town, it beat standing by the hummus at parties.

Turned out crime was fun.

"Suddenly I'm feeling very hungry," I said.

Rachel sighed. "Oh, if your drama class could see their little Socks now."

• • •

I hadn't been lying, I was hungry. I never lie about food.

"We have to be ready to follow him," said Rachel, future spy extraordinaire. "Maybe we should just get milkshakes."

"Double cheeseburger," I said. "Oh, and a chocolate milkshake. Good idea. Oh, and fries."

"Okay, two fries," said Rachel. "And a strawberry milkshake."

As the one who'd ordered the cheeseburger, I was in charge of the tray while Rachel was in charge of finding a table where we could sit and watch Brad-Dave-Chris at our leisure and from a safe distance.

The only problem was that she couldn't locate him at all, let alone find a table.

"What if he just popped in to use the bathroom and left while we were buying food?" Rachel asked.

"Nobody uses the bathrooms in McDonald's except drug addicts—they're disgusting."

"Well, he could have gone to the bathroom to do drugs," Rachel said. "It's not like we know him all that well. In fact, you're attracted to the dangerous type. Look at Twizzler."

I scanned the circular tables and the expanse of yellow tiles. There were a ton of kids, laughing around circular tables over crumpled wrappers and greasy boxes, but none of them was the man I was quite literally *after*.

"Don't talk like Twizzler was the guy I married who sold me for crack," I said. "Twizzler was the guy I talked to by the hummus whom you later told me had a close personal relationship with glue. The arts and crafts cupboard was more his girlfriend than I was. And maybe Brad just went upstairs."

"You made up a name for him?"

"You made up a *drug problem* for him," I reminded her and marched up the stairs.

Upstairs there were booths. I looked around for our quarry in every one, squinting to make out individual faces among the squashed-together groups until people started glaring back at us.

"I don't see him!"

"I don't see him either," said Rachel, chewing on her bottom lip. She looked really annoyed. She had Colin—she didn't have any interest in this new guy, but Rachel didn't like to fail at anything, even at pretending to be a spy.

Besides, she'd felt the same rush I had, giggling and running in pursuit, having a break from the Sunday afternoon boredom. It was a bit deflating to have it all end like this.

I looked down the stairs, leaning against the rail, to the floor below.

Then I saw a head of really nice-looking brown hair.

"There he is!" said Rachel. "But is he coming up, or is he going to sit down there?"

"He seems undecided," I said, leaning out further.

He had a tray with him and was sort of bobbing about the place. I leaned out against the railing as far as I could go in case he made any sudden moves. Silently, I ordered him to make up his mind—all this wavering about was unmanly. He should be more decisive. What I needed was a man of action!

As if he could hear my psychic berating, he started suddenly up the steps.

I wasn't expecting this. I was leaning too far over the railing.

I flinched.

The moment stretched out, as if time itself had slowed to savor my unbelievable humiliation. Endless seconds passed as the tray slid from my hands: there was the moment when its weight was still against the sweaty tips of my fingers but it was already irredeemably lost; the moment when the tray was flipping, its red plastic bright in the fluorescent lights; and the moment when I fully realized what was going to happen and felt my stomach turn in a slow churn of horror.

There was the moment when the boy whose name I didn't know looked up, just before the tray hit. His eyes were wide and bright blue, narrowing. He saw me.

Then the tray hit in an explosion of food and milkshakes.

Rachel hit the ground beside the railing, hiding herself from view. I looked down at her in frozen horror—she had her face buried in her knees.

I had a very strong urge to hide, too. Only the boy had seen me when he looked up, and he knew exactly whose tray had hit him. Hiding would just be like putting my head under a blanket and pretending I was invisible.

Not that it wasn't tempting. I have never been so embarrassed in my whole life.

"Oh, wow," I called down feebly. "I'm really sorry."

There was a napkin dispenser on the table by the stairs. I took a paper napkin from it and wandered hopelessly down.

The boy had dropped his own tray when my tray had hit. His chicken nuggets had spilled out and were lying in a heap with Rachel's food and mine, reproaching me.

"Wow, I am really, really sorry," I repeated, just to stress this important point, and cringed with every step down.

"You said that already," said the boy I didn't know at all, had been stalking, and had now assaulted. He didn't sound angry, just dazed.

Then again, he had just been hit on the head with a tray.

There were fries hanging on his shoulders like decorations. His T-shirt and his hair were splashed with sludgy brown and pink, and when he blinked I saw that there was milkshake stuck in his eyelashes.

"That's because I am really, really sorry," I said and waved my napkin like a tiny paper flag of truce. I reached out and dabbed ineffectually at his T-shirt, because wiping his milkshake-stained face seemed invasive.

Whereas stalking him had been totally acceptable behavior.

"Um," he said. "Thanks."

I lowered the now soggy square of brown and pink. "You're welcome."

"Could you, uh, give me a hint on where you found that

28

napkin?" he asked. "I think I could use just a few more."

"Yeah, I can totally cut you in on some napkin action," I said.

Okay, he wasn't yelling, and he hadn't accused me of dropping the tray on purpose, which would have been a horrible lie, or stalking him, which would have been a horrible truth. Things were not so bad.

"You look very familiar," he said.

"I have one of those faces!" I yelped. "It is just one of those things! One of those faces . . . things."

At that unpromising moment, a voice behind him said, "Sam?"

"Oh, God, Colin," I said. "I mean. Colin, great to see you!"

There he was, in the flesh and at the worst possible time— Rachel's maybe-boyfriend Colin, standing in McDonald's looking tall, handsome and even more puzzled than usual.

"Oh, hey, I didn't see you there," said Colin, who had obviously gone mad and was babbling nonsense. "Uh, has there been some kind of accident?"

"McDonald's: its vengeance strikes from above," said the boy. "Could you point me to those napkins?"

"Right," I said. "Follow me."

My victim followed me, and so did Colin, as if it was any of his business. Some of McDonald's staff, who had been busy staring at the horrible spectacle with fascination, came over to clear up the mess I'd made, and I was at the top of the stairs before I realized that I'd led the boys straight to Rachel.

"Look who it is!" I shouted immediately. "COLIN! That's who it is! Right here!"

Rachel got up so fast she kind of wobbled as she rose. "Hi, Colin! Good to see you!"

Colin regarded her blankly. "What were you doing on the floor?"

When a guy is dating a girl, he thinks he owns her, I thought with passionate resentment. What right did Colin have to ask such a personal question?

"Oh, I dropped something," Rachel said, quick-thinking as a future spy should be. "But I have it now. In my pocket. So that's all right."

"What was it?" Colin asked.

"Er . . . gum," said Rachel.

Colin kept smiling, but the boy I'd stalked gave Rachel a very doubtful look.

"Here are your napkins!" I said and shoved a big mass of them directly in his line of vision.

"Um . . . thanks," he responded, and took them.

A few dabs of the paper against his face showed that the milkshake had dried a bit too much. Unfortunately the strawberry one had scored a direct head hit—he had a stiff, vaguely pink widow's peak.

"I think maybe I need to go to the bathroom," he said eventually. He caught his reflection in the metal of the napkin dispenser. "Is my hair pink?"

"Slightly pink," I told him. "In a manly and stereotype-defying way."

"I'm definitely going to the bathroom," he said, draping the napkin over his hair like a veil. "In a manly and stereotype-defying way."

He sloped off with the napkin still on his head. There was a good chance he might be crazy.

Of course, I hunted strangers through the streets, so who was I to judge?

"This is lucky," said Colin, settling with Rachel in the nearest booth and stretching out both arms to get one around Rachel's shoulders.

"It sure is. And not at all suspicious!"

Rachel laughed a little hysterically. Colin, a simple soul, looked at her and then laughed politely too.

This was going to be my punishment, then. I was going to have to spend the afternoon with a boy I'd ambushed and assaulted, witnessing the spectacle of Rachel romancing Colin, the so-dim-he-was-flickering bulb.

Well, I deserved it, and I would have to accept it. I slid round to the other side of the table.

"What have you guys been doing all day?" Colin asked amiably.

"Nothing!" Rachel yelped.

"All day," I added with great firmness.

"Sounds boring."

"Yes, that was our day," I proclaimed. "Very, very boring. Tedious. Almost unbearable, really!"

Rachel proved she was one day going to rival Mata Hari by stretching and murmuring, "Missed you," in his ear just when Colin was starting to look a bit suspicious.

Of course, that meant that Colin started nuzzling her and murmuring to her. They started rubbing their heads like seals in love, and I wondered if I had done something terrible in a past life to deserve this, before recalling that I had actually done something terrible to deserve this only ten minutes ago.

"So I might go down and get something to eat," I said, staring at the fascinating wall behind them.

"Want me to get it for you?" asked Colin's friend.

He had returned. He'd returned damp.

It was a good look on him. He really did have excellent shoulders.

Not that I really noticed. Shoulders were a delusion and a snare. Shoulders had been what got me into this mess.

There was a small pause. Not that I was staring. I was thinking deep thoughts.

"It's no trouble," he added. "I'm getting a Coke myself."

"I'll get you a Coke," I said. "And new chicken nuggets. Least I can do."

He smiled at me. It was a crooked, brilliant smile.

"I'm a bit off milkshakes just now," he added.

"Ray, this is Sam," Colin said. "Sam, Rachel."

Rachel and I exchanged looks. Hers was tolerant, mine not so much.

"Yes, thanks, Colin, we've met!"

"Sorry," said Colin ridiculously. "I didn't know."

"Er," said the boy. "I think he means me."

Rachel and I both looked at him. "Uh?" I said intelligently.

"I'm Sam," said the boy.

"You can't be Sam," I said.

He smiled again. "Please don't make me say it."

"Say what?"

"Don't make me lower myself by saying the old Dr. Seuss line. You know. Sam I am. Oh, well, there I go. Sorry about that."

"Don't be sorry," I said. "Dr. Seuss is a classic. And Sam I am, too."

"What a coincidence," said Sam.

"Her name's Samantha really," put in Rachel, in a noble effort to make me sound more feminine and alluring.

"Even more of a coincidence," said Sam. "Well, the thing is, my mother wanted a girl."

"Really?" Colin asked.

We all gave him pitying looks.

"Yes, Colin," said Sam, straight-faced. "I had to wear pink until I was four. Also, I had the sweetest ringlets."

I couldn't help it, I laughed.

Sam's eyes turned back to me. "So, fancy a Coke?"

"I think I do," I said.

"Cokes all around," Rachel commanded, nudging her true knight in the ribs. Colin sprang to obey. "Well, well," Rachel said, as the boys went down the stairs. "What have we learned today?"

"Er," I said, stealing another dazzled glance at Sam's excellent shoulders and wondering if this counted as narcissism. "Crime pays?"

I hoped that this wasn't going to lead to some lifelong stalking compulsion. I had a picture of myself in ten years' time, still making my move by buying binoculars and following guys while wearing a ski mask.

If I hadn't gone over to talk to him, though, none of this would have happened. Possibly it was time to be less shy.

But not more criminal.

"We've learned that I am always right." Rachel smiled like a cat. "Like a leopard on an antelope, baby."

Lost in Translation

BY MICHAEL LOWENTHAL

IN NINTH-GRADE Spanish, Patricio couldn't say his own name. A wide-jawed redhead with skin the shade of moonbeams, he seemed stymied by his Anglo facial features. "Pat*rrrr*icio," Señora Fuentes growled, modeling the correct roll of Rs. "*La lengua. La lengua*. Use the tongue!" But for all her urgent coaching, Pat still couldn't introduce himself.

"Pat-dicio," he spat earnestly, then shrugged and flashed his front-teeth gap, and even Señora had to forgive him.

Try to see him as I did that first day: on the room's left side, over by the windows, so the sun sparked his cinnamon-sugar hair. It was kind of parted in the middle, kind of not, disheveled and perfect and winging over his right ear as though he'd just woken from a nap. He squinted in the glare, providing my first glimpse of the dimples that flickered at his nose's bridge when he was frustrated or laughing or—instantly, I imagined it—having sex. He'd come to class as Pat Banner, the wrestling-team stud: cocksure, suave, untouchable; but as Patricio, stuttering his way through this alien vocabulary, he was thrillingly waifish and exposed.

I doubt Pat noticed me that day. He had to, though, in the following weeks, because if his accent was the worst in class, mine was the best. My father had been a cultural attaché in

34

Bogotá, and my family lived there till I was three; by ninth grade, my Spanish knowledge had dwindled to *sí* and *no*, but the music of it lingered in my brain.

Señora Fuentes was a crusader for *español*. The most glamorous teacher at Lewis High School—impeccably coiffed and rouged, stiletto-heeled—she viewed our failures at fluency as ethnic denigration. With an Argentine propensity for drama, she latched on to Pat and me as examples.

"Patricio," she demanded one mid-September Monday, strutting model-like before the blackboard, "*Repite por favor: 'A mí me gusta el béisbol.'*"

Patricio tried to state his fondness for baseball, but it came off like a drunk saying the alphabet backwards.

"*¡No! Escúchame bien*, listen close." And then Señora, hands on her high, elegant hips, repeated the sentence at *Sesame Street* pace: "*A mí me gus-ta el béis-bol.*"

Pat scrunched his nose, the indentations at the bridge as dark as scars. He tried again, but the language was elusive.

"*Ay ya yay*," Señora lamented. "*Chicos*, what are we going to do? *Patricio tiene la lengua gorda.* But maybe Carlo can say it right. Would you, please, Carlo?"

I feared offending Pat with my proficiency, but I couldn't defy a teacher's request. I spoke the words, my accent deft, impatient crispness balanced with lush exuberance.

"*Perfecto*," Señora cheered. "*Perfectíssimo!*"

I hardly registered her praise. I was fixed on what she'd said about Patricio, that he possessed "*la lengua gorda.*" She'd meant it as stammery, tongue-tied. Literally, it translated that he had a "fat tongue."

• • •

I was young for my class, having skipped the second grade. Sometimes I blame that difference for my trouble fitting in, but I suspect another year wouldn't have changed things much. I just wasn't good at being a kid.

I tried. I eavesdropped on the cool guys' conversations, panning for nuggets about the trends of 1981. But the fickle logic of adolescence foiled me. I couldn't have told you why The Knack was awesome and the Village People worthy of scorn, why Pumas were cool shoes and Stan Smiths for geeks.

On weekends, while other kids skated or watched cartoons, I marched on the Capitol. It was the first year of Reaganomics, and growing up in suburban Washington, D.C., the chances for dissent were plentiful: the nuclear freeze, Central America, handgun control. My jeans were speckled from painting protest banners.

The big rally that fall was Solidarity Day. Downtown swarmed with disaffected unionists. I joined the Liberation League, a group of college students, and we marched behind the thuggish Truckers for Justice. We got so near to Pete Seeger we could count his banjo's frets. The real triumph was finding a T-shirt to add to my collection. (PREVIOUS HOLDINGS: BREAD NOT BOMBS; A MAN OF QUALITY IS NOT THREATENED BY A WOMAN SEEKING EQUALITY.) The new one was a green shirt shouting DEFEND ATLANTA'S CHILDREN, NOT EL SALVADOR'S JUNTA. Genius! Twenty-three black kids had been killed recently by a madman in Atlanta. Why was the U.S. propping up a murderous regime in El Salvador instead of stopping the slaughter here at home?

Monday was misty and cool—windbreaker weather—but I wore just the T-shirt anyway, the goose flesh on my arms a badge of pride. At the bus stop, kids stared quizzically. By school time, the stares turned to sneers.

Before Spanish, Tim Jeeter challenged me. "Junta?" he said, pronouncing it with a hard J, seedy and suggestive. "What the hell's a junta?"

"Not '*djun*-ta,'" I corrected him. "'*Hoon*-ta.' It's a military government."

"I still don't get it. What does Atlanta have to do with El Salvador?"

Other kids joined in the jeering. "Defend hooters?" one snickered.

I shrank.

And then, in sauntered Patricio, all smile and squint lines and casual backhand swipe of the nose. He glanced at my shirt, seemed to sniff the air like a danger-sensing dog. "Hey, man," he said. "Dig your shirt."

They were the first words he'd ever said to me. In those early lonely weeks of school I'd hoped for acknowledgment, but I'd never dreamed of such deliverance. He had swooped me from the fire, untied me from the railroad tracks.

For the whole of class I stared at Pat. When Señora asked him to conjugate *poder* and *querer*—irregular verbs he flubbed for the hundredth time—I attempted a reciprocal rescue. "*Queero*," he guessed, and I mouthed, "*Quiero*," but he never thought to look in my direction.

After class I tailed him to his locker. "Hey," I said. "Thanks. Thanks a lot."

Pat's brow creased in the same pattern as when Señora stumped him. Then he looked at my chest. "Oh. No problem."

I spun the numbers on the neighboring locker's dial. "No offense," I said, "but with the trouble you have in Spanish, I was kind of surprised you even know what a *junta* is."

"A what?"

Then it hit me: Pat couldn't pronounce *junta*, let alone argue why El Salvador's was evil. He had no clue what my T-shirt meant. Why, then, had he shielded me? Maybe he had a soft spot for underdogs in general. Maybe his soft spot was more specific.

• • •

I spied on Pat, pestering mutual friends with questions. I didn't find out much, but in my imagination the bits of story bloomed: Pat was adopted; he was allergic to walnuts; he had never lost a wrestling match.

I'd been attracted to guys before, but that was all skin and quickened breath. This was deeper. My toes curled when Pat said my name. I got teary at the thought of his hairline. When I pictured something as innocent as holding his hand at the movies, my brain's folds seemed to unfurl and snap back into a new design.

In Spanish, we learned rule-flouting verbs, exceptions that were listed in our textbook. "Don't question," Señora told us, "memorize." But no one had ever given me a primer for my passions. Could I trust the broken grammar of desire?

In my fantasies over the next few weeks, I spent so much time with Pat that, seeing him in person, I'd forget we weren't best friends. I concocted excuses to approach him. I'd found a pen on the floor—had he lost one? His surfer shorts were rad—could he tell me where he'd bought them? Pat generally greeted my buddyness with a "Wait, I *know* I know you from somewhere" look. I should've been angry or disheartened, but I was grateful to be granted an audience.

Then, just when I thought all hope was lost and that our brief connection had been a fluke, he astonished me with a show of thoughtfulness. In October, Anwar el-Sadat was assassinated, and Pat brought me *The Washington Post*. "I know you're into politics," he said. I'd read the paper already at home, but I studied his copy, every word, unable to keep from grinning despite the grim and bloody news.

A week later, a Friday, Pat followed me when Spanish class let out. "Carlo," he called. "Wait up, Carlo." After a pause,

MICHAEL LOWENTHAL

during which he seemed to search the air for subtitles, he
wished me a good weekend in not-too-badly butchered
Spanish: "*Tienes el bieno fin de semana.*"

"*Tú también,*" I managed. "That means . . ."

"I *know*," he said. "You too."

• • •

Around Thanksgiving, our entire grade was bussed to the
Smith Center, a nature retreat in western Maryland, for an
overnight of hands-on science. I was nervous about rooming
with my classmates. They'd see me get dressed; they'd hear
my bathroom noises. Who knew what secrets they might
guess? But my fear was balanced by the prospect of being close
to Pat: hearing *his* noises, watching *him* get dressed.

The teachers split us into groups, and Pat and I were
separated. All day we bushwhacked, collecting specimens. We
poured plaster casts of possum tracks, brewed sassafras tea.
Dinner was army-style in a giant mess hall, where we then
watched movies on a sheet hung from the rafters. The
entertainment was supposed to sedate us, but the main
selection —*M*A*S*H*, with its buxom Major Houlihan—only
fanned our hot, hormonal flames.

Later, in the boys' bunkhouse, the air was galvanic with
arousal, as though sex was a gas seeping from hidden vents.
Tim Jeeter expounded on the merits of big tits versus small.
Then Keith Rosen took a poll as to whether pussies smelled
like tuna fish or burritos. No one would admit to first-hand
knowledge.

I don't remember who brought up the Smurfs, the tiny blue
gnomes that were the latest cartoon craze. Did they have
gnome-sized privates, someone wondered? If they had pubic
hair, was it blue?

I had claimed the bunk below Pat's upper berth. Now the

springs creaked, and Pat leaned his head over the rail. "Forget the Smurfs," he said. "You know what grosses me out?" Silence shrouded the room. "Red pubic hair. Fire crotches. They're nasty."

Giggles of assent. Mock upchucking.

A teacher knocked on the door and warned us to settle down. Within minutes phlegmy snoring could be heard.

I lay awake, confounded by Pat's remark. He himself had such lustrous red hair—*pelirrojo*, Señora Fuentes called him. Was he saying that he grossed himself out? (I knew the feeling; my body betrayed me, too.) Or could his pubes be different from the hair on top of his head? He might be blond down there, or brown, or Smurf blue.

The next day, on the ride back to school, I was devastated to learn that Pat had hooked up with Stacy Stokes, a girl known for her bouncy, precocious breasts. While I was tracking mammals, they'd gone to third base.

I was miserable, and envious, and turned on. For days after I would jerk off to the vision of them doing it, then get so fraught I couldn't finish, then finish anyway, pretending I was Stacy.

Spanish class was both comfort and punishment. Pat sat, as always, by the windows, mullion shadows like prison bars on his face. Señora Fuentes continued her crusade. As beginners we were condemned to the declarative: *I am, I go, I say, I do.* But Señora hinted at tricks we'd later learn. "It's really the subjunctive," she said once, when asked to translate a phrase. Then dismissing the thought, she offered a more simplistic version.

The word "subjunctive" goaded my curiosity. I asked Señora after class what it meant, and, gratified by my interest, she revealed the tense of contingency, of *what if*? In Spanish, she explained, verbs took different forms when referring to fantasy. She taught me key words—*quisiera*, *pudiera, tuviera*—plaintive, vowelly cries for help.

For weeks, while the rest of class tackled the simple future, I filled up my notebook with a more advanced endeavor: if I were to tell Pat, to kiss him, if he were mine . . .

• • •

After New Year's, a surprise: Pat invited me to his home. It felt like extra credit for my efforts.

Pat's small house sat off-kilter on its lot, as though it had been wide-load-trucked there and the driver, in a rush for his next job, never bothered to position it correctly. Shrubbery choked the yard. The neighbors must have thought the place an eyesore.

When I walked in, that Friday afternoon, I tingled with a tourist's edgy thrill; Pat's house was the shocking opposite of my own. The furniture was chintzy and undusted. Trinkets adorned the walls. No books.

His room was up some stairs, tucked into an unfinished loft. Actually, the loft itself was the room. There was no door, no clearly marked boundary, just a bed plunked amid a space of splintery wooden studs. I couldn't decide if the rawness was sad or hopeful. Pat said his dad, for years, had promised to finish the room.

He elbowed a heap of dirty laundry from the bed, kicked off his shoes, and lay down. I lay down next to him, in the skinny space he left, and finally, for the first time, we really talked. School stuff at first, petty gossip: who'd been caught smoking in the bathroom. Eventually we steered toward the personal. Pat asked about my dad—"He was an ambassador or something, right?"—and the lesser truth didn't dim his awe. I asked Pat about being adopted. He said sometimes he wished he were an orphan. His folks, when they bothered to be around, got on his case. They hated Stacy. His dad called her a slut.

"So, do you guys . . ." I ventured, unable to help myself.

"Me and Stace? I really shouldn't say."

As let down as I was not to hear the nitty-gritty, I was relieved by his secret-keeper ethos.

For dinner we fried corned-beef hash and gobbled it in front of the TV. During a commercial break, I called my mom and told her not to worry, that I was at a friend's and I'd probably stay the night. She asked if adults were present, and I promised her they were. I figured Pat's parents had gone away for the weekend, or maybe worked the night shift.

We watched sitcoms until midnight, then retired to Pat's loft. I hoped at last to solve the riddle of his pubes. He ducked behind the plywood that separated his "bedroom" from the john. I heard the gurgle and then squirt-squirt of his peeing, followed by an agonizing pause. I sat on the bed's edge, picturing dead babies to drain my hard-on. When he came back he was shirtless but wearing baggy full-length pajama pants.

"You can take the bed," he said, and burrowed into the laundry on his floor.

Not having pajamas of my own, I slipped under the covers wearing my jeans. I nuzzled the pillow—Pat's pillow—and numbed myself with his scent's anesthetic.

• • •

Saturday we woke late and wolfed huge bowls of Count Chocula cereal. We lounged in front of the TV again, then napped the way only boys can do just after sleeping ten full hours. Eventually we walked into town. We killed time. We did "stuff." I was so lost in telling myself to memorize every moment that I didn't notice much of anything.

At day's end, Pat didn't ask if I wanted to stay again, and I didn't ask if I could. I just did.

His parents still hadn't shown. No one watched us. We could have been on the moon. Again I slept in my clothes, wanting badly to strip bare, but petrified. Pat sprawled on the floor below me, his limbs twitching all night like a puppy's.

Sunday brought the same aimless bliss. We didn't need the crutch of "activity." Being together was all: *¡Compañeros!*

When night came, I sank into depression. We dined on corned-beef hash for the third day in a row, but this time the routine sagged with nostalgia. Would things ever be this good again?

I was lacing my shoes to go home when Pat stopped me. "It's late," he said. "Stay another night."

"What about school?"

"We'll go together. We'll take my bus."

And the teetering earth was righted on its axis.

We stayed up till two, listening to records I pretended to know. I confessed to feeling different from the other guys at school. Friendships were important to me, I said. *His* friendship.

Pat understood. He was different, too, he said. And as he yawned his way to sleep, he mumbled something cryptic about a "special school for people like us."

My brain sizzled. I dreamed of a vast classroom full of Pats: chisel-jawed redheads with winning smiles. We'd study love poems in all the world's languages!

I sucked a breath. "*Te amo*," I almost said.

In the morning we rode to school together. I was a mess in my four-day-rumpled clothes, but I relished my classmates' stares, proud of each wrinkle and stain. That afternoon, in Spanish, we couldn't talk; Señora Fuentes sprang a pop quiz. I caught Pat's attention, though, when he handed in his answers, and he knighted me with a secret smile.

I burned to ask about the "special schools" comment. And kept burning for weeks. Then for months.

Pat never invited me home again.

He wasn't cold—when we passed each other in the halls, he punched my shoulder and called me Carlito; we ate lunch together when we could. But on weekends he was busy. His father had grounded him to help around the house; Stacy booked his Saturday nights. "Maybe Sunday," he sometimes said, then didn't call.

Had I murmured something in my sleep that put him off? Or was he terrified, like me, of wanting more?

• • •

Spring shed its grace on Washington, D.C. The city flushed pink with cherry blossoms, pollen optimistic in the air. The first day warm enough to wear shorts, Pat saw me and called, "Hey, *hombre*, nice legs." I convinced myself I could do it, I could ask him.

I picked the day before Easter break, reasoning that if things backfired, I wouldn't see Pat for a while. I set the date on my calendar and counted down.

When the day arrived, world politics intervened. Argentine troops invaded the Falkland Islands, overtaking a squadron of British marines. Señora Fuentes canceled her lesson plan to expound on imperialism's evils. She insisted we say "Islas Malvinas" instead of "Falklands." She lectured the full hour, past the bell. And then Pat sprinted out; I couldn't catch him.

By the end of vacation, ten thousand Argentines occupied the Malvinas. The British navy sailed south at full alert. Because of my activist's reputation, I was expected to take a stance. Loyal to Señora Fuentes, at first I supported the Argentines. But Tim Jeeter accused me of hypocrisy. "Defend Atlanta's children," he mocked, "not Argentina's junta."

I wasn't the only conflicted leftist. The Liberation League convened an emergency meeting. Some students called for picketing the British embassy; others threatened to quit if we sided with Argentina.

As General Galtieri and Prime Minister Thatcher traded ultimatums, I finally issued one to myself: I must talk to Pat by the beginning of the month.

I waited until the final hour, the night of May first. I locked myself in the guest room in our basement. I took my noteboook so I could jot down anything important Pat said, and a Rubik's Cube for nervous fidgeting. As I worked up the guts to lift the phone, I twisted the cube, trying to match reds with reds, blues with blues. The manufacturer boasted of forty-three quintillion configurations, but only one, of course, was correct.

In a blind, breathless rush I dialed Pat's number.

Yes, he said, he was alone; he could talk.

Alone, I scribbled in my notebook, then added, *TALK!*

"Crazy stuff in the Falklands, huh?" I started.

"*Las Malvinas*," Pat corrected. "*¡Por favor!*"

I noted that his accent had improved. "You're right," I said. "Don't report me to Señora."

The line was staticky. Breath. Trepidation. I had two languages, but neither one was helping.

"So, um, Pat?" I finally asked.

"Yeah."

"What I was wondering was . . . well, you know how when I slept over that time, you mentioned a special school?"

"Um," he hedged. "What exactly did I say?"

I wrote *special*, then added a question mark. "A special school. For people like us?"

"I guess I'm not sure I know what 'people like us' means."

"Right," I said. "I mean, me neither. That's what I wanted

45

to ask about. I wondered how you think we're similar."

I could picture him in his derelict loft, his brow creased in sexy puzzlement. I cranked the Rubik's Cube; three yellows locked in line.

"I don't know," he said. "Don't *you* think we're similar?"

"Yeah," I said, brightening. "But I feel different from other people. People besides you."

"What about those hippie protest freaks?"

"They're not really freaks," I said.

"Nah, it's cool. But you've got to admit, they're kind of freaky."

"Okay, so am *I* freaky, then? Because I do these things. Well, I don't *do* them. They're more like *feelings* I have? And I'm wondering if maybe you have them, too."

"What kind of feelings?" he asked.

Here was the line: if I crossed, I'd *always* be across.

I wanted to, but didn't, say *love*. I said *like*. "I like you a lot . . . you know, in *that way*."

Silence.

I doodled in the notebook, my palms greased with sweat.

Pat finally coughed and started talking, and the music I heard, the sweet resurrecting song, was: "Come on, Carl, of course you're not a freak."

How long did that harmony ring—a split second? Two seconds? Three? I would've sworn it was time enough for a room full of monkeys, typing randomly on as many keyboards, to compose all of Shakespeare's love sonnets.

Then Pat said, "I'm flattered, I really am. I like you a lot as a friend. But I don't, you know . . . not like *that*. Not at all."

I lost my wind. I almost wished he'd screamed "fag" and slammed the phone. I wished he'd never speak to me again. Then I could hate him back for how he hated.

I spun the Rubik's Cube, careless of pattern, letting entropy do its dirty work. Eventually Pat said bye, he'd see me Monday. I stared down at the notebook, which trembled in my hands, my words as illegible as monkey scrawl.

• • •

The next day, Sunday, a British sub sank the Argentine cruiser *General Belgrano*. News reports showed the ship engulfed in flames. Because of the oil that slicked from the wreckage, even the sea appeared to burn. Three hundred and sixty-eight Argentines drowned.

In school on Monday, kids gossiped about Keith Rosen's having felt up Lisa Kelly. They traded crib notes for afternoon tests. Didn't they know the world was on fire?

I stumbled through the halls, stupefied. At lunch someone asked what was wrong. What could I say? I'd seen my future; it crushed me. I shrugged and blamed my tears on allergies.

I considered skipping Spanish, but why bother? I couldn't skip the rest of my life. I claimed a chair at the very back of the room.

I had promised myself I wouldn't look, but I did. Pat was in his usual spot. He wore a Sex Wax shirt, his surfer shorts and Pumas with no socks. When he turned to me, I yanked my gaze away.

Señora Fuentes was slumped over her desk. Hair had pulled free from her bun, and skewed like a defunct engine's wires. Wet mascara blotched around her eyes.

"I'm sure you've heard," she began, barely audible. She rested a wobbly hand on her heart. "Forgive me," she said, "today I can't—" and sobs consumed the rest.

I had never seen a teacher cry. She wept and wept, beyond the point of shame. "My brothers!" she cried. "*Perdidos*— everyone lost."

I looked then at stoic Patricio, who stared out the window,

away. Backlit by the sun, he was centered in a force field, golden-red as the highlights in his hair. He tapped a rhythm on the desk with his pencil—maybe the drumbeat of The Knack's newest song? I could hear it, but I couldn't guess the tune.

Confessions and Chocolate Brains

BY JENNIFER R. HUBBARD

MY FRIENDS WONDERED how I could fall in love with a guy who gave me chocolate brains for my birthday. The brains had peanut-butter filling, and Connor ordered them from a medical-supply company that also sold life-size skeleton models, eye charts, and T-shirts with the digestive system outlined on them. I liked the candy brains not only because I loved chocolate, but also because they symbolized the dream Connor and I had, that we were going to become doctors someday.

"It's disgusting," Annie said, eyeing the box when I offered her some. "You mean you bite into those things and stuff leaks out?"

"Not 'stuff,'" I said. "Peanut butter." I held out the box to Monica, who shook her head.

"More for me," I shrugged, and by the time Connor came over that night to study calculus, I had eaten a third of the box.

• • •

Connor and I started our open-book calculus final by sitting on the couch with the TV on. We liked to ease into our homework, calculus being like a cold pool that you *could* just dive into if you wanted to flash-freeze your nervous system,

49

but if you had any sense you would lower yourself into it an inch at a time.

Of course, when I sat next to Connor, the only calculation I was doing was measuring the space between us in heat and electricity. When he first sat down and Mom looked in on us, that space was the width of my hand (with fingers spread). Gradually we edged closer, until there was maybe half an inch between his blue-jeaned leg and mine. His arm rested on my shoulders, his skin hot against the back of my neck.

My grandfather stalked into the room. "Shove over," he said to Connor.

We moved over. Connor took his arm from around me, and Gramps dropped on to the sofa cushion next to him.

We all stared at the screen. I was so close to Connor that I could feel his heart beating, hear how his breath had shallowed and sped up. My grandfather glowered at the end of the couch.

"Sarah! What's this crap you're watching?" Gramps said.

I honestly had no idea. I'd been paying attention only to Connor, calculating the narrowness of the gap between us, breathing the scent of his soap. But on the TV screen in front of us, a guy dressed in camo fired off a machine gun.

"He'd never be able to hold that weapon," Gramps said. "Firing over and over like that. It'd be too hot to hold!" Which was as much as I'd ever heard about Gramps's experience in the war.

Connor's eyes slid sideways, toward me.

"Why are you watching this, anyway?" Gramps went on.

"I don't know," I said, thinking, *Because Connor's thigh was about one centimeter away from mine, and I wasn't actually watching the screen, thank you very much.*

"Where's the remote?" Gramps leaned forward and saw my

birthday present on the coffee table. "What the hell are those?" He stabbed a finger at them.

"Brains, sir," Connor said. The only time I ever heard Connor say "sir" was when he spoke to my grandfather.

"What? Speak up."

"Brains, sir! I got them for Sarah."

"Brains?" Gramps raised his eyebrows at me, and I nodded. "Well." He hooked one out of the package with a long, white-bristled finger and popped it into his mouth. We watched him chew and swallow.

"You're a very strange young man," he said to Connor, and licked peanut butter off his teeth.

"Yes, sir."

"Is that some kind of fad now? Chocolate brains?"

"No, sir."

"I didn't think so." Gramps grabbed the remote.

"It's because we're going to be doctors."

I poked Connor's thigh. The rule about dealing with Gramps was, *Never volunteer information.* The less Gramps knew about my dreams, the less material he would have for hollering questions at me about why the hell was I doing this or why the hell was I planning that.

"We really need to get going on that homework!" I said, jumping up. Connor jumped up, too, and we left Gramps on the couch, popping another brain into his mouth.

* * *

"I don't get it," I groaned, rolling over on the bed onto the papers full of Connor's diagrams and explanations.

I hated not getting calculus. I'd always been good at school. In chemistry, I knew the reactions backwards and forwards. In bio, I'd been the one who drilled the parts of the cell into Connor's head and helped him remember all the steps of protein synthesis. Now, with calculus, he was the one whose brain made all the connections while I floundered in the dust.

Numbers used to be sure and definite and straightforward. They didn't change; 4 was 4 and 77 was 77. But the further we went in school, the stranger things got. I suppose my first hint of trouble came when they threw "imaginary" numbers at us. I mean, seriously, imaginary numbers? And now I was drowning in a pool of derivatives and integrals. Now I could hardly find numbers at all in the homework: it was all ds, xs, ys, and squiggly symbols.

"Take it step by step," Connor said. "Like, in problem fourteen . . ."

"Forget problem fourteen." I threw an arm around his neck.

"Fine with me," he said and kissed me. "You're the one whose exam isn't done."

"I can't think about it any more." I'd just begun to kiss him again when my phone trilled.

"Don't answer it," Connor whispered.

"That's Annie's ring. If I don't pick up, she'll just keep calling."

Connor groaned while I scooped the phone off my nightstand. "Yeah?" I said.

"Bridesmaid Emergency," Annie said.

"What do you mean?"

"We got the dresses, and they are *repulsive*."

"What? No. Emily said she knows how bad the dresses usually are, and she promised . . ."

Annie cackled. "Just wait till you see them. We're all going to look ridiculous."

"But Emily has such nice clothes, and she promised . . ."

"Apparently there's something that gets turned on in the brain when you become a bride. Some kind of filter that makes you inflict horrible dresses on your friends and delude yourself that they look good." Someone screamed in the background. "You hear that? Monica just tried hers on."

"Where are you?"

"At the bridal shop on Vega. Come on over and get fitted, and see the horror that is your dress."

We hung up. "Change of plans," I said to Connor. "The bridesmaid dresses are in. You want to bike over to the store with me?"

"No," he said, reaching for me again.

"Later." I kissed him once more and hopped off the bed. "Annie says they're awful, but you know how dramatic she is. Let's go see."

"Sarah," Connor said, "I don't give a crap what the dresses look like."

"Don't you want to see how I'm gonna look?"

"You could wear trash bags and you'd look great."

"Keep saying stuff like that, and I'll let you be my boyfriend."

"I heard your current boyfriend is a great guy—bought you chocolate brains and everything." He tried to pull me back down on to the bed. "So exactly how humiliating is it that you'd rather look at these dresses than make out with me?"

"These are *bridesmaid* dresses," I said, yanking a comb through my hair. "Almost nothing comes out ahead of that. And hey, you beat calculus hands down."

I felt only a small pang about leaving my exam half done. I still had a day and a half until Monday morning, right? Plenty of time.

• • •

Connor biked over to the bridal shop with me, but he left without even coming inside. The store was a flurry of lace and measuring tape, veils and mirrors. Monica stood in front of a triple mirror while a woman with pins in her mouth knelt at the hem.

"Whaaaaat?" I said.

"Told you," Annie piped up from a nearby chair where she had collapsed in a bundle of fabric.

"What's with the color? Is it *supposed* to be that color?"

"It's called pineapple," Annie said.

"Who picks out pineapple as their wedding color? And what's with that thing on the shoulder?"

"It's a bow," Monica said.

"It's too big to be a bow. It's like a giant cabbage landed on your shoulder."

"It's not the bow that's the problem." Monica brushed a bit of it away from her cheek. "What I don't like is the asymmetrical neckline. I'm too lumpy for a dress like this. It looks like half of it's missing or something."

"You're not lumpy," Annie and I said together, automatically.

Both Monica and Annie looked sallow, even jaundiced, in the mustardy color. I could only imagine how my olive skin would look. We'd all look like candidates for the hepatitis ward.

"What about Emily's sister?" I said.

"With her posture, she can carry off almost anything, including the lopsided neckline and the weirdo bow, but the color looks muddy on her." Annie scrolled through a menu on her phone. "Mon, let me take a picture and send it to Emily. Just in case the sight of us actually *in* these dresses can bring her to her senses."

The woman on the floor finished pinning Monica's hem and stood up. "Oh, I think they're very flattering," she said.

54

"We know you mean well," Annie said, waving the woman away. To us, she muttered, "She's *paid* to say that."

• • •

The dress did look as bad on me as I thought it would, the bow resembling a second, less-defined head sitting on my shoulder, the color giving my skin a reptilian hue. I collapsed into the chair next to Annie.

"What did Emily say about the pictures?"

"That she's all tied up with wedding stuff; she'll get back to us later."

"I can't believe she's actually getting married." Emily was only a year older than Monica and I; she was the same age as Annie.

"When I tell people she's getting married at eighteen, they all ask if she's pregnant. And I say, 'No, just stupid.'"

I snorted. "Don't you think she and Brian are good together, though?"

"Oh, Brian's fine. But he's only nineteen. They're talking about the *rest of their lives*. I don't even know what color sheets to get for my room next year, and they're making lifetime decisions."

"I know." I thought about pairing up with Connor for the rest of my life, and something squirmed inside me. Not about Connor himself—because right now, I loved being with him. But it was bad enough to think of the commitment it would take to become a doctor: the years ahead of me, laid out in a planned track. I didn't want to lock up too much of my life too soon.

• • •

I took another stab at calculus that night, but didn't get very far. Monica and Annie said that the exam should be easy since it was open book, but I told them what Connor and I had always said: *These exams are worse because what open book means is that the book can't save you.*

I couldn't work on it anyway, because I had to answer a Frantic Bride call from Emily. I didn't have the heart to complain about the pineapple monstrosities while she freaked out about the fact that forty of Brian's relatives still hadn't RSVPed and the caterer was demanding the final count, and Brian's uncles were too busy arguing about who was going to drive whom to the ceremony and whether Brian's cousins could afford to miss their karate class, and nobody wanted to sit in a car with Great Aunt Sophie for three hours. And then I had to soothe Emily's worries that her hair wasn't going to look right because she'd just cut it, and what on earth had made her cut her hair so soon before the wedding? She just knew she was going to look totally ugly and weird. Her older sister had had a terrible hairdo on her wedding day.

"It looked like a giant toadstool on her head," Emily moaned.

"I promise you, your hair will not look like a toadstool," I said. *And I promise you, I will never ever get married if this is what it's like*, I added silently. "You're going to look beautiful. Everything will go fine. Everyone who needs to be there will be there."

And she believed me for about three minutes, before she started agonizing all over again.

By the time I got off the phone, exhausted from surfing the giant wave of Emily's emotions, I glanced at the calculus book and couldn't even bring myself to pick it up. Tomorrow, I promised myself, and popped a chocolate brain in my mouth. Maybe the peanut butter would be good for my neurons.

• • •

On Sunday afternoon we met at Connor's house, and shuffled

through the pages of our calculus books. Then he started rubbing his foot against my calf, and I stroked his shoulder blade, and then the books were on the floor and his tongue was in my mouth. Emily interrupted us with another Wedding Freak-out Call, and we revisited the exciting world of calculus where Connor tried to explain why I should care about a bathtub being filled at one rate and simultaneously emptied at a different rate.

"Let's just turn off the faucet and be done with the stupid problem," I said. "That's what any fool would do if they were worried about the tub overflowing."

"Well, it's not just bathtubs." Connor was always straining to show me how calculus could be used in real life. "Imagine if you had a leaking tank."

"If you have a leaking tank, you shouldn't be adding anything to it, don't you think?"

He sighed. "Okay, let's start over. If—"

My phone went off again, Annie this time. Connor said, "I'm gonna throw that phone in—"

"—a leaking bathtub," I finished, clicking on the phone. "Yeah, Annie, what's up?"

"We have head things," she said.

"What? What are you talking about?"

"For the wedding. We have these things we're supposed to wear on our heads."

"Hats?"

"No, not hats. Hats would be something normal people could at least recognize. These are big poufy things that clip on to your hair."

"What are they? Bows? Flowers?"

"They don't look like anything you've ever seen before."

"Imagine if a yellow marshmallow exploded," Monica yelled in the background. "That's what they look like."

"So we're going to wear exploded marshmallows on our heads?" I said. "Are you sure?"

"Ohhh, very sure. Emily told us herself, and what's more, she thinks they're the cutest, most clever things *ever*."

Connor tapped his calculus book. "You know I have to go to work in half an hour, right?" he said.

"Oh, Annie, look, I have to finish this exam. Talk to you later."

"Well, if you don't object to looking stupid at the wedding . . ."

"Annie, I've seen the dresses, remember? We were already going to look stupid."

In the half hour we had left, Connor managed to help me unravel one of the seven remaining problems.

"What do I do about the other six?" I asked, frowning at the blank spots on my page.

"You can do them," he said. "Just take your time."

"Maybe you can help me when you get back?"

"I'm working late tonight." He kissed me, hunted out his car keys, and paused in the doorway. "But you can stay here a while longer, if you want."

I smiled at him. Something about the way the doorway framed him, the way he jingled his keys, the piece of hair that stuck up just over his left eye, made me want to snap his picture right then.

"I'll be fine," I said. "I'm not stupid, and I have your notes to go by."

• • •

Nine-thirty. I had to leave; neither Connor's parents nor mine wanted me staying here this late. Yet all I had for these last six problems was a big smudge, the sign of repeated erasing.

I dropped Connor's notes and mine, and stared at the folder where I knew he had stored his completed exam. I would just look at the first line of Connor's answer, I told myself. As soon as I saw where he was going, I'd be able to take the next step myself.

No, I decided. As much as Connor and I worked together, we had never just plain copied from each other. We'd joked about a guy at school who also wanted to be a doctor, and who was known for cheating: *What's he going to do in surgery, read the instructions off the back of his hand?*

"Sarah!" Connor's mother called up the stairs. "Do you need a ride home?"

"Um, in a minute, thanks!"

I was out of time. And so I looked.

I copied down Connor's first line, but I didn't see what to do next.

I'm so tired, I told myself. One more line, and I'm sure I'll see how to do this.

My phone beeped then—Mom, calling me home. I stared at my test paper, unable to imagine several more hours at home alone, wrestling with these unbelievable problems. I looked at Connor's paper, at his nice, neat, worked-out solutions.

My phone beeped again. I could hear Connor's mother shuffling around at the foot of the stairs, her footsteps and the clink of her keys.

I started scribbling.

I wasn't worried about the teacher seeing that Connor and I had solved the problems in exactly the same way. She knew we worked together, and we were both A students, and we both knew our stuff when she called on us in class. Although it took me longer to get the material, I always did learn it eventually, and I could answer any question she might have about how I'd solved my problems. I had never just copied blindly from Connor; he'd helped me figure things out. He'd taught me how to solve the problems myself.

Until now.

Enough, I told myself, as I packed my book bag for the next day and set it beside my bed. The calculus was done, and I wasn't going to worry about it any more. I had plenty of other things to worry about—like having to wear an exploded marshmallow on my head and an asymmetrical pineapple dress on my body at Emily's wedding. Like Gramps using up all the hot water tomorrow morning if I didn't get in the shower first. And Gramps was hard to beat, since he didn't sleep much and was always up by 5 a.m.

When I closed my eyes, I still saw equations, scribbled figures, variables. I had calculus poisoning of the brain, I told myself, rolling over in bed.

Hopefully, you didn't need calculus to be a doctor.

• • •

On Wednesday, we got back our calculus exams. Connor and I both had our usual As. My paper said nothing about copying; the only mark on it was the A.

I stuffed my paper in my pack, and Connor and I walked over to the bridal shop. "I want you to see this monstrosity," I told him.

"You'll look fine."

"Keep saying that. You have to see the dress now so you can prepare yourself. That way, you'll be able to keep a straight face on the wedding day."

When I came out in the pineapple concoction, complete with what Annie had called "the head thing" wobbling above my forehead, Connor looked up. He'd been sitting in a pink vinyl chair next to a three-way mirror, studying his shoelaces, but when I swept out of the dressing room, he lifted his chin.

"Well?" I said.

His eyes skipped over the dress and fixed right on my face. "Beautiful," he murmured.

• • •

My grandfather turned out to have an unexpected appetite for brains—the chocolate-peanut-butter kind, at least. Connor and I came home from the bridal shop to find one lonely brain left in the box.

"I can't believe they're almost gone," I said.

Connor peered into the box and smiled. "If you eat that, will you have no brains left?"

"Ha ha. You want to split this with me?"

"Nah, you go ahead."

"Oh, come on. At least take the occipital lobe."

He bit into one end of the brain I held up for him. I licked a stray thread of peanut butter from his lips and popped the rest of the candy into my mouth. He kissed me as soon as I swallowed.

"Break it up," Gramps said, shuffling into the living room. "Where the hell's the remote?"

"Haven't seen it," Connor answered.

Gramps squinted at him. "What are you doing here, anyway? Do you live here now? You ought to pay rent."

Connor laughed, but his face flushed. I took his hand. "I'm at Connor's just as much, Gramps."

Gramps just grunted. I led Connor up to my room, where we had to keep the door open, but sometimes we could kiss a little before anyone passed my doorway.

Connor flopped on to the bed. "What'd you get in calculus?"

"A. You?" As if I didn't know.

"A. See, I knew you could do it." A grin spread across his face. "You must've been up all night Sunday."

I took a breath, the peanut-butter brain seeming to have grown to a bowling ball in my stomach. "Not too late," I said.

"The last one was tricky, wasn't it? I heard a lot of people got it wrong."

My face was heating up. I sat on the desk chair and said, "Mm, sort of." And I was thinking, *I should tell him.* He probably won't even care. He won't, will he?

But what if he did? He sat there, open-faced, smiling at me. Connor had never cheated, as far as I knew.

He never had to, a little voice whispered in my brain. *He's too smart.*

So had I been, until Sunday night.

But was "never needing to" enough? Was that all that had kept me honest?

Forget it, I told myself. It's over and you didn't get caught, and nobody cares. It's not like you didn't try to do the problems the right way. It's not like you couldn't have figured them out yourself eventually, if you'd had another week.

"What's the matter?" Connor said.

"What?"

"You look kind of . . . strange."

"Strange how?"

"I don't know. Are you okay?"

"Wonderful. Amazing." I pushed stray hairs off my damp forehead. I took a deep breath, thinking, *Tell him. No, don't tell him.*

"You sure?"

"Yeah." I sat down beside him and laced my fingers through his. "Yeah, I'm fine."

It was like I'd stolen something from Connor.

That's exactly what it felt like. When his lips touched my neck, his hand stroked my hair, all I could think about was the fact that I'd copied from him. And worse, that he didn't know I'd copied from him. First I was a cheater, and now a liar, too?

"What's wrong?" he said. "I know something's wrong with you."

"Nothing. It's just—my mom is going to walk past any second, I know it."

I should stop making a big deal out of this. It wasn't grand larceny. Connor wouldn't even care. At least, I didn't think he would care.

Probably not.

• • •

Emily's father let us all have wine at the wedding-rehearsal dinner, which was probably a mistake. Annie took Monica and me aside after the dinner, and we huddled on the steps of the restaurant. "Tomorrow we'll be doing this all over again, except then we'll be dressed like idiots," she said.

"With poufy things on our heads," Monica moaned.

"And Emily's going to be *married*. Like a grown-up." Annie shuddered.

"Things'll never be the same again," I said.

"Oh, look at you, pretending like that's such a tragedy," Annie said. "Don't tell me you aren't about *this close* to getting married yourself, Sarah."

"Whaaaat?"

"You and Connor are practically married already."

My face, already heated with wine, seemed to ignite. "No, we're not."

"Oh, come on. I bet he's buying you a diamond any second."

"God, Annie, we've still got another year of high school. And Connor can't afford a diamond."

"All you need is a down payment." Annie gulped wine, her eyes bobbling a little, the way they did whenever she'd had too much. "You know what? I asked him out when we were freshmen."

"What?"

"Connor. Before he started going out with you. I asked him out."

"I never knew that!" Monica said. "What happened?"

"We went to a movie," Annie said, her eyes avoiding mine. "We had a great time. But then—nothing."

"You went out with Connor?" I said, still unable to digest it. I thought I knew every guy Annie had ever seen, or thought about seeing, or fantasized about seeing.

"It was while you were in Chicago with your family—and I didn't say anything because it was just that once. I told him I wanted to see him again, and he gave me the 'You're great but I just want to be friends' speech."

"Ugh, I hate that speech," Monica said.

"There was no point in bringing it up, it was too humiliating. And then later, when you started going out with him—what was I supposed to do? Say, 'Oh, by the way, I once went to a movie with him?' It wasn't like anything much happened."

"Did you kiss him?" I said.

"Whoa," Monica laughed.

I expected Annie to say, *No, of course not.* Hadn't she just said that nothing happened? But she stood silent, staring out across the restaurant's parking lot. Metal car hoods gleamed coldly under the lights.

"Annie!" I said. "Did you kiss him?"

"Well, yeah," she said. "I mean, that was all. Just one kiss. Like I said, it never went anywhere."

I turned and walked back into the restaurant, where people had clumped up into quiet groups. I dragged Connor away from Brian's side.

"What's up?" he said.

"Did you go out with Annie?"

"What? What are you talking about?"

"Did you go out with Annie when we were freshmen?"

"No."

"You didn't? To the movies?"

He blinked at me, and then something flashed in his eyes. "Oh! Yeah, I forgot all about that." He stared past me, at the velvety wallpaper. "That's right, we went to a movie once." His eyes refocused on me. "What about it?"

"Why didn't you ever tell me?"

"I didn't even remember it."

I closed my eyes. The wine burned in my stomach.

"You're not actually upset about something that happened three years ago, are you?"

"Connor."

"What?"

"I copied your calculus test."

"What?"

I opened my eyes. "The last six answers, the ones we didn't get to, I copied them right off your paper."

He pushed the hair back off his forehead. "Sarah, what's with you tonight? You're acting crazy."

"Didn't you hear me? I copied your answers."

"Yeah, I heard." He looked past me again.

"What do you—think about that?"

"I think it was stupid. You didn't learn anything that way, and we both could've gotten in trouble."

"I know."

"The teacher could've thought I copied from you."

I hadn't thought of that before, but he was right. "I wouldn't let you take the blame if that happened."

"Great," he said, his voice dead as a flat tire.

• • •

As I came down the stairs the next day, teetering on my golden shoes, Gramps said, "In my day, girls knew how to dress."

"In your day, I'm sure bridesmaid dresses were just as ugly as they are now." I concentrated on each step, thinking that a bridesmaid with a fractured ankle would ruin Emily's day. Not to mention mine.

Gramps rifled through the chocolate-brain box, as if hoping the empty ruffled cups would magically reveal a leftover brain we'd overlooked. I glanced at the door. Connor was usually early, but today he was on the verge of being late. And after the silent car ride home last night, I was wondering whether he'd show up at all. Then again, Connor had never failed to show up in his life.

The doorbell rang. I exhaled and said, "Bye, Gramps, Connor's here."

"Ask him where to get more of this candy," Gramps hollered after me.

"You ready?" Connor asked, not meeting my eyes.

"Yeah." I decided to try a joke. "Can't you tell? I mean, you don't think I'm just wearing this to the church and I'm going to change into some *other* hideous dress when we get there, right?"

He jingled his keys without laughing. "Let's go, then."

We were in the car, his eyes on the road and mine on the side of his face, when I said, "Can we at least talk about this?"

"Okay."

I licked my lips. "I'm sorry."

"What I can't figure out is why you did it," he said. "You're smart enough. You didn't need to."

"I did need to. I *could not get* those last problems."

"Then why didn't you leave them blank? You still would've passed the course."

"We have to do more than pass. We have to get good grades to get into a good college to get into a good med school." I swallowed. "I never knew you were so strict about rules. I seem to remember you forging an absence note so we could go to the beach last year . . ."

"It's not about rules," he said. "It's just—I thought I knew you. Knew what you would and wouldn't do. I never guessed you would cheat on a test."

"I never did before."

After a minute of silence, I said, "I thought I knew you and Annie, too."

"What's that supposed to mean?"

"I can't believe I never knew you two went out!"

He jerked the wheel to the right and shifted the car in to park. Turning to me, he said, "You never knew because I didn't remember it. It wasn't important. It's not like she was ever my girlfriend, or . . ."

"I think she has a crush on you," I said. "I think she has for a long time. And I didn't even know that until last night."

"Annie? No way."

"You should've heard the way she talked about you. She does."

He frowned as if trying to absorb that piece of information. "Well—but I'm with you."

"Even though I'm a cheater?"

He laughed softly. "Yeah, even though."

"And even though I'm dressed like the Pineapple Freak Queen of the Eastern Seaboard?"

"Well, that's giving me second thoughts . . ."

I poked him in the shoulder.

He said, "We're going to be late for this wedding."

"I guess you're right."

He shifted back into drive and we rolled onward, toward the church. "Connor," I said, "I've felt horrible ever since I finished that test. I didn't know what else to do. I was desperate, and I was so sick of looking at those problems, and I knew your answers would be right, and . . ."

"School's only going to get harder," he said. "Wait until we hit med school."

"Are you trying to make me feel worse?"

"No," he said. "I'm just wondering what I'm going to do when things get tougher."

"Well, if it's calculus, I know you won't be copying from me."

• • •

Annie met us on the front steps of the church, her face reddening when she saw Connor with me. "Am I the only one with a hangover?" she said. "I don't even know what I said last night. It seems like I was just blabbing on and on about all kinds of—"

I touched her arm. "It's okay. Where do we get ready?"

She smiled with relief and led me up the stairs. I hung back, holding Connor's hand until the last possible second, letting my palm, fingers, fingertips slide away from his.

"See you on the inside," he said.

"I'm counting on it."

Iris and Jim

BY SHERRY SHAHAN

WHEN SHE WAS wheeled into the day room, attended by her IV drip, Jim thought she was the most beautiful girl he had ever seen. She seemed absolutely pure, evacuated of all evil, honed to perfection. Her head was an imported melon covered by the finest filo pastry, stretched and rolled thin. Her cheeks were egg shells. Concave. The hair on her head was shredded coconut. The hair on her body was dark and fuzzy, like the mold on Gorgonzola. Her skin was the color of Dijon mustard—that wonderful brownish tinge that comes from lost vitamins and minerals. She was everything *gourmet* Jim had denied himself.

According to the nurse, her name was Iris and this was her eighth admission in three years—her parents checked her in, she put on some weight, she went home, she lost it. This time, she'd done a two-month fast and then eaten a carton of laxatives. Jim was impressed, he felt encouraged; apparently, it was possible to go through the program and not be totally brainwashed.

When Iris looked at Jim, she wondered what he was doing on the ward. Not exactly no-boys-allowed, but he was the first male anorexic she'd ever seen.

When Jim looked at Iris, he couldn't help but imagine what life would be like in their own tenth-floor apartment, no elevator. Living room with barbells, rubber balls, wrist weights with Velcro strips. Medicine cabinet with over-the-counter laxatives (chocolate squares, capsules, herbal mixtures). Diuretics in timed-release tablets. Digital scales, fine-tuned to a quarter-ounce. Disposable enema bags. No kitchen. Ultimate control over their bodies.

Iris smiled at him; her T-shirt said YOU ARE WHAT YOU EAT.

"Everyone's on a diet," she said softly, "and all they do is gain weight."

Jim nodded.

"The nurses are jealous of my figure," she continued. "Most people are. Even Dr. Chu. Why do you think he started this program?"

Jim couldn't think of any other reason.

"They won't be happy until everyone on this unit looks like the Pillsbury Dough Boy."

Jim sighed.

After dinner, Jim opened and closed the metal chairs 350 times before stacking them against the wall. Then he focused on questions to ask his nutritionist: how much does the average toenail clipping weigh? How many calories do you burn clipping them? What happens to the saliva I swallow?

Therapy filled the following days.
    Occupational.
    Individual.
    Group.
    Movement.
    Art.
    Plus lectures. "The issue isn't food," Dr. Chu droned on. "It's about seeking perfection in an imperfect world."

Dr. Chu gave Jim permission to join a few patients on twenty-minute walks around the hospital grounds. Monitored, of course, by the physical therapist who made sure no one jogged.

Jim stared at his lunch: a sandwich (with crust), an apple (with skin), and a lettuce salad with a little packet of oily dressing. He portioned his sandwich with a knife and fork, careful not to touch the bread in case calories could be absorbed through his skin—the reason he'd never used shaving cream or aftershave.

He tried not to look surprised when Iris asked the nurse for a bullion cube. "This potato doesn't have any flavor," she said. "May I have a cup of hot water, too, please?"

Bullion sloshed over the potato melting the excess butter. Iris ate the potato and left her floating butter. The nurse didn't make her drink the bullion because it wasn't on her menu.

At dinner, Iris used her finger to wipe a pat of butter on an asparagus spear, then sucked an adjacent finger, pretending to remove the excess butter. The buttered finger scratched an ankle, and the calories were absorbed by a yellow sock.

Iris gave up her wheelchair on the eleventh day.

Iris and Jim shared secrets. Jim told her how he'd stayed up the night before the weekly weigh-in, drinking gallons of water so the scales would show an increase in weight, which he'd pee away later. Iris told how she'd smuggled fishing weights on to the ward and sewn them into the hem of her hospital gown. "As long as the scales show a weight gain," she said, "we have an argument against the doctor raising our calories."

After lights out, sometimes at two, sometimes three or four, depending on the schedule of the night nurse, Jim sat on Iris's hummingbird feet while she did sit-ups. She rode his bony spine while he sweated out push-ups.

"Was it good for you?" he'd ask afterwards, collapsing from exhaustion.

The next weigh-in showed that Jim had not put on the required weight. Dr. Chu summoned Jim into his office "to chew the fat."

"We monitor your weight very carefully," he said. (It's our job to make sure you gain as much weight as possible while you're here.)

"Did you hear me, son?"

"Uh-huh."

"We can't let you go home until your weight stabilizes." (You're a prisoner until you gain a thousand pounds.)

"Do you understand, son?"

"Uh-huh."

"Since your chart indicates no weight gain, even after we've raised your calories another 200 per day, the staff can only conclude you've been exercising after hours." (We have closed-circuit cameras and hidden microphones in your bedroom.)

"Are you listening to me, son?"

"Uh-huh."

Jim found Iris in the day room playing solo Scrabble. Four Ss spelled *slim*, *slender*, *slight* and *svelte*.

Iris smiled at him. "I got *emaciated* on a triple-word score!"

"They're on to us," Jim said, sitting beside her. "Guess all that water before weigh-in didn't make up for exercising."

"Salt pills. Then we'll retain more water."

"Tomorrow's my mom's birthday and I have a two-hour pass," he said. "I'll buy some."

"Wrap them in a tissue," Iris said, "and put it under your arm. Nurses never check armpits."

Jim savored these conversations with Iris; he relished them.

Sandy and another bulimic strolled by sucking orange wedges.

"Quitters," Jim murmured.

"No willpower," Iris whispered back.

Before visiting his family, Jim stopped at a drugstore and bought a packet of salt tablets.

A display of boxed chocolates by the register gave him an idea. He headed to the Home Remedy aisle and grabbed a carton of laxatives, then paid for a small paintbrush and the latest copy of *Weight Watchers*.

He set the laxatives on his dashboard during his mom's birthday party. They were a melted mess by the time he returned to the hospital. In the parking lot, he used the brush to paint the pages of the magazine with laxative. Then he checked in at the front desk. Pockets were turned inside out. Shoes shaken. Cuffs unrolled. Frisked, like a felon. Thankfully, the salt tablets didn't drop. Sweat kept the tissue in place. No one questioned the magazine.

"Have you seen Iris?" he asked the nurse.

"Took her to ICU an hour ago."

His heart slipped. "Is she okay?"

"Her resting pulse shot up to 250 beats per minute," the nurse said. "That girl's a cardiac arrest looking for a place to happen."

Jim didn't bother to ask if Iris could have visitors. He knew the answer. He also knew the hospital layout better than most of the staff since he used to jog the halls late at night.

He found her in Room 602. She wasn't under an oxygen tent. Good sign. She had an IV drip and a heart monitor. Her eyelids fluttered lightly.

"Iris?" he whispered, moving closer.

"Jim?" Her voice was thin as angel-hair pasta.

He held a limp hand. "How're you feeling?"

"How do I look?" she asked, eyes still closed.

"Like a delicately carved skeleton," he said.

She smiled. "Come closer."

Jim lowered the rail and slipped under the sheet. He was about to give her the magazine when the bouncing ball on the screen went flat and a siren sounded. Nurses stormed the room screaming medical stuff Jim didn't understand, although, "Get the hell out of that bed!" seemed clear enough.

A nurse slapped at Iris's arm and jabbed it with a needle.

Jim watched from the foot of the bed and stuffed pages of *Weight Watchers* into his mouth. He choked down the table of contents. He finished off a laxative-lathered essay, "Hunger Pains."

The bouncing ball reappeared on the monitor, slowly at first, just a simmer, then full boil.

While Iris began to breath comfortably, he finished off "Feed My Lips" and "Food for Thought."

His darling had pulled off another near-death experience; Jim had never hungered for her more.

The Last Will and Testament of Evan Todd

BY SAUNDRA MITCHELL

FADE IN:
ESTABLISHING
Here's the thing.

I'm trying to compose my first shot.

It needs to be memorable, which makes me want to go static. But static is . . . well, static. People like to start a story right in the middle. I like it, too.

But this time it's my story. I have one chance to get it right.

If I had my camera, I'd cut this whole voiceover. Sure, yes, some of the greatest movies ever let the narrator VO all over the place. Still, it's out of style.

But I don't, so . . .

For establishing, I could start at the hospital. Lots of lights, lots of unfamiliar sounds.

A doctor leans over and slaps my cheeks—not hard. It's kind of weird. Pat-pat-pat, and then she peels open my eyelids.

"Fixed," she says.

Another doctor, or maybe he's a nurse—his scrubs are sea green instead of blue, whatever that means—unfolds a cotton blanket. It steams when he spreads it over my waxy feet.

I'm naked, completely naked. They brush my penis aside like a lank rope of seaweed, scrubbing my thigh with bloody iodine. There's a cut, and they slide a thick tube under my skin. They slide another into the thickest part of my arm.

Someone sighs and says, "Sixty-six degrees. His lungs are probably shot."

"We could try ECMO," one of the yellow-scrubbed doctors says. She sounds young, like she could be in my class.

"Jesus, Hernandez, I hope he's insured," the blue doctor says, and laughs.

He snaps open a silvery blanket—it cracks and flashes like lightning, obscuring everything. That's the transition.

Or I could start with the nightmare, which isn't really a nightmare. I don't jerk up, or gasp. I'm not even sweating.

I sigh, I roll over in my bed and I look at the clock. It's three in the morning, and tomorrow is my first day back since I fell through the ice.

And what pulls me from dreams to waking is this hook in my skin. It tugs, drawing me toward something I should know but I don't.

It's that sensation—like when a word is on the tip of your tongue, or you almost remembered the capital of Hungary. It's just that, and the blue glow from my clock reflecting on my face.

See? Static—so if I'm going static, if that's how I'm establishing the first scene for the last year of my life, then let's go.

Let's melt that digital glow to an unearthly blue, one that's dark, one that shimmers with imperfect light. We'll see a silver bubble. One, then two, like pearls rolling up from the shadows.

And we'll sink down and see long fronds of seaweed waving in the blue, then focus on a silkier patch of it. It's golden instead of black-gray; down a little more and you'll see it's my hair. It waves in the water as another pearl drifts from the underside of my chin.

This is me, Evan Todd, dead, drowned under the ice at Miller's Pond.

And let's pull back, until you see my bare shoulder. Until you see my back. Until you see me looking in the mirror—it flashes like the silver blanket at the hospital did.

My clock glows in the reflection: 3:47—I have school in three hours.

I wash my face and raise my head again and I need to make this really clear.

Maybe you see me, winter-gold and brown-eyed, and taking breaths and splashing myself with cold, clear water from the tap.

Maybe that's what everyone sees.

But let's establish it right here: when I look in the mirror, I see Evan Todd, blue and pearled and drifting, drowned at Miller's Pond.

I did not survive.

FADE OUT

FADE IN:

Chelsea Bennett leans against my locker. A green balloon bobs above her head, suspiciously similar to the silver and blue balloons I saw stuck in the hawthorn tree outside.

"I thought to myself," Chelsea says, winding ribbon around her hand, "Evan's not going to get enough attention when he comes back to school so let's draw some more!"

Even though she sounds sarcastic, she hugs me hard enough to make herself squeak. Chelsea's body isn't slight; everywhere she presses against me is lush. Her flyaway curls tickle my chin; she smells like star anise and sugar.

"Thanks," I say when she finally lets me go.

"How was the bus?"

"It reminded me why I quit riding the bus."

She watches me spin the combination lock, leaning her head against the metal. It's like my hands are the most fascinating things she's ever seen. Her eyes cross slightly when I start again. "When can you drive again?"

"Not sure," I say, hesitating, then spinning the combination to the beginning once more. "It's not a rule, exactly. More like a guideline."

Chelsea says, "Move," and pushes me out of the way. With three quick twists, she opens my locker, presenting it to me with a flourish. "Your books, sir."

When she bows, I catch a glimpse of myself in the smooth, silver pendant around her neck. I'm still and blue there, too. So much for the hope that my bathroom mirror at home was broken. Yeah, that common reflective malady, the one that shows you things that aren't there—happens to everybody.

Too roughly, I duck past her and claim my books. "Thanks."

Chelsea catches my hand. She flattens it between both of hers. Her green eyes are so wide, I see the shadow of myself in them. She asks, "Evan, are you okay?"

"I'm good, I'm great," I say, threading my fingers through hers.

"If you're not ready," she says. She steps closer, and she is heat. I swear, I see it coming off her. She's a desert mirage, shimmering, beckoning. "People will understand."

This is when I do something I shouldn't. I smile—not a sin—and then I kiss her forehead—which is. Burning up on her, it's the first time I realize how deep the cold reaches beneath my skin.

"Evan," she says. Her breath is a caress against my throat.

Breaking away with a smile, I squeeze her hand, and stroke her chin. I back against my locker to close it, then shoulder Chelsea. My sleeve pops when it rubs against hers. "Really. I am so good."

I feel her sink down. Fuck, I hate myself.

"All right," she finally says, forcing summertime into her voice. "Let's go, Living Dead Boy. Your adoring masses await."

I wish she were kidding.

The locker room opens on to the common area in our school. It has too many jutting walls and angles to be called a diamond, but you get the idea. We walk past the Wall of Fame, a grid of eight by tens that start out black and white, and end in color.

Notable Alumni, the wall brags—we have an Olympic gymnast from the seventies, and a NASCAR driver from last year. Stonard's not a huge school; it takes fifty-seven years to fill three rows of four.

The white, high pitch of lilies overwhelms me. When Chelsea spins me toward the trophy cases, I see why.

"Are you for real?"

"So real," Chelsea said, pushing me along. "You're not getting the full effect, though. Mrs. Cross banned the candles after the first day."

Let me frame this:

The trophy case is the center of the common area and baseball is its centerpiece. Gold and green banners hang on either side of it; bronzed baseballs stud the lowest shelf like footlights. The rest is pictures and trophies—a metric ass-load of trophies.

We can't compete in basketball, even though that's Indiana's state religion. There's just something inherently short here; we're a compact people in Stonard. The tallest guy in school is an underfed six footer who plays percussion in our marching band.

But we can play some baseball, damn it. The Stonard Vipers have gone Semi-State or State every year for twelve years running. I've been on the team since my freshman year. Allegedly, maybe, I'm supposed to be team captain next year.

And there's a shrine to me in front of our State trophy.

A shrine.

My stomach turns. Plastic-clad bouquets, teddy bears with bats, cards, notes, somebody's letter jacket—that's just crazy. And right there along the edge, proving Chelsea honest, a few wax crescents cling to the tile.

I can't bring myself to pick up even one of the cards with my name inked there in bubble letters. This is some kind of a theater—a show I've never seen.

"I can't confirm it," Chelsea says, releasing her helium balloons to hover over the pile. "But Seb Mancuso says you appeared to him in a slice of Friday Pizza."

"Very funny."

"Oh, Evan." Chelsea throws her arms around me, pretending to be playful. "When are you going to give it up and just walk on water?"

It's when she touches me that I realize the ache of cold again. She bands me with fire; I want to push my hands up the back of her shirt and pull her into my lap.

I turn—maybe my body has decided for me, but the trophy case catches the light. Its transparency clouds, clear to silver; it becomes a mirror for the hollow, dead weight of my eyes.

Yes, I stole a kiss, but I manage to peel Chelsea off before I molest her in the hallway. She's almost my best friend, so I feel her deflate. I know the shadows that catch in the corners of her smile.

No matter how warm she is, no matter how alive, I have to stop getting her hopes up. It's never going to happen; we're never going to happen. I love her like crazy.

I want to keep her in my pocket; I love setting up stupid jokes so she can knock them down. We have the best time, as long as I ignore the crush, and she tries to hide it. We were a lot better at this before I died.

"Oh my god, Evan's back!" Shelby Howard cries from across the room.

And in an instant, I don't have to be good at pushing Chelsea away; a weirdly adoring crowd does it for her. I mean, these are my friends, or really good acquaintances—anyway, they come to my parties. I go to theirs. I have no idea who they are.

I try to catch Chelsea's gaze. Over Shelby's head, I mouth, "Save me."

Chelsea presses a hand to her chest, echoing infatuated delight when she mouths back, "Oooh, Evan Todd!"

I'm on my own.

CUT TO:
"Hey," Tyler says. Hunched over his trig book, he inhabits his desk like he might ask for a toll to cross his bridge.

I spill into the seat beside him; instead of answering, I stare at the board. In the milky cloud of dust that remains, I can see the ghosts of equations past—all stuff I missed while I was in the hospital.

Tyler hooks his fingers under his book, raising one edge of it. He hesitates, then drops it, turning to me. "Hey."

"Oh, hey," I say. I roll my eyes up like I'm thinking, like I'm trying to remember. "Oh yeah, Tyler. Tyler Ross, right?"

The dark mass of his hair wavers when he ducks. His fingers twitch on the edge of his book; I want to angle on his pinkie—the one I broke in freshman year with a wild pitch. It bobs, flickering, like a spider sounding the lines in its web.

"Sorry I didn't come to the hospital," he finally says.

"Me too," I say. I have no grace.

Tyler sprawls back. With a monumental effort, he raises his

head. "Olivia's having a party at her dad's cabin Friday, you in?"

"Fuck no."

"Fuck you, then."

"That's what I told your mother," I say, and I can't help it. I crack the ice of a smile first.

"Your mother didn't say anything," he answers. "I pay her to shut up."

We both smile, but we're almost feral. Everything's tight in Tyler's jaw; my spine is steel.

Yeah, I'll go to his girlfriend's party, and he'll clap me on the back and throw me another beer—we're friends. Best friends.

He was there when I fell through the ice.

DISSOLVE TO:

FLASHBACK—MILLER'S POND

All I remember is burning.

My lungs burn. My thoughts burn.

Scalding, I think I know that this is down, not up.

I exhale silver, not breath.

Where is up?

Where the hell is Tyler?

CUT TO:

"Welcome back Evan," Mrs. Golini says and jerks me back, to trig. Trig, on the first day back, one seat away from the Vipers' star third baseman.

"Thank you," I say. I stretch out on my desk, sprawling elbows and knees and smile. Brightly, even.

She slips a folder onto my desk, patting the top of it. "The lessons you missed; if you need help just let me know."

I nod and look at Tyler. "Ross can catch me up."

"Wonderful," she says.

Her voice melts into the background, something about haversines or tangents, but it's all just noise. My gaze drifts from the board to the windows. Outside, winter rises in a silver haze. Snow swirls through the air; when it touches the pavement, it dies.

My bones ache. They splinter at the joints so ice can slip into the marrow; nothing melts there. Mrs. Golini's voice warps, a slow wave that comes around me and I drown again. Down deep, there's a pressure that slips hard fingers into my ears, and wraps around my heart—it doesn't beat, it quivers.

The gasping stops. Sometimes frigid is fire; as soon as I burn inside and out, I stop struggling. Up or down, doesn't matter . . . there's an awareness of drowning, but no urgency. It's quiet, down deep. Still.

The hook in my chest yanks me to the surface again. The deep, secret green of the water spills out of me, and suddenly, I smell—coffee?

"Evan!"

Waters clear, and I blink to see Mrs. Golini's hazel eyes far too close to mine. Startled, I jerk away. Metal screeches in the distance as I scramble to my feet. "Get off! Get off!"

Clawed fingers reach for me. "Evan!"

"Don't touch me!" I draw back, then my shoulders crack. My sternum splits. Some fire-hot grasp wrestles me down, but down is tile instead of a weedy sea of blue. My knees crack against tile and that pain wakes me.

Twisted in their desks, everyone watches.

"Shut up." Tyler's voice is behind my ear. His breath spills across my skin, and just for the heat of it, I do exactly what he says.

Mrs. Golini trembles, but her back is straight. Her voice is firm. "Tyler, help Evan to the nurse's office."

FADE OUT

FADE IN:

"I didn't mean to scare her," I say.

Tyler, from the far corner, agrees. "He was trying to get away from her."

It's not until now, now that I've seen myself from outside—not in a mirror, outside—that I realize my mother looks like me. There's a ghost of my dark eyes there; her mouth is wide and shaded like mine. And right now, it's turned down.

"I was afraid this was too soon," she says.

From the nurse's bed, I swear to her, "It's not. I was going crazy at home."

This is the wrong thing to say, considering I just lost it in trig. The clinic is just off the main office, and I hear people talking beyond the door. My name floats to the top of conversation. People are concerned.

Mom looks at the floor, tugging her chin in thought. "I wonder if Dr. Strickland has an opening?"

"I'll apologize. I was going to apologize anyway."

"Evan, your intentions are good, but if you had a seizure . . ."

Tyler could help, but he's leaning on the wall and watching the conversation I can only half hear.

"They would have called an ambulance."

"Honey," she says.

I cut Tyler another look. Chewing his thumb, he drifts further away. I mutter, "I think I just fell asleep."

When Mom frames my face with her hands, her expression ripples. Instead of going on, quietly frustrated, she frowns. Turning her hands over, she presses one to my forehead, the other to the side of my neck. "Evan, you're freezing."

An answer spills out of me; it pours out of my mouth before I can stop it. "Yeah, I know, I'm dead."

"Evan!"

"I'm sorry."

"Get your things," Mom says. She reaches for her bag, but I catch her hand.

"I'm sorry! I'm fine. Mom, please."

To prove it, I stand. I clasp her hand between mine. I'm ready to beg.

My memories of the ER are insubstantial; ghosts of something that happened to me when I wasn't there.

But waking up in the hospital was agony, and it was real, and mine. At first, I was a twilight machine, fed by thick coils of tubes cut and thrust into my veins. I drifted toward awareness, vague and lost. But those tubes were gone when I woke up.

It was dark.

Swathed in tape and gauze, bound wrist and ankle with thick straps that cut into my skin, I couldn't move. I couldn't even scream. The faultless rhythm of the ventilator demanded my throat for my next breath.

I lay like that for hours; I *thought* it was hours. Inside, I screamed for hours, and no one heard me at all.

"I promise you," I say. "I fell asleep."

She hesitates. I don't know what that is in her eyes, if it's hope or fear, but finally she picks up her purse and says, "Dr. Strickland probably can't fit you in today . . . but I'm calling her when I get home."

This is good; this is great. And I tell her that as I see her out, like she just stopped by to pay a visit. From the corner of my eye, I catch Tyler slinking back to class. He hunches his shoulders and hurries.

I'm pretty sure I won't see him again until Saturday.

DISSOLVE TO:

Tonight, Dad comes to my door after work. Straight to my door, too. I hear him come in, then heavy, blanket-familiar footsteps right to me. A while ago, he quit coming inside without knocking.

Instead, he arrives, leans against the frame, crosses his arms over his chest. Casual, like he's visiting my office before heading to the water cooler.

"Big day, huh?" he asks.

I spread my arms. "I'm going to my own funeral, check it out." My desk is a haystack of cards and notes, little balloons on sticks and stuffed animals. "Chelsea helped me dump the flowers off the custodian's dock."

When he's nervous, my dad coughs out a laugh, heh heh. "Learning anything?"

"Yeah, it looks like I'm 2 good 2 b 4 gotten."

"Wisdom for the ages." Heh heh.

A guilty itch starts at my edges; maybe I don't know half these people, don't recognize the handwriting, couldn't match it with faces. But I fell through the ice and they caught their breath. They deserve some kind of respect.

I swivel toward Dad. "Olivia's having a party this weekend."

Dad sheds his discomfort with a smile. "Getting right back into it. That's a Todd, right there."

"Since I can't drive, I'll probably stay over."

"Don't do anything I wouldn't do." I think he wants to call me Sport or Champ but he doesn't because I'm not seven any more, which he knows. And I can almost mouth along with him when he adds, "You have protection?"

He's asked me that before every party since ninth grade. Sometimes, I wonder if he wants me to say no so he can hand me a twenty with a wink and a nudge. We're pals, my dad and I. We never talk about anything.

"I'm covered. Thanks," I say with a thumbs up.

"Good deal. I'll tell your mother," he says. Then he's down

the hall, off to change his work clothes.

It seems like we've had this conversation a thousand times. Even when I came out to him, it was painlessly friendly.

ME

Yeah, Dad, I'm pretty sure I'm gay.

DAD

(*Heh heh*)

That's all right then. You have protection?

ME

Yeah. Uh, yeah.

DAD

Good deal. I'll tell your mother.

And he exited, down the hall to change his work clothes. Later, Mom asked a bunch of questions about falling in love. If I had. If I wanted to. Then, as she stood, she asked, "Did I do something . . . ?"

Before I could say no, she answered herself.

"What a stupid question." She kissed me, both cheeks, then brushed my hair from my face. "I love you, beautiful boy."

"I love you, too," I said.

Now she worries because I haven't brought anyone home. Well, actually, now she probably worries because I drowned in Miller's Pond and told her I was dead. I swivel my chair again, stealing a look at the darkened mirror in my bathroom.

A silver bead of water streaks down my cheek.

And on that note, I go back to my funeral.

DISSOLVE TO:

Though the air still hazes with frost, Olivia's party spills out in rings around her father's cabin.

Up in the woods, everything's barren; leafless branches

stretch toward a bitter black sky. A haze hangs between us and the stars, so glittering white lights strung everywhere make up the difference.

"Evan," Olivia crows when she sees me.

Olivia is gorgeous in a camel wool coat, two shades lighter than her skin. The buttons gleam, competing with the rhinestone flowers hiding in her hair. I swear, when she shakes her head, I see the blue part of my lips in every bauble.

She swoops over and clasps the back of my neck. Two bright spots of crimson light my cheeks—not a blush, but her lipstick. Olivia loves that trick. "Evan, Evan, Evan Todd, look at you."

"Hey, sexy, you come here often?" I ask. I dip my head, but I don't wipe off her kisses. They drive Tyler nuts, and I figure he owes me.

Waving me off, Olivia tugs on my knitted hat. "Fail."

"It's twenty degrees out," I say.

Her laughter is warm. "But there's cider inside. Wine, a pony keg . . . mixers if you're good to me."

"Aren't I always good to you?" I ask, then slip my hands into her sleeves. She shrieks, barely saving her drink when she jumps back.

"Oh, no, you are not freezing to death at my party," she says. She grabs me by the front of my coat and drags me inside.

The music's so loud, I feel every filament of the beat on my skin. Bodies crush close, to talk, to dance, begging me to slip into the teasing heat. The coats are shed in here, revealing tropical cuts, bare backs, bare arms. I feel like a vampire. I want to drink them all up.

Caught in currents, I spin around to say, "Hi," or to surrender hugs.

"Brrrr, sweetie!" Sinjai says, clasping both my hands between hers.

Morgan pulls me close. "So good to see you!" She rocks me against her chest until Olivia peels me away.

"You're a whore," Olivia says lightly.

Shrugging, I smile. "I'm just friendly."

She pulls me into the kitchen. We don't stop at the impressive array of liquor bottles or red party cups filling the counters—she leads me into the pantry.

It sounds intimate, but it's not. The pantry is almost as big as the kitchen; instead of appliances, it has shelves. Lots and lots of shelves, filled with jars of homemade jam, fruit and pickles. It smells of cinnamon and of something vaguely earthy in there, and as Olivia turns, her spiced perfume slips into the mix.

"So what's going on with you and Tyler?" she asks abruptly.

I watch her rise on to her toes, slipping fingers into dark reaches. With a shrug, I start to rub out the smear of her kiss off my cheek. "Wish I knew."

Olivia ticks her tongue. "Don't give me that."

"I don't know!"

Producing a dark bottle, she twists off the cap. Slow, deliberate motions, the metal band flashing between her fingers. "He's been worrying himself crazy. Have you seen the circles under his eyes?"

I laugh. "I haven't even seen him, let alone his fucking circles."

"He's been sick over this," she says. She takes a sip from the bottle, then hands it to me. "Sick over you, texting me at all hours. Having nightmares."

The smooth, golden burn of Jamaican rum is almost as good as drawing heat from touch. It's like a swallowed ember, glowing dimly in my chest. "Well, I can't tell it from here. Did he move his locker?"

With pursed lips, Olivia waits for the bottle before she answers. "He's been using mine."

"He's skipping trig, too." I point at her. "He was there on Monday, haven't seen him since. And he's gonna get busted off the team if he flunks it. I can't help him there."

Rubbing the bottle against her lower lip, Olivia shakes her head. "I don't know what . . ."

"Liv," Tyler says behind me. His voice shimmers like oil on water.

"Look who's here," Olivia says.

He answers with a kiss, dipping her back until she has to scramble to keep the bottle upright, propped on his shoulder. The air arcs electricity when he rights her, when he tosses me half a glance. "Hey, Ev."

Olivia starts, "Maybe you should—"

"Dance with you?" He slings his arm around her shoulder, then kisses the back of her neck. It's the only skin her coat reveals. "Any time, let's go."

Wedging past me, Tyler shrugs, as if to say, "Hey, when the lady says she wants to dance . . ."

With a touch, Olivia palms the rum into my hand, and she's spirited into the pulsing body of her party again.

It's funny; she actually takes warmth with her, and sound. The pantry makes a hollow echo of my breath. Before the walls can close around me, jarring me up with green tomatoes and apple rings, I slip into the party, too.

I used to know how to do this. I can fake it.

CUT TO:

"No," I say, raising my voice. With a finger pressed into one ear, I lean closer to Sinjai. "I'm still in physical therapy now, but I should be able to play by spring."

Her nails press into my arm as she presses closer. "Oh! We were all wondering!"

"Oh, yeah, I'll be good by then!"

Before I can elaborate, Chelsea sweeps by, and in a tangle of high-pitched greetings and partings, she extracts me from Sinjai's company and rushes me through the patio doors.

"I'm so cold," she complains, huddling me into a dark corner. The stonework wall bites into my hip. I steady Chelsea's shoulders to keep her from shoving me onto the lawn, and she shoves both hands up the back of my sweater.

Serpentine heat streaks across my skin, and I pull her closer. "Then why did you bring me outside, loser?"

"Quieter," she says. She lays her cheek against my chest, and absurdly, I want to ask her if my heart's beating.

A useless question. I know it is. I feel it fluttering in my throat, hungry at my temples for more of her heat. Her breath sinks through wool to my skin, a bright, white point of warmth that slowly spreads.

She shifts, melting to fill all the spaces between us. As the edges of her nails glance across my shoulders, she complains, "I'm warmer than you are."

"I coulda told you that." Rubbing my cheek against her hair, I tighten my arms around her. "Livvy's got a fire going inside, I'm pretty sure."

Her breath stops, hitches, and she presses against me. "I know."

"Hey," I say, when the weight between us changes.

"I was so scared." She turns her head, rubbing her brow against my collarbone before looking up at me. "You went and died on me, and I never . . ."

Cold collapses around me. It's like the weight of water, like trying to run through it. I think, I'm sure I don't want her to say what's coming next. I manage a quiet, "Chelsea . . ."

"Seriously, Evan, I know I talk all the time, talk, talk, talk, babble, even, I'm babbling right now, but I don't, I can't, you have to know." She stops; I hope. Then she goes on, this awful, unstoppable hitch when she says, "Evan, I love you."

"I know."

She stiffens; her hands fall—ghost touches down my spine to escape my sweater. "Oh, really?"

Mumbling, I nod. "I was trying to ignore it."

The subtle fall stops. Chelsea jerks back. Her eyes glitter, a hard and angry grace note to the set of her jaw. "Wow."

"I didn't mean it like that," I say, but when I reach for her she deflects my hands. "You know it's not you. You're amazing."

Her posture suddenly perfect, Chelsea smoothes her shirt and glares at me. That's one of the amazing things about her— she's not ashamed. She won't look away. "Why can't I be your exception? It happens all the time!"

I hate that I'm the reason she's trying not to cry. "If anybody could be, it would be you. I'm just not . . . I just don't . . ."

"God, you take advantage of me!" A ripple wavers out from the middle of her lips, and she fights it with angry blinks and shoulder bobs. "Hugging me, putting your arm around me, God, I am just . . ."

Trapped on the stage of the patio, I shove my hands in my pockets and try to hide in my raised shoulders. The music still plays, and an uncomfortable spotlight of attention turns its glare on me. "Chelsea, I never lied to you."

At first, it seems like she has no reaction at all.

Then, she slaps me.

It's a white hot moment that fades to black, and by the time I turn to find her, she's lost in the sea of the party.

ANOTHER ANGLE

The funny thing is, I'm the one standing there with the sting of her hand on my face, but everyone's looking at me like I'm the sinner. Staring, really. Asking with their eyes, What did you do to her, asshole?

"'Scuse me," I say.

Girls I've known for ever lower their gazes. They shrink and angle away, parting to let me pass through them, but not without dirty, defensive looks. Not without accusing glares. Cutting through them, I feel their heat at a distance.

For the first time since the ice, I have fire of my own. It's small, just a faint glow, but it pulses in my wrists and my hands and my spine.

My hands make fists, and I don't apologize when I bounce off J.P., our second baseman. Drink sloshing, he bristles and turns, but to hell with him, he's in my way.

"What's your problem?" he starts, but I cut him off.

"Have you seen Chelsea?"

His expression changes. Oh, Chelsea, oh yeah, that one— it's the subtle life of a party at work. Everybody knows when something happens, even if they don't know what that something is, kind of like a bruise you don't remember getting.

Subtly sympathetic, he nods toward the stairs to the loft. "Went that way with the pussy posse."

"Thanks," I say, and thump his back harder than I need to as I head that way.

The last thing I want to do is get into this in front of a bunch of people, but I'm hacked off and feral and pissed. I'm not going to raise my hands or my voice. I just want an explanation.

It's probably the movies; how good it looks up on a screen when beautiful women coil and strike. How bad guys try to earn it, like it's proof of their heat. But you know what? Getting slapped is humiliating.

Before I'm halfway up the stairs, the landing above me explodes. A thundering wave of shouts roll through the air— one is Tyler, for sure. I can't make out what he's saying, but I see him slam his palms into Nick Blake's chest.

A two-step stagger, and Nick lunges back. Their collision vibrates through the wooden steps; I feel it buzz the soles of my feet. Rushing up I grab the first scarlet jacket I come to and yank him back.

"Get off me!" Nick rages, and surges. It's like trying to hold back a landslide. He almost slips free. I scramble to haul him back again.

I can't tell who's caging Tyler. All I can see of him is arms and a haze of dark hair. He's got his arms banded back around his shoulders. Hands locked. Laced. Tight. Unbreakable even as Tyler heaves and twists against them.

Straining, his teeth bared, he snaps at Nick, "I will drop you."

"Come get it!"

Sharp with adrenaline, I haul Nick off his feet. "Knock it off!"

For a moment, they still siege and seethe, but they're going nowhere. There's another flash of temper, and then it's gone; they're still pissed, no question, but they're probably done trying to kill each other. Without the prospect of more blood, onlookers drift away and I finally remember to breathe.

"Let go," Nick says, his tension unspooled. I wait, just another second, then release him. With a warning look, Nick straightens his shirt and bounds down the stairs.

Once he's gone, I ask Tyler, "What was that all about?"

"Forget it," he says, and brushes past. No explanation. No

eye contact. Whatever's shifted his tide, it's pulling him farther and farther away from me.

"Well, that was exciting."

The comment comes from the guy who held Tyler back, and I finally get a good look at him.

His letter jacket is blue and gold, a cougar on his sleeve. Gold floss spells out Ex Beauchamp across his heart and his varsity letter glints with swimming pins. I would have guessed basketball. But we've played all over Indiana, and I don't recognize his school. He's a stranger, completely random.

"It's not a party till somebody throws a punch," I say.

"Then this is definitely a party."

I look past him at a wall of closed doors. Chelsea could be behind any of them, but I'm hitting that long slide from angry to tired.

"Sorry, am I in your way?" Ex's face is kind, his brows thoughtfully apologetic, and he moves to let me pass.

I shake my head. "Nah, just trying to figure out if I'm coming or going."

We shake hands, clap each other on the shoulder, because that's how you thank a stranger for breaking up a fight with you. Then I skim past, playing a shell game with the doors. I know two are bedrooms, and one's a studio—Olivia's stepmother paints landscapes.

The middle bedroom opens. Carrying a bundle of used paper towels, Sinjai steadies them against her chest when she comes out. She narrows her eyes and reaches back to pull the pale pine door closed.

It doesn't catch.

When Sinjai walks away, I peer through the open wedge between door and frame.

Surrounded by wads of tissue, Chelsea sits on the floor. She's blotchy, slumped against the wall. But in spite of sailing a sea of Kleenex, she has an almost-smile for someone I can't see.

Fuck it. I'll talk to her later.

CUT TO:

THE NEXT MORNING

We've always had a system.

After one of Olivia's cabin parties, Tyler and I get up first thing and haul out the beer bottles and makeshift ashtrays. While we do that, Olivia drives home any leftover guests, and then midway to noon, Tyler's dad shows up with his truck to clear out the rest of the mess.

Some of the parents bitch about it under their breath, but not too loud. We haven't had one drunk-driving accident since Livvy started throwing her parties back in freshman year. Nobody with alcohol poisoning. No drunkenly fatal stunts like train dodging, or car surfing or ghost riding.

Yeah, pretty much the only student at Stonard that's died in three years is me.

And I was sober at the time, so . . . hate the methods, but they work, right? Anyway, Mr. Ross walks in as usual. I guess because I've been thinking about it lately, I suddenly realize how much he looks like Tyler. How much Tyler looks like him. He's the salted, aged version, with silver wings at his temples, a roughness around his jaw, but the smile is the same.

"Plausible deniability?" he asks with a grin.

I shake his hand and vow, "We played checkers all night."

"Good enough." Laughing, he tosses Tyler a box of trash bags and turns to survey the damage. It's not that bad. We'll be out in an hour at the most, as long as we can find the vacuum. "How about this spring, Evan?"

Gathering cups into towers, I nod. "I'm probably playing."

"Good enough, good enough," Mr. Ross says. He gestures

at Tyler, cheerful. "I dunno what that one would do all alone out there."

"I know how to play," Tyler says. Black plastic snaps in the air.

"Sure you do," Mr. Ross agrees. He makes a face, sweeping popcorn off the couch and on to the carpet. "Ross and Todd, though, that's a team."

"I dunno," I say lightly. "I'm looking forward to giving him hell when he's captain."

Before Tyler can deny becoming captain, his dad does it for him with a snort. No words at all, just a sound that speaks all doubt.

My pile of cups is becoming a pyramid. "I'm voting for him. He deserves it."

Mr. Ross says, "Sure would like to see State again."

"I'll get the sweeper," Tyler says.

I bow my head when Tyler leaves, then ask his dad, "Is he okay?"

Taking his time, Mr. Ross finishes putting the chair back together. Sliding the cushion into place, straightening the whole lounger so it's perfectly angled to catch the morning light. Finally, he says, "He's got his moods."

Unsettled, I stop and almost look at him. Sideways, my right eye meets his left, leaving space to give us cover if the truth is ugly. "Maybe seeing me like that did something to him. If he talked to somebody . . ."

"He needs to man up, that's what he needs," Mr. Ross says.

That's all; that's the end. I'm not Mr. Ross's buddy any more. And honestly—I'm a little relieved.

DISSOLVE TO:
Home and showered, I wrap myself in a towel and stand in front of my blanked mirror. At the edges, condensation rolls

down, peeling away strips of steam. I'm still safe, shrouded in the hazy middle.

"Evan," my mother says from my bedroom door.

"Yeah?"

Her footsteps fall soft and familiar. I hear her touching the things on my dresser. Straightening them. "How was the party?"

"It was all right," I say, flattening my hands on the counter.

"Did you have a good time?" she asks.

A bead of water wells at the top of the mirror. It pulses, almost alive, growing and straining until it's too heavy to cling to the glass any more. It doesn't reveal me. It only threatens to.

I listen to her sit on my bed. Resigned, I say, "I guess."

"I'm sorry it wasn't more fun for you," she says. There's something distant, distracted in her voice. She segues suddenly, cutting past frames of small talk to ask, "What you said at the nurse's office, Evan. It's bothered me all week . . ."

With the heat of the shower slipping from my skin, the shadowy ache of cold starts to spread again. I reach for my robe, trying to shake it off. "I thought you were going to call Dr. Strickland."

"Don't change the subject," she says softly.

Bundled in my robe, I turn out the light and lean against the wall. I feel her on the other side of it; I don't have to look to know she's hollowed with worry. "I'm not. I just thought you were."

"I did. We have an appointment." She sighs. "You have an appointment."

I don't want to wear the weight of her grief. She should leave, go away, let me reclaim my room—just be downstairs and not up here. Anything I have to say will let her down. What kind of prick makes his mother cry on purpose? "Okay."

"Come here."

"Ma, I'm not even dressed."

"I thought I bought you a robe."

The instant irritation is familiar and normal and it almost makes me laugh. Rolling against the wall, I peer around the corner at her. "What?"

Hands folded in her lap, she raises her head to look at me. "How are you, Evan?"

My mouth says, "I'm dead."

She snaps up and flies from the room.

FADE OUT

THE END

Headgear Girl

BY HEIDI R. KLING

CHER'S LIST OF NO'S

1. No gum
2. No peanut butter
3. No nuts
4. No grape juice
5. No hard candy
6. No dark soda
7. No raw carrots (no big loss)
8. No drama camp
9. No Eve
10. No Dad
11. No brother
12. No Jesse
13. No chance for a lead in the play
14. No freaking life!

I'm not kidding when I say I look like a wimpier version of Long Duck Dong's uberdork girlfriend in *Sixteen Candles*. If you haven't seen the greatest eighties movie of all time, get thee to the video store and rent it now cuz that's *so me* and if you've already seen it, I won't have to go into a long boring descriptive scene where I stare at myself in the mirror and tell

100

you all about my hair color (clown) and eye color (dirt) and boob size (can't complain). I won't have to tell you today is my first day of sophomore year, and I'm standing here on my curb in the direct Indian summer heat, sweat dripping down my forehead onto the leather strap holding my headgear and neckgear in place. I won't have to explain that yes, I mean THAT KIND OF HEADGEAR. The real-deal, full-on, eighties-style headgear—Google it for a visual cuz it's practically an artifact by now, and if you've never laid eyes on it then lucky you. But of course my orthodontist dug up this hideous thing because I have some rare and extremely serious case of "imbedded incisors insert-long-and-boring-dental-term," which basically means I have vampire fangs that supposedly only medieval torture devices from Orthodontia Archives can help yank out of my gums and down into my mouth to join my more normal teeth. Phew. Got that?

So Mom bought Dr. O.'s toilet of crap—even though I wanted a second opinion—and, because I've never won an argument with my mother in my life, I'm standing here alone, unable to move my head, waiting for the Giant Yellow Twinkie. No, I'm not six but since I have no car or license here I am, but that's not as crucial as the fact that my teeth are encased in barbed wire and my perm-gone-bad bozo bangs are puffing out from under the strap.

I'm freaking out cuz none of my friends have seen me yet.

Not even Eve, not even George.

Especially not Jesse, who looks like Young Paul Newman and whose baby blues rip my heart out of my chest every time I let myself think about them. Since I've hidden out like a California-teen version of bin Laden in his cave all summer and because they've all had decent things to do, I'm terrified our reunion will be a re-enactment of the villagers chasing Frankenstein with their fiery sticks.

If my orthodontist were here, he would be standing here dead.

The only thing that makes the whole girlfriend-of-Long-Duck-Dong scenery worse is that my BFF since pre-school, Adamless Eve, is sitting on Said Bus sure-as-Sherlock as gorgeous as she was at the end of the last school year before she bid me "Ta ta" and headed off to Musical Drama Camp. Yes, the one my mom couldn't afford to send me to because of monetary reasons due to my date from hell with the Evil Dr. O. and because Dad drained our bank account and moved in with Sally. (But that's another horrible story for another horrible day.)

Honk! Honk!

Here it comes, with all of its exhaust-exhaling delight.

BOARDING THE TRANS-FAT-LESS TWINKIE . . .
No, Ms. Busdriver-wishing-you-had-a-Camel-straight-dangling-from-your-cherry-red-lips, no, I don't need the disabled level lowered. No, please stop lowering it. Yes, I can walk up two stairs without—Oops. Nope, I'm fine. (Bang knee against door. Feel large bruise swelling up.) Oh, yeah, yeah, freshman idiots, laugh it up. It's so funny. I'm such a freak. Yes, I'm drooling. Yes, this is headgear. No, it's not illegal. Fascinating that your aunt had to wear something freaky like this. I'm glad you feel sorry for me. No, I can't move my head to see the spitballs firing in my direction. Yes, I just cracked my hip on the metal rod jutting out from the vinyl seat. Yes, I can see your beat-up black cowboy boot sticking out in the aisle and no, it's not funny to trip the girl with the freaked-up orthodontia, and Eve, will you pretty please scoot your gorgeous butt over and make room for Frankenstina?

(Gasp!)

A VOICE: Cher? Is that YOU?

102

CHER (ME): Duh.

EVE: *(swooshing hair in slow motion)* Oh. My. God.

CHER: Thanth.

EVE: I just didn't realize . . .

CHER: Yeth.

EVE: Why are you talking like that?

CHER: *(points to mouth without moving head)*

EVE: Your mom seriously is making you wear that to school?

CHER: Obviouthly.

EVE: Poor you! Poor Cher! Does it hurt? I'm sooo sorry! *(rests gorgeous head on Cher's thick shoulder)*

CHER: Ith no big deal.

EVE: Huh?

CHER: *(louder)* ITH NO BIG DEAL.

EVE: *(bats eyelashes)*

CHER: Howth camp?

EVE: Huh?

CHER: CAMP!

EVE: *(lights up)* Camp was totally totally, amazing. So I was cast as Sandy, in *Grease*, 'cept it was this role reversal experimental thing where Sandy was a boy and Danny was a girl. I mean, I never really thought about it before but you know both of those names could really go either way, kinda androgynous, you know? So anyway, I was Boy Sandy, and this amazing guy—super hot, super cool, also super gay, major pity—was Girl Danny. So we just played around with the whole idea of *changing* for someone you like, like you know how in *Grease*, at the end of the movie, Sandy totally changes into like that hard-core chick and wears the black leather jacket and Afros out her hair and wears the super tight leather pants and smokes and stuff?

CHER: Tho Boy Tandy did that inthtead?

EVE: Kinda. Well. It was a bit different than that, but yeah, pretty much, it's kinda hard to explain. I'll show you the DVD okay. Oh, Cher, I so wished you were there! I totally missed you and with no computer and only snail mail it was like I missed everything. So what did you do all summer?

CHER: (*points to headgear*)

EVE: That's it?

CHER: (*points to headgear again*)

EVE: Didn't you see Newman or George?

CHER: (*blushes*) NO!

EVE: The whole summer?

CHER: (*blushes deeper, points to headgear*)

EVE: So *no one* has seen you?

CHER: (*eyes fill with tears*)

EVE: This is worse than I thought. I'd hug you but I don't want to get caught . . .

CHER: (*shrugs large shoulders*)

EVE: What about the play?

CHER:

EVE: Can you take that thing off for auditions?

CHER:

EVE: Just please don't bring up the chair thing again, okay?

CHER: (*drool slides down chin*)

EVE: (*wipes it off with her sleeve*) Oh fucksicles.

As the bus rumbles through our tiny NorCal foothill town passing 4WD trucks with gun racks and RVs filled with grandpas on fishing trips, and my teeth clang together like cymbals, I try not to think about being cast as a piece of furniture in my first play. It was a long time ago, and who cares if it was the jumping off point of twenty-five more plays of being typecast as inanimate objects, right? And Eve's being super sweet. Super supportive. It's just . . . somewhere in the deepest Hades of my stomach, molten lava burns with jealousy as I listen to her ramble on and on about the hot guys she hooked up with and how she got a standing ovation on closing night. It's not what you're thinking; I don't hate my best friend. I mean, look at her! Listen to her! And no, I'm not *in love* with Eve either, in a creepy, she-stalker sort of way. I just want to *be Eve* and am woman enough to admit it. To myself anyway. And I've read enough pop psychology books (under the covers, by light of flash) to know it's not really because of who *Eve* is. She's innocent. She was just born that perfect vanilla-smelling way. It's because of who *I* am: a total loser. Someone who, fresh out of the shower, still somehow smells rotten. Someone who is bound to have a whitehead on her chin when talking to the hottest guy at school. Someone who inevitably trips on her eighth-grade graduation gown (fuchsia might I add) as she walks up the *one* step to the podium. Someone who at birth was destined to be the only girl in high school forced to wear headgear at the age of sixteen.

"HEADGEAR GIRL, AGE SIXTEEN" should be the headline of some cheesy rag instead of the real-life story of a real live girl, but here I am in the flesh. A live specimen. A pedigree geek-freak.

Which is why I like theater. It's the only place I fit in and, even if I don't get the best roles—Tree in Forest, Maid #3, Butt-half of a Donkey, Soldier Who Dies in Act I, Set Changer Dressed in Black, Servant #2 with no lines—at least they let me in the door. At least they don't shoosh me away. At least in theater class, *I exist*.

And I know what you're thinking: Oh, yeah, here comes the story of the classic geeky girl who's wearing headgear on the chilly first day of school but when she gets it off in the spring, flowers will bloom and she will look like Angelina Jolie. I'll be crowned Prom Queen next to Brad Sherman, who's a shoo-in for the real Brad, and blah blah blah. Sorry to disappoint. But no, this isn't that story.

So now you're probably thinking: if it isn't *that* story—the one where the gorgeous girl takes off her glasses and brushes her hair and suddenly she's one of Leo DiCaprio's model girlfriends—then this must be the story of the ugly girl who has the great *personality* so everyone loves her and she is the most popular girl at school because beauty is inner and all that other totally false crap? Nope. Try again.

I don't have an interesting personality. I'm not the class clown. I'm not even funny at all. (At least not intentionally.) So basically I'm the worst kinda geek imaginable: I'm Napoleon minus the Dynamite. How's *that* for a description?

• • •

Things go from bad to worse when we get to school.

In the hallways, I'm greeted by either shocks of disgust or open mouths wagging in complete disbelief. Eve graciously walks next to me toward our first-period drama class, where our favourite teacher from last year, the way-awesome Ms. Tea is sitting on the stage flipping through some notes. We're the first ones here. Thank God.

Ms. Tea blinks and wiggles her tiny pug nose slightly when she sees me, but quickly and only once. Either she's an incredible actress (for sure) or she's been pre-warned via the office via my mother not to balk and run away at the sight of me (most likely).

"Good morning, Cher. Good morning, Eve."

"Morning, Ms. Tea. Did you have a good summer?" Eve sing-songs her way into the front row as her white eyelet skirt floats through the air behind her.

"I did, thanks. How about you girls? How was camp, Eve?"

"Utterly. Ridiculously. Fabulous."

"That good, huh?"

Eve nods like a bobble doll. "The play we did, it was like this reverse *Grease* where Danny . . ."

While Eve fills an attentive Ms. Tea in on her adventures at musical camp, trickles of other kids enter the theater. I glance toward the door each time—peripheral vision, of course—half hoping he is, and half hoping he *isn't*, in this class.

I get back into listening mode, cuz obviously I can't be in talking mode. "We're doing *Wild Oats* this fall. But I don't think we'll do role reversal."

"Seriously?" Eve gushes, "Cuz I know how to do it. I may be able to take a lead role *and* assistant direct. Did I tell you I directed a one-act at camp? It was so amazing and . . ."

While Eve fills Ms. Tea in on directing the one-act, I stare straight ahead wondering how in the world I'll even get cast as furniture in this show.

What's the show? *Wild Oats*. Perhaps it's about a farm. I could be a fence.

A barbed-wire fence? They could build it around me like that human toilet costume George wore last year and I could just stick my face through a cutout hole. I don't need any lines. I won't even have to move my neck for that.

I open my mouth a millimeter. "There any fentheth in *Wild Oath*?"

The normal females stop talking and look over at me.

Ms. Tea's eyes are warm. "What did you say, Cher?"

"I THED, ARE THERE ANY FENTHETH IN THE THOW?? I COULD BE A FENTH!"

Eve throws her delicate fingers to her forehead. "Fences, Cherrie? She's saying the word fence, Ms. Tea. Right, honey?" She looks at me like I'm a pathetic stray dog she's found instead of her best friend. Then she tilts her face back toward our teacher. "She wants to be a fence."

I don't *want* to be a fence. I said maybe I *could* be a fence.

"Cher? I don't know if there's a fence in this show. You can still try out for a normal role."

"But with thith thing on maybe I . . ."

Eve leans forward and stares intently. "It's totally bizarre Ms. Tea and it's probably because I've known her my whole life, or maybe it's just because I'm so good with dialect and learning foreign accents and stuff? But I can *translate* Cher's new headgear voice into regular English. I can do it the whole semester. For the show even!"

A burble of giggles fills the stale theater air and I see George out of my peripheral vision laughing it up.

"Paris, girl, you rock. And uh, Sonny, why is your face caught in a bear trap?"

"Headgear." Eve nods with a shrug.

George's green eyes dance. "You said it was bad. But wow, baby, wow!"

"George!" I say, in my one happy second of the day.

"Boy George! You made it back for auditions! How was your summer and I *have to have to* tell you about camp . . ."

George, with his bushy eyebrows, straight-legged chinos and crisp pink polo shirt is the picture of upper-crust cool and class. "Cher, even stuck in a bear trap you are lovely as ever." He kisses my hand. "And darling Paris, I see you have a new chihuahua in your bag?"

Eve pets the stuffed animal tucked into her fluffy white purse. "You like?"

George grins. It's so great to see him. "I likesy. Yes, I do."

Eve's eyes widen. "Cher, scoot over one so Georgie can sit down. Thanks. So I can't believe you were in Europe all summer! How was France? Totally amazing, I'm sure? The clothes! The food! Did you bring me anything? Next year you and Sonny and Newman *have* to come to camp—of course we couldn't all room together, but we could be counselors and at night we could sneak out and . . ."

As Eve fills George in about sneaking smokes on rickety piers under starlit skies, on jealousy-inducing backstage love triangles and on late-night skinny dipping, I suck on the metal rod across my lips, suck back some drool and try and wish myself there, minus this face-cage and plus summer-tanned Jesse.

"Where's Newman?" Eve asks, like she can read my mind. My stomach bursts into flames and I almost choke on my own spit.

George gently picks an eyelash from Eve's dimpled cheek and holds it in front of her bubblegum lips to blow and make a wish, which she does with a giggle. "Just passed him on his board," George says to me, patting my bumpy knee and trying to avoid staring at my mouth. "He'll be here, Sonny. Promise."

Can a stomach really do an Olympic vaulting event?

"Whyth he telling me? I don't care."

"She doesn't care," Eve explains loudly. I glance toward the door. It's not too late to run. To hide. To try and avoid the inevitable. Stop beating heart. Now.

George faces our teacher. "Ms. Tea, it's so fabulous to see you after such a long summer. I just wanted to let you know that Mr. Newman is on his way. Yes, I'm offering a pre-apology that you can accept upon his arrival."

Ms. Tea raises her eyebrows in our general direction.

"Jethe," I say.

"Jesse," Eve translates from George to Cher back into real life.

When Ms. Tea waves her hand through the air, it's not in a condescending way like the other teachers do, like they want to fill in the moving air with a roll of the eyes and the word "kids" uttered sarcastically. Ms. Tea just means, "Whatever, guys." She finds us amusing and talks to us like we are people instead of teenage alien life forms, which is so rare and why we love her. And let me explain something else to avoid further confusion:

All of us drama-geeks have nicknames.

They started last year. Boy George made them up, handed them out and they stuck like ABC gum.

I'm Sonny because of the obvious: Sonny and Cher, as in, "Ha ha ha, I haven't heard that before." George even made us a duet in last year's talent show, but I had to be Sonny and he was Cher with the full wig and high heels and "I Got You Babe." The audience was roaring at our bellbottoms and my thick brown stache that Jesse helped me attach with makeup glue, so I accept the Sonny cuz when Jesse says my name it sounds more like Sunny, like maybe he thinks of warmth and happiness and daisies when he thinks of me, which is . . . okay, totally fine.

Eve's George-name is Paris, as in not the famous city with the Eiffel Tower, but as in everyone thinks she's the most popular girl at school because she's rich and gorgeous and skinny, but inside she's really a sweet drama-geek like the rest of us. So it's just in jest because she's not at all like the real drink-driving, stints-in jail, slutty, not-the-city-in-France, other famous Paris.

Boy George named himself, although he bares no resemblance to the cross-dressing, VH1 "Bring Back the Eighties," "Karma Chameleon" singer at all. His real name is George and he looks like your average prep. Clean-cut hair in that popular style where it sticks up a little in the front with gel, polo-shirt wearing, tucked into tan chinos, retro topsider shoes, preppy boy. He's on the tennis team and the yearbook committee and is, of course, the king of drama club. The "Boy" in the "George" thing is meant to be ironic because he's always insisting he isn't gay even though he has a soprano voice, listens to the *Cats* soundtrack on his iPod on repeat and I *think* drools over Jesse (especially when he wore that white tank top to play Stanley) but then again you'd be dead not to.

Jesse is Newman, because, chills, I can hardly think it without swooning—George thinks he looks like the young Paul Newman, which he totally does. When George first named Jesse "Newman", I hadn't seen any YPN (Young Paul Newman) movies. Then I rented some.

Okay. *Butch Cassidy and the Sundance Kid*? My dream in life is to re-enact that "Raindrops Keep Fallin' On My Head" bicycling scene with Jesse one day. The only part of that amazing movie that made no sense was how the girl could stay with grumpy Robert Redford when it was so obvious YPN had the hots for her? Then again, both YPN *and* RR being in love with you? Not a problem I've ever had to deal with.

Then the jail movie? Where YPN is wearing the blue jail jumpsuit that matches his denim-blue eyes and he's talking about the eggs in that "come hither" voice? COME ON!

I've never seen blue eyes like that in my life.

Except on Jesse. Which is why Boy George is *always* right and is meant to be completely worshipped at all times.

So that was pretty much our group last year: Boy George, Newman (YPN), Paris and me, rocking on faux velvet chairs and lovin' life, pre-headgear.

But that was last year. B.F. Before Freakenstein. And I have no idea what's going to happen now.

The first three theater audience rows fill up quickly with laughing and chatter, and "What did you do all summer?" So far it's not that bad. 'Course no one can see me, except Ms. Tea facing me on the stage.

Ms. Tea stands up. "Welcome to Advanced Drama!"

Hoots and hollers come from the whole class. We all adore

Ms. Tea, who's dressed today in a long, flowy floral skirt that looks like it's from Indonesia or somewhere. She's twisted her long, black hair into a floppy bun on the top of her head with a multicolored scarf. Her feet are bare, as always.

"For those of you new faces out there, I'm Helen Teacake. I wouldn't mind if you called me Helen, but the administration would, so please call me Ms. Tea."

The class laughs. Told you everyone loves her.

"Take off your shoes, if you'd like," she continues. "Make yourselves comfortable. I want you all to feel at home here in our theater." A scrambled ruckus begins as sneakers are ripped off, followed by a lovely green-room/locker-room scent that isn't all bad because it reminds me of last year and this theater, my favorite much-better-than-real-home place in the world. I take a deep breath to take it all in: smelly socks and dusty plush seats. It's the first time I've felt okay since they strapped me into this thing.

I slip out of my pink Converse Hi-tops, and hope my bare feet don't reek too badly. After surveying for ABC gum, I tuck my feet under the red, velvety theater chairs.

Eve slips out of her sparkly flip-flops. I watch her rosebud-pink toenails wiggle gleefully in the air.

Ms. Tea continues. "I hope you all had a fabulous summer and are excited for this fall's theater arts class. I know I am."

Eve's hand flies up.

"Yes, Eve?"

"Can you announce the play, please, Ms. Tea?"

"It's called *Wild Oats* and it's a comedic western."

The class buzzes as Eve's hand shoots up again.

Ms. Tea shoots me a wink. "Yes, Eve?"

"When are the auditions?"

She clears her throat. "Monday next week."

Ms. Tea lets out an exaggerated sigh as my BFF since

preschool's hand flies up again. This time she doesn't call on her, because she's watching the door slide open as Jesse slips in.

My heart nearly leaps out of my silver mouth when I see him. His dirty blond hair is longer than it was last school year, grazing the collar of his pink TEEN IDOL shirt where he's written in black marker below the pop singer's silk-screened face, "SUCKS." I cover my metal mouth and smile, fidgeting around to ensure Eve's head is blocking me. I sneak another peek. Only Jesse could get away with that. I mean, we know it totally sucks, but *Teen Idol* is totally popular. But since he's Jesse, he can get away with anything. His chipped, yellow skateboard is tucked under his arm, and as my eyes can't help but slide down his body, I notice he's wearing his old Converse, too.

Gulp.

"Sorry, Ms. Tea," Jesse says in his way-too-cute voice. "I crashed my board on the way to school."

I'm sure Ms. Tea's raising her eyebrows suspiciously, but I can't take my eyes off Jesse. "Are you all right, Mr. Blake? After your accident?"

"Sure thing, Ma'am."

Jesse and Ms. Tea have this thing. It started when we did *A Streetcar Named Desire* last year. Jesse played Stanley, Eve played Blanche DuBois, and I played Cop #2. A dialect coach taught us southern accents and since then, Jesse speaks only with a southern twang while we're in class.

Ms. Tea grins coyly. "Do you need to go to the nurse's office?"

Jesse looks down at his skinned knees. "No need for that, Ma'am. Just internal injuries."

Our teacher shakes her head, laughing. "Take a seat then, Mr. Blake. I'll let you off with a warning this time, but if you're ever late for one of my rehearsals it's straight to the office for you."

"Will never happen again. Promise you that." He taps the bridge of his baseball cap in her direction and then, by a total twist of freak-fate, he looks right at me and we have a brief flash of eye contact.

Please don't see me. Please don't see me. Please don't see me.

I jerk my neck straight ahead, but can still see Jesse out of the corner of my eye as he continues to scan the room. Either he didn't recognize me or he doesn't want to recognize me. I can handle Eve's nausea, other kids' wild-eyed pity, Ms. Tea's wonder, but I can't handle Jesse looking at me like that, like I'm someone to be pitied, instead of the girl who used to be his friend.

Heat rises on my cheeks as his stare burns in our direction.

"Hide me," I whisper to Eve as I bend over, head over ankles, smooshing my metal face into my backpack. I move it around a bit, feigning business, but then panic and unzip it so fast that I catch my finger in the metal strip. Blood oozes out, and I wipe it on my blue and white P.E. clothes, staining my tiger-orange gym shorts dark purple. When I zip my backpack back up in the now silent room, it causes even more of a commotion.

"You okay, Cher?" Ms. Tea asks with genuine concern.

I freeze, still bent over, my eyes glued to my (indeed they are) stinky bare feet.

If I stay down here long enough, surely she'll start talking about the play again and Jesse will find somewhere else to sit. "I'm fine," I mumble.

Eve speaks up on my behalf yet again. "She's okay. She's taking off her shoes."

I crank my neck to whisper, "Thank you," which she interprets as a devilish green light to commit the worst best-friend fraud on the planet. I watch in horror as she stands up, smoothes down her gauzy skirt, tucks a piece of her Barbie-doll hair behind her ear and faces the audience of our classmates.

"Okay, guys, here's the deal. Cher got head- and neckgear over the summer, which her psycho mom and Evil Dr. O. are making her wear all the time. Even to school. Even to play rehearsals. So even though she looks super weird and freaky, it's not her fault. So let's not make a big deal about it. K?"

How could the day get worse?

Two letters: P.E.

So I change into my gym clothes and head into the basketball gymnasium where all the normal kids are dribbling basketballs. Of course, I'm late arriving due to the fact I had to rip the neck of my T-shirt open to make space for my enormous mechanical head.

Of course, they've already picked teams for the basketball "drills."

Coach Boots, the bald JV basketball teacher, grimaces so hard at my appearance that thick blue veins stick out of his neck and I'm thinking he may have an aneurysm.

"Uh. Ms. . . .?"

"Ther Johnthon," I say.

"Cher. Do you have a doctor's note?"

"No."

The wheels in his Mr. Clean's bald head are churning.

"No doctor's note?"

"No."

Some kids snicker. My bodyguard/translator is not in this class.

"Quiet! So can you participate in that . . . uh . . . thing?"

I shrug.

"Would you rather sit on the bench for today?"

Sit on the bench instead of running up and down the squeaky b-ball court for an hour?

"Maybe that would be good."

"What, hon?"

"I THED okay."

When I turn to walk away I hear even more snickers and then a gasp. I turn around as a girl I recognize from last year's art class runs up next to me.

"Cher, right?" She has brown hair and kind eyes.

"Yeah?"

"Are you having your monthly visitor?"

"No."

"Are you sure? Because there's blood all over the back of your shorts."

What? Oh my God.

"Really? Cuz . . ."

Oh sheesh. The zipper cut from drama!

I have to turn my whole body around to check and see if the class is staring, which of course they are.

"ITH FROM A CUT ON MY THINGER!" I announce. Why? I have no idea. I guess I don't want them to think I'm a human Freaksicle who also forgets to bring tampons to school.

Everyone stares until finally Coach Clean blows his whistle and the gym fills with the horrific sound of echoing bouncing balls and "Here!", "I'm open," and "Nice shot!"

I slink back on to the bench and cross my legs tight.

I pray that someone misfires a newly blown-up ball straight at my face and shatters my walking prison into a million pieces.

Of course, no one does.

• • •

I've survived mostly on liquids the entire summer because I can only open my mouth an inch. So Mom's been making me this juice/fruit drink in the blender. She puts in a cup of orange juice, half a banana, and some yogurt and presses blend. I told her it wasn't going to work for school, but did she listen? Of course not.

I'm sucking the luke-warm gunk through a straw when Eve plops down beside me at our favorite wall outside in the quad. It's a relief to be with someone who understands what I'm saying. I guess it's like how a mom can decipher her toddler's gibberish when nobody else can. Another talent gold star for Eve. Or maybe she just knows me?

"You aren't athamed to be theen with me?"

"Hell no!" Eve blurts out, smacking on some minty gum. "How's your day going?"

My eyes roll.

"What happened?"

"Everyone thought I wath on my period in P.E. becauth I wath wearing bloody thortth. Remember the zipper debacle in theater?"

"Shit! You serious? God I'd *die*. That sucks ass."

"Tho embarrathing. Good thing wath Coach Clean took total pity on me becauthe of the obviouth," (point, point) "and let me thit on the bench and watch."

"That's cool."

"I gueth. Tho aren't you eating?"

"No way. Now that you've lost all that weight, I need to as well."

"Eve! I wathn't *trying* to lothe weight. I jutht can't eat. You know how dithguthting protein powder ith? Try thucking down thith fruit drink thing!"

I shove the straw into Eve's face and she shoves the mug away. We start laughing (well, she's laughing, I sound like a hog in heat), and the mug slips out of our tangled hands, lands on the grass and rolls down the hill. Straight into Jesse's back.

"Holyshitballs."

"Hide me."

I duck behind Eve's suede vest, careful not to tangle my wires in her angel-food hair.

"Doeth he know it wath uth?"

Eve speaks in a low, slow voice. "He's looking around, but I don't think he sees us. Shit. He's looking at me. What should I do? Okay, I'm waving at him. Oh no, Cher, he's picking up the mug and walking over . . . Hi, Jesse!"

Should I flip my other leg over the wall and run?

What are my options?

"He's coming," Eve hisses.

So I do it. I fling my other leg over the wall and jump down, smashing my face into the concrete as I skim down the flat wall. I squat down just in time.

"Hey Eve . . . what's up?" That voice. Melt.

"Nothing much." Smack, smack, smack.

My nose is pressed hard into the wall. No one's walking down the ramp, thank God.

"I'm returning Sonny's mug." Sonny's? Did he just say my nickname?

"Oh, that's not Cher's."

Jesse says in his eye-twinkling voice, "Nice try, Barbie. This mug says 'Property of Cher.' So do you know where she is?"

Property of Cher!? I'm going to *kill* my mother.

Eve's voice is all sparkly now, too. "Haven't seen her," she plays along.

"Well, okay then. I'll see you at After-School Club. Oh, and Barb?"

"Yeah?"

"Tell Sonny I said hi," Jesse says.

Pause.

Pause.

Pause.

Smack, smack, smack. Bubble pop. "Fuuuuuuuuuuck."

"Ith he gone?" I whisper, peeking over the wall on my tippiest tiptoes.

"Fuckin' Aaaaaa . . ."

"Tho it'th thafe to come back up now?"

"I think so."

"Ith Newman gone? Totally, completely gone?"

"He's back down by the picnic tables joking around with his smelly skater friends."

When I see she's telling the truth and the coast is totally clear, I swing my pink Converse All Stars over the wall until I'm straddling it.

"Giddee up, cowgirl," Eve oozes.

"Funny." I gingerly take the mug from Eve's delicate fingers.

"He thed to thay hi to me?"

Eve nods. "Totally."

I stroke the side of the YMCA plastic mug where his fingers had just traveled and it's like looking into a crystal ball at the county fairgrounds.

I see his soulful reflection in the green-room mirror as I put on his stage makeup. I see him running his fingers through his thick mess of hair when he can't remember a line. I feel our fingers touching carefully, as if by accident, as we run the light board during rehearsals. If it wasn't for this stupid mess of wires, we may have had a chance this year. Tears burn in my eyes. "He'th even cuter thith year ithn't he?"

She flips her mane to the side. "That's the fucking understatement of the year."

I don't like the sound of her voice when she says it.

119

Nor the expression in her eyes as she watches him lean back and laugh into the air about something one of his punk friends said.

"Eve?"

She's still staring at his back. "Yeah?"

"Don't even *think* about it."

Cotton-candy pink, she faces me. "No. For sure not. YPN? Totally not my type. Plus, well, I know how you feel about him . . ."

My eyes narrow suspiciously, but I'll let it go for now. She did cover for me just now and she is my Barbie doll BFF. She would never do anything to hurt me.

Jessie kicks a knit hacky-sack into the air. It bounces off his knee and he rockets it back up into the air.

I hold the "Property of Cher" tightly to my chest.

I am *never* washing this mug again.

• • •

"Okay, then what?" I'm yacking with my green-room spy, aka 007 Boy George.

The egg timer buzzes, and I quickly add five minutes while Mom's in the bathroom.

"I'm telling you, *nada*. Barbie and Newman sat by each other, which is *not* unusual because you weren't there."

"No holding handth? No making out? Nothing?"

"Making out? Cher, you are seriously paranoid. *Nothing happened*."

I'm still suspicious but let it slide. "Tho what are you doing for your monologue at auditionth tomorrow?"

"Ms. Tea said we're reading cold from the script."

"Really?" I had a monologue from this cool theater book I found at the library all memorized and ready to go. But I wasn't sure I was going to do it. I mean, I slur the words I say.

Add a dental lisp to my long list of horrific traits.

BUZZZZZZ.

Egg timer again. This time it's post-toilet-flush and Mom hears, too.

"Okay, Cher. Hang up," she says, moving her flabby arms in slow circles like a kid acting out a choo-choo train.

"Mom, come on, jutht a thec. I jutht have to athk George about—"

My evil mom comes over, grabs the phone from my hand and says, "Goodbye, Cher's friend," and hangs up on George. Just like that.

God, I could *kill* her sometimes.

"Why did you do that?"

She's still pumping her arms in the air. "Ten minutes on the phone is the rule, Cher. It's time for dinner. Besides, I don't know what you possibly have to talk to your friends about at night. You've already been with them all day.

Just because she doesn't have any friends to talk to doesn't mean I don't.

"I haven't been with them all day. I had to go to the orthodontitht, remember? I mithed my firtht drama clath, we were talking about auditionth . . ." My eyes burn. If Dad were here he would take my side. He'd say, "Mellow out, Carol. Your salad's not going to wilt if it sits five seconds longer."

"Oh. Well," Mom says, finally resting her arms. "You can call him back after dinner then. But I'm setting the timer."

We glare at each other, willing the other to say something else to escalate this argument into a full-on Cher-sprints-into-her-room-and-slams-the-door fight. I don't have the energy tonight, so I shrug and flop down into my usual seat at the dinner table.

Mom grabs her salad off the counter and we settle in for

one of our famous silent dinners. She crunches on dry lettuce and a tiny piece of steamed chicken breast while I barely choke down a yogurt smoothie with ultra-thick protein powder mixed in.

We don't bother with the "How was your day?" thing any more.

It goes without saying we both know that the other one doesn't give a crap.

And without Dad keeping the peace and Jason around for comic relief, it's too depressing to even attempt to make small talk at the dinner table.

When we're finished eating (sucking), Mom says that I can be excused to go up to my room to finish my homework. I remind her that she said I could call back George. She rolls her eyes, flashes five fingers, and then vanishes into the living room to lie on her back and do a thousand grunting stomach crunches.

Sometimes I think the silence is more depressing than all the yelling and screaming, and Dad and Jason should just ditch Sally-the-Perfect-Aerobicized-Realtor and move back in. But then I look at mom with her angry stubborn expression and her slick new workout clothes and I know that's *never* ever going to happen.

● ● ●

So I was ill-prepared for auditions, but in a way I guess more prepared than some, because it turns out we weren't reading cold from the script. We were reading cold from *our* script.

The script of our lives.

Ms. Tea was all prancy and dancy and peacock-feathered-proud as she paced back and forth on the edge of the stage—downstage as us theater geeks referred to the spot, where if you weren't careful, one could easily teeter off into the audience and land on the lap of a greasy icky football coach's lap whom you just know is sitting in the first row so he can peek under the actresses' skirts. Perv.

Not that that's ever happened to me.

So she says, "Instead of reading from the script, I want you to read from your heart."

Eve's hand immediately flies up. "Our heart?"

"Exactly. I want this to be a free-flowing exercise. I want you to share with your audience a feeling—personified. Whether it be fear, love, admiration, shame . . ."

Shame. I got that one nailed.

I raised my hand, "How long doeth it have to be?"

"Under two minutes."

I nodded while everyone else looked at me like I had just announced I was leading the Nazi Fan Club and . . . Who wants to join?

A harsh whisper in my ear. "Dude. Cher, we need to talk her *out* of this, not agree to do it, especially as compliantly as that."

George.

I shrugged.

After the day-week-month-summer I had, who cares? I had plenty to say and maybe now someone to say it to.

"Who'd like to go first?" Ms. Tea asked. Her eyes glided over the crowd and fell on me, full of pushing-milk-toward-a-hungry-kitty kindness. Full of her knowing I had something to say. "Cher?"

Faux red velvet rocked back and forth nervously. Nobody volunteered to take my place, and I imagined nobody wanted to be privy to what I was about to confess; they were about to get an earful.

Scampering up the side stairs and slumping into my spot, I stood downstage center, under the spotlight, cleared my metal-tasting throat and focused on dictation the best I could. And yeah. It reads clearer than it actually was. Headgarial Hazard . . .

The Cher Monologue

CHER: I'm not kidding when I say I look like a wimpier version of Long Duck Dong's uberdork girlfriend in *Sixteen Candles*. If you haven't seen the greatest eighties movie of all time, get thee to the video store and rent it now cuz that's so me and if you've already seen it, I won't have to go into a long boring descriptive scene where I stare at myself in the mirror and tell you all about my hair color (clown) and eye color (dirt) and boob size (can't complain).

(Cher pauses for audience laughter after gesturing toward spoken body part)

And if things weren't fabulous in the looks department before? Well, they are full-on sucky now. Because on top of all of this . . .

(CHER pauses again, waving a hand from Top-to-CherBottom. This time there's no laughter. Instead Cher hears a rubber shoe scuffing the auditorium floor; instead she notices one awkward cough. The lights are so bright she can't tell who it came from, but her face reads that she has an idea. Jesse's awkward cough gives her the strength to continue on with her monologue.)

I got this.

(CHER points to her headgear.)

124

And I talk like that lame bear from Sesame Street. Headgear Girl—me. I'm a freak. Or, since freak is not politically correct by even Quasimodo's standards, I'm not what you would call "normal" whatever that even is nowadays. And I get that. I do. But guess what? Under all this metal, under all this slurping and beastliness? I'm me. I'm Cher. And besides . . .

(*An uncharacteristic jetting of sharp hipbone meets a sly, nearly confident cock of the head as Cher hits the note of her final delivery.*)

Paranormal chickth are all the rage right now, right?

After. After. After I rubbed a piece of my shirt between my fingers in a vain attempt to figure out if this was real or just some sort of crazy nightmarish daydream, I finally got brave enough to glance out at the audience. Even in the shadows, even with the glare from the spotlight, I catch their expressions: Ms. Tea's, Eve's, George's, Jesse's.

They were all looking at me like blank-faced dolls waiting for their mouths to be painted with smiles or frowns. Like they didn't know whether to laugh, cry, clap—and needed an artist to tell them. So I just sort of stood there awkwardly rubbing rubbing rubbing that material, waiting for Ms. Tea to tell us what to do next.

She's the director. She's the artist.

And then I think, why should I wait for Ms. Tea's order?

This was *my* monologue.

This was *my* creation. If anything, I am its monster.

So I bent over in the most outlandish Shakespearean bow—Falstaff at his finest—and in my ears rang the most delicious round of applause. An applause so thick and rich it rivaled the curtains that hung behind me.

When I arched back to standing, a swan-like grace infiltrated my body, Jesse ran up on stage with a dozen roses pledging his undying love and . . .

Okay, who am I kidding. Truth is, I almost fell over backward, caught myself just before falling on my ass and after mumbling a most self-deprecating Elvis-style "Thank ya, thankya verry much," I flop back into my seat awash in a sea of "Good job"/"nice going"/"That was awesome."

The standing ovation part?

Totally true.

Never Have I Ever

BY COURTNEY GILLETTE

THE TRICK WAS to get out. So when Mrs. Robinson suggested Alfred, I went. Mrs. Robinson was the Junior Honors English teacher. She was always piling fliers on our desks—literary magazines, contests for young adults, calls for high school poets, writing camps, seminars. Things that made us feel older than we were. On my own, I had sent two stories and four poems to literary magazines, and all of them had been rejected. When I told Mrs. Robinson this, she frowned.

"That doesn't matter," she said, "Really, it happens to the best of us. Maybe instead of a contest you'd like to take some classes?"

"What kind of classes?"

"College classes," she smiled, then dug around on her desk for a purple and gray brochure. "Here. This is a weekend retreat upstate. I've never had a student go, but maybe you'd be interested?"

I thumbed through the brochure. *Academic classes for advanced high school students, in disciplines of creative writing and literature.*

"Really?" I said. It was exciting. To be told to do something as a writer. So far, I only knew I was a writer because I wrote. I was seventeen. I wrote poems and stories in long rambling documents on our computer. I made collages from magazines and concert stubs, scraps of poetry or novels smeared across the pictures. My boyfriend Tommy was in art school. The closest I got to being an adult was going to visit him, spending days in the city walking around.

I sent in the application before telling Mom. This is how I did things with her. I told her what I was doing, and then waited for her to say, "no." When she said "no" I did it anyway.

She was at the computer when I told her. I had made dinner. I had enough money to pay for the weekend from my job at the bookstore at the mall. I figured this was like a responsible teenager's version of running away.

"I have something I want to do, the second weekend in July," I told her. I was hanging on the door jamb that separated the kitchen and the living room. Our computer was wedged on to an old night table, next to the couch.

"Yeah," she answered, not looking at me. "Is it with Tommy?"

"No, it's upstate. At a college. It's a writing thing."

I could see her furrow her brow, then lower her head to rub her hand against it.

"Okay."

"I already applied," I said quickly. "It's $375 for the weekend. I can pay for it."

"A writing thing?"

Last winter, Mom had found my journal—the biggest breach of trust being that she had gone looking for it—where I had written poems about wanting to have sex with my best friend, Rebecca. I wrote stories about what it would be like, in so many different ways: if we were both vampires, if we were both college students with our own apartments in the city; if we were living in the eighteenth century and were being courted by men who we had to hide our affair from. Mom flipped out, lectured me on how dirty it was to write about sex and to write about sex with a girl, and was I a lesbian? And why did I have a boyfriend? And were we having sex? And she couldn't handle this right now, she said, not with Dad gone, I just had to stop, and it didn't matter that she had found my journal—it didn't matter, it was already done—and she was going to talk to the guidance counselor at my school. And take down those posters of girls, and no you can't go to that show in Philadelphia. And why, Amber, why why why why why?

Mom turned from the computer and looked at me.

"It's academic," I said. "A poetry class. A fiction class. A literary criticism class."

She shook her head. "How did you learn about it?"

"Mrs. Robinson."

These were the golden words. Mrs. Robinson was the kind of teacher who, even though it was our junior year, and even though by this point parent-teacher conferences only happened when kids were failing, Mrs. Robinson called at your house when you did something well. When I was the only student to get a B on our first essay—a critical look at epiphanies in Eugene O'Neill's *Long Day's Journey Into Night* (I had gone through eighteen drafts of it, having been warned by Tommy that she was the most harsh on your first paper)—she called my Mom to tell her.

Mom and I hadn't talked about writing since the sex poems. She never told me that Mrs. Robinson called. Mrs. Robinson had told me when she handed the papers back to us.

"I can't pay for it," Mom added.

"I can, I know."

"When is it?"

I told her.

"How would you get there?"

I shrugged. This I hadn't thought of. We shared one car

between the two of us—her driving to work, then after school when she came home, I drove myself to work on the nights I had to be at the bookstore. No way would she let me drive up there.

"I'll take the train."

She snorted. On the screen was her email account. Emails from my father with subjects like *Money*, *Money again*, *Money for dental*. "That's too far."

"It's like four hours."

I had no idea where it was. It was a guess. I just knew it wasn't here.

She looked at me, then turned back to the computer. "We'll talk about it."

I went to the bank and sent them a money order the next day.

• • •

I could take the train there, but then I had to take a taxicab to the school, which was about twenty minutes away. Mom called the college to ask if there were any other students taking the train that I could split a cab with, but the coordinator said there wasn't.

"How else are they all getting up there?" Mom demanded.

"Their parents," the coordinator responded.

Mom didn't ask me about it again. She gave me fifty dollars for an emergency and told me to call when I arrived, and call before I got on to the train back home.

• • •

Alfred was a hamlet, too small to even be called a village. They were hosting about fifty high school students that weekend for various academic things. Astronomy. Political Science. Fine Art. Writing. There were only eight of us in the writing group—all girls—and I was the first to arrive.

"Your roommate's name is Katie. She's from Buffalo." My warden, a chunky girl named Kelly, told me this in a chipper voice. She placed big, long "annnnnnd"s between her sentences and rarely made eye contact. I kept a permanent smile on my face, not sure how to address her otherwise.

When Kelly left, I poked around the dormitory. The closet, the matching desks, the squat bureaus. It was so plain, yet all I ever wanted. I ached to leave home. An hour or so went by as I lay on the bed, reading. When I got bored, I took out my iPod, turning the volume all the way up so that I could hear it through the tinny speakers, which I propped up on the bureau by the door. I was opening and closing all the drawers, just to snoop, when someone appeared in the doorway.

"Is that Sleater-Kinney?"

I whipped around. A tall girl with short black hair was peeking in. She held herself almost perpendicular to the door jamb before slinking into the room.

"Yeah," I smiled. "It's *Dig Me Out*."

"Oh, my God," she said, flopping on the bed where I had left my book. "I love that album."

"Are you Katie?"

"Mira Albany," she smiled, extending her hand. I shoved a drawer shut with my hip and leaned forward to shake.

"Amber."

"Pleasure," she grinned, holding my gaze. A thudding sound from the stairs interrupted us. A girl wearing a blue bandana popped in the doorway, throwing a heavy duffel bag in front of her steps. A mess of dreadlocks peeked out from under the bandana.

"I thought my parents would never leave," she huffed. "Do you guys smoke?"

"Yeah," answered Mira.

"Kinda," I said.

The girl was rummaging in a purple bag on her hip. "I saw kids outside. We can smoke here cause they don't know who's eighteen or not."

Mira sat up. "Are you joking?"

The girl smiled. She had pulled a box of Marlboro Lights and a small blue lighter from her bag. "For serious. I guess it makes sense. This is college, right?"

Mira ran down the hall for her cigarettes, and while we waited, the girl in the bandana pointed a finger at me.

"Amber?"

"Yeah."

"Cool. Katie. We're roommates."

"Oh," I smiled. "From Buffalo?"

She rolled her eyes. "The one and only."

Mira waved from the stairway and we went to join her. Outside, two girls were sitting on the porch smoking. One girl had long brown hair, and the other one wore huge gold hoop earrings and her hair was pulled back into a tight ponytail. They were loud and laughed in giant whoops. When we walked by them, they went quiet and stared us down. Later we would find out that they were Kiana and Jackie. They were both from New York City, one from Manhattan and one from the Bronx. To me, being raised in New York had to be the urban equivalent of being raised by wolves.

Just as Mira and Katie lit up their cigarettes, a blonde girl wearing the telltale purple sweatshirt of a warden appeared.

"The orientation is in fifteen minutes in Gould Hall. Do you need directions?"

"We'll figure it out," Mira quipped. The warden sniffed, then looked at Katie and I.

"It's the red building behind the cafeteria," she stated. "Don't be late."

As she walked away, Katie made a face at Mira. From a few feet away, the girls on the porch guffawed.

"Who pissed in her yogurt?" Mira scoffed. "God."

Katie gave me a cigarette, and as I puffed on it, I looked up at the trees that lined the one side of the campus. *I'm not at home*, I thought happily. It was ecstasy.

They crammed a lot into our first day, after orientation and lunch. Everything was printed on lavender paper—our schedule, our assignments, the rules. The writing group became an awkward clique that traveled from class to class: a literature class where we read Hemingway's *Hills Like White Elephants*, a poetry class where the professor insisted we call him Steven and cursed liberally. Kiana and Jackie kept to themselves, scowling at anyone who tried to talk to them; Joan was Mira's roommate and kind of a suck-up; Lindsey chewed gum loudly; and Terry took notes in a tiny red notebook that I thought made her look like a real writer.

That night, the warden reminded us of the curfew rule— everyone could stay up late, but you had to stay in your room after 11 p.m. I had put on a pair of boxers and a T-shirt and was thinking about writing in my journal when Katie came back from the bathroom and got her cigarettes.

"Are you going to bed?"

I froze, looking at her quizzically. She laughed. "Everyone's hanging out in Lindsey and Terry's room. C'mon."

We snuck quietly in our socked feet down the hall to where a bit of light spilled out from the crack of the door. The building was old, with big wood hallways that reminded us of *Girl, Interrupted*. We all wanted to be beautiful, suicidal Angelina Jolie when she was single and wild. In their room they had started playing Never Have I Ever. My insides clenched immediately, knowing that I was a virgin who would probably pale in comparison to their experiences. Mira looked particularly cool, leaning back in a pair of tiny gym shorts, the kind from the seventies, and a white tank top. Her shoulders were dotted with freckles. *She looks hot*, my mind reeled, and I gulped, wanting to shake off my own thoughts. She smiled broadly at me when I came in with Katie, clicking the door behind us. Then she patted the floor next to her by the bed, and I sat down, my heart beating wildly.

The game was simple: everyone holds up both hands, fingers splayed. One girl proclaims something she's never, ever done (kissed her friend's boyfriend, given a blow job), and the other girls who have done this thing, they put down a finger. The peer pressure, the confessions, the hollering and laughter—it quickly escalated, and we were in a fast kinship, the kind of immediate bond that only girls can build. When Katie said, "Never have I ever had sex," we all sat quietly watching the girls who could fold down a confident finger: Kiana, Jackie, Mira and Lindsey. In the gossip that followed, it came out that Jackie had lost her virginity when she was eleven. The boy was twelve.

"*What*?" Terry gasped. Most of us were wide-eyed.

Jackie shrugged half a shoulder, tanned and peeking out from the oversized Tweety bird shirt she used as a nightgown. "It doesn't matter what age we were," she sneered. "We were in love. I loved him so much. Everyone in my neighborhood had sex like that."

"But you were eleven," Lindsey announced.

There was a slight flinch, but then she jutted her chin out. "So?"

The look of scorn plastered on Kiana's face as she glowered at Lindsey made it seem like she might have lost her virginity when she was really young, too.

My fingers hadn't moved during this question. Sex was something that I told Tommy I just didn't want to do. In and out, up and down—it looked boring to me. Couldn't we do everything else? Couldn't he eat me out, and couldn't I pour chocolate syrup on his dick before going down on him? Tommy was happy to fool around in so many ways, not minding that I wasn't interested in straight-up sex. I didn't want anyone to ask me about it, though. As the game continued, I focused on the few things I could: French kissed, sucked dick, gotten drunk. Check, check, check, I let my fingers drop with an anxious pride. Yes, I had done these things. Only Joan was more prudish than me. She sat in the middle of us and pouted, lamenting her abundance of "never evers."

"Here," I told her, shifting so that I could put my legs out in front of me. "Never have I ever shaved my legs more than twice."

"What?" Katie laughed.

"No fucking way," Mira said, crawling forward to look.

"It's true," I said. My leg hair—light brown and soft, barely grown in some places. I had shaved a handful of times before deciding it was a waste of time. I was seventeen, I had a boyfriend, I was a feminist, why bother?

"That's gross," Kiana said, shaking her head. Joan was grinning, her index finger folded down in her happy palm.

Meanwhile, I was dying to say it, I was dying for someone to say it. *Never have I ever kissed a girl.* Maybe it was said, but the want, the need was just so deep that I don't remember it, that I mentally hyperventilated over such a moment of coming of age. I didn't care about giving blow jobs, or losing it, or the gross places girls had gone to fuck their boyfriends. I wanted to talk about girls. I wanted to say that I had kissed my best friend, slipped my tongue in her mouth. That I loved her so much. More than Tommy, I thought. But different. But yes.

No one asked. I didn't ask. It hurt, like holding your breath until your lungs felt scarred.

Only when Joan had fallen asleep on a stray pillow, and Terry was getting anxious about how early we had to get up for class, did Mira turn to me and ask quietly, "How long have you been with your boyfriend?"

"Seven months."

She nodded, then gave me a sideways smirk. "Have you guys had sex?"

I blushed hard, making her laugh. "No," I said, "No, I just . . . we do other things. But sex, I just . . . I don't know."

"You don't want to?"

"I can think of better things to do than the whole insert tab A into slot B," I gushed, and she buried her head in my shoulder, laughing.

"Girl," she cried, "You are crazy."

Peals of laughter erupted from Kiana and Jackie. "I'm serious!" Lindsey was saying. "He looks just like Johnny Depp!"

"Who?" Mira demanded.

"The boy from the Astrology group. Who sat at our table at dinner."

"You mean Astronomy?" Katie smirked.

"Whatever."

"He's okay," Kiana conceded. "I've got my eyes on that fly boy who had on the Knicks hat." Here she fanned herself with her hand.

"He *is* fine," Jackie agreed.

"Where do you think their dorms are?" Mira asked, leaning forward with a glint in her eye.

Katie laughed. "You wanna go for a visit?"

"You know," Mira shrugged, "it's a long weekend. And that boy with the Knicks hat was *hot*."

Jackie and Kiana cackled, leaning forward to give Mira a high five. I laughed along, I did. I was trying to picture the face of the boy in the Knicks hat, but I couldn't place it. My mind swam with the faces of the other boys who had been in the cafeteria—just boys.

"Who do you think is cute?" Katie asked me. I rolled my eyes.

"I've got a boyfriend," I said. Mira shoved my arm playfully.

"Yeah, we know. But still. Who's your crush?"

I was trying not to look, I realize, but I could see her nipples underneath her shirt. She had no idea, I thought. I was stuck in the isolation I always felt when I checked out girls.

Just then, the door swung open. Jackie screamed, and Lindsey scrambled up to her feet.

"You girls are still awake?" It was Lisa, the warden. Her face was a scowl. She was wearing long cotton pajama pants with little lambs on them.

"Yeah," Kiana answered.

Lisa glared at her, then straightened, pointing at the door. "You're here to take college classes, and even though you might think college is all about staying up late, it's not. Your first class is in, like, five hours. You all need to go back to your dorms."

We exchanged glances, and Joan was the first to slink past Lisa, squeaking apologies. The rest of us stood up and followed. "Bitch," Kiana mumbled as we walked back, to which Mira and Katie laughed loudly. Before Lisa could say anything, though, we were back in our rooms, the doors snapped shut in her face.

• • •

I never thought that writing could be exhausting, but after two days of classes, I was beat. They kept us constantly busy, herding us from Comparative Literature, to lunch, to a lecture on Memoir, to our Poetry class, then to dinner. After dinner was the only time we could do our own things.

Tommy I talked to on the phone once while I was there. I had a phone card, and one of the wardens let me use the phone in her room while everyone else was downstairs, watching a movie. When I came out of the room after hanging up, there was heated talk coming from downstairs, in the lobby.

"This is completely irresponsible of all of you. You are here at Alfred by the recommendation of your families, your teachers. People who trust you."

I crept to the top of the stairs and watched from the banister. Mira, Terry, Kiana, and Jackie were lined up against the wall. Three wardens were across from them, along with a woman with a black bob whom I recognized as the Director. She was the one speaking. Mira noticed me above them, but didn't register it—her face was a deep scowl, which made her look younger than any of us, like a baby. Other girls who had been watching the movie crowded around the doorway in their large T-shirts and flannel pajama pants. Slippers. Flip-flops.

When Lisa saw me, they all turned and looked. The Director whipped her head around to look at me.

"You need to come down from there," she said sternly.

I quickly came down the stairs, thinking of defenses, even though I hadn't done anything. "I was on the phone with my boyfriend," I said quietly, darting looks at my warden.

The Director, though, had turned her attention to Kelly and Lisa. "I need to speak with you and the other interns."

Kelly nodded. Lisa even uttered a "Yes, Ma'am." To which Mira rolled her eyes.

We were all told to go to our rooms for the rest of the night. Lindsey was on the stairs in front of me when we were herded up.

"What happened?" I whispered.

She glanced to see that Kelly and Lisa were ahead of us, then shook her head. "They went over to the boys' dorms and then walked around in their bras. Pretty dumb."

"Are you kidding?"

Lindsey shook her head. "It just sucks that we're all on lockdown now."

In our room, Katie wrote in her journal, the reading lamp clipped to her bed shining warmly. I shifted in my own bed, opening and closing my book.

"How much trouble do you think they'll be in?"

Katie shrugged, her pen still bobbing across the page. "I don't know."

After a few minutes, she added, "The program ends on Sunday. I can't imagine they'd send them home now."

"Yeah." The book I had brought—*Letters To A Young Poet*, which I had already read, but brought in the hope that one of the girls would see me reading it and think me cool—was covered in cellophane and stuck to my bare legs under my shorts.

"It's kind of dumb," I added. I wanted to be more specific, to say it was dumb to go to see the boys. If we had all walked around here in our bras, just us girls, we probably wouldn't have gotten into trouble. I thought of the awkward sight of Mira Albany, lanky in her white cross-my-heart bra, the way the fabric would cut across her small breasts. How Jackie probably wore a bra that was black, or purple, or brown. It was probably made of silk.

Katie didn't say anything.

The next morning at breakfast, Mira, Jackie, Terry, and

Kiana had to eat with their wardens. They looked pissed off. Their wardens just looked nervous.

I went back to the buffet to get more strawberries. From across the room, I saw Mira get up from her table and walk quickly toward me. I paused, pretending to pick good strawberries from the rotten ones.

Mira slid her tray next to mine.

"Are you in trouble?" I whispered. Mira shook her head, smirking. She glanced dramatically back at her table, then turned to me, her head bent low. She began spooning yogurt into the same bowl her oatmeal had been in.

"Whatever," she said. "How fucking stupid. They threatened to call our parents."

"They didn't?"

"Nah." She dropped the scoop back into the yogurt, and some splattered on her hand. She licked it off. "They're just gonna tell them on Sunday when it's over."

"That's dumb."

"Totally."

Mira's warden was now on the other side of the buffet, picking out an orange. She watched Mira, then looked away when I noticed her. Mira and I tried not to giggle.

"Hey," Mira whispered, both of us sliding our trays slowly toward the end of the buffet. "You never told me who your crush is."

I felt my heart clamp shut, just for a second. "Oh."

Mira laughed, her eyes and mouth both wide. "I bet he was with us last night."

I tried to smile. She stood up taller, looked at the warden, then smiled at me. "I totally made out with John."

Here I had to smile. What else could you do?

We were back in Poetry, our last class. When we came in, there wasn't an assignment on the whiteboard. Our notebooks were still in a pile. It was just George, sitting on the table. He nodded at us as we came in. I wondered if he knew about the bra incident.

"Something different today," he said. "I know I promised you the most poetry writing you could cram into a classroom, but today, we're not gonna write."

He slid the pile of books closer to him. "Today, I want you to share them."

"But what about the ones you said we never had to show?" Jackie said, clutching at the strap of her bag across her chest. "The ones at the back of the book?"

George held up his hands like he was surrendering, closing his eyes. "Those," he said slowly, "you do not have to show anyone. I'll keep my word. But I'll take a shot in the dark and say that those poems may be the best of what you've written here."

"You read them?" Joan squealed.

"No," George laughed, "No, honest to God, I haven't read a damn one of them."

"You better not have," Jackie deadpanned, and everyone giggled.

"He means that your best writing happens when you're totally uncensored." Everyone swiveled their head to look at Mira, who had taken her usual seat at the desk at the back of the room. I'd sat on the table next to her, and beamed—so close to her.

George picked up the first of the notebooks, glanced at the cover, then held it like a frisbee.

"Albany." He nodded.

She leaned forward, gracefully catching the notebook between both palms. He tossed the others back to us—Joan and Katie, Jackie, Kiana, Terry, Lindsey. Mine he tossed last, just as I had stood up, walking toward him to retrieve it, afraid that if I tried to catch it it would just land on the floor.

"Here are the rules," he said. "Everyone can read a poem. Just one. No feedback. No workshopping. Not a word. Then when everyone's read, we can discuss."

Everyone nodded. "Just one?" Kiana asked. He nodded. "Make it a good one."

He hopped from the desk and went to the front of the room. "I forgot to rearrange," he said, and there was a loud dragging noise as he pushed a table away to the edge of the room. We hopped off our tables and followed suit, creating a semicircle of awkwardly placed tables, with a blank space of dirty green linoleum floor in the middle. From down the hall there was the sound of a power washer, echoing off the emptiness. George shut the door with his foot, then clapped his hand.

"Sacrificial lamb?"

Jackie hopped down. I thought about flipping through my notebook, finding the poem I wanted to read, even though in my heart I knew which one I was going to share. There was the safe poem, the one about my mother and the divorce, the one I knew everyone liked from workshop. But there was a poem at the back, one that I wrote after we played Never Have I Ever, a poem that scratched at me like an itch. That was the one for me.

Jackie, for all her swagger, rocked her leg back and forth while she read. Her poem was peppered with pauses, full phrases that got caught in her mouth, a cocked eyebrow at the end. Kiana let out a whoop and we laughed and clapped. "*Girl*!" Kiana started, but George threw an arm out like a referee.

"Nope!" he said. "Next!"

It went like that, some people popping forward—Kiana, then Terry—others needing a few moments of peer pressure. After Katie read, I nervously put my hand up and made eye contact with George, smiling.

He made a hand motion telling me to go ahead.

"I hope she reads that one about her mom," Kiana said, eliciting another bug-eyed look of exasperation from George, and giggles from the rest of us.

"This one," I said, "is called 'Back of the Book.'"

If the back of the book is for no one to see,
then dear Jesus
I want you.
Like the one whose lips I knew in February,
like the body I pulled close in March,
but closer still.
You're taller than me
I wonder how I'd fit into you
chin to collarbone
sweetness jammed up against my heart.
I'd call you baby
I'd hold your hand
I'd hold you in your
Sleep
Everything's a dream, though,
just mirage, imagination,
unless I tell you.

Unless I open my mouth.
Unless you open yours first.

I closed my notebook with one hand and sauntered back to my seat. Kiana and Katie hollered, and Mira had a grin on her

143

face a mile wide. It made me laugh. George was clapping, smiling down at the ground.

"The back of the book," he remarked. Kiana gave him an exaggerated hush, and we all laughed. The only person who hadn't read a poem yet was Mira.

She slid from her spot on the table and walked forward. Then she looked at George. "Do I have to read something I wrote this week?"

George shrugged. "I suppose not," he said. "If you have something else."

"I do," she said, and turned to put her notebook on the table to her right, long arm stretching to reach. Then she closed her eyes, took a breath, and began. Her poem, from memory, started out loud, with short words sewn together, a pace that slowed, her eyes meeting ours, then quickened, a dramatic pause, a careful gesture forward. It was about being an adult in another life, why being a teenager sucked because she had been here before—a poem drawn with what-ifs and tongue-in-cheek metaphors, and the ending—an ending about love, about how sad it was to be a girl who had loved big but couldn't find anyone her age to love big, too.

"*I keep thinking*," she slammed, "*is it you? Is it you?*" She turned her gaze, eyes meeting mine, a funny smile on her lips. "*Is it you?*"

I nearly missed the ending, my brain wrapping around the look she just gave me. She's just performing, my brain told me, she's just showing off. That wasn't about me. That wasn't about me.

Everyone clapped and some hooted. I clapped and laughed at the same time, giddy with admiration for Mira. She brought her lanky form back to the table and hopped up beside me.

"That was fantastic," I told her, and she responded by leaning her head on my shoulder, then burying her face there.

And I don't know what did it, I don't know what came over me, but I turned and kissed her on the head. Just small. But enough. George was saying something to us all at the front of the room. When I kissed her, she lifted her head, and anticipating disgust, I found her face lit up with surprise. She grinned.

"I don't know what you are all planning to go to college for," George was saying, "but poetry is something you should continue. Major in it, minor in it, write it on the sly, but for goodness' sake, keep writing," he begged us. He led us in a discussion of our poems, asking some of us to repeat lines, to talk about images, to ask how we thought up a particular line or part. When we talked about my poem, Jackie whipped her head around.

"Was that about your boyfriend?" Everyone laughed. I opened and closed my mouth a few times, eyebrows raised.

"No, actually." Everyone laughed again. Jackie made her eyes wide at me, like, can you believe this girl?

"Who's it about?"

"That might not be important," George interjected, but everyone ignored him.

"It's about your crush, isn't it?" Mira was giving me a sly look. I threw my head back when I laughed, bright red.

"Who's your crush?"

"I fear this discussion has veered away from poetry, ladies," George said. "What is it about the poem that makes you want to know?"

"Because," Katie said, "it was about wanting someone before you get them. Right?"

I nodded.

"That's the best part," Kiana mused.

"*Sweetness jammed up against my heart.*" Joan tapped her pen. "I wrote that down, I loved that so much."

"What did you mean by that?"

I shrugged. "It's just how I picture it, I guess. What I want."

"Who you want," Jackie corrected, causing everyone to laugh again.

Mira hadn't taken her eyes off me the whole time. We had moved closer, so that our thighs touched. And sure, other girls were sitting this way, too, but I wanted this to mean something. It was a difficult thought, one that I didn't want to let myself think and kept cutting myself off at—it's nothing, I thought feverishly, this is nothing. This is coincidence. She doesn't like you. And even if she did, what about Tommy?

Tommy was the most dreadful thought. It was like they couldn't even compete. If Mira were a boy I would not have been flirting at all; I wouldn't even have dreamed of it. But Mira, with her mop of black curls and awkward tall body, her daring, the way she paid attention to me . . .

I didn't know what I wanted to happen before Sunday, nothing or anything, but suddenly Sunday seemed way too close.

· · ·

For our last night, they took us all out to dinner in town. While we waited for the reservation, milling about on the small sidewalk—the wardens looking like nervous sheepherders—Mira found a stairwell around the corner and sat there to smoke a cigarette. "I'm right over here," she said loudly, waving her arms at her warden, who nodded, then blinked. I had followed Mira over because my cigarettes had run out and she said I could have some since she had taken one of mine the first day there.

Pulling out two cigarettes, I reached for one, but she pulled them away, a sudden smile lighting up her face.

"Wait a minute," she said.

"What?"

She cocked her head at me. "I will give you this cigarette on one condition."

"Technically that is *my* cigarette, since you owe me." I was glowering at her, but it quickly became a laugh. "What?"

She pinched the cigarettes close to her chest. "Tell me who your crush is."

"Oh, God."

"Tell me!"

I looked away, smiling, but the slight pause bloomed into an awkward moment of silence. Mira stared me down.

"It's complicated," I said finally. I turned to see what comment she'd throw at such bullshit, but she just kept looking at me. I put my hands out in front of me.

"Have you ever liked two people at once?"

"Yeah," she said.

"Well, what if they were really different? Like, so different they couldn't even compare?"

She squinted. "That'd make an easy choice, though. You'd choose the better one."

I bit my lip. "It's not like that. It's like . . ." I exhaled. "It's like, Tommy is my boyfriend. But my crush is a girl."

I held my breath. She nodded.

"Have you been with a girl before?" Her voice had dropped to a whisper, even though everyone was half a block away.

"My first kiss was a girl."

She raised her eyebrows, a quick smirk.

"But have you ever slept with a girl?"

I shook my head.

"Do you want to?"

"Yeah," I whispered.

She nodded. "Me too."

"You do?" My laugh was too loud for our conversation. I

147

clapped a hand over my mouth and moved back. She smiled.

"I think about it a lot. I mean, but I don't know anyone, who, you know, so."

I nodded.

"There are, like, just two hundred kids in my whole high school. I know everyone. I grew up with all the girls. They're all . . ." She frowned, then she turned, putting both cigarettes in her mouth and lighting them. She handed one to me and I took a drag, turning my face to blow away the smoke.

"They're seating us now," Lisa called to us.

Mira held up her cigarette. "Can we come in a minute?"

Lisa scowled. "They're seating us *now*."

"Jesus Christ," Mira mumbled, taking a drag on the cigarette. I watched her for what to do.

"We can save them," I offered.

She rolled her eyes. I felt awful, like the closeness I had just felt for her was being violently pulled away.

"Okay," she said, stubbing hers out on the wall. I did the same and we carefully slipped them into the box.

Walking toward the restaurant, she turned to me and put her hand on my wrist. "Sit with me, yeah?"

"Of course," I said.

• • •

We were all on curfew after the bra incident, so while the kids from the other groups roamed the halls and watched movies in the common room, we were made to stay in our rooms after nine. In our room, Katie was reading a magazine and listening to her headphones. I wrote for a while, and I wondered if I should have called Tommy. I felt guilty, and then I looked at Katie.

She took out one of her headphones. "Are you okay?"

"I told Mira," I said. I had confided in Katie about my crush at lunch after our last Poetry class. I was going to burst otherwise.

"Oh, my God." She pulled out her other headphone and scrambled off her bed, coming to sit on mine.

"So?"

I told her about the conversation we had, before dinner. Afterwards, Katie sat back on her palms.

"I so knew she liked girls."

I shrugged. "You really can't always tell."

"Yeah, but still." She bit her nails. "How'd you leave it?"

"I don't know. I mean, we didn't talk about it at dinner. Obviously. And it's not like I could get any more alone time with her now."

Katie thought. "Yeah, you could."

"How?" I asked, incredulous.

She shrugged. "Sneak out later."

"But the wardens are like police out there."

"Not after they're asleep."

I thought about this. "How late do you think I'd have to wait?"

"Like midnight? Maybe one?"

"Wouldn't Mira's roommate tell?"

"Joan?" Katie laughed. "C'mon, she probably sleeps like a bear. Mira even says she snores."

I nodded, then flopped back on the bed with a sigh. "Oh, my God, I couldn't. I have a boyfriend."

"So?" Katie laughed. "It's not like you're going to fuck her." I held my breath. Katie's eyes bugged out. "Wait, are you?"

"I don't even know what that means!" I wailed. Turning over, I pushed my face into the pillow and yelled.

There was a swift knock at the door. Our warden Kelly poked her head in.

"What's going on in here?"

"Boy talk," Katie chirped, a sweet smile on her face.

Kelly smiled back and closed the door. "Keep it down, okay."

We burst out laughing.

"Just go talk to her," Katie said, lowering her voice. "C'mon, you can't start that conversation and not end it."

"I should just let it go," I mumbled.

"Yeah, but then you're just gonna obsess over it." She pointed a finger at me. "It's like, find out if she likes you now, or spend the next like ten months wondering if you should drive up to Vermont and ask her yourself."

I laughed. Katie took off her watch and began jamming the buttons. "Here," she said, "I'm gonna set my alarm for midnight. You can decide then."

"You're the best," I said.

"Anything for love," Katie chortled, and my heart swelled and felt sick at the same time. Love? This was a crush. Tommy was love. But I was beginning to doubt the difference.

• • •

I didn't sleep much. I kept waking up every few minutes to check Katie's watch, which she had left on the floor between our beds. Finally, when it said 11:57, I fiddled with the alarm to turn it off and gingerly got out of bed.

The hallways were dark, except for a mix of moonlight and fluorescent street lamps coming in from windows at both ends of the hall. Downstairs the light in the common room had been left on and shone orange light through the banisters.

My heart was thumping quickly even though I had rehearsed it a million times—if anyone asked, I would say I was going to the bathroom. Mira and Joan's room was actually the door across from the girls' bathroom, so I could, if I got caught twisting their doorknob, say I got confused. I tried to

150

imagine Lisa or Kelly believing me, but shut off my imagination when it got that far.

At their door, I kept my hand on the doorknob a long time. I hadn't thought it this far. After what seemed like for ever, pins and needles forming in my bare feet, I slowly twisted the knob and pushed the door open, praying it didn't creak.

Mira was, luckily, sleeping in the bed closer to the door. She stirred, and I held my breath. Her body turned over toward me, and I saw her squint, then sit up quickly, then squint again.

I held a finger to my lips. She smiled. Getting out of bed, she pulled on a pair of jeans, then looked at me. "Let me get my cigarettes," she whispered.

I stepped back from the door, the racing fear in my heart turning to giddiness. Mira Albany, my heart sang, Mira Albany, Mira Albany.

She came out into the hallway and slowly pulled the door shut behind her. She then stood very close in front of me, our faces nearly touching.

"Where should we go?" I whispered, trying to make my voice as far from audible as I could.

"The bathroom?"

"Someone could come in."

She turned away from me, and when she did so, she put her hand on my hip. I thought I might die.

"The boys' bathroom," she said. "C'mon."

At the other end of the hall was the boys' bathroom, smelling of bleach, the blue cakes of cleaner untouched in the urinals. She lead the way to a rectangular window at the other end, by the shower stalls, and pushed it open a sliver. I leaned against the wall, the tiles cold on my shoulder. She turned toward me, and I thought I would lose everything—my ability to speak, my ability to see.

She took her cigarettes from her back pocket and pulled out the two we had started earlier. "Here," she whispered, and I liked it that we were still quiet, that this was still a secret.

I put the cigarette in my mouth and she struck a match, the sudden light coming between us. I closed my eyes as I inhaled, then pulled back, blowing smoke toward the window. She lit her own, shook out the match, then tossed it out the window.

"I'm so glad you came and got me," she said.

"I had to," I smiled.

By the tiny light of our cigarettes, I could see her smirk. "I'm kind of impressed. I didn't think you were the kind to sneak out."

I shrugged. "It was Katie's idea."

"Katie?"

I realized what I was revealing here, and quickly sucked on my cigarette. "Well," I said, "she knew who my crush is." The next words came to me and I said them with a cool look of nonchalance. "She wanted to make sure that I got to see her."

Mira tucked her chin into her chest and laughed. Looking back at me, she whispered, "I guess your crush isn't Michael Strout."

We both laughed, and the sound echoed off the shadows. I looked at the door for a moment, remembering the danger of where we were and what we were doing, and felt momentarily panicked again. We both smoked in silence. Then I reached up to smudge my cigarette out on the concrete of the window pane, and flicked it outside.

"Amber," she said. And when I turned back, she kissed me.

Mira was only the fourth person I had ever kissed in my whole life, and it was awkward, at first. Her teeth banged up against mine. I found myself putting my hand on her hip, and she slowed. I bit her lip, and she pulled away, a small laugh.

We looked at each other, and then she kissed me again, and her hand slid under my T-shirt and my breath caught in my throat. I tucked my mouth against the warmth of her neck. I could hear her breath quicken, and when she spread her full palm over my stomach, I sighed.

"You're beautiful," she whispered, and I grinned into her neck.

Was it cheating? Was this cheating? Was I cheating? It seemed a whole different plane. I was 400 miles, a six-hour train ride, three states from home.

As if reading my thoughts, she pulled back and looked at me. "Is this okay?"

I still had one hand on the back of her head, her hair brushing against my fingers. "Yes," I said. "No. Sure. I don't know." A nervous burst of laughter passed my lips. She smiled, leaning forward to kiss me again. We pressed up against the wall, my bare foot crushing her pack of cigarettes on the tile floor.

Outside, someone coughed. My shoulders seized up around my ears, and she whipped her head around, her fingers tight on my hip.

"Shit," she breathed.

"Who—' I said, but she squeezed me where her hand was and I shut up.

There was the creak of the door to the girls' bathroom down the hall, then a gentle bang when it closed.

"We should go back," I said.

Mira hadn't relaxed and was continuing to stare at the door with hard eyes. I ducked to pick up her cigarettes and held them out to her, nodding to the hallway. "C'mon, c'mon."

"Okay," she said, "I'm coming."

I pulled the door open slowly and we slipped out. It was disorienting, to be among the shadows of the hallway, our eyes adjusting to the dark. Mira held her hands out behind her as we walked along and I took them, lacing our fingers together. We were close to the door to her and Joan's room when we heard the toilet flush, the sink go.

We froze. I had let go of her hands to push her along, when the bathroom door opened. As she sprinted the last few feet, a voice behind us hissed. "Albany."

We whipped around.

Kiana was bent toward us. She was wearing an oversized T-shirt with splatters of glow-in-the-dark paint on it, and her hair was wild from not being in a ponytail.

She hurried toward us. "What are you doing?"

"Nothing," Mira whispered. She looked from me to Kiana, then turned and slipped into her room.

I looked at Kiana. She had a perplexed look on her face. "What were you doing?" she asked again.

My legs felt weak. What *had* we been doing? "Nothing," I whispered, then, after a pause, "We were having a cigarette."

Kiana sucked her teeth in the quietest manner possible. "Right," she smirked. Then she turned to go back to her room.

"Kiana!" I whispered, louder than I intended. She turned around and looked at me.

"We were having a cigarette," I repeated.

From one of the rooms where the wardens slept, there was the sound of someone shuffling about. Kiana made an about-face toward her room, and I turned, speeding toward my room and quickly shutting myself inside.

Katie was asleep, her arm splayed out above her head, her jaw slack. In the dark, her dreadlocks looked serpent-like. A teenage Medusa.

In bed, I stared at the dark of the ceiling and listened to my heart race. I kept trying to memorize it—Mira Albany's lips, Mira Albany's hand on my hip, where her palm had touched my stomach, how her breathing had shifted, how it felt to bow my mouth to her neck.

I had never so fiercely wanted to keep a memory that I also wanted to erase.

Tommy and I had talked about cheating once. Or rather, we had talked about girls, and how I liked them. It was the day Tommy told me why women wear high heels. We were sitting on one of the faux leather couches that had cropped up around the mall, fake plants and coffee tables, like the mall was part hotel. The couches were usually filled with department-store clerks on their lunch breaks, or groups of teenage girls rummaging through their bags to talk about what they had bought. That day we had found a couch all to ourselves and were people-watching. When he asked me what kind of girls I thought were cute, it took me a long time until I saw someone who I found attractive.

"Her," I whispered, nodding toward a girl walking out of the music shop. She had short messy hair and a mean face. She was wearing combat boots and cargo pants, vaguely boyish.

"Really?" Tommy asked.

"Yeah," I said, "I mean, she looks like she could be gay or something. Maybe."

"What about girls who don't look gay?"

"What about them?"

"Don't you think they're hot?"

I made a face. Tommy scanned the people walking by, and then smiled. He turned to me, trying to look nonchalant.

"Girl who just came out of Sunglass Hut. By the escalator."

I turned. There was a girl in one of the short skirts that were in all the magazines this month. Hers was black, and she wore it with black tights and dark-gray high heels. The purse on her shoulder was some kind of designer thing with big gold clasps on it. She wore her hair in a tight ponytail, smudged make-up around her eyes.

"In the heels?" I asked, skeptical.

"She's smokin'," he laughed. I rolled my eyes, smiling. We both watched her get on the escalator. She looked around her with an air of boredom, like she couldn't wait to leave the place.

"You know why women wear high heels, right?"

I looked at him. "Ugh, no. They're so pointless."

Tommy smirked. "They're not. They have a purpose."

I raised my eyebrows. He continued, "They raise the woman's ass. And they do something to the legs, or the calves, maybe. Believe me, there's a reason women look good in heels."

I turned back to the escalator to look. The girl with the ponytail was on the second level now, and I watched as she walked above us, passing the T-shirt shop and the candle boutique, the same bored expression on her face. I tried to watch her ass, to see if it looked especially desirable, or different, than the ass of any other woman on the face of the earth.

I didn't notice anything, but I blushed, unabashedly checking out women like this. I felt small butterflies of desire bloom in my stomach.

"Do you check out girls a lot?" Tommy asked. A few moments passed, then I shook my head.

"Not really. I mean, sometimes I see girls who I think are cute. Like when we're in the city."

He nodded, looking a little hurt. I scooted closer to him, leaning my head on his shoulder.

"It's not about you, though," I said. "It's different. Like . . ." I thought for a few moments. "If you were on a diet of just strawberries. Sometimes you might see a box of blueberries, and it would look good."

Tommy was quiet. "But what if you stop liking strawberries?" he asked.

I burst out laughing. He turned his face from me, scowling at the potted plant beside the couch we sat on. "Oh, Tommy," I laughed, putting my arms around him.

"I'm serious," he said.

"Listen. I like you. I like you a lot. And I like you now, and I'll like you tomorrow, and for a long, long time. As long as you like me back."

"I like you, too," he said quietly.

"Lucky for you," I added, "I love strawberries. *Love* them."

He blushed, and I kissed his cheek, lingered there, then kissed him full on. When we pulled away from each other, he held my hand. I felt good and safe, like I wasn't lying. He knew I liked girls. Someday I would date girls. Right now, I was dating him. I loved him.

That night at Alfred, though, before I went to sleep, I decided I wouldn't tell him.

• • •

The breakfast on the last day was more casual. Kids' parents had started arriving, and they were all eating in groups, showing their mothers and fathers around campus, introducing their new friends. Some people's families just ate breakfast and left.

I ate breakfast by myself, although both Katie's family and Lindsay's family came over to say hello and invite me to sit with them. I gestured to my book and said that I was okay, thanks. At noon, one of the wardens was going to drive me to the train station for my 12:30 train back home. I wouldn't get in until eight. There were two hours to wait between trains in New York, and Tommy had talked about coming up to meet me, so we could hang in New York for a tiny bit, then go the rest of the way back together. I was relieved that the idea hadn't panned out. The idea of seeing him in four hours was too much.

My true reason for sitting alone was my hope of talking to Mira. Every time someone entered the cafeteria, I looked up, waiting for her to come through the swinging doors. Joan had come down with her mom. They were sitting at a table by the window. I thought about asking Joan if Mira was still asleep, but I didn't want to be rude. Or desperate. Kiana had come to say goodbye. She was with Jackie and Jackie's cousin, a gorgeous guy in his twenties who had come to drive them both back to New York. They were as loud and raucous as anything. The wardens seemed relieved to not be in charge of them any more. I waited for her to say something when she said goodbye, but she didn't. She and Jackie and I exchanged emails, and Jackie said that if I was ever in the city we should hang out together. I loved it, that suddenly New York was a possibility, a city with friends to visit.

I watched Joan and her mother bring their trays to the clean-up station. They were about to leave when Joan stopped and dug through her purse, pulling out a folded paper. She scanned the cafeteria, then brightened when she saw me. She walked over quickly, her purse flapping behind her.

"Hey," she said. "Are your parents coming?"

I shook my head. "I have a train at 12:30."

"That's so cool," she said. "I don't think my mom would ever let me take a train so far by myself."

I shrugged. "It's just six hours. It's not so bad."

She nodded. Then she held the paper out for me. "Mira asked me to give this to you."

"Is she upstairs?"

Joan looked confused, then shook her head. "Oh, no. She left way earlier. Her dad came."

"She left?" I knew I sounded dejected. I hope I just sounded crazy and not, well, heartsick.

"Yeah, he came at like eight this morning. She wasn't even packed yet, but they left right after that." Noticing my hurt look, she added, "I don't think she got to say goodbye to most people."

"Right," I said. I put my hand on the paper and slid it closer to my tray.

"Well," Joan smiled, "Have a good summer! I wrote my e-mail address in your poetry book, yeah?"

"Yeah, totally," I said, returning a smile. She put her arms out and I stood up so we could hug. I gave a polite wave to her mother and waited until they were safely out the swinging doors before folding open the paper.

Inside, Mira had written her e-mail address and her phone number. *Sorry I didn't get to say goodbye*, she wrote. *Call me if you want to, it's gonna be a long summer, yeah?* There were some words she had erased, and over the gray smudges she wrote, *I crave your lips and will dream of the night ours met. XX, Mira*

I swooned. I read the note over three times before I realized I was holding my breath. Mira Albany! My heart swooned. Mira Albany! I thought about calling her now, but she wouldn't even be home, she'd still be in the car with her father. I rummaged in my bag for a pen, determined to write back to her immediately, fresh with the fever from her words. Looking up, though, I noticed that most of the families were gone. The few faces that remained were unfamiliar—graduate students and some wardens from other courses. The digital clock by the mascot said it was 11:30.

I tucked the letter into my journal, deciding I could write to Mira on the train.

• • •

159

It was frightening how much I thought of Mira with a giddy joy, and how that joy could so quickly be crushed by the thought of Tommy at home—stable, good Tommy. This weekend, we would probably go out to dinner. Either the diner by his work or the new burger place by the mall. Or maybe we would go to one of the fancier cafes in town. We would watch television. We would swim in the pool at his parents' house. We would fool around in the middle of the day when no one was at his house, the same patterns of sucking dick and finger fucking that we had been doing for what suddenly seemed like a long and boring amount of time. I was trying to treasure the memory of Mira, to remember her hand and palm and mouth, without overplaying the kiss. Tommy paled in comparison to the deep thing that I felt when I recalled Mira.

In my journal, I drew a box of blueberries, the tiny fruits with their star tops tumbling over the sides. Then, in giant box letters, I penciled the words "Oh No Oh No Oh No" until there wasn't any more room on the page.

Dirty Talk

BY GARY SOTO

BORED ALMOST TO the point of tears, Tiffany Tafolla sat on the living room couch with a pillow on her lap. She looked up at the mantel clock: 10:37. She sighed and gazed out the front window. She wished *something* would happen. A cold Saturday morning in January, the fog was as gray as cement. How did people drive through such a brew?

She recalled seeing an old science fiction movie with her Uncle Richard. It was about fog that killed people, and it was one of Uncle Richard's favourites from the 1950s. As she finished her box of Milk Duds, she knew that the movie was no good, no matter how much Uncle called it a classic. At age nine, she swore none too quietly, "This movie is *@!*." Her uncle, who had also been devouring Milk Duds in the dark, halted his pleasurable munching and glared down at his niece. He licked his lips, as if preparing to scold her for her language. But he only winced, shook his head at his niece, and wiped her mouth clean of chocolate.

That was five years ago. Now, on the couch, Tiffany uttered, "That girl looks like a duck. Her *#&@!* legs are too short!" She was watching a rerun of *Dance Your Ass Off*, and Tiffany thought nothing of her outburst. The girl she cussed at deserved it! She had no business on television, especially with such a great partner! The guy was hot!

"I'm bored," Tiffany admitted after releasing a yawn that could have inflated a balloon. She tossed the pillow in her lap aside, spooking awake her cat Maxi, and got up from the couch. She reached for the remote control on the coffee table before pressing "off"—the girl with short legs disappeared.

She was four steps into the kitchen and ready to confront the breakfast dishes, her one chore for the day, when her cell phone rang.

"**&#," Tiffany muttered. She pulled the cell phone from her pants pocket and checked the phone number: Beatrice Rodriguez, her best friend. She took the call. "Hey, girl, what the +!@!*. You were supposed to call at nine." They had plans to go the mall and scour the stores for good-looking guys. It would be something fun to do on a winter day.

"You know what that &!@!* Manuel did?" Beatrice bawled. "He's sharing that *!@!* photo he took of me eating a burrito. It's on his Facebook page!"

"Shisty rat!" Tiffany slurred in anger, her face heating up beneath a layer of multicolored cosmetics. She scowled as she remembered the photo. Beatrice was struggling with a burrito—the cheese was clinging to her chin like dental floss— when Manuel, her goofy boyfriend, clicked the photo with his cell phone. And now he had posted it on his Facebook! *!@!*.

"I hate him!" Beatrice bellowed. "I'm never going to talk to him again. He's a *!@*!"

"Yeah, he is," Tiffany agreed as she looked down at Maxi purring at her ankles. She tickled the cat's scruff with her toes. "I got to clean up the kitchen, but I'll be over in an hour." She snapped shut her phone in anger, uttered, "*$%@*!" and, rolling up the sleeves of her red hoodie, faced the dishes piled high as an Egyptian pyramid. She squirted blue detergent into a plastic tub and picked up a sponge—one side was spongy, the other side rough. Her make-up began to loosen from the steam of the hot water and her anger at Manuel for pulling such a trashy trick. How dare he put that image on Facebook! "That's his girlfriend," she roared to the black frying pan. "What's wrong with him?" she asked the plates covered in hardened egg. "How could he do that!" she yelled at the spoons and forks. Her heart beat angrily as she pushed the *frijoles* down the garbage disposal. She ground them for a long minute.

Finished, Tiffany reapplied her make-up, sprayed her neck with perfume, and put on a long wool coat that reached below her knees. She pulled on a Raiders cap and black gloves, and made her exit.

"Man, it's cold," Tiffany complained with a shiver from the porch. Nevertheless, it was good to get out of the house and have a purpose greater than watching television. She would run over to Beatrice's house and make her feel better. Tiffany clapped her two gloved hands together and sprinted off the porch, leaping with her arms out like wings. She felt happy doing this, the spring and leap off the porch. If only she could really fly!

"*!@!*," she heard from the neighbor, Mr. Ramirez, a heavy-set man who could break a sweat just picking up a tool from the ground. He was in his driveway fooling with his pickup truck. In the bed of his truck sat Frisko, his pit bull rescued from the animal shelter. Frisko sported a pirate's patch over his permanently injured eye and a collar studded with nails.

"Hey, Mr. Ramirez," Tiffany greeted, her white breath unrolling like a cloud from her mouth. "It's =*&! cold, huh?"

"You got that right," he hollered from behind the small wooden fence that ran between the properties. He complained about the starter and, gazing into his tool box, muttered, "Where's my socket wrench? *!@!*."

163

"Do you think Frisko's cold?" Tiffany asked. She felt sorry for the dog because, unlike Maxi, he had to sleep outside on an old army blanket.

Mr. Ramirez looked momentarily at the dog. "*!@!* no. The dude is built for cold."

Tiffany walked across the frozen lawn, turned, and walked backwards a few steps, her house slowly disappearing in the fog. Down the street, she ran into Mrs. Clarke, her former babysitter, who had spent a few months in jail for passing bad checks. But that temporary lapse of good judgment didn't color Tiffany's opinion of Mrs. Clarke. No, everyone was doing bad—passing worthless checks, making late rent payments, and committing outright thievery. Only last week one of their neighbors caught a teenager breaking into his house. The multitasking teenager, reported the neighbor to the police, was on his cell phone talking to a friend while he was shimmying through the back bedroom window.

"A $&*!=* cold day, huh?" Mrs. Clarke offered up as conversation. Bundled in a couple of coats, she was raking leaves in her front yard. When she smiled, she revealed an empty space where a tooth should be lodged. Her ratty hair looked as if it had been pulled at by a blackbird.

"Yeah, it is," Tiffany answered in return. "I can hardly see where I'm *!@*! walking." She laughed and thought, I just cussed. She sprinted down the street, trying to build up heat beneath her coat. But she stopped when an elderly woman asked in Spanish if Tiffany could help her.

"Like what?" Tiffany asked roughly.

"*El arbol de naranja*," she began to explain. She pointed to the tree at the side of her house. "Would you be a dear and pick a few for me?"

Tiffany eyed the house and the string of Christmas lights hanging from the eaves. There was an orderly squad of cactus plants in coffee and soup cans on the porch. And were those two bulky plastic garbage bags filled with aluminum cans? Bundled cardboard for recycling? Her parents had warned her about such a ploy—a nice woman begging for help and the next moment you, an innocent victim, are tied up in a van and going somewhere nasty.

"Nah, I ain't got time," Tiffany answered. Under her breath, she swore, "*!@! no."

Tiffany walked away, throwing back a few Tic Tac breath mints. But as she sucked on those wintry pellets, she became troubled by her manners. The old lady could have been her grandmother—she was Mexican and brown as a penny. She had long ropy braids like her grandmother, too. *Why did I do that?* she wondered. She was just a little old *viejita*. She just wanted a couple of oranges from her tree. She spat the Tic Tacs from her mouth. She didn't know why she did that either.

"Whatever," Tiffany concluded, feeling a brief pang as she walked down the street.

• • •

A few minutes later she was at Beatrice's house. She rapped on the front door where a plastic Christmas wreath still hung, and pushed the door open when no one answered. Her face was immediately enveloped by the over-warm living room. Tiffany expected Beatrice's eyes to be pooled with tears when she arrived. Where was the mascara running like sludge down her cheeks? The pouting mouth? Where were the shoulder-heaving sobs and the box of Kleenex on the coffee table? Instead, Beatrice's eyes were bright with laughter.

"You should see what that #@!*# girl is wearing," Beatrice said, her hand on her stomach.

Tiffany glanced at the program on television. A chubby girl in an orange tank top was standing in front of a 360-degree mirror. Tiffany had a tank top not unlike the girl's somewhere in her drawers. But on her, it looked cute. On this old Barbie doll with stringy hair . . . ugly.

"I thought you would be all sad?" Tiffany asked as she sat down next to Beatrice on the couch, ready to raise her arms and hug her best friend. She rested her hand on Beatrice's knee.

"Nah," Beatrice answered without looking at her. Her eyes were on the television and her smile was undulating like a wave.

This was not what Tiffany expected. No, she expected a heart-to-heart talk—and she would have it! Tiffany took the remote from the coffee table and pressed the off button. The chubby girl, flanked by Stacy and Clinton from *What Not to Wear*, disappeared, though their images clung at the back of Tiffany's mind. Right then, she decided to get rid of her orange tank top.

Beatrice turned to Tiffany, her mouth open and snarling. "Why did you *!@*! do that? I was watching!"

"I want to hear about Manuel," Tiffany answered, scooting a few inches from Beatrice, who scooted a few more inches away. It looked like a face-off.

"Hear *!$%@*! what?" Beatrice tried to swipe the remote from Tiffany's hand, but Tiffany was quick enough to swing it behind her back.

"Give it to me!" Beatrice scolded. "I mean it!"

"Nah, tell me first."

"Give it to me, I said!"

Tiffany didn't like the rage on her best friend's face, or her struggle against Beatrice's arms snaking around her waist trying to get the remote. Beatrice seemed genuinely mad, but about what? That Tiffany had turned off the television? Still, Tiffany braved repeating herself. "I want to hear about

166

Manuel." She was going to add how Manuel was such a *!&*! but she decided that she should just keep those words inside her.

Beatrice stopped, caught her breath, and softened. Her hands came to her mouth as she hid her smile. She bowed her head and stomped her feet on to the carpet. She looked up at Tiffany. "I'm going to be famous."

Tiffany offered a confused look.

"Like really famous," Beatrice said as she bounced on the couch. She explained that within twenty-four hours Manuel's photo of her eating that cheesy burrito had jumped from Manuel's cell phone to a friend's cell phone. The image had jumped like a virus from cell phone to cell phone—all this before Manuel posted the image on Facebook, where it was being eyeballed around the clock. Beatrice had received phone calls and text messages confirming sightings in Rhode Island. There was a chance that her image would leap over to England by nightfall.

"That's terrible," Tiffany remarked.

"Terrible?" Beatrice arched her eyebrows. "It's like everyone's going to know my face."

"But with a string of @#!&! cheese hanging from your chin?"

"Yeah, but still!"

"Still what? Don't you think it's like ##@!& embarrassing?" Tiffany peeled off her gloves, as if getting ready for a bare-knuckled fight with Beatrice about how embarrassing it was.

"Tiffany, my face is going everywhere. People will be text messaging me internationally." She reached down to a bowl of peanuts and threw a few into her mouth. She spoke with her mouth open, revealing the crunched, semi-crunched, and uncrunched peanuts. "It's like I'm finally going to be famous, like that girl on television."

Tiffany remembered the chubby girl in the orange tank top. If that was fame, Tiffany figured, they could have it.

Silence filled the room.

"What's your *!@*&! problem?" Beatrice finally asked. "And give me the remote!"

Tiffany was hurt. She had walked in the terrible cold to comfort her best friend, and now that friend was scolding her? "I was just trying to be supportive."

Beatrice snapped on the television. Stacy and Clinton were dumping clothes into a garbage can and criticizing the woman in the orange tank top. Beatrice hoisted a smile to her face.

"I got to go," Tiffany said in a clipped voice. Her friend didn't seem to need comforting. *What Not to Wear* could do that for her.

"Nah, girl—don't go!" Beatrice apologized for her outburst.

Tiffany felt a little better and sat back down. She scratched a mustard stain on the leather couch. She flicked the flakes into an ashtray on the coffee table. "Are we going to go?" Tiffany asked.

"Go where?" Beatrice asked, genuinely puzzled by the question.

"To the mall."

"Can't do," Beatrice replied. She reached for another handful of peanuts. She poured a few into her mouth, chewed a little, shook the remainder in her palm like dice, and said, "I got to take care of Jenny's baby."

Jenny was Beatrice's older sister. She had the baby with a guy who was now in prison—two years to pump weights for stealing a Hummer, a vehicle so poor on gas mileage they laughed that car dealers couldn't give it away.

"Jenny's staying with us," Beatrice added.

"Your sister?" Tiffany looked around. "Where is she? Asleep?" Jenny was known to party until dawn.

"At the mall or something," Beatrice answered. She tossed the remaining peanuts into her mouth. "The baby's asleep."

Just then, Jenny's baby came tottering into the living room. Her eyes were large and her light-brown hair tousled. Her cheeks were pink from just waking up.

"She is so, so cute!" Tiffany sang. "Come here, sweetie." Tiffany raised her arms for the baby to come.

But the baby just stood there. She yawned and rubbed her eyes with her fists.

"You can't get any cuter! I swear!" The baby is about two, Tiffany figured. "What's her name?"

"Maria," Beatrice answered and frowned. "Give me a *!@*! break! Ain't there enough Marias in the *$@*! world?"

Tiffany stiffened at her best friend's outburst. It was cruel and ugly. "No, we need all the precious Marias in the world. It's a classic name."

"Classic?" Beatrice muttered.

"Classic and symbolic," Tiffany defended.

"Whatever." Beatrice sulked, slouched into the couch, and changed the channel.

Tiffany was irate. How could Beatrice think of her niece as just another Maria? She swallowed the cuss words that almost shot out like lightning in her friend's direction. How dare she speak about her little niece in such a manner! Instead, Tiffany resolved to be calm and asked, "Does she talk yet?"

"Like a *$!@# parrot," Beatrice answered as she sat up. She made cooing sounds at the baby. "Maria want a cracker? Maria want a peanut?"

Maria clapped her hands and did a little jig, turning in a circle like a toy. Her large eyes squinted. Her smile revealed her tiny, white teeth. She then ran to Beatrice, who hugged her and pushed a peanut into Maria's mouth. The smiling baby began to chew on the peanut and immediately began to choke.

"Baby's okay?" Tiffany asked, her brow pleated in worry.

The baby's oval-shaped face began to turn red and her eyes, already large, seemed to get even larger. Drool seeped from her lower lip.

"Are you okay, Maria?" Tiffany asked as she went to her knees and placed a hand behind the baby's back. She tapped the baby's back and said, "Cough it up. Be a good girl and cough it up." Tiffany wiped the drool on her sleeve.

The baby appeared startled. A pinkish hand went to her mouth and came out slimy.

"She can't breathe!" Tiffany shouted. She rubbed the baby's back and tapped it softly and then harder when the baby's face began to turn purple and a single tear rolled down her cheek.

"Do something!" Beatrice cried as she leaped from the couch on to the floor. "Jenny's going to be mad!"

Tiffany turned the baby upside down like a salt shaker. She shook the baby, cried in panic, "Come on, Maria, cough it up," and drummed her fist against her back until the peanut flopped on to the carpet. Tiffany righted the baby and set her on the couch. The purple in her face slowly drained to a pinkish flush while she gasped for air.

"Man, you scared us," Beatrice yelled at Maria. She dabbed roughly at the drool on the baby's chin. "Don't do that again!"

The baby rubbed tears from her eyes. She sneezed and put her fingers into her mouth.

"Poor thing," Tiffany said in relief. "She could have choked and died." She could feel her heart racing and noticed that her hands were shaking. She locked her hands together, but they still trembled.

The baby pushed out her pudgy arm and opened her palm. She made a noise with her lips that to Tiffany sounded like, "Please."

"No, no peanuts for the bad girl," Beatrice scolded. But she reached for the bowl of peanuts and pushed a handful into her own mouth.

"She's not bad. It was just an accident." Tiffany pouted at the baby, cooed precious words, and took her hand into hers as she sat down next to her. She lifted the baby in her lap. "Huh, sweetie, just a little accident. A boo-boo."

The baby looked up at Tiffany and, reaching upward with her stinky hands, cooed sweetly, "*!@#*."

Beatrice laughed and pointed. "Did you hear her? This little gangsta girl's already using bad words!"

Shocked, Tiffany gazed at little Maria's mouth. How could such a sweet darling thing cuss? She lifted the baby from her lap and on to the couch.

Maria smiled and repeated, "*!@#*!" She clapped and smiled. She shimmied off the couch and helped herself to the soda on the coffee table.

"Are you going to let her drink soda?" Tiffany herself liked sodas, but knew enough about healthy habits to understand that a soda was really a poor choice for a growing baby. "Don't you think she should drink milk or juice?"

"She can drink anything she wants," Beatrice replied defensively. "Huh, home girl? Show Tiffany how you dance."

Baby Maria began to wag her head from side to side in imitation of Beatrice, who was towering above her. Maria then began to move slowly around the coffee table, clicking her fingers. Beatrice clapped her hands over her head, the baby duly following along. When Beatrice shook her bottom, the baby did the same. Then the baby tripped and knocked the glass of soda off the coffee table.

"*!@$&!" Beatrice yelled. "Look at what you done!" She raised the flat of her hand and yelled, "I should spank you."

The baby ran from the living room.

"You wouldn't spank her," Tiffany said.

"But look at what she did?" The soda was quickly disappearing into the carpet. Beatrice hurried to the kitchen for a dish towel.

Tiffany began to slip on her gloves. I'm out of here, she thought. She felt remorseful and sick, but for what? What was it exactly? That Beatrice was proud of her burrito-eating image spreading across the country, or the soda-drinking baby who already had bad words in her vocabulary?

"Where you going?" Beatrice asked as she returned to the living room holding a damp and twisted dish towel.

"Home to do some work," Tiffany answered with a little push behind her words.

"You're jealous, huh?" Beatrice snarled. She began to twist the towel.

"About what?" Tiffany asked, one hand on the doorknob. She was upset by her friend's tone of voice. She also thought for a second that Beatrice might snap the dish towel at her.

"About me." There was an anger pushing out of Beatrice's eyeballs. Would smoke from her nostrils follow? "It's because I got Manuel and you ain't got nobody. It's because everyone's going to know me."

"Eating a burrito? With cheese hanging from your chin," Tiffany said, anger building up like a fire in her own heart. "Is that what you want to be known for? Get a life!"

"Jealous," Beatrice hurled at her friend. She snapped open the dish towel and knelt to clean up the spilled soda. "That's what you are—jealous!" In a frenzy, she began to rub the spill.

Tiffany turned and opened the door, the cold wintry air rushing against her face. She left as Beatrice continued to heave insults about how stuck up Tiffany was.

"You can think what you want," Tiffany tossed at Beatrice,

and closed the door behind her. She hurried down the street in scissoring steps that could have cut metal.

• • •

The fog was thick, and even thicker than earlier. A pair of yellowish headlights appeared in the road, briefly lighting up what was for Tiffany a dark day. She had lost her friend, and feared for baby Maria. She imagined the toddler eating peanuts and drinking a soda while seated inches from the blaring television. If I could only rescue her, Tiffany thought. If only I could stop her from saying those bad words.

Tiffany thought about how she herself had learned them. How did she start? In the theater with her Uncle Richard? From her parents, who sometimes used profanity? She hated herself, and hated herself even more as she walked toward the house where the old woman with the orange tree had asked her for help.

"She's a nice woman," Tiffany told herself. "She just wants oranges." Right there, Tiffany promised herself not to talk to Beatrice, even if she became famous. Her lower lip was trembling as she began to cry. She closed her eyes and saw little Maria clapping her hands over her head. The poor thing, she thought.

A car passed, again lighting up the foggy day. But the light receded, and she was once again alone in the fog. "I'll just use nice words," she told herself. Words like "rose," "garden," "pretty clouds," "jasmine," and "love." She could feel her face lift in happiness as she recited these words. She thought of the *other* words—the cuss words, the profanity, the hip-hop slang, the funky language of the school yard—and she could feel her mood darken. She could even feel her face change into something hateful.

Tiffany stopped in front of the old woman's house. There

was a yellowish glow behind the front window and the faint lilt of Mexican music. Without being asked a second time, she took it upon herself to pick those oranges. She entered the yard, got a bench leaning against a fence, and boosted herself into the orange tree.

"Kitten," she piped as she picked the first orange. "Candy," she hummed when she plucked the second one. "Jam . . . birthday . . . pony," she said as she plucked one orange after another, until the pockets of her big coat were filled and her mouth was singing a new vocabulary.

Abstinence Makes the Heart Grow Fonder

BY JENNIFER KNIGHT

"IT'S ALWAYS THE drummers, isn't it?" Kelly said wistfully as we spied from around the timpani at my crush.

"What are you talking about?" I hissed. He was only feet away and I didn't want him to see us gawking.

"I mean, when have you ever seen a clarinet player with abs like those?"

I shook my head, giggling. "You do have a point there. But I'd like him even without the abs."

"The hair then," Kelly sighed. "It's gotta be the hair."

I rolled my eyes, watching Chris tap away on his drum pad, pretending to listen as one of the color guard flirted with him. His dirty blond hair was long and carefully tousled, as if he'd just gotten out of bed and woken up looking like a shampoo model.

He did have nice hair.

"It's everything," I said quietly, turning away.

Kelly turned as well and crossed her legs. "He's going to ask you out soon."

My heart did flip-flops at the thought, but I squashed the feeling back. I'd been hoping that very thing ever since our first football game when Chris had sat by me on the bus instead of one of the color guard, like he normally did. Ever since then, when his amber eyes had melted into mine, I'd been hooked. Borderline obsessed.

Hence the spying.

"You're making things up," I accused Kelly. She was a major band gossip and thrived on rumors. I knew for a fact she started many of them herself, so I didn't put much stock in her assertion that Chris Harper—hottest drummer on the planet—would ask me, the trumpet player and overall basket case, out anywhere.

"No," Kelly said. "I'm sure this time."

I scoffed.

"What makes you so sure?"

"Well, for one thing . . ." She stood and gathered her books. "He's headed over here."

I felt my eyes turn into golf balls.

"And for another, he's got a flower."

My mouth hit the linoleum floor of the band room.

Kelly gave me an excited wink and skipped off to join a group of flautists chatting near the lockers.

I sat frozen on the floor, nestled inside the curve of the timpani set, trying to believe what Kelly had just said. Was she messing with me?

"So is this your secret lair?" a husky voice said from above me.

Chris.

I gaped and he grinned.

"Somehow I thought it would be bigger," he said.

I laughed stiffly, instantly nervous. "No, we prefer the storage room—more privacy."

He smiled at my lame joke and came to sit down next to me, his elbow propped up on his knee. "This seems plenty private to me. If Kelly hadn't just popped up, I wouldn't have guessed you were down here."

I giggled idiotically.

"What were you two doing anyway?" he asked.

I bit my lip, trying to come up with something besides the truth. "Gossiping."

He seemed interested. His light-brown eyebrows twitched up. "About me?" His voice was low, intent, and his eyes smoldered into mine. I was now having trouble breathing normally. How did he *do* that?

"Not everything is about you, you know," I said with as much bravado as possible.

A crooked smile pulled at his lips. "And that's why you were spying on me, is it? Because you *weren't* talking about me?"

Oh, God, no! He'd seen us. Fire rippled down my spine and filled my entire face. He chuckled at my reaction.

"It's all right," he said coolly. "I *am* hard to resist. It's both a blessing and a curse." He sighed heavily, casting a wicked grin at me.

I silently cursed myself for being so obvious.

"This is for you, by the way," he said after a moment.

I looked up and saw a sunflower emerge from behind his back. "Drama club was selling them in history class, so I bought one."

I took the thick stalk and sniffed the sunny flower, now totally elated rather than embarrassed. He'd bought a flower for me. I looked up into his oaken-colored eyes and murmured my thanks, thinking I'd somehow have to immortalize this flower.

"What are you doing tomorrow after school?" Chris asked. His eyes bore a tinge of doubt in them now. The contrast to his normal confidence was devastatingly adorable.

"Nothing," I said, feeling like a loser for not having plans.

"I'm going to the beach with my cousins," he said. "They flew down from Maine and they want to see the ocean."

"No better place for that than South Beach." I shrugged. Was he asking me out or wasn't he?

"Actually, we're going down to Cape Florida," he said. "Less crowded and fewer boobies hanging out."

"Like you'd mind that." I nudged him playfully in the arm.

The crooked smile cropped up again, stealing my breath away. "Well, *I* wouldn't mind, but my twelve-year-old cousin might. And her dad."

More inane giggling from me.

Chris eyed me again with that hint of vulnerability playing in his gaze. "Do you think you might . . . want to come with?"

Every nerve in my body fluctuated from numb to electric several times as I took in the meaning of his words. Chris Harper was asking me out—on a date!

In my eagerness to scream *Yes!* I began to sputter unintelligibly.

"It doesn't have to be a date or anything," Chris qualified, seeming nervous. There was a small flush of pink on his cheekbones.

My high punctured itself at once.

"But . . ." I started, gaping at him as even my sunflower seemed to wilt. "I want it to be a date."

Chris's face lit up. "Really? I didn't know if you—"

"I do!" I cut him off. "I want to go out with you."

Chris chuckled. "Well, great. We'll drive down together. Is that okay?"

"Perfect," I breathed.

Another heart-stopping smile and his eyes delved into mine, removing me from time and place, making my entire body tremble.

And then his cell phone buzzed. He blinked and snapped it to his ear.

"I gotta go," he said, hanging up. "My ride's here."

I just nodded, still dazed.

"See ya, Liv." He touched his knuckle to my cheek as he passed, leaving me breathless.

Within seconds Kelly was back, her eyes wide and sparkling with excitement.

"Spill!"

• • •

The next day took too long to pass. In the morning I saw Chris in the band room before class, blushed like a fool and ended up walking face first into the doorframe. We ate lunch in the same separate groups as always—him with the percussionists, me with the brass section—and I tried not to drool as he entered a chin-up contest with Chili, the bass drummer. As the end of the day neared, time slowed and slowed, dragging out until I was sure someone had stopped the clocks.

But eventually, twelve o'clock came and I was free. Free to fly to the band room like my hair was on fire and see Chris. I entered with my heart doing gymnastics in my chest. I knew that if today's date went well, I'd have every chance of getting a kiss from him—my first real kiss. Then I could die happy.

I found Chris leaning against the wall twirling a pair of drumsticks between his long fingers. His eyes flickered and connected with mine as I came in. He gave me an easy smile and met me by the lockers, leaning against them casually. I wondered fleetingly if he ever stood up straight or just went from object to object, leaning.

"Ready?" he asked, stuffing the drumsticks over his shoulder into his backpack.

I could only nod. My body felt drunk with nerves.

"Excellent. My car's out front."

I followed him out to a sparkly, baby-blue Lexus convertible parked on the curb and got in. As soon as we hit the highway he rolled the top down, letting the sun beat on the top of our heads.

Chris was, as always, a breeze to talk to. I was able to keep up a decent flow of conversation—broken only when I stared too long at his profile or had to prevent my hair from trying to fly down my throat and suffocate me. The hour it took to get to Cape Florida felt like minutes and I was surprised when we slowed down at the parking lot, the smell of the ocean and the spotty shade of the palm trees washing over me. Excitement fluttered through my chest as romantic beach fantasies made their way with my mind. There was no place more romantic than the beach, right?

Chris honked the horn, snapping me back to reality.

"Hey!" he said, waving at a small group of people already unloading their car. "My cousins," Chris said to me softly.

Oh . . . right. *They* were here. No sex on the beach for me today . . .

Chris parked and jumped out of the car. I followed, feeling awkward and more than a little dejected. I felt like his cousins were intruding on my date.

I watched Chris hug his family as I shuffled my feet near the car.

"Liv," Chris said, waving me over. "This is my Uncle Charlie." He pointed to a tall, red-faced man with a lot of facial hair. He thrust his beefy hand out and shook mine roughly. Chris pointed to another tall, rather hairy man who looked very similar to Uncle Charlie, but wore glasses and a slathering of thick, white sunscreen on his nose. "My dad," Chris announced. "You can call him George."

I thought briefly that I'd rather die than call him George, but I shook his hand with a shy smile.

"And my cousins, Jenny, Cara, and Mike." He pointed to

three kids, the oldest of which was a girl who looked a few years younger than me with yards and yards of thick, auburn hair—the kind I would have killed for. The other two were younger and might have been twins.

We all headed down to the beach, the kids flitting around, kicking up sand, Chris helping his father tote the huge ice chest, and me trying to sedate myself. I was so nervous. We passed between the thick tangle of saw grass and mangroves—swatting mosquitoes the entire way—and finally reached the beach. I'd only been to Cape Florida once before and I was too little to remember it, so I was surprised when I saw how tiny it was. The beach was just a small crescent of pristine white sand that came to a rocky peak on one end. A white lighthouse stood in the distance, surrounded by palm trees and the ever-present mangroves.

The best part was that it wasn't nearly as crowded as the beaches I was used to and it all felt very secluded with the wall of trees to our back.

Chris and his family set up camp near the water, laying down blankets, erecting chairs, rubbing sunscreen on the kids. Uncle Charlie and Chris's dad (who I had decided to call Mr. Harper—*not* George) heaved themselves into their chairs, cracked a couple of beers and dissolved into lazy conversation.

Chris gave them a withering look. "How boring can you get?" he mumbled. I tried not to stare as he pulled his shirt over his head to reveal his thin, but not too thin, chest. He was perfectly tanned and I was instantly self-conscious of my own complexion, only slightly darker than a chalk stick.

My hands were shaking so badly as I wrestled with my shirt, I felt like I was having an episode.

"Well, what did you have in mind?" I asked him, unbuttoning my shorts.

He shot a quick grin at me and bent to pick up a short, oval-shaped object that looked like a tiny surfboard.

I eyed it warily. I didn't like where this was going.

"What is that?" I asked.

"A skim board." He slipped it under his arm and cocked his head for me to follow him to the water's edge. "The trick is to get it going a bit before you jump on."

"Get it . . . going?"

"Yeah, watch." He tossed the board into the surf and chased after it, hopping on and skating about ten feet before coming to a graceful stop. He bent and pried it from the water, walking back toward me with a jaunt in his step now—clearly he knew he'd impressed me.

The kids had gathered around me now, eager to see it again.

"Chris, let me try!" one of the little ones shouted, the girl.

"Sure thing, Jenny. I'll get you going, okay? Just chase it and then try not to fall down."

Everyone laughed but me. He wasn't expecting me to actually get on that thing was he? I was the opposite of coordinated when it came to sports, which is why I'd chosen the marching band as an athletic outlet since all I had to do was walk.

But Jenny had no fear. She crouched next to Chris, poised to chase after the skim board when he tossed it.

"Okay, don't kill yourself," Chris murmured to her.

"Just throw it," Jenny said with a roll of her blue eyes.

He did and Jenny raced after, catching up with it in seconds and riding even longer than Chris had. She whooped and we all cheered when she hopped off unharmed. She jogged back to us with the board over her head.

"Me next, me next!" shouted the older girl, who must have been Cara.

"Nope, it's Liv's turn," Chris said, giving me a warm, yet wicked smile.

"No, no, she can go," I said eagerly. Too eagerly. Chris noticed and now I was done for. Endless mockery.

"Come on, wimp, Jenny just did it no problem and she's ten."

"Yeah, well, kids are resilient. If she fell, she'd survive. I, on the other hand, will likely break something."

"Then don't fall."

"As if I could control it."

A devil smile. "I'll start you off, how about that?"

I stood silently, debating. The kids and Chris were all watching me; even Uncle Charlie and Mr. Harper were watching. Even though I knew this could only end in disaster, I also didn't want to be a dud on our first date.

"All right," I sighed. "But none of you laugh when I fall."

He was already chuckling.

I stood at the ready, waiting for Chris to toss the board.

"On three," he said. "One . . . two . . . *three!*"

He threw it and I ran after, dreading with every bone in my body what would happen when I caught up.

I came within range of the board and jumped on. Immediately, the board flew out from underneath me and I went down, skidding across the sand on my butt. I came to a stop after about two feet and toppled over face first into the water.

I was tempted to stay underneath and drown, but a pair of hands pulled me from my watery grave and yanked me to my feet. It was Chris, of course, laughing uncontrollably along with his cousins, all of whom were screaming with giggles.

"That was awesome!" Chris laughed. "Epic!"

I shook his hands from my shoulders. "Well, I'm glad I could provide some comic relief," I snapped. I was completely humiliated and annoyed with everything. This day had not gone at all how I had planned. No romantic beach, no playing in the water, no kissing in the sand . . . just a rash on my ass from where the sand scraped me and a bruise to my ego. That kiss I'd been hoping for was looking pretty remote.

"Aw, don't be that way," Chris said. "I fall all the time. I just got lucky."

I wrinkled my nose at him and started off toward Uncle Charlie and Mr. Harper, thinking I'd rather be "boring" than humiliated.

"Nice one," Mr. Harper said, snickering. He looked so absurd with his white nose and thick glasses, magnifying his olive-green eyes to the size of kiwis.

I tried to laugh, but I might have sounded snotty.

"Turn around," he said. "Let me see your war wound."

Oh, yeah, because I so want to show you my ass, I thought. But I obeyed, looking at it for the first time myself. My entire right butt cheek—besides what was covered by my suit—was red and swollen as though I'd dragged it along sandpaper.

So, not sexy.

Uncle Charlie and Mr. Harper both winced, making ouch-that-looks-like-it-hurts noises.

"Yep," I said, sitting down on the blanket with a grimace. "Nothing like a good ass burn to really put you in a good mood."

More guffawing from the men.

For a while, I watched Chris help the kids skim board and was comforted by the fact that they did fall several times, though not nearly as spectacularly as I had. Just as I was about to give up entirely on the possibility of salvage the day, Chris started back toward me.

"Wanna see the lighthouse?" he asked, holding a hand out to help me up.

"Sure," I said. I was just glad he wasn't making fun of me any more.

As we started off toward the rocks, I heard a call from behind us. "Keep your pants on, there's kids on this beach!" Mr. Harper's voice.

I flushed scarlet, avoiding Chris's gaze.

"Sorry," he said. "My dad's kind of a dork."

I shrugged.

"You're mad at me," Chris said.

I whipped around to look at him. "Why do you say that?"

"The whole . . . skim board thing. I didn't think you'd take it so hard."

I sighed, deciding to let it go. "Well, I did warn you." I smiled to show I was over it. "I'm kind of defective when it comes to athletics."

We were nearing the lighthouse now, and what few people there were on the beach tapered away until we were all alone.

"In truth," Chris said, "I thought it was cute."

I scoffed, feeling my face redden. "Oh, please, that was probably the least cute thing I've ever done in my life."

The lighthouse loomed overhead, throwing us into its cooling shade. Gulls cried from the rocks, dipping in and out of the frothy surf as they fished. It was very secluded where we stood, enshrouded by mangrove trees on one side and the vast ocean on the other. We stopped walking and I tried to calm my nerves by focusing on something other than how cute Chris looked with his hair wet.

"I want to kiss you so bad right now," Chris said. His husky voice was low and there was a note of uncertainty in it.

I had to lean against the lighthouse for support. My voice came out as only breath when I spoke. "So why don't you?"

"I thought you were angry," he admitted.

I shook my head, begging him with my eyes to come closer.

He did. He braced his hands on the lighthouse, leaning over me, surrounding my body with his. I felt his hips against mine, his breath on my cheek. I closed my eyes and awaited the euphoria I was sure was coming.

A light touch; gentle, careful. I leaned in, eager for more. He responded, taking the small of my back and pulling me even closer; his lips were soft perfection on mine. I never wanted this to end.

But all too soon, he pulled back, just as breathless as I was.

"I've been dying to do that for weeks," he whispered with a sinful grin on his moist lips. All I wanted to do was kiss them again.

"Me too," I admitted. It was so easy to admit. We both knew exactly how the other felt, somehow. As though we'd already said it a thousand times.

"We'd better get back," he said, nuzzling his face against the skin right under my jaw, kissing it.

"Well, when you do *that* . . ." I muttered. I turned and caught his lips once more, unable to stop myself. Saltwater and the taste of his breath, his wet hair between my fingers—it was all I could do not to moan in frustration when he pulled away yet again.

"My dad's going to bust in on us if we don't get back." Chris smiled apologetically.

"Okay," I said. I was trembling so violently, I was scared I couldn't walk.

But Chris took my hand as we made our way back down the beach and I was sure that with his hand in mine, I'd be able to walk endlessly.

• • •

186

A three-day weekend prevented me from seeing Chris (he was hanging out with his cousins all weekend) so when Monday rolled around I was a half ecstatic, half nervous wreck. What if he'd decided that I was too clumsy for him after all, or too dorky, or too boring? What if he ignored me?

My fears were wasted. The second he saw me, he was at my side and he hardly left it for the rest of the week. He even started picking me up from my house and taking me home from school. It was a development that allowed us ample make-out time in his car.

By Friday, I was sure I was in love with him. But he was the first guy I'd ever dated, ever kissed—at least with my mouth open—so I wasn't sure if what I felt was love or just infatuation. Whatever it was, I was addicted to it and every kiss made the wanting stronger.

• • •

Friday was a game day, which meant I'd get to spend all evening with Chris. At six o'clock, with the setting sun glowing outside the window and the smell of sweaty bodies, dirty bus and brass polish engulfing my senses, Chris and I cuddled into each other at the back of the bus.

For some reason, football games had always been a kind of aphrodisiac for me. Maybe it was the excited energy pulsing through everyone or the sweet smell of sweat in the air, the darkened bus ride home when anything could happen and nobody would know . . . I'd always had fantasies about having someone to fool around with on game day and Chris was the perfect person to do it with. We made out pretty much incessantly all the way to the football field, stopping only when the parent at the front of the bus would squawk, "Hand check!" We'd throw our hands into the air along with everyone else, giggle like fools and then proceed to try and suck each other's face off.

I was on an endorphin high all throughout the first half of the game. Whenever the drum line played, I felt butterflies and Kelly nudged me in the ribs too many times to count, whispering that Chris was staring at me. Even when it started to rain, I couldn't be in a bad mood.

"I think you should go back there and talk to him," Kelly said, pulling her poncho over her head.

"We're not allowed to," I said, though the idea was certainly tempting.

"Oh, come on. He's been staring at you all night, practically *begging* you to go up there. Just pretend you have to give him something and then hide behind the bass drum for a while."

"I don't know . . ."

"Ugh, you're such a goody-goody," she scoffed. "Go flirt with your boyfriend!"

"He's not my boyfriend," I hissed. It was true, he'd never asked and we'd only been together for a week. "Besides, how much can I flirt when I'm wearing this?" I plucked at my band uniform in disgust. "It's like a giant banner saying, *Don't screw me!*"

Kelly snorted. "Well that can't be helped. Besides, it didn't stop you from making out the whole bus ride."

"I have to walk by the color guard," I groaned, watching them daintily slip their ponchos on over their skin-tight costumes.

But Kelly wasn't hearing it. "They're wearing ponchos too, now get going before we have to get ready for the halftime show." She nudged me out of my seat.

I passed my section leader and said I had to go give Chris something. He eyed me suspiciously, but let me pass.

"Careful on the stairs," he warned.

The rain was really coming down now. I caught Chris's eye

as I climbed the metal stands and did my best to give him a sexy wave and a wink.

And then my worst fear came to pass.

My leg fell through the gap in the stands all the way up to my thigh. I screamed as my ankle twisted painfully. For a split second I was sure I would fall right through and land in the putrid mud beneath.

Luckily, I was too big to fit all the way through the slat. But I *was* stuck and my leg hurt like hell.

"Oh my God!" someone shouted. I was right next to the low brass section at the top of the stands and several of them got up to gawk at me.

"Are you okay?" one of the tuba players asked me. His hands hovered around me and I could tell he was trying to decide if he should try to pull me out.

"Yeah," I grumbled. "But I think my leg is stuck."

He straightened and called out, "MR. MILLER! LIV IS STUCK IN THE STANDS!"

Complete humiliation.

Why was this happening to me? First the skim boarding incident and now this? Couldn't I just have one ounce of sex appeal around Chris?

Our band director, Mr. Miller, hurried up the stands, followed by the drum majors, the color guard captains and a few random people who'd happened to be passing by at the time.

My face must have looked like a radish.

And then, to make things even worse, Chris was suddenly there, crouched down next to me.

"Are you hurt?" he asked. "What happened?"

"What do you think happened? I slipped." I was in no mood to be nice. My ankle was twisted and my leg was in serious pain; the entire band was staring at me and I wanted out. Now.

"That's what you get for being so skinny," Chris said as he wiped my wet hair out of my eyes.

"Can you pull her out?" Mr. Miller asked.

"I can try," Chris said. He locked his hands underneath my arms and tugged, but the movement made pain shoot through my leg like a knife and I yelped. Chris released me.

Mr. Miller sighed. "We're going to have to call the fire department to cut her out."

My mouth hit the floor.

"No don't!" I gasped. "Chris, try again. I can take it. Just *pull*!"

"No, we don't want to hurt you," Mr. Miller said.

"I won't sue you, if that's what you're afraid of."

He gave me a look and turned to the drum majors. "Get the band ready for the halftime show and I'll take care of this." They nodded, and started shouting at the band to ignore me and put on their hats and gloves.

"That means you too, Harper," Mr. Miller said.

Chris looked reluctant to leave, which was sweet, but I'd rather have died stuck in those stands than have him watch as they sawed me out.

"Just go," I said, wincing as pain shot through my leg.

He touched my cheek and went back up the stands to get his drum. The band filed out of the stands, stepping around me like I was a puddle of mud. Some people murmured words of sympathy or gave me pitiful looks as they stepped over me, but most gave me looks of the utmost horror, as if they were thinking to themselves, *Thank God that isn't me!*

Ten minutes later, the band was on the field and the fire department was trooping up the stands. The flashing lights had attracted the attention of most of the school. I felt like some sort of beached whale, stuck in the sand and totally helpless.

190

After much staring and prodding, the firefighters decided that their only option was cutting me out. They even had to evacuate all of the people from the stands, just in case the vibrations from the saw made them collapse.

Oh, please let me die in the fall if it happens . . .

Ten more minutes and the entire school was watching as a burly firefighter revved up a chainsaw and began excavating me. If the vibrations hadn't hurt my twisted leg so bad, I might have been more embarrassed. Mostly, I was just relieved when one of the firefighters tugged me free and laid me down on one of the benches.

I wasn't as hurt as I thought I was. As soon as my leg was free, I felt much better. I watched from inside the paramedic's truck as the band performed a rinky-dink rendition of *James Bond* and *Mission Impossible* without me.

Afterwards, Mr. Miller popped his head around the side of the truck.

"How's our girl?" he asked the paramedic who was bandaging my ankle.

"Just a sprain. Nothing a few days of rest won't cure."

"Wonderful," Mr. Miller said. He turned to me. "I've called your parents. They're waiting at school to pick you up."

"Great," I grumbled.

He seemed to realize I wasn't in the best mood, so he mumbled something about checking on the score and scurried off. I was more than glad to see him go and even happier when the paramedics let me limp back to the stands and rejoin the band.

Everyone cheered when I showed up, which made me smile and want to kill myself at the same time.

"Do you always fall this much or is it just around me?" Chris's voice in my ear. I turned and he planted a kiss on my lips.

"Just around you, I think," I said with a sigh. "It's extremely embarrassing, just so you know."

Another of his devil smiles. "Like I said before, I think it's cute."

"I think you have cute and defective mixed up."

He chuckled. "You're far from defective." His eyes raked over me, a greedy glint in their tan hues. He leaned in, making me glaringly aware of everyone watching us. "I can't wait to get back in that bus," he breathed in my ear.

My heart stopped. I was amazed that I no longer felt stupid and mortified, but sexy and excited. I wondered again how he had the power to spin my mood with so few words.

He touched his lips to my ear, sending tingles down my spine, and made his way back up to the top of the stands, where the drum line stood.

Kelly was in my face next, hugging me. "Well, that totally backfired," she said and I smiled, dazedly.

"No," I said, "actually, it didn't."

When we got back to school, after turning in our uniforms and packing up our instruments, Chris pulled me aside. "I want to see you this weekend," he said. "I don't think I can go two days without kissing you."

I flushed with pleasure; I'd just been thinking the same thing.

"Come over to my house tomorrow night," Chris said. "We'll watch a movie and hang out."

"Okay."

"When's your curfew?"

"Well, I have to go feed my aunt's cat at some point," I said, just remembering that I had to drag out to the Redlands tonight to do just that. Maybe I could guilt my mom into doing it for me since I'd just endured the most humiliating night of my life and now had an aching ankle. "But I don't really have a curfew." I'd never had a reason to stay out late before.

Chris's handsome face split into a grin. "Excellent."

● ● ●

At sunset the next day, I limped up to Chris's front door. I had gotten my mom to feed her sister's cat, so I had the whole night to spend with Chris—a thought that sent my mind spinning a million different fantasies. None of which involved clothing.

I could hear drums pounding from one of the rooms upstairs and my heart followed suit. I rang the doorbell. Mr. Harper answered, looking just as goofy as ever. I wondered how someone so strange could have created a son as sexy as Chris.

Speaking of whom, Chris bounded down the stairs and tugged me up in his arms—right in front of his dad. I patted his back awkwardly, not wanting to look like some sort of slut in front of Mr. Harper.

"I missed you," Chris said in my ear.

My heart melted and I forgot all about Mr. Harper.

"Me too," I said.

Chris began to lead me up the stairs to his room.

"Keep the door cracked," Mr. Harper called after us.

"Okay, Dad," Chris mumbled. We rounded the corner on the second floor.

"And the lights on!"

"Yeah!" Chris rolled his eyes at me.

Chris's room was small and cluttered with computer games, books, folded laundry, drum pads, and drumsticks. His twin bed was squashed into the far corner and a TV sat on his dresser across from it.

It was obvious that we would be sitting on the bed.

"Nice room," I said, fidgeting.

He snorted. "It's a mess, but it works." His eyes flickered to the bed and then fixed on the rack of DVDs next to his computer desk. He cleared his throat. "What do you want to watch?"

"I don't care."

Chris grabbed a random title and stuffed it into the DVD player. He sat on the edge of the bed, skipping past the commercials. I sat next to him, carefully, making sure not to get too close. I became aware that we hadn't so much as touched each other since entering his room. I wondered if he was as nervous as I was. It was the first time we had been completely alone.

On a bed no less.

I grabbed one of his pillows and propped it against the wall, leaning back, watching as Chris adjusted the volume and crossed the room to the light switch. He hesitated for a moment and then flicked it off and shut the bedroom door.

My body felt so numb and shaky I might have been having a mini seizure. He crossed the room in the darkness and came to sit next to me.

Still no touching.

"Won't your dad get mad about the lights?" I asked.

"You can't watch a movie with the lights on."

Apparently if he did get mad, Chris didn't care. I didn't mention the door.

The movie started, but I couldn't have been less interested. The silence between us seemed to beat at my ears and a thick electric tension grew between our bodies. I was aware of every movement he made, wondering when he would at last reach over and touch me.

Thirty minutes into the movie and my heart had not given up its frantic pounding. I wanted so badly to cuddle into Chris's side, but he still hadn't so much as held my hand. I didn't want to be the one to make the first move.

An hour in and the tension was so thick it was almost a solid object between us, electric and nerve wrecking. I was hyper-aware of him, his arms folded tightly, his lips pressed together in a straight line, his eyes staring vacantly at the screen.

He seemed to notice I was staring at him because he turned. His eyes caught mine and locked there.

"Liv . . ."

That was it. The moment his lips broke and he said my name, I couldn't take it any more. The need to kiss him was so intense I couldn't think of anything else. I grabbed his face and kissed him fiercely, elated when he responded by kissing me back, just as eagerly. He pressed me back on to the bed, his hands roaming everywhere, his lips never leaving mine.

I was scared when I felt his hands at the buckle of my jeans, but I wanted it at the same time. I let him touch me, relishing in the feeling of my heart pounding next to his. I could almost feel it through my shirt, feel his breath mingle with mine . . .

Things were going fast. My shirt came off. Then his. His jeans were on the floor before I could blink and mine were around my ankles. Nothing was said; neither of us had to discuss what it was we wanted—our bodies spelled it out for us. We were close to naked on his bed, kissing and fondling, driving each other crazy . . .

And then a knock on the door brought us back to reality.

I was so surprised I almost screamed.

Chris flung himself off the bed, cursing.

"Put your clothes on!" he hissed.

I obeyed, buckling my bra, struggling with my jeans and trying to find the right holes to put my arms through in my shirt. Less than thirty seconds later and I was decent, if disheveled.

Chris glanced at me, making sure I was dressed, turned the light on and opened the door.

His dad was standing there—not angry as I had been expecting, but snickering with his eyes on his watch.

"What do you want?" Chris snapped.

"Oh, nothing," Mr. Harper said lightly. "I just wanted to see how long it'd take you two to get your clothes back on."

I winced, putting my face in my hands.

"Twenty-three seconds," Mr. Harper said, tapping his watch. "Not bad." He gave his son a clap on the shoulder and strolled back down the hall, guffawing to himself.

Chris's back was rigid as he closed the door with a sharp snap and came back to the edge of the bed. I scooted up next to him, laying my chin on his shoulder.

"I guess it's kind of a good thing," I murmured after a while. "I don't know if I would have been able to stop if he hadn't . . ."

"I know I wouldn't have."

I gulped.

"Do you even have . . ." I didn't want to say the word condom. It felt so real saying it aloud. It was one thing to be swept away with the moment in the darkness of his bedroom, but to discuss having sex out loud, in the light—it felt way too serious for something that had only been going on for a week.

Chris shrugged. "My dad gave me one when I turned thirteen, but I wouldn't hold much stock in that."

I wouldn't either.

"Do you want me to take you home?" Chris asked with a sigh.

I shook my head. I never wanted to leave him.

"Let's finish the movie," I said.

"I haven't even been watching it." Chris shot me a guilty grin, which I returned.

"Start it over. We've got all night."

• • •

The next month that passed was like one big game of foreplay. Football games turned into fondling sessions, movie theaters became two-hour kissing sprees; the car, his bedroom, school hallways . . . we made out everywhere like a couple of sexed-up idiots.

But we were very careful, after that first time, to keep our clothes firmly on our bodies. Though we never discussed it, it seemed that we were both waiting for the two-month marker to try having sex again.

The second month was achingly long, filled with more torturous football games, movie nights in his room, and dark car rides home at one in the morning. We even went back to the beach before the weather turned too chilly, although he didn't make me skim board, claiming I was enough of a hazard to myself without adding water to the picture.

I began to wonder just how I'd gotten so lucky. Chris and I seemed to fit together perfectly and denying myself the pleasure of expressing just how much I loved him became more and more difficult, the harder I fell.

• • •

The night we went for it again was the night of our two-month "mini-versary."

We'd just gotten out of a movie and were walking to his car.

"You have something in your hair," Chris said, reaching up to grab what I assumed was popcorn or M&M's from my hair.

God, I was so dysfunctional. Couldn't I at least eat without spraying myself with food? It was, after all, a basic human function.

But as Chris picked out whatever was in my hair, he

suddenly kissed me, sending a bubbly feeling through my veins. When I opened my eyes, he was holding a little silver ring in his hand. The metal was shaped like a pair of hands clasping a heart, with a delicate crown on top.

"It's a Claddagh ring," Chris said. "When you wear it with the tip of the heart facing away it means your heart is free, available. And when you wear it like this . . ." He slipped it on my right hand with the tip of the heart facing inward. "It means your heart's been captured. You're taken."

I gazed up into his eyes, touched.

"I thought you might like it."

"I do!" I breathed. "I love it. I love you."

It was the first time I'd ever said it out loud. I hadn't even realized it at first, it felt so natural. But I knew that the "L" word sometimes scared guys and I was instantly petrified that I'd made a terrible mistake. That Chris would yank the beautiful ring back off my finger and run screaming from me.

But he did pretty much the opposite.

He cupped my face in his hand and smiled.

"I love you back."

• • •

In the car, we played our favorite game: stoplight make-out. By the time we got close to my house, I was more than ready to give in to him at last.

As we kissed in my driveway, I pulled back for a moment.

"It's still early," I said. "I don't have to go yet."

One of his signature wicked smiles crossed his face. "What did you have in mind?"

"Well . . ." I let my hand travel down his flat stomach. His eyes widened.

"But, we have nowhere to go," he said, groaning.

"This sucks."

I pulled away, thinking hard.

"Your place is out," I said. "I've been caught with my pants down one too many times to try that again."

Chris snickered. Though we'd kept our clothes on since that first time, his dad still had the nasty habit of coming to "check on us" once every fifteen minutes.

"What about your room?" Chris asked.

"Not unless you *want* my dad to kill you," I said. My parents were easygoing about me and Chris, but they weren't that chilled out.

"What about a hotel room or something?" he suggested.

"I don't know any hotels that'd rent to teenagers. Plus, I'm broke."

Chris deflated. "Yeah, me too . . ."

We dissolved into silence, wracking our brains.

"Could we just . . . do it in here?" Chris asked tentatively.

"Oh yeah, that sounds super comfy."

"Naw, come on. We can lean the seat back and the windows are tinted. Nobody would see. Besides, where else have we got?"

I wavered. "Well, maybe if we found someplace quiet."

Chris's face suddenly lit up.

"I know the perfect spot!"

He threw the car into drive and shot off down the street. It wasn't until we passed a pharmacy that I remembered something vital.

"Umm . . . Chris?"

"Yeah?" I could hear the excitement in his voice.

"You weren't planning on using that old condom your dad gave you, right?"

It was clear from his silence that he either hadn't thought about it or that was exactly what he'd been planning.

"We need to get some new ones," I said.

He gave me a pleading look.

"I'm not taking any chances!" I said indignantly. "Pull into the next pharmacy you see and go get some."

"Why do *I* have to do it?"

"Because you're the one with the penis."

"You're the one with the *womb*," he retorted.

We glared at each other at the stoplight, trying to make the other one give in. Finally, I sighed.

"We'll both go in," I said. "That's the only way it's fair."

He scowled for a second and then said, "Yeah, I guess so."

He pulled into a twenty-four-hour Walgreens and we scurried out, holding hands a little too tightly to be normal.

We went inside and straight to the Family Planning aisle, which held the condoms and—ironically—the pregnancy tests. I guess that was so you could properly visualize the consequences of not using a condom.

We stared at the wall of contraception before us, slightly awed.

"Well?" I asked. "Which one do we pick?"

Chris gave me a sarcastic smile. "Extra-large of course."

I snorted. "Oooh, how about vibrating pleasure?"

"Let's not get complicated, here," Chris said practically.

I giggled.

"Whatever is the strongest anti-baby condom is what we want," he said firmly. "See any that says anti-baby?"

"No, but I see 'ribbed for her pleasure.'" I giggled at his withering glare.

"You're not taking this seriously," he accused.

"No, I am, I am." More irrepressible giggling.

"Trojan Gold," he said, taking a box. "Extra thick."

I covered my mouth with my hands, blushing and snickering incessantly.

"Will you stop that and help me choose?" he said, exasperated.

I tried to calm myself, but only ended up snorting loudly and dissolving into more laughter.

"I'm sorry," I said.

"You're the one who wanted to do this."

"I know. I'm sorry. I'm stopping."

He gave me a narrow look. "How about grape-flavored?"

I burst out laughing, and this time he joined in. We went to the counter with the Trojan Gold in hand and flushed like crazy when the cashier gave us a knowing wink.

• • •

Back in the car again, Chris steered us into a remote area in the Redlands. Palm tree nurseries, abandoned dusty roads and the occasional house were all that was out here. I recognized the area because my aunt lived close by and I drove down this way occasionally to feed her cat if she was out of town. The absolute darkness had always given me the creeps and tonight was no exception, even with Chris here. That, compounded with the thought of what we were about to do, sent my heart into hyperdrive.

Chris shut the car off and we both stared at the windshield for a moment, silent.

"Are you nervous?" I whispered.

"Are you?"

"Maybe," I admitted.

"We don't have to . . ." He gave me a worried glance.

I shook my head, my eyes locked on his. "I want to."

Chris put his hand on my cheek, bringing me closer to him. He kissed me gently, his flawless lips parting mine, and his hands traveled down my spine, tickling me in the best way possible. I couldn't believe we were actually going to do this.

I'd always imagined it would be like in the movies—lying before the fireplace, limbs tangled, a whole night wrapped up in one another. The car wasn't exactly romantic, but it was all we had. And it was all we needed.

As before, our clothes came off and our breath was heated, ragged in our throats. My mind was swimming with Chris, his scent, his smooth bare chest underneath my hands. I clutched his back as the pleasure threatened to consume me.

We stopped to roll the seat back, laughing a little as we fumbled with the condom box. And then, as we were giggling and trying to figure out the mechanics, the unimaginable happened.

Red and blue lights from behind us, the rude whoop of a police siren.

"Oh my God," I said, whipping around from underneath Chris to look out the back window.

He cursed savagely, trying to both put his jeans back on and get into the driver's seat at the same time.

I was busy searching for my shirt. "We're going to be arrested!" I whimpered. I could feel tears in my eyes.

"Stop crying or it's gonna look like I'm raping you." He threw my bra at me.

I only cried harder as I fumbled with it.

"Aw hell," Chris muttered. "I'm gonna get tazered."

"Where's my shirt!" I screeched, eyes wide as I saw the cruiser slowing.

"Here, I was sitting on it."

I was still quite disheveled when the cruiser came up next to us and Chris only had one leg in his jeans. The cop parked and came around to the window. Chris, amid a stream of cursing, rolled the window down.

The cop looked bored out of his mind. "License and registration," he drawled.

Chris rooted around in his jeans for it, while I hurriedly struggled into my pants, flushing down to my toes. The cop took Chris's ID and scanned it for a moment. Then he popped his chewing gum and gave us a glare. "No weapons or illegal substances, right?"

"No," Chris said.

The cop grunted and clicked a heavy black flashlight on. He directed the beam around the car. I watched his eyes fall on the condom box on the dash and then on the underwear squished down by my feet. I could have died in that moment. Then he directed the light at me and I squealed, ducking down behind Chris. I didn't even have my shirt on!

"Hey!" Chris protested as he shielded me.

The cop directed the beam in Chris's face.

"You guys need to find a motel to do this stuff in, all right?"

I groaned, half crying, half wishing for death. Images of Motel 6, ratty bed sheets and hookers assaulted my mind. I felt like complete trash.

"All right," Chris muttered.

The cop eyed me and I gave a frantic nod.

"Good. Now move on outta here."

Having sufficiently humiliated us, and completely ruined the mood, the cop handed Chris his license, got back into his cruiser, and drove away.

I put my face in my hands. I was beyond mortified. I couldn't even speak.

Chris sighed. "This is ridiculous. We should be able to find someplace private without constantly being interrupted."

"I know," I grumbled. "I'm sorry."

Chris turned and stared at me. "Why are you sorry?"

"I don't know, I'm . . . defective. If you were with any other girl this wouldn't be happening."

Chris took my hand. "I wouldn't be with any other girl. This isn't your fault. We just need to do this better. We need someplace where nobody's home to interrupt us, where it's quiet and dark and just . . . empty."

And then I remembered something. Something I should have thought of way before now. But coming out here had brought it all back.

"Oh my gosh," I breathed.

"What?"

"I'm so dumb."

"You're just now realizing this?"

I elbowed him in the side. "No, you're going to love me in a second. I can't believe I forgot about this until now. I'm so stupid."

"I already love you, so just tell me."

I half smiled at him, thrilled to hear the words "I love you" pass his lips again. "My aunt has a house out here," I said.

He stared at me.

"And?"

"And she's had to go away for a couple of days," I said excitedly. "Oh, my gosh, Chris, I know where she hides the key to her house. Her *empty* house."

He was gawking at me.

"This whole time . . . you knew this the whole time?"

"Yeah, but I didn't remember until just now. I feel like such a moron, I've been feeding her cat now and then for years. I just haven't done it lately because my mom took over, remember? If it had been any other time, I would have thought of it." I was bouncing in my seat, so happy. Finally, after two torturous months of waiting—of being good—and after all of my completely unsexy mishaps, being caught by Chris's dad, pulled over by a cop, and utterly humiliated. *Finally*, we could have some privacy!

Chris just sighed and threw his hands over his face. "You know what? I think you were right about something."

I gave him a questioning look.

"You *are* a little defective."

• • •

It was close to one in the morning when we pulled into my aunt's abandoned driveway. Her house was ancient and wooden, always smelling of cedar mingled with must. It was quaint, with a brick fireplace jutting into the sky and a cobblestoned walkway littered with statuettes of cats frozen in mid-pounce or batting at some imaginary bug. A vast field lay behind the house and the shadows of two great blackberry trees stood still and quiet in the front yard. I took the key from under a large stone by the porch.

My heart was doing somersaults as I unlocked the door.

Everything felt strangely surreal, as if this was only a dream. I half expected to open the door and find my aunt home early, ruining everything.

But the house was as dark and empty as I had hoped. We stood in the foyer, shuffling our feet and refusing to look each other in the eye.

"Where do you want to go?" Chris asked.

I didn't want to use anyone's bedroom. But the couch was definitely not romantic and with a house full of beds it seemed silly. And then I remembered that the attic had recently been remodeled into a guest room.

Perfect.

I towed Chris upstairs into the attic. My eyes went straight to the bed beneath the window. The half-moon shone through the pane, casting it in a white, almost ethereal light.

Chris took my hand and led me toward it. When he kissed me, it was as though my life had been leading up to this moment, and it kind of had. I'd dreamt of this since I knew what love was and now, thanks to my aunt's empty house, it was as perfect as I could have imagined.

Chris lay next to me on the quilted bedcovers, our breath coming quickly and our hearts beating too fast. It felt like every other time we'd tried to make love in the past, only this time, we weren't interrupted.

Somebody's Daughter

BY SHELLEY STOEHR

Kayla

I told my mother—I was crying and everything—I told her
that *everyone* has their belly button pierced, and if she didn't let
me then it was her fault if Brian Kepler didn't like me, and it
was absolutely *necessary* that I get my belly button pierced
before his party tonight, and you know what she did? She laid
there on the couch with her eyes closed, doing her deep
breathing thing that nobody else's mother does, I mean, *really*,
and then she said, "Party?"

Oh, shoot, I kinda forgot to tell her about that. I was kinda
stuck then, because my mother never let me go to a party
where she didn't know the parents. I knew I had to make up
a story in a hurry so she'd let me go. I didn't want to lie
because she always said that lying would be the worst thing I
could ever do, but on the other hand, I couldn't tell her details
about the party because Brian's parents were going out of
town. That's why it was such a big deal—there were going to
be no adults, and a keg and the pool and everyone who
mattered was going to be there, and Rain said she was going
to lose her virginity Saturday night—oh, I shouldn't say
that!—and if Brian were to ask me, I would too, *only*—I
thought—*he won't ask if my mother won't let me get my belly
button pierced* . . .

"Just a little birthday party. You know Brian. You know how much I love him. Please, Mom!" I said, adjusting her pillow.

She winced when I moved her, but then she sighed, so I knew her neck was hurting more than usual. Her pain was bad, I knew it, because otherwise she'd totally be sitting up, leaning forward on her hands, looking into my eyes . . .

And then, I never could've gotten away with even a small lie, but all of a sudden it was so easy, because she was lost in her world of hurt. So I said, "It's his birthday! He invited me specially! It's almost like a *date!*"

"Are you asking if you can go?" She was happier than she was letting on. I knew she really wanted to believe someone like Brian would ask me out. She was crazy that way, thinking I was totally special and everyone liked me, and that all the boys must love me.

I started rubbing my mother's foot. She sighed with relief, and I said, "So I can go, right?"

"I don't know, Kayla, it's not a good time."

"It's never a good time with you!"

"I'm sorry, I'm so sorry . . ."

Okay, so sue me—she was weak and I needed to go to the party Saturday night, and not only that, but also get my belly button pierced. I knew if I kept at it, kept pushing her, she'd give in, if for no other reason than guilt over being sick and being afraid that it made her a bad mother. I knew how she thought, and I also knew my father would only say "ask your mother," so it was all or nothing if I really wanted Brian to love me back—and I did, believe me I did, I wanted that more than anything. It was only the most important thing in the world.

So, I didn't want to take advantage of my mother and her weaknesses, what with her pain and her guilt and her wanting me to have everything—but my love for Brian was so real, so powerful. I knew I could get him to like me if I just had this one chance and did it right, and so I said to my mother, before she could recover herself and get her head straight about what was "best" for me, "So can I get my belly button pierced before the party Saturday? I have the form; you just have to sign and Rain's mother will take us."

When my mother opened her eyes, they were full of tears, and of course I felt like shit, but I didn't give up. I just gave her my saddest daughter in the world look.

She signed the form.

I won. And I felt like throwing up.

Rain

My mother didn't come home that morning. She'd promised she'd be home for the weekend, but she didn't show up Friday night. Saturday morning she called. "I'm performing at Dancespace tonight!" she said. "Remember that piece—"

I didn't remember. I didn't want to. Tears slid over my cheeks.

"You can come to the city and see me tonight and stay at my friend Wendy's apartment. You can sleep on the couch, I'll take the floor."

I was quiet. What was I supposed to say to her? There wasn't anything I could say. Nothing would bring her home like I wanted.

"Are you happy for me?" She was begging for it to be all right that she was doing what she wanted to do.

"Yeah, Mom, I'm proud of you. You're really making it on your own now."

She sighed, with relief, it sounded like. "I am. It's wonderful to feel the real me peeking out again, you know? Not a wife or a servant or a—well, I'll always be your mother, of course. Can you make a ten o'clock train?"

"No thanks, Mom. I have plans already."

"Oh! . . . Oh."

"Remember, Brian's party, the one Kayla's been flipping out over for weeks? I told you about it. You said you were going to take Kayla and me to get our belly buttons pierced before the party! And you said you were going to be here!"

"Well, Rain, I'm sorry, but this performance is important to me. I have to dance. I just have to. It's my spirit, it's my soul, it's—"

"I know. I gotta go." I waited to say, "Love you, Mom," until after I'd hung up.

Then I slumped against the wall, slid down to the floor, wrapped my arms around my knees, and softly cried. My father came in, sat next to me, put his arm around me, and held me while I cried harder. "She never wanted to be my mother!" I said. "I ruined her life."

My dad patted my back. "You could never ruin anyone's life." He got up. The last remaining flap of hair on top of his head was standing on end.

I smiled. Getting up, I asked him if he wanted some juice.

"The usual," he said.

I made him a strong screwdriver that was mostly vodka, two ice cubes, and a splash of OJ. "Can you take Kayla and me to get our belly buttons pierced today? Mom was gonna do it," I said as if it was no big deal. I didn't want to scare him off.

"I don't know, noodle. I'm not feeling so well today." He took a long swallow, then stared down at his hand, which was still shaking. After finishing the drink, he was steadier. "I'm not so sure I approve of you mutilating your body anyway," he said.

"But Dad . . ." I poured on the guilt while I poured

210

him another drink and just orange juice for myself.

He sighed, beaten. "Yeah, okay, I guess. If I'm feeling better. I think I'm coming down with something."

He said that every day, and I paid no attention. "Oh, Daddy, you're the best!" I said, and meant it. If it weren't for him, what would I do? Sleep on some stranger's ratty couch in New York City? Not me. I hated my mother, and I hated dancing, too, hated it! Daddy would never take off to "find himself" when I needed him. He would never do that to me.

"I'm gonna shower. You, eat something! You're too thin!" he said, peeling my arms off where I'd thrown them around him and topping off his drink before heading upstairs. "And make some coffee!" he yelled down.

"I'm gonna call Kayla and tell her she can come over."

He didn't answer. I knew what he was doing, he was crying. Crying over my mother. Crying over the reality that we were left out of her new life, and because he had a pounding headache, and he had to deal with me and my friends—he had to make me happy now, and I knew he could hardly stand the responsibility.

Setting my face to "impassive," I stopped thinking, and busied myself with making a pot of coffee. I decided to start drinking it black. Thick and black to grow me up, and I wasn't going to tell anyone, even Kayla, that I was nervous. Not because of the pain, exactly. I didn't mind pain. I was worried I might accidentally cry, and I didn't want anyone to ever see that.

Casey

I remember being in a hurry to get to the party. My mother was taking forever, and I said something like, "Mom, you look fine. Mom, you're beautiful! Leave your hair alone! You're fine! It's not like you're going in."

"Is that a threat, Casey?" she said. "Because you should just be glad you have a mother who will jump up on a moment's notice."

"Can we go now?"

"Where's the fire, Casey, huh?"

"Mommy, *please*."

"What's really going on?"

"There's nothing going on, Mom, let's just go. Please!"

To tell you the truth, I didn't know if something was going on or not, I just knew that Rain called me and said she wasn't going to the party if Kayla wasn't going, and Kayla was crying when I called. *She* wasn't going to the party without her belly button being pierced. "It's not fair!" is what she said. "I never get what *I* want!" I asked did she mean I shouldn't go to the party either because I didn't get my belly button pierced and she just said, "You wouldn't understand, Casey. You're only fifteen." I was like, "Thanks Kayla, why do you have to say that to me? You said age was just a number." She goes, "I was talking about Brian and me, sweetie," and I thought *I'm not your sweetie and you're only sixteen anyway*, but then I said, "Okay, but Brian won't care if you have a ring through your belly button, you're beautiful and smart and we should go to the party," and she said, "I guess." So I called Rain back then because she usually drives us everywhere, but *she* said no way was she driving tonight because she was going to have fun for once. I was like, "I can't do any drugs, my mother made me promise," which was maybe half true. Rain was all yellin' and shit then, saying, "Who said anything about drugs? Don't be such a baby, Casey. Tell Kayla to get her Mom to drive us." So I was like, "Whatever," but only to myself and after I hung up, while I was calling Kayla back, who only started crying and saying maybe she shouldn't go to the party at all but then she said she was getting a text, and it was Rain, and whatever it said calmed Kayla down, so she said to me, "Casey, could your mother drive us?" I sighed. I really, really didn't want my mother to drive us because she was going to act the way she was now.

"Okay, I'm ready. Is there anything between my teeth?"

"Mom, you're just driving, you're not going in, *please*, please, pretty please?"

She sighed. She rubbed toothpaste on her teeth, and I did the same. We saw each other in the mirror, stopped growling at each other, and grinned.

"I love you, Mommy," I said.

"I love you too, Casey. Let's go. Does my hair really look okay? Do you think I should grow it out?"

"You're beautiful. You're the best, Mom." I pretended to ruffle her spiked hair, which of course you couldn't really do because it would probably bite your hand; that's just what I thought because it was so stiff with mousse, and also because it belonged to my mom and she got really mad if you touched her hair. Plus *she* would bite you herself if you rubbed her the wrong way. *Me too*, I thought, and let my chunky black bangs fall over my eyes. When I was twenty-one I was going to have my incisors sharpened into fangs. My mother didn't believe me when I told her that, but she'd see.

"Do you need help?" she asked me when we were in her car, an old Mustang convertible that coughed and eventually started.

"Mom, I think I can buckle my own seatbelt."

She leaned over me anyway. I rolled my eyes and pushed her away.

"Remember what I told you," she said.

"I know, Mom, I'll never ever, no matter who offers what drug to me or how old I am, I'll never do it. I promised you that already!"

"Just checking. Maybe I should check in with Michelle, see how she's doing."

"Please, Mom! Kayla will have a cow if you go in her house and get all chummy with her mother before this party and we're late because of it. Please, just drive please."

I was thinking, as we drove in the warm night air, how good it felt to be driving with my mother, and going out with my best friends, and going to my first kegger. I was also, I admit it, thinking, if someone offered me an Oxy, I'd probably take it.

Rain

Before Casey's mom, Nancy, picked me up, I remember emptying my dad's ashtray and putting it on the kitchen counter. Taking one of his cigarettes out and lighting it.

Coughed some. Felt a little woozy—then a lot, like I was going to throw up and/or pass out. I sat down quickly on the floor, putting my head between my knees until the feeling passed. I stood up and inhaled from the cigarette again. It had an awful taste, like soot, but the second hit was smoother than the first, and I figured I could get used to it.

Next, retrieved the vodka from the coffee table, poured a shot into a glass, added a splash of OJ like my dad had taught me, and gulped.

Whew. Fuck. 'Nother head rush. Sat down on the floor *again*, cooling my bikinied butt on the tile. In a minute I was already on my feet again, because I always get up again, and I always will no matter what. Fuckin' remember that, World!

As I started my second drink, I was feeling way better. Less tense. Smooooth. I swiveled my hips and ran my hand over my belly, savoring the warmth, appreciating my body, which was slimmer than it'd ever been, and strong. I didn't even want to put something on over my bikini, I wanted to go to the party just like this, slinky and warm and smelling of smoke. But you—I mean, Casey's mother—would freak, I was sure of that, and then she wouldn't take us to Brian's house. *Who does she think she is?* I thought. Mothers.

I looked down at the red spot around my belly button piercing. The vodka sure cut down on the throbbing. I wished it didn't look so new.

Upstairs in my room, I fumbled through my makeup and found a cover-up stick, which I smeared around the new piercing. It worked pretty well at covering the red. I looked at myself in the mirror. Swiveled my hips again—thought, *Look, Mom, I'm dancing. Just like you!* Thinking about my mother killed my buzz, because she said she'd come home for my piercing and my first big party, and she didn't. I was a little sad, maybe even a lot.

"Oh, fuck that," I said out loud. I tripped rushing, angry as hell, to my mother's closet, got up with my knees still burning from the rug, yanked a spaghetti strapped, low-cut, tie-dyed long dress from Target off its hanger and pulled it on. My chest hung out all over the place—good! And it was too long for me, I mean, to be a short dress on me. So I found some scissors. I was all, Fuck! as I wrapped my fist around the blades and held on for a moment, stopping myself from crying. Crying is a waste of time, like being scared. All that shit.

Gotta grow up, Rain! Not a little mommy's girl anymore. I sniffled, then pronto pulled it together and cut down the dress to a mini. A mini-mini. The vodka I'd drunk made me cut a jagged edge, but it was okay.

No one was going to be looking at my hem anyway.

The phone rang. "Mom?" I said, a sudden rush of hope flooding my heart—hoping she was waiting at the train station for a ride home.

Stupid, Rain.

I hung up on whoever it was because it wasn't her. Felt my heartbeat slamming in my chest and tears starting again because it seemed like I wasn't just on my own tonight. *No one* lived here anymore. Not even my Dad, not really.

Well, that night I decided I would be someone else. Someone popular and most importantly, never ever afraid. I was going to run the show from now on.

I hurried downstairs, leaving all the lights on as I went, because in spite of the hard, all-together, strong person I was, I was maybe still a little scared of the dark. I admit it, okay? So fucking sue me.

In the kitchen, I tossed the pack of cigarettes and my dad's lighter into my tote on top of my towel, did a shot of vodka straight from the bottle, and left the lights on in the kitchen and living room as I passed through to the front step to wait for my ride. I felt better already.

Kayla

I was at the party, finally. It wasn't what I thought it would be like. I felt weird. Everyone was looking, and I didn't like to be looked at, not *that* way. I was Rain's best friend, but I wasn't like her, I wasn't brave. Meanwhile, she was acting like more than her usual self, like she was possessed or something.

"Come on, Kayla," Rain whispered. "You want Brian to notice you!"

I looked around the hot tub. Brian wasn't noticing me, that was true. He didn't even know I was there. I wanted to pretend he was looking at me out of the corner of his eye, and he wasn't talking to me because he respected me too much to grab my breast the way he just did that other giggling girl. *Oh, shit, I am a loser*, I thought in a panic. I couldn't believe it took me two beers and this stupid, insanely stupid, visit to the hot tub for me to realize that. Where was Casey? I wanted to just go home, so I stood up.

Like an idiot, like a little baby, I wanted to cry, and I was just standing there, shivering, when Rain stood up next to me, and she was all, "Oh, yeah, you go, Kayla." Then the next thing I know, she was bumping my skinny hip to make me dance and then everyone was looking and we looked so stupid. *Shit, Rain stop!* I couldn't say out loud. I couldn't say it!

Rain's afraid of the dark, she said? Big whoop, fear is my life.

Rain didn't stop. Before I could even say, "Let's go," she pulled off her bikini top! Before I could even grab her and pull her under the water and ask her what she was on and why she was acting crazy, before I could even—

She pulled off *my* top! Holy shit! My nipples were cold and hard, and I didn't feel good, but now Brian *was* looking, and he had forgotten about the other skanks, and he was cheering us on!

Someone handed me a jello shot, which I swallowed down, and then a beer, which I chugged down, and then I—little, meek, pathetic eleventh-grader at a senior party, not-even-invited girl—wiggled my hips, and danced with Rain.

She told me, "They want to see a show, Kayla. Should we give them a show?"

My head was swimmy. I saw Casey coming toward us, and she looked concerned and nervous and as if she was about to put a stop to Rain and me dancing. For a moment I was torn between the comfort of my old self, promised by Casey, and the promise of following Rain's lewd behavior and branding myself in Brian's mind for ever—but then Brian's best friends Kris and Jason from the basketball team, they got in the way so I couldn't see Casey anymore. All I saw was how happy Rain and I were making the boys and I was thinking, *Brian will never forget me*, and when Rain squirted me with beer, I squirted her back with the beer that magically appeared in my hands, and those other girls who were in the hot tub before *disappeared*, fucking *disappeared*! It was all Rain, it was all *me*! We play-fought, and everyone was cheering, everyone loved us.

We put on an awesome show. Rain spread beer foam on me and you won't believe this, but I licked it off her stomach, because that's what the crowd wanted! They loved me! Afterwards, when I was sweaty and breathless and drunk, Brian—Brian Kepler!—guided me out of the hot tub and tied my bathing suit top back on for me.

"I think you've had enough of the wild side," he said. He smiled at me! He *liked* me, *me*!

"Come on," he said, "let me get you a beer."

His arm slung casually over me, Brian and I walked to the keg, if you can call what I was doing walking. Really, it was more like floating.

Rain

I didn't care. *Let Kayla go*, I thought.

Crap, that was mean. Of course she should've gone with Brian, he was everything to her. I felt like crying. I didn't want to be so angry all the time. Kayla didn't do anything to me.

"Come on, come on!" some guy yelled. He pushed a wine cooler into my hand, and I was back out of my head, into my body. I lied when I said I didn't like dancing. I didn't like it taking my mother away, but at the party, I could totally see why she went. The crowd! The excitement! The rush of power! I was in control, and all those people I didn't even know couldn't take their eyes off me. Swivel hips, get a cheer. Shake shoulders, feel the music in my bones.

I remember though, it ended—the faces and the yells faded back, and I was not Rain who was in charge of everything, who put Dad to bed, who got Kayla her guy, who gave Casey a feeling of life-without-Mom-up-her-butt.

I was little Rainbow, six, dancing in the living room with my mother. The furniture pushed out of the way. Daddy at work. Mommy lifting her leg with ease, spinning, then spinning me, dipping me. She couldn't take her eyes off me. I copied everything she did. We were a team. I was special. I was light. The light in her eyes and the glow in her cheeks . . . our fingers touched and it was electric and I *loved* to dance . . .

I snapped back to my place on the hot tub, and the eyes on me and the attention I was getting—and the music suddenly seemed too loud, pulsing like the heart of a beast, my heart in time, but not my real heart or my good, Rainbow heart.

I saw my breasts, wet with sticky spray and then someone else sprayed me with his beer. Foam bubbles popped on my chest, my stomach.

"Take it *all* off!"

"Come on, baby!"

More beer spray. Laughter. Yelling. I didn't feel safe anymore. I was alone. I was, oh God, oh shit, I was scared. Those people, they were too close. I could see their teeth. They wanted to eat me alive. Everyone was yelling at me! Seemed like everyone. I didn't know who they were! I couldn't believe I took my top off, but I couldn't stop, couldn't show any fear. *They'd like that*, I thought.

Not fun, not fun, oh Mommy, what do I do now? I thought. I didn't cry though. I remembered I was running the show, and that made me feel better, stronger.

Someone pushed another wine cooler into my hand. I vaguely remember gulping the last one back and then pouring the remains over my head while the crowd screamed with delight.

Then thinking, *Not fun, not fun anymore* . . .

I stopped dancing, stumbled out of the tub and spun around. The party, the crowd, were a blur. All those boys wanted something from me, and I didn't have anything left to give! Couldn't they see, couldn't anyone see that they took and took until there was no Rainbow, not even any Rain left? I stumbled back, but there wasn't anywhere to go. It felt like something had wrapped its claws around my throat, strangling the breath out of me. I saw spots. I needed air, but I couldn't ask for help, I was strangled and oh God, then I was so dizzy. When would it end? Who would save me now? I'd always saved everyone else. I didn't know what to do with myself now that I needed me.

Everyone was still looking at me, jeering. Kayla was gone. Casey was gone. Blurry, spotty, shaking—I couldn't even see where I'd put my bikini top, and I was starting to feel like puking. My heart was beating faster. I dropped the bottle in my hand, and it sprayed glass on to my legs and bare feet, and into the hot tub and it made me jump, and when I did, I fell.

I knew I was going to crack my head open, but then—a miracle! Someone caught me. Someone big and shirtless and red-headed.

"Going somewhere?" he asked.

It was as if he saw only me. He was deaf to the boos as he carried me away from the hot tub. He wrapped me in a fluffy towel, and my head drooped with embarrassment. When he lifted my chin with his finger, I saw the other kids had scattered from the tub and the spilled glass, and from me, and man oh man, I was so glad for once to be forgotten. I was so relieved not to have to control the situation any more.

"Here, drink this. It'll relax you," the boy said.

Although I knew I'd probably drunk enough already, I didn't care—I did need to relax. I wanted to forget. I wanted to do anything the boy who saved me asked. I wanted to swallow my fear back down and keep it there. So I gulped back the red, sickly sweet punch in three swallows. It was strong.

"Good girl," the boy said, taking the empty cup.

I gladly gave myself up to Red's protection. I watched someone cover the hot tub with a board. My striptease dance was already forgotten, and the crowd had moved on to dancing "Cotton-Eyed Joe," sans moi. Gratefully, I leaned my head on Red's shoulder, and shut my eyes. He rubbed circles on my back, and everything was okay.

Casey

My stomach was crampy and hollow because I didn't even eat dinner before going to that stupid party where I didn't know anyone unless you count the two crazies who were dancing in the hot tub and I didn't. Count them. Stupid supposedly-my-friends girls who left me on my own. Alone.

Stupid humidity and stupid hair I tried to blow dry straight at home, but after a half-hour—how long was I here? Whatever. My hair puffed out, from pageboy to Afro. I tried to push it behind my ears, but it bounced back out a frizzy mess and I didn't even wear my bathing suit—that's how much of an idiot I was—I totally forgot.

It was their fault, Rain and Kayla, Kayla and Rain, Rain, Rain, Rain, Kayla Kayla Kayla, Kayla and Rain. Why did I think they'd really want to hang out with me? They just wanted a ride to the party I think.

"You don't look so good," said the girl next to me, and she should know cause she looked fine, with chocolate skin I could just eat, I swear, and legs that went on and on and made me think, *I am so over Rain Rikowsky.*

Pushing my hair behind my ears again, I was all like, "Aaargh fuck!" when it wouldn't stay put, and I got up and went over to the pool and just bent over and dunked my head in. It was nice under the water, sounds all dull and the chocolate girl's voice was like, whoo whoo whookay? And when I looked up over my head, she was all swirly like a sundae. When she grabbed me by my hoodie—the one with the skulls and the sparkly roses that said Rock On and Tough Girl—she yanked me up and I was like, "I'm fine!" I laughed as I flipped my sopping hair back, where it finally stayed, except for my bangs, which dripped pool water in my eyes and made them burn.

Fucking Rain had taken her top off, and *Oh! Oh my God, that's funny!* I thought. I was giggling so hard when Rain suddenly took Kayla's top off, too—princess Kayla—I was like, "Look!" to no one in particular, and then a mob surrounded the hot tubs and I couldn't see my supposed friends, my supposed love of my life, not that she knows it, stupid Rain Rikowsky.

I stumbled. Chocolate girl said, "I'm Ebony," and she was there to hold me up! She took me by the arm and led me to the fence, and let me slide down, and then she slid down next to me and I was like, *Mom, if you could see me now,* only that made me want to cry, because I knew I fucked up getting so fucked up and my Mom was never going to shut up about this, you know?

So I stared into chocolate girl's eyes, and she said, "I'm Ebony."

"I remember," I said, but I didn't remember anything.

"Tell me, how much did you do?" she wanted to know. I liked her accent. She was soooo pretty . . .

I didn't think she was going to narc on me, but still, I was like, "Do what?"

She didn't push me, she was just all, "You are sooo wasted," and so I shrugged and pulled my hood up, just 'cause whatever.

I took Ecstasy and smoked pot and had some white wine, I knew that, but all I said was, "You're soooo pretty."

She kissed me.

Holy crap, I thought, *she kissed me!* I was still sitting there, trying to wrap my head around that when she said, "Come on, I've got something for you," and I took her hand and I thought, *Sorry, Mom,* and *Screw you Rain, if you even care,* and then . . .

I went.

Kayla

Here's what happens when a heart breaks: you feel it in your back and around your ribs. The focal point is in your heart, a heavy coldness that spins inside, jagged edges cutting out your center, your self. The pain extends around like a rope, tying all of you into the loss.

Your stomach feels empty, even though you've just eaten a small mountain of chips and spicy melted cheese, hoping to fill it and be a normal teenager again, when you'll *never* be normal or quirky or pretty or promising or lovable . . .

You can't fill yourself, and you grasp with your fingers, without even thinking about it—your fingers open and close, reach and pull. You want to get something, anything inside. Even if it's anger. Or self-loathing.

Nothing can go right when your heart is breaking. You get out your paints to try and show the darkness inside on the outside, and the brush flies out of your hand and is lost under the bed where you can't reach without getting a splinter in your belly. "Jesus fucking Christ, give me a break!" you yell in a whisper at the ceiling and at *all* the gods of all the religions who let this happen to you.

You get out another brush and paint anyway, but the color over color over color turns to mud, and it only drags your spirit into the mess of your aching body and the final picture doesn't cover the hole inside you—it makes you cry. Before long you're wailing as you try to paint the canvas, and fail, and start painting yourself brown and ugly like you feel.

You feel like everything you've worked for—hoping and dreaming and praying so hard—it was all a lie, a great cosmic lie. The way you felt just hours before the party—swollen with excitement, fat with pleasure, open to possibilities, at one with the whole fucking fabric of the universe or some shit, well, it's all gone now because it wasn't just waking up and not remembering, and it wasn't just finding the only boy you ever loved in the room with your best friend—it wasn't just your innocence . . .

It was all of you.

Nancy

I woke up with a start at 3 a.m., sitting straight up and shaking my head, as if a bucket of water had just been thrown on me. I rubbed my eyes frantically. I remember thinking, *Something's wrong! Casey!* and hurrying to her room. She wasn't there. Grabbing my keys and my cell, I was dialing her number as I slid my feet into my Berks. She didn't answer, and I left a quick, "Where the hell are you?" message before fumbling with the door downstairs, which—Shit!—always stuck in summer. I threw my shoulder against it and finally smashed through, ran to my car, left the house door open behind me and didn't care.

Brian Kepler's house was quiet. Too quiet.

"Casey!" I yelled in the backyard. "Casey! Casey!"

Backyard strewn with empty and broken bottles. Pool table in the garage, felt torn. Running, slipping, running, shouting.

"Shut up or I'll call the cops!" I heard from the house behind the back fence.

I should've called the cops, but I ran into the house through an open door instead, dialing as I went. "Casey!" I yelled into the house and the phone at the same time. Stupid voicemail. Stupid party. Stupid mom.

Upstairs, I threw open doors. Threw open one, and Kayla was in a boy's bed, but no boy. She was sleeping, tucked in all nice.

"Kayla! Kayla! Wake up! Where's Casey? Where's my daughter?"

Kayla opened her eyes, snapping awake the way I had back at home. "Mrs. Shaw?" Kayla fumbled under the covers. "Oh God," she said.

"Looking for these?" I said, throwing her underpants at her. "Where is *Casey*?"

"I don't . . ."

"Forget it! You're useless. You stupid little—' I didn't say *bitch*, but I was thinking it as I left the bedroom and continued throwing open doors, shouting as I left the doors open, revealing girls and boys making out, having sex, passed out in vomit, stoned, stupid. "Casey!"

The door at the end of the hallway opened, and a boy, *Brian*, that was who it was, *Brian Kepler*, I thought.

He tried to stop me from going in. "You can't—"

"Casey!" I yelled, pushing past the boy, into the room.

I froze.

"Look, I don't know what happened, but I told them they have to go. I don't know—"

"Shut UP!" I yelled in Brian Kepler's face. I noticed the top button of his shorts was undone. He wasn't wearing a shirt. "Don't you move," I told him.

God help me, I forgot about Casey when I walked into that room. All I saw was Rain Rikowsky, eyes shut, legs spread. (I don't know how to say this, I'll just do it.) A boy with his shirt

225

off and shorts around his ankles, pumping on top of her. A couple of half-naked boys, boys with their zippers undone and their hands moving fast, groans, shouts and cheers swallowed when I'd burst in. The boy on the bed jumped down and grabbed his shirt off the floor, tried to run. Brian Kepler stopped him. I tore a handheld video camera out of another boy's hand.

"I think you broke my thumb!" he yelled at me. I slapped him.

"Shut UP!" I said, rushing to the bed and throwing a stained bloody sheet over Rain's lower body. I rushed to her head. I said, "Rain, honey, wake up. Rain, are you there?" Her head lolled. Someone snickered, but mostly the boys were trying to get away. Many did escape. But Brian threw camera boy down and shirtless boy against the wall. For about half a second I wondered whose side Brian Kepler was on. He seemed to be on ours. But I hated him.

I called 911. I gently stroked Rain's face.

"Oh God," I heard from the door. It was Kayla. "Rain . . . Brian . . . oh God oh God oh God oh—"

Brian tried to hold on to Kayla, but she shoved him, sudden power bursting out of her. She ran to Rain and held her hand. I dropped the camera I'd confiscated. I looked at Kayla. "Where's Casey?" I tried to say, but it was hard to talk. I couldn't get a breath, and I couldn't stop crying and I couldn't find the ground with my feet any more.

EPILOGUE
Casey
"Hey," I say to Rain in the courthouse hallway. I haven't seen her since the night of the party, and now here we are. It's okay, I guess. I mean, it will be. I hope.

"Hey," Rain says with an awkward smile that says she's sort of happy to see me, *but* . . . "You changed your hair."

I run my hands through the longish strands of my hair. "Well, you know, the black—"

"I thought it looked more blue . . ."

"—was kinda growing out anyway. You like it?" My mother and I had a girls' night last night, mostly to chill me out, but her too, in preparation for the trial starting today. We wanted to give me credibility, too, so we bleached out my hair, and then put in chunky gold and strawberry-blonde highlights. Very normal high school student, very not who I am, but whatever. It's important for my friends that I look presentable for this trial.

"Been two weeks without a drink," Rain's father says to my mother, digging into his pocket. He pulls out a tin coin. He shrugs. He seems smaller than I remember.

My mother squeezes his arm, and Rain leans into him. She bites a nail. She seems smaller, too.

"You wanna take a walk?" she says.

I shrug and nod.

"It's okay, Mom," I say before my mother can say what I know she's thinking, which is something like, "Do you think you should?"

"My mother is afraid of me knowing the truth," I say to Rain as we escape down the hall.

"*I'm* afraid of knowing the truth," Rain says as we leave through the heavy front door. "And I was there."

"I'm sorry," I say. I'm sorry for what happened to her. I'm also sorry I wasn't there to save her. I'm embarrassed it had to be my mother. I'm ashamed.

Rain brushes her hand against my arm like she's checking I'm real, and I touch her hand with my fingertips like I'm checking *she* is.

"So, your mom is writing a book about us," Rain says as we walk around the corner. She takes a pack of cigarettes out of her coat pocket.

"Yeah. Not sure how I feel about *that*," I say.

Shrugging, Rain offers me the open cigarette pack, and I see that instead of cigarettes, it's half full of joints. Shaking my head, I look at her, shocked. We're on a pretty busy street, we're about to go into a courtroom for the trial of Rain's rapists.

"Oh, right," she says, smiling an old, familiar, kinda evil grin. "You're doing the sober thing too, now." Rain laughs, bitter, and I cringe. I know that to her it's too little too late. But what does she want me to do?

I don't know what to say, so I get out a regular cigarette of my own to cover up my embarrassment. She hot-boxes the joint, and we're quiet.

"Girls," says a steady voice out of nowhere. Kayla's mom.

Rain holds the joint low and behind her back as Kayla hugs her. I notice Kayla gives Rain a look. While she hugs me, Kayla says, "Mom! I'll see you inside!"

Mrs. Crew leaves, and a tear slips over Kayla's pale, now nearly translucent, face. I can see the veins beneath her skin as she shakes her head.

"Oh, fine," Rain says, carefully extinguishing the joint on the sole of her boot. She puts the roach back into her cigarette pack. To Kayla, she says, "I'm saving this one for you, blondie. It'll make you eat. You know, starving yourself to death won't make this go away. It happened. Deal with it. I am."

"Really? Because you seem *so* well adjusted," I say in Kayla's defense, before Rain breaks her.

I can hardly look at Kayla—talk about getting smaller. Kayla's fingers look like tiny twigs, fleshless, as she puts them against Rain's face. "We'll be okay," she says.

Rain rolls her eyes, but I can see she's about to cry. She snuffles, sucking it up.

Same old Rain.

Kayla—same old Kayla—puts a hand on the back of Rain's and my head and pulls us together. Our foreheads touch. It's corny, but nice. "We will always be okay, no matter what. We'll always be together, too," she says, and with that, she links arms with each of us, and we walk into the courthouse together.

Margo Ferkel's Two-Hour Blitz of Badness

BY JILL WOLFSON

HOW CAN A girl be bad with a name like Margo Ferkel? That's a cartoon character's name, red nose and big, floppy feet that she's always tripping over. Or maybe the title of a highly evolved religious figure from a country high in the Himalayas. *In a rare audience today, Her Holiness the Margo Ferkel shared a message of hope and wisdom for the ages.*

But behind her name of hard consonants, I saw Margo's potential, a streak of longing to be more than just the daughter of Irv and Ann, a desire as desperate as my own to break out of the stultifying expectations of our Philadelphia blue-collar upbringing. We lived on the same street, a one-block string of brick homes, houses with shared walls and tiny lawns and marigolds in a line dance that screamed of conformity. The only way to tell the houses apart was by the front-door screens, Margo's decorated with an F in wrought-iron filigree, mine with a W.

It wasn't that we were great friends. Even in that bastion of consistency, we had our differences. To me, our looks said it all. Margo was blonde, pale, fragile-looking, bland, the salt to my pepper. I was dark and sharp-featured, all points and nervous energy. But Margo and I had been thrown together since infancy. Our parents took Israeli folk-dance lessons together; our dads were in the same weekly pinochle card game and the moms played mah-jongg together. That's the way things were in our neighborhood. Kids weren't over-booked with music lessons and sports. You were bored a lot, so it wasn't unusual for me and Margo to wind up in each other's room looking for something to do. Especially in the summer. Especially that summer, when we had gotten too old for the street game of kick-the-can and were too young for any kind of job except babysitting.

That afternoon, my mother was at the hairdresser's and I was entertaining Margo with the details of my new life philosophy. She was transfixed. Margo may have been a year older, but in terms of self-assurance and social cache, I was the shit, just coming off my reign as queen of sixth grade. I had had a great realization recently, one of those shifts in understanding that cause your whole world to come tumbling down. Now I was rebuilding it to my own specifications. Margo hung on my every word.

"Here's the secret: grown-ups can't read your mind," I pronounced.

"What do you mean?"

"I mean, they can't. Parents and teachers can't get inside your head and know everything that you're thinking or planning to do."

"I know that."

"You know it, but you don't really *know* it. You only know it like you know the words to a song or something superficial like that. Because you *act* like they do know everything. I was like that until I had this big explosion of *getting* it, really understanding that they don't know crap about what's really going on in my head. So, I can do anything I want. All I have to do is widen my eyes and lie my head off. They don't suspect. Especially since I've been such a good girl for my whole life."

I turned my eyes into two round pools of innocent indignity and pressed my palm to my collarbone. "Me? How could you think it was *me* who took that five dollars?"

"You didn't!" Margo practically shouted.

"Stealing was hard at first. I thought I'd puke. But then—I don't know—everything becomes easier the more you practice it."

A few months earlier, I had started keeping a journal of all the bad things I had gotten away with. "If I show it to you, you're not going to tell your parents, are you?"

Margo shook her head almost violently, and I knew I had a willing student.

"Number one: stealing the money out of my mom's bag. Number two: writing a note and passing it around class. *If I ever get big, floppy tits like Mrs. Atkins, shoot me!* Three: cursing my grandmother behind her back, the F word."

"You didn't," she spat out.

"I did."

"That's really bad."

"I also let Alan Brickman kiss me."

"Where?"

"Behind the girls' room at the rec center."

"No, I mean *where*?"

I stuck out my tongue and took it on a slow, sloppy tour of my lips. After allowing some time to let that transgression sink in, I asked, "So what's the worst thing you ever did?"

I watched Margo's eyes. She didn't know how to control them yet, hadn't practiced that flat innocent look like I had, so I knew she was about to tell the truth.

"I watched TV on Shabbat."

"No!" I said with admiration. It wasn't a particularly big deal to me, but Margo's family was religious. This was a major violation of the rules, maybe even on the same level as cussing a grandma. I didn't think Margo had it in her. Here was an opportunity to drive home my point, to be the teacher to this willing student.

"And did your parents somehow find out?"

"No."

"And did God send down lightning to punish you?"

"No."

"See! You can do whatever you want, whenever you want. You just have to be sneaky about it."

I took her by the hand and led her downstairs to my father's liquor cabinet. I had been eager to add this one to my list. "My personal favorite is Seagram's Seven." I poured a capful and handed it to her. Then I removed the cap from a vodka bottle and filled that cap with whiskey as well.

"Are you sure they won't notice it's missing?" she asked. My answer was to tilt back my head like I had seen my father do and swallow. She did the same, and we both fought the urge to cough it back up. "Nectar of the gods," I said.

"Delicious," Margo agreed.

After that, it was just a short, easy downhill slope to more bad behavior. Lunch was my idea. The first bite of a salami sandwich washed down with a gulp of milk—the unholy pairing of meat and dairy on a bed of whiskey—unleashed the wildness in her.

"Fuck," Margo said.

"Fuck a duck," I added.

"Fuck a big fat shit damn piss mother-fucking duck."

She wasn't laughing. She was dead serious. "What else? What's next?"

Back in my bedroom, from under the mattress, I pulled out a magazine that I had stolen from my cousin Harriet's creepy new husband. "He may be my cousin, but he's a total sleazebag." We were on our bellies in bed, hip to hip, turning pages. "Look at those bazooms," I said.

"Knockers," she agreed, then without pausing said, "You know what would be really bad?"

"What?"

"If we kissed."

I sat up. "You mean, me and you. You and me."

"Yeah, so we can practice to be with boys. But I want to be the girl."

"Okay, I've already kissed a boy, so I know how they kiss. I'll be the boy."

We leaned toward each other. Our eyes closed, our lips met. I felt the awkward pressure. It wasn't much different than kissing Alan Brickman. "Next, tongues," I ordered. She tasted like salami, so I knew I did, too.

"Now touch this." She pointed and I put my hand over the right side of her chest, felt the hard softness there. When I said in a low boy voice, "Yum, bazooms," she started laughing and then I started laughing back and we couldn't stop. We were shaking with it, bouncing on the bed, hair flying, our feet in each other's faces.

"That was really bad!" I finally managed to say.

"Next time, we can be even more bad."

Almost two hours had passed since this blitz had begun. I had my mother's schedule planned almost to the minute. She would be back soon, so we probably had time for only one more thing. "Let's make it good. What do you really, really want to do?"

"You decide. Your choice."

We were still lying in the bed, my hand resting on her leg. The skin was so smooth, almost hairless. I pushed her aside, sat up and pointed to my own legs. Just the week before, I had gone to the school nurse and while taking my temperature, she took note of the thick, dark hair on my arms and legs. "Hmmm," she had said casually. "You must have a lot of testosterone in your system."

I couldn't get that out of my mind. "I wanna shave my legs," I announced. "My mom says I'm not old enough."

Margo nodded with sympathy. "You're old enough. Definitely. Me, too."

"My mom will be so mad."

"My mother will *kill* me."

"They don't have to know. Just wear pants."

"But it's summer."

"That's why we need to shave our legs!"

With that logic to spur us on, we locked ourselves in the bathroom, which was hardly big enough for two. Margo sat on the closed toilet lid. I opened the medicine cabinet, watching her image in the mirror swing by, and then disappear. My mother always used an electric shaver, dainty and pink, *Lady* something. It wasn't here. But I spotted my father's razor on the first shelf, thin, sleek and gunmetal gray. "Ta-da!"

I called up the mental image of my dad shaving and fumbled with the razor, twisting the handle until the hinges dropped open like the halves of a peach. I tipped the old blade into the trash can and inserted a fresh one from a new pack. To cover up my uncertainty, I kept talking. "The secret to a really good close shave is a fresh blade. And of course, the shaving cream. You do the honors."

I handed the can to Margo, miming how she was supposed to shake it first. Then I positioned myself on the edge of the sink, balancing on my bottom and resting my extended right leg on her lap. I felt the pleasure of the pepperminty smell, the pressure of her hand as it smoothed the cool cream into a thick layer on my legs.

"Like that?" she asked.

"Perfecto. Don't forget here." I pointed to my inner thigh.

"You're sure you know what you're doing?" she asked as she sprayed the cream on her own legs.

"Of course. I've watched my mom and dad shave hundreds of times. Thousands."

Maybe I had convinced myself that I wasn't lying, or maybe I was just eager to look nonchalantly bad. I didn't stop to question or plan. I reached down and drew the blade across my right thigh, down the leg and up the left one. Then I reached over and did the same on Margo's legs, plowing through the shaving cream like a shovel through snow. And for a split-second longer, the snow remained white, freshly fallen, until a thin line of red, a worm rising to the surface of the bank, made itself seen. A worm and then two worms and then four and then eight growing thicker and fatter. There was no pain, not even a sting, just these hideous, twisting snakes spilling their red guts all over our legs.

Margo screamed. She was a screamer. That's another way we were different. "Stop it!" I ordered, and when she didn't, when she kept screaming and accusing me, when she pushed aside my offer of a towel and her high-pitched hysteria multiplied in volume in that tiny bathroom, when blood and shaving cream were flung everywhere, the floor, the walls, the mirror, I felt myself go blank, a strange, dead calm inside. I slapped her across the face.

"I wanna go home!"

"So, go," I said. "Go!"

The front door slammed behind her and I settled into cleaning up the horror film around me. I bloodied three towels, a half-roll of toilet paper and used up most of my father's styptic-stick, which turned from white to putrid pink. I dabbed, painted and winced until the snakes shriveled into dried-up worms that could be contained by half a box of plain old Band-Aids. The bathroom mess took even longer, but by the time my mother came home with her newly set hair, the towels were in the washing machine and the trash can was emptied. It was bathroom beautiful.

"I cleaned the bathroom for you," I announced with an extra measure of cheeriness.

"What?"

"You're always complaining that I'm a bathroom pig, so I cleaned it."

"Well, miracles never cease." Mom planted a kiss on my forehead. "I thought Margo was coming over."

"She did already."

"And you girls had fun?"

"It was all right. She's not, you know, the same kind of girl as me."

All that night, I waited with dread for Margo's parents to come pounding on our front door. I would be the bad one. I made their daughter do all these terrible things. I almost killed their daughter. I was the ringleader. But they didn't show up that night or the next one or the next week. That's when I realized that Margo didn't tell them and wasn't ever going to tell them. We were bonded in blood, in badness. We never talked about that afternoon, or anything else. If one of us saw the other sitting on her front stoop, we waved and walked in the other direction.

• • •

Right before school started that fall, the Ferkels moved, not too far, but two miles was a different world, a slightly classier neighborhood with more space between the houses, a different school system, a different rec center and a whole different circle of pinochle and mah-jongg-playing adults.

Over the next few years, I heard things. Margo joined the school band, then gave it up. Her parents divorced; it was ugly. She took a part-time job in a donut shop. But by my sophomore year in high school, even tiny bits of information about her dried up.

I had another new boyfriend by then, but things didn't work out too well with him. I flunked math, then history, switched from the college-bound track to vocational. Then I dropped out, got a waitress job, another boyfriend, got stoned a lot, lost another job, another guy. Don't get me started on the problems with my parents. Things happen to me. Things that aren't always good. Disappointments, lies, crises, numbness, betrayals, hurts, treachery, things that a lot of my so-called friends say that I only bring on myself.

I don't like thinking about the past too much. But every once in awhile, I find myself wondering about Margo Ferkel and about the scar that she probably has on her inner right thigh. It would be jagged, raw-looking, the same as mine, slowly fading and softening with time. I'm running my fingers along that scar right now, wondering if Margo ever does this. Does she feel the bumps? Does she remember? Does she miss a time when being bad—the worst bad that you can imagine—is kissing a girl, locking a bathroom door and shaving your own legs?

Nude Descending a Staircase

BY JENNIFER FINNEY BOYLAN

Dead

THE PHONE RANG in my mother's house. It was Aunt Nora. She said, "Eleanor, you'll never believe what happened. I just died."

My mother checked the clock. It was late. "Nora," she said. "What are you talking about?"

"I know what you're thinking," Aunt Nora continued. "But listen. I'm dead now." She paused. "Don't worry. It doesn't hurt. That's what I wanted to tell you."

"Nora," my mother said. "You're not making any sense. Of course you're not dead. You're on the phone."

My aunt made an irritated sound. "I knew you'd act like this. I *knew* it!"

"Nora. Are you listening to me? I want you to put the phone down. I want you to go get yourself a glass of milk. Will you do that for me, please?"

"You want I should get some milk?"

"Put the phone down and get yourself a glass of milk. When you have the milk, come back to the phone."

My aunt put the phone down begrudgingly. My mother, alone in her big house, sat on the edge of the bed and listened to the sounds of Nora moving around her apartment. Whatever it was she was doing, it was clear she hadn't traveled in a straight line to the refrigerator. My mother heard furniture moving, a toilet flushing. Aunt Nora was singing something to herself.

My mother thought about hanging up and calling me. Aunt Nora and I had been close when I was little. She was going to name me after her, in fact, until my father talked her into calling me Jennifer. Still, Nora and I had an understanding. We were both a little crazy.

But Aunt Nora was more than a little crazy by the time she called my mother and announced her own end. "I have the milk, Eleanor," she said. "I'm still dead."

"Did you drink it?" my mother asked. "Did you drink the milk?"

"I drank it. It tastes like milk." There was a pause. "Being dead doesn't change the way things taste."

"Nora," my mother said. "I want you to stop. I want you to drink the milk and go to sleep. I'll call you tomorrow morning."

"Why should I need sleep?" Aunt Nora said. "I'm dead. I'm not tired."

"Just drink your milk and go to bed. Will you do that?"

"All right," my aunt said, unconvinced. "Good night."

"Good night."

My mother hung up the phone. It wasn't exactly unusual for Aunt Nora to talk like this. All of my mother's brothers and sisters were troubled. Shamus had frozen to death on a freight train in Oregon. Caeli lived above a liquor store in Boston, and played one of those electric organs that supplied its own percussion. Sean, who no one had seen for seven or eight years, was rumored to have swelled up to the size of a bus, mainly because he was working as a night watchman and sat around eating potato chips. My mother was normal, almost exaggeratedly so, which in some ways made her the craziest of all of them.

Aunt Nora was the oldest. She was the only one who remembered the Civil War. The family had emigrated to America through Ellis Island in 1925, spent a couple of years in Boston, then decided to go back to Galway. By the time they got back, Ireland was down the drain. So they turned around again and came back to the States. A week after that my grandfather deserted the family for good. He turned up forty years later in the New York City morgue. He'd died on the Bowery with my Aunt Nora's address and phone number in his pocket.

My mother and Nora were the ones who had to go and identify the body. They didn't tell my sister Lydia or me about it. They took the train up to New York City and walked from Penn Station over to the morgue, which is on East 33rd Street. There's a big sign in the lobby in Latin. Loosely translated, it means, "Here is the place where all laughter stops. This is the place where the dead bring life to the living."

They were led into a room and the body was rolled out in its drawer. He had long, greasy, dirty hair. My mother couldn't say for sure whether it was her father or not. She hadn't seen him since she was a teenager. But then they noticed that his middle finger on the right hand was missing above the knuckle; he'd lost it in an auto body plant in the twenties. On the basis of this, they nodded. It was him, all right.

The medical examiner wanted to know what they wanted done. We don't want him, the sisters concluded. He abandoned us our whole lives. Now that he's dead, we'll abandon him.

So my grandfather was buried in a pauper's grave on Hart Island, in New York's Upper Harbor. The island is New York's potter's field, operated by the Department of Corrections. Prisoners in orange uniforms bury the dead in pine coffins in a long row, six coffins piled one on top of the other. Guards stand there with their guns trained on the gravediggers. I wrote a story about Hart Island one time. Most of the facts I got right, but I also threw in some stuff about a girl who's lost her father. At the end of the story, a chimpanzee wearing the father's clothes comes in on a unicycle and teeters in the moonlight.

The morning after my mother got the phone call from Aunt Nora, she got up, drank her coffee, then called her back. Nobody answered the phone. A few hours later, my mother finally called up her friend Happy and the two of them went over to my aunt's apartment to see what was what. They got to Nora's place and rang the bell. No one answered.

My mother had the key. She opened the door.

The place was empty.

For a while my mother and Happy combed through Nora's apartment, nervously searching for signs. But there weren't any. Aunt Nora was gone. Which was very strange, since she did not drive and did not like to leave the house even to walk around the block. Sunshine made her chilly.

Finally, one of them found a small piece of paper, which explained that an ambulance had been there during the night. Happy called the hospital. Aunt Nora had been admitted. Apparently she'd had the wherewithal, at some point, to call 911 and explain the situation.

It was mid-afternoon before my mother finally arrived at Bryn Mawr Hospital. There was my Aunt Nora, tied to her bed. She broke down in tears when she saw her sister.

"Eleanor, I'm so sorry," she said. "The milk didn't work."

Mardi Gras
The year I turned fifteen, my parents announced their intention of going to Mardi Gras, and leaving my sister Lydia and me at home alone, unsupervised. We were old enough to

be trusted, they said. But in this they were wrong.

"So we're going to be totally on our own," my sister said, reviewing the facts. I could see that her thoughts were not unlike my own. "Is that what you're saying?"

"Well, your Aunt Nora will stay here during the evenings," my mother said. "Just to make sure you're safe."

The announcement that Aunt Nora would be present did not immediately dislodge our plans to have the world's biggest party while my parents were gone. For some reason, we figured she'd be fine with it.

Aunt Nora was at work at the Bridal Salon when our party started. There was Darryl and his older brother Jonathan. There was Anne Niemeyer, who could ignite her own farts with a butane lighter. There was Dominique Leith, who had had three abortions. There was Lisa Yarrow, who had a Volkswagen and a pet rabbit. There were Lee Monahan and Steve Moe Hunter, who had bandanas. And there was Perry van Roden, who had been held back a grade for reasons that were not clear. I wanted with all my heart to get someplace alone with Perry. As night descended upon my parents' house, I realized that all I really wanted out of the impending bloodbath was for Perry to put one hand on my cheek and kiss me. "Jenny," he'd say. "You're so pretty."

By eight o'clock, there were perhaps a hundred ninth and tenth graders out of control in the house. I only knew about a dozen of them. Teenagers were descending on the house like crows dropping down on roadkill.

Kerrill Ferguson—who had a cool mom—had provided the keg. He walked around asking people for money for it. He kept at it for so long that in the end he made some money off the deal. Now and again he went over to the keg with a paternal demeanor and lovingly agitated its pressure pump with his large and hairy forearms.

My sister had disappeared early in the evening, and at about nine o'clock I went looking for her. I went up the long stairs to the third floor and found Perry van Roden alone in my room painting a mural on my bedroom wall with oil paints. He was singing some Rolling Stones song to himself as he painted. "You gotta move!" he sang. "You gotta move!" After taking a good look at the mural he was drunkenly painting, I realized he was right. We *were* going to have to move.

"Perry," I said. "What are you doing?"

He grinned. "Everythink's *yalla*," he said. It was clear enough: Perry was absolutely drunk. "Everythink's *green*."

Perry reached down and squeezed another tube of oil paint on to his hand. He squeezed it so hard the paint made splattering noises as the air glurted out of the tube. He scratched his cheek with this same hand, and a giant glob of blue paint now smeared across it.

"Ugg," he said. "Everythink's *bloooooo*."

"Perry," I said. "You want me to go get like some aspirin or something?"

He looked startled. "Aspirin," he said, and started laughing. "*Aspirin!*" Perry van Roden's knees buckled and he fell to the floor laughing.

"Perry," I said, kneeling down toward him. "Get up. Please."

He opened his eyes, and then reached up for my face with one hand, and drew me down to him, and we kissed. It was nice, the kiss. But it was not exactly what I'd had in mind.

"C'mon Lydia," he said softly. "Let's do it."

I pulled back. Lydia?

"It's me," I explained. "Jenny?"

"Lydia," Perry said again, and pulled me toward him. We kissed again, but to be honest, being called by my sister's name kind of wrecked it.

At that moment, from downstairs, I heard my aunt's voice. "Jennifer," she said. "Jennifer, come down here."

I left Perry laughing on the floor. I walked down the creaking stairs to find Aunt Nora standing in the hallway. She looked small and frightened.

"Jennifer," she said. "Where is your sister? Who are all these people?"

I didn't know what to tell her. They were good questions.

"Did your parents say it was all right for you to have this many friends over?" she asked, unsure. "I don't remember anyone saying anything about this."

From upstairs, suddenly, came the sound of a door swinging open. "Lydia," a voice moaned. "Lydia."

A moment later, Perry van Roden appeared. He was only wearing his underwear. Streaks of oil paint were smeared all over his body.

"Lydia," he moaned. *"C'mon! Let's do it!"*

My aunt screamed. A moment later she ran into my parents' bedroom. I heard the door lock behind her. It sounded like she was weeping.

I stood where I was, aware of the degree of trouble I was now in, alone. A moment later Perry van Roden, my love, reached the bottom of the stairs, and moved forward to embrace me. I was fifteen-years-old, my aunt was calling my parents long distance, and I was holding an almost naked boy in my arms for the first time. He buried his face in my hair.

"Oh, Lydia," Perry moaned, stroking my face. "I'll love ya till the day you die."

Plums

There was a three-year interval between the time that Aunt Nora decided she'd died and the time that she actually did. She spent the time in between in a series of hospitals, each one less cheerful than the one before. My mother and I would visit her, walk her around the ward. She'd whisper to us, "Watch yourself. Some of the people in here are really strange." One time we sat in a kind of courtyard next to another couple who was visiting a woman in a wheelchair with a tracheotomy. Every now and then mucus would burst suddenly out of a hole in the woman's neck. Aunt Nora sighed and suddenly imitated the entertainer Jimmy Durante. "It's humiliatin'," she said. "It's mortifyin'!"

My mother and I weren't sure who'd make it to the funeral. She didn't have many friends left. When we got to the funeral home my cousin Declan, Caeli's son, was standing there in a blue suit and a long ponytail. Declan is about ten years older than me. During the war he went to Canada. By the time Carter gave everybody amnesty, he'd acquired some unusual beliefs. For one thing, he only ate plums. For another, he spent about two months out of every year living in the desert in Mexico eating the hallucinogenic cactus, peyote. For all that, he was a respected scientist. He wound up teaching organic chemistry at Sarah Lawrence.

We walked across the room to say hello to cousin Declan. The only thing in the room besides the three of us was my aunt Nora, stretched out in a casket and wearing makeup. The night before, the funeral home had called us and asked us for a photograph of Aunt Nora. So they'd know what she was supposed to look like. It took us a while to find one that worked, since Aunt Nora hadn't looked like she was supposed to look like for a long time. My mother, turning boxes of photographs upside down, had muttered, "She never looked like she was supposed to have looked like."

Cousin Declan hugged my mother. "She's okay," he said. "She's part of the universe now."

Declan and I shook hands. We hadn't seen each other since

his first wedding, more than twenty years earlier. "How've you been, Jenny?" he asked me.

"Good," I told him. "I'm good."

We stood there for a while, the three of us, then we turned to look at Aunt Nora, all stretched out. We didn't say anything. After a little while my mother started to cry. She ran her fingers through Aunt Nora's hair.

"Poor thing," she said.

Later, we all drove out to the cemetery. While we sat in our limo, my mother laughed suddenly. We looked at her. She said, "You know, I was just thinking of that song Nora used to sing when she was in the hospital. You remember the one? 'Where Am I Going to Live When I Get Home?'"

She started to sing it. It sounded like a country and western song.

> *Where am I going to live when I get home?*
> *My wife threw out everything I own.*
> *She ain't what she said.*
> *I wish that I was dead.*
> *Where am I going to live when I get home?*

"Well," cousin Declan said. "She knows now. All right?" The phrase "All right?" asked as a rhetorical question turned out to be one of my cousin's signatures. I wondered if he'd picked it up in Canada.

My mother just shook her head. "It's funny," she said. "There was a time in her life when she was a happy person."

We stared out the windows. It was raining. We didn't talk for while.

"The Yaqui Indians have a name for a day like this," said cousin Declan as we pulled into the cemetery.

"Yeah?" I said. "What's that?"

"Minas Derendah," he said.

"What's that mean?" The car stopped. A man with an umbrella opened the door.

"It's kind of hard to translate," cousin Declan said. "All right?"

After the ceremony we went to a local brew pub called John Harvard's. Years earlier it had been called The Covered Wagon. I'd had my senior prom there. Before that I'd seen Count Basie and his orchestra perform in the same place. The spot where the Count's piano had once been was now occupied by an enormous copper kettle containing thousands of gallons of ale.

"So, Eleanor," cousin Declan said, after our beers had arrived. "I wanted to tell you I'm getting married."

"You are?" said my mother. "That's great. Who to?"

"This woman," cousin Declan said. "I met her on a vision quest."

We all sat there in silence for a while. There was a table of secretaries next to us who all burst into laughter at something. Finally my mother said, "Well. Isn't that nice."

"I wanted to invite you to the wedding." He looked over at me. "You, too, Jenny. If you want. It's going to be in California. During the equinox."

"The equinox," my mother said. "And when is that again?"

"September twenty-first," said cousin Declan. "I want you to be there if you'd like to come. You should know, though, we're going to have a vision quest as part of the ceremony. All right? I don't want you to be uncomfortable."

"Of course I wouldn't be uncomfortable at a vision quest," my mother said. "Not if it makes you happy." She supped her beer, then thought about it. "Now what would this involve exactly?"

Declan chose his words carefully. "Well, we'll all be camping out. This is near Big Sur. The ceremony itself will be performed by a shaman in a teepee. Then we sit in the sweat lodge."

"A sweat lodge," my mother said, fascinated. "Jenny, have you ever been in a sweat lodge?"

"Not yet," I said.

"Oh, wait," my mother said. "September twenty-first is the Philadelphia Flower Show. Darn it." She looked at me. "Jenny, you'll just have to represent the family."

Declan finished his beer. For a guy who ate only plums, I thought, he sure could put away the beers. "What do you think?" said my cousin. "Can you make it?" He smiled strangely. "I'm telling you, it'll be something to remember! All right?"

"All right," I said, and at that moment saw the future in all its completeness.

Seven months later, I was in a teepee by the Pacific Ocean watching cousin Declan exchange vows with a woman named Dakota. I was wearing a long blue dress. You could hear the waves hitting the shore as the two of them said their vows. As it turned out the ceremony wasn't all that mystical—the shaman read from the Book of Common Prayer.

After the wedding, a big fire was lit outside and people danced around it playing drums. Cousin Declan came over to me and gave me a giant hug. I could feel his ribs through his poncho. "I'm glad you're here," he said. "You and me, we're the last of the Mohicans, all right?"

Dakota was standing by the fire with her arms spread wide. I noticed she had a ring on every finger. The shaman approached her, beating a drum.

"It's important," said cousin Declan. "Family."

The shaman was wearing some sort of headdress that had once been part of a goat. He began chanting.

It's humiliatin', I thought. *It's mortifyin'.*

Sad

One day as I looked out the window at the lovely red trees of autumn I imagined that I saw someone drop an anvil out of a window, an anvil tied to a long rope whose nether end was firmly affixed to my own leg. I saw the anvil disappear. I saw the rope rapidly playing out. I felt the knot suddenly tighten around my leg. The next thing I knew my head fell down on the desk. A student came into my office but I couldn't talk to him. After a while he went to get the department secretary and the secretary got the department chair and the chair called security and security called an ambulance. For the next few months I spent some time resting and thinking over my recent mistakes. During this period my mother wrote me lots of cheerful letters. She reminded me that, in spite of all of this, there are good things in the world and that it's important to keep sight of these good things and not to forget them. I noticed she didn't mention any of these good things by name. I didn't figure I was one of them.

The window in my room at the Maine Medical Center was open, and a hummingbird buzzed among some red flowers outside. My husband was staying at Ronald McDonald House. I smelled the smell of burning leaves, heard the sound of rakes moving across suburban lawns. Now and again I sang my aunt's little song.

Where am I going to live when I get home?

One of the things that's surprised me since I came out of the hospital is the fact that almost everyone I talk to has some sort of similar story to tell. Oh, for heaven's sake, they tell me. I've had times when I thought I was never going to be able to leave the house again. A good friend of mine told me about a period she went through when she took five showers every day. Another friend told me about going to the beach in Florida one time and staying inside with the shades pulled down for six days. Someone else told me he went through a time when he slept less than an hour every night, lying there the rest of the time frozen in self-loathing, insomnia and horror.

I think sometimes about Perry van Roden, covered with oil paint. I think about my grandfather, buried in an unmarked grave on Hart Island. I think about my aunt, so relieved to find that her own death did not hurt.

Mostly, though, I think about how fragile we are, how full of love and imagination and hope, and how simply all our little boats can crash upon the rocks. It is a world full of easily broken people, people like my aunt and me, who worry whether or not they're insane. Maybe like you, whoever you are.

Strudel

For weeks before my eighth birthday, Aunt Nora was upstairs in her attic apartment, playing with my present. Whatever it was she had bought me had batteries, that much was for sure. I could hear the thing beeping and whistling as its gears turned and its wheels moved it around the floor.

On the big day, the doorbell rang and I went to the door and opened it. A horse was standing there. "Hi, Jenny," the horse said. I could tell that the voice actually came from my father, who was hiding behind the horse, not very effectively as it turned out, because I could see his legs. The next thing I knew, my sister and her friends jumped out from behind some hedges and everyone shouted, "Surprise!" It was very exciting. Moments later, lots of eight- and nine-year-olds were riding a horse around our yard.

The only problem, of course, was that I didn't like horses. My sister rode them and my parents went off every weekend to watch her ride while I stayed home and ate pancakes. I didn't like the way they smelled, I didn't like the noises they made, and above all I didn't like having to watch one walk around and around in circles with my sister on its back.

So after a while I left my parents and my sister and all of her horsey friends and the horse itself and went back inside. For a while I thought about eating the cake by myself, but I knew this wasn't a good idea because it would too self-evidently declare my sadness. There wasn't any rule against being sad in my house; you just weren't supposed to be public about it.

From the attic came the sound of singing. I walked up the stairs and found the door to Aunt Nora's apartment open. She wouldn't live with us much longer. Sunlight filtered down the stairs.

"Is that you, Jenny?" she called.

I ran up the stairs to find her in a kind of Japanese kimono she'd made for herself. She bowed to me. "Honorable niece," she said.

In her arms was a doll she'd sewn herself out of a sock and some yarn. It had feline ears and long whiskers and luxurious eyelashes. "Her name is Mao-Mao," she said. "She's a kittygirl."

It was the most wonderful gift in the world. I hugged the kittygirl as hard as I could. I was consumed with astonishment, unable to speak.

She put a needle on the hi-fi. She'd recently purchased a novelty record by a bandleader named Eddie Lawrence called "Old Vienna." As his band performed Strauss waltzes, Eddie Lawrence performed a monologue about a strudel-eating contest. The climax of the story was a moment when a giant strudel went out of control and rolled down the Matterhorn, thus destroying Old Vienna once and for all. *Zee giant strudel slid down ze mountain and viped out ze entire population! Und zey put up a zign, zaying, "By order of zee emperor, zere will be no strudel eating on zee mountain today."*

Aunt Nora walked in her kimono to the window and looked out at my parents and my sister and her friends riding their horse in circles around the yard. Light slanted through the window and shone upon the floor.

"Ah!" Aunt Nora said wistfully. "Zat was Vienna!"

The clock in the corner softly chimed the hour. I lay on the floor for a while longer and listened to a story about an avalanche of strudel.

Scrambled Eggs

BY LIZ MILES

[Signs in]
Tweet, bloody tweet. What's happening? Who knows?
　Imbusyshopping: Mornin my precious. How are you?

@Imbusyshopping: I'm doing good ta . . . except for a
bruised, breaking and bleeding heart
　Imbusyshopping: Poor darlin . . . wanna banana yum-
　yum milkshake? *pouring a delish heart-fixer just for
　you*

@Imbusyshopping: That's so sweet of you but I'm cooking
eggs, burning toast and melting mounds of butter . . .

@Imbusyshopping: . . . and I don't even care if this pus-
volcano explodes on my face. And I don't care if I put on a
hundred pounds.

Yes, cruel world, I'm having high-chol eggs for breakfast.

So, tweeters, how shall I cook them? Answers in 140
characters, obviously.
　Imbusyshopping: In a creme caramel of course sweetie!
　Eggs and cream keep anyone's lips smilin all day :-)

Halibut4: Oh! I've got an amaaazing book on eggs. I can send you 40 recipes. At least!!! I'm emailing some ideas now. I mean, Now!

@Halibut4: Thanks Hal! And thanks for the link to A Thousand Saucy Salad Dressings *smiling*. One day . . . I'll try some. Promise x
Ramraidit: Cook them eggs on my ass, honey

@Ramraidit: *fingers up* Creep.

looking in cupboard for bourbon None left. No eggnog for breakfast then.

So how shall I cook these eggs, breakfast tweeters? Come on. Wakey-wakey!
Tooley14: Down. Sunny-side down.

@Tooley14: Not up?
Tooley14: No, down.

@Tooley14: Who are you? Do you follow me?
Tooley14: Or scrambled. If your day is really crap, scrambled. If your day is dead before you even get up . . . scrambled.

TinyDeeDee: Yoo hoo! *waving* Bad night darling?

@TinyDeeDee: Oh Dee! My heart's broken . . . He was staring at a blonde ALL night. I went to the bar and saw him in the mirror drooling at her.

@TinyDeeDee: . . . size zero, mincing toes—you know—and

dancing like a you-know-what. Jesus.
  TinyDeeDee: *hugs*

@TinyDeeDee: And then . . . Casper tried to pretend he'd just "sort of thought she was familiar." Can you believe that!
  TinyDeeDee: Do you still think Casper's the One? *firm sisterly hug*

@TinyDeeDee: I don't know. I don't know what to do, Dee. *dabs puffy, teary eyes with balmy tissue* I just want some "sincerity".
  TinyDeeDee: It's not like you're looking for the ideal then? You're not asking for the world are you?

@TinyDeeDee: You know what. I am. I want a guy who loves me just like I love him. That's ideal. And I want It. Casper is/was It.

@TinyDeeDee: Oh Dee . . . I can't see how I can trust him now *more tears* I've probably driven him away anyway.

@TinyDeeDee: He keeps sayin I'm drinking too much. Wouldn't buy me more than two Manhattans and a daquiri all night.

@TinyDeeDee: Tight bastard.
  TinyDeeDee: I'm so sad for you, Amy. I'm sitting here hugging me like I'd hug you.
  Ramraidit: You're avatar is HOT! HOT! HOT!

@TinyDeeDee: I'm going to block that creep. I'll ram his tweets down his throat.
  TinyDeeDee: Who's that bugging you Amy?

@TinyDeeDee: Some idiot called Ramrod or something. Doesn't matter. Anyway, I yelled at Casper for wanting the blonde. Then he walked out.
  TinyDeeDee: Has he texted or called this morning?

@TinyDeeDee: No. I'm worried sick, Dee. I'm shaking. I can hardly eat anything. I thought I should have protein . . . but I can't face it.
  Halibut4: Just so you know: 1 boiled egg = 6g protein. Your protein RDA depends on your weight—I'll email a protein calculator link now.

@Halibut4: Thanks for the emails, Hal. Real sweet of you. Got any cocktail recipes?
  TinyDeeDee: What are you going to do? You should call him. Casper's fit. Some other girl'll have him.

@TinyDeeDee: I know, Dee *weeping uncontrollably* I'm probably too late. The one cute guy I've really loved. Casper and me—oh fuck! *dropped egg on floor*
  TinyDeeDee: Call him. You've got to. Don't waste a second or you'll regret it. Ring now.

@TinyDeeDee: I don't know . . . I think it's too late.
  TinyDeeDee: Call him! Just sign out and go and call. NOW!

@TinyDeeDee: Okay Dee, I'll go and ring. I promise.
  TinyDeeDee: Do it Amy! Or you'll lose him!

@TinyDeeDee: I will. I'm shutting my laptop now . . . I'm picking up my mobile.
  TinyDeeDee: Good luck Amy! Chow hun.

TinyDeeDee: See ya DeeDee
   Tooley14: You're lying to yourself.

@Tooley14: err . . . what?
   Tooley14: You don't care. Do you?

@Tooley14: Who are you? Your profile says nothing. You look sort of kind though. Maybe. Is it you in the avatar?
   Tooley14: Do you really care?

@Tooley14: About my guy? Course I do. But on days like this . . . Sometimes I don't know. Do you care about stuff?

@Tooley14: Do you? You look sort of depressed. Are you?

@Tooley14: Looks like you're gone. Who the fuck are you anyway?

Better get on with this *ringing my man. Correction: ringing my Once-upon-a-time man*

• • •

TinyDeeDee: I've heard nothing all day from you Amy. Nothing here, no DM. I'm getting worried.

@TinyDeeDee: Helo
   TinyDeeDee: Hello! At last! What happened? What did Casper say?

@TinyDeeDee: Helo brup
   TinyDeeDee: What? Your tweet isn't coming through right.
Bum bum burp bum bottom botty

TinyDeeDee: Amy? You okay? You been drinking? It's only noon, kiddo!

Buuuuuuurrrrp

TinyDeeDee: Amy?

@TinyDeeDee: Amy has a big botty

TinyDeeDee: Who is that? Whoever is pretending to be Amy . . . fuck off!

@TinyDeeDee: OMG . . . It's me now. Me, Amy. It's okay . . . just a sec. Oh Maddi

@TinyDeeDee: Sorry, Maddi's been playing with my phone again. *telling Maddi off*

@TinyDeeDee: She's been in my bag again. I told Mom she's got to have a phone of her own. Mom says five is too young. Like . . . not.

@TinyDeeDee: She found my mini yesterday . . . just stopped her tipping the whole Campari down her throat *laughing*

TinyDeeDee: What a minx. But tell me Amy . . . what happened? Do you wanna DM/email?

@TinyDeeDee: It's okay, Casper doesn't tweet. He's just a Facebooker (likes to be Mr. Exclusive I suppose) *sigh*

TinyDeeDee: What happened?

@TinyDeeDee: He sent a mega-bunch of flowers, "Perfect Pink Radiance for your Perfect Lady," $55. I looked them up. Card said: Trust me (ha-ha)

TinyDeeDee: $55! That's wonderful! Sooo happy for you. *jumping up and down, happy-happy*

@TinyDeeDee: But Dee—who'd send something like this unless they felt guilty!
TinyDeeDee: That's maybe not always, always so. Is it?

@TinyDeeDee: I've met cheaters before. I've seen the love-rat pattern. But I can't tell Casper to go. I can't just finish it. I love him.
TinyDeeDee: Why don't you pop round and see him now . . . have a heart-to-heart?

@TinyDeeDee: Can't do it, Dee. He'd see that as like social terrorism. Arriving without texting first? No way.

@TinyDeeDee: I've got a plan though. I'm going to test him. I'm going to see where his heart is . . . behind those pecs or in his jeans.

@TinyDeeDee: I do sort of trust him. But I've got to KNOW. He's real soft and loving. Like when my dad . . .
TinyDeeDee: Yes, I know sweetie. How is your mom?

@TinyDeeDee: She's okay 'cept when, like yesterday, Maddi said: "Daddy coming home from Afstan?" or something. It set mom off.
TinyDeeDee: Poor little thing. Your mom too. Tragic. You too, Amy. I'm so sad for you all. *sniffing for real*
TinyDeeDee: But Amy. What's the plan?

@TinyDeeDee: I'm going to set it up so we go to the same Greenwich club. The wiggle-ass is always there. I'm going to create an opportunity.
TinyDeeDee: An opportunity for what?

@TinyDeeDee: For Casper and Wiggle-ass to talk—to see what Casper does. I'll dance with him and get us dancing near to her.

@TinyDeeDee: Then I'll say I'm going for a pee. Then I'll wait for a while *smiling*
TinyDeeDee: Cunning plan. You gotta tell me what happens. *sisterly kiss*. It'll be fine. Gotta go and write up this rank college report now.

@TinyDeeDee: OK. I'll be back tweeting on Sunday. *hugs*

Ramraidit: Hey, you wanna share that big botty, Babe? Come sit on my knee. Warm me up huh? Share those big soft buttocks? LMAO

@Ramraidit: If you weren't so sad I'd block you. Moron.

DM from TinyDeeDee: I'm DMing cause I'm worried about that nerd @Ramraidit. Block the creep. You can't trust people like him here.
DM to @TinyDeeDee: It's okay, Dee. No worries. And I sure won't tell him where I live. *laughing*

@Tooley14: You still gone?
Tooley14: No. I'm here. Listening. Mainly to you.
Tooley14: JJ—my older brother—was shot in Kabul.
Tooley14: What happened to your father?

@Tooley14: A bomb killed him and three of his mates. I got to go. I don't tweet about that.
Tooley14: Sure thing. It's like a knife that digs deep isn't it—talking about those things. I know. It keeps turning.

Tooley14: Just existing is hard, isn't it? And some days . . .

Tooley14: . . . not existing seems right. The only way.

Imbusyshopping: *biggest hug in the world* Amy, honeypie, I'm SO sorry to hear what you just said. So sorry.

Halibut4: I'm very sorry to hear about your tragic loss.

Thanks guys. It was a while ago. Okay, I'm going. I got to make a date with my boyfriend.

Ramraidit: Do you fancy a smoochy dance with me, Babe?

@Ramraidit: Sure, yeh! I like to dance with weirdos

shaking my head
[Signs out]

• • •

TinyDeeDee: How'd it go? *waiting to hear how the plan went*

TinyDeeDee: I'm getting worried. You alright, hun?

Ramraidit: I'm thinking of you and listening to ♫ Fatboy Slim—"I See You Baby (Shakin That Ass)."

TinyDeeDee: Get in touch when you can, Amy. I'm waiting, thinking of you.

TinyDeeDee: Am seriously worried about you.

[Signs in]
Nothing. Damn blonde.

Slut.

Six vodkas n no boy no more.

Walking home on my own :/ 2 o'clock and Mom's gonna be climbing the walls.

Who cares?

I'm listening to ♫ Lady Gaga—"Bad Romance".

slips on kerb Shit.

Gonna jump in the river.
   Ramraidit: Hey, you dweeting? I bet you're singing to me, Babe. We're dancing, hey!

@Ramraidit: Yey! This song I'm listening to is so for you.
   Imbusyshopping: Honey-child, you should be in bed, safe. Home-sweet-home. Call a taxi or your mommy, young lady.

Whoop! I'm vodka'd! I'm Casper-less!

@Imbusyshopping: Ooh Busy-wizzy, the street's all shiny, jeweley in the rain.

@Ramraidit: I'm dancing down the street. Here's one for you . . .

@Ramraidit: I'm listening to ♫ Avalanches—"Frontier Psychiatrist." LOL

Oh . . .

feeling sick

callin taxi . . .
> *Ramraidit:* Do you want my address Babe? You can rest your pretty little vodka-shot body right here next to me.

[Signs out]

• • •

[Signs in]
No college. Taking day off. Feeling ill.

Lonely.

No Casper. No dad.

Sorry but I'm crying. I'm doing it. Public crying. Alone. What's happening? Oh *sort of laughing* I'm sipping a Campari. Missing Casper. Missing my dad. That's what's happening.
> *Tooley14:* We're all lonely.

@Tooley14: I know. But I lost my guy forever last night. And Dad's gone.
> *Tooley14:* You're lonely because you think no one loves you any more?
> *Tooley14:* Love's an illusion. A fog people hide in.

@Tooley14: A fog? It didn't feel like a fucking fog. It felt nice.

@Tooley14: Are you a nice guy? Or are you like Casper? Or maybe you're like Ramrod?

TinyDeeDee: AMY, what have you been doing?? You DID go home in the taxi didn't you? (just read your last-night tweets!!)

@TinyDeeDee: I think I'm losing it, Dee. Tiny sweet Dee. *thumping head*
Halibut4: Oh! I've got a humble hangover cure. Bloody Mary: tom juice, horseradish, shot of vodka, squeeze of lemon, 2 drops Tabasco, celery stick x

@Halibut4: Thank you, Hal. But I'm sipping something like an anemic Bloody Mary already. I don't like tomato juice.
Halibut4: *blushing and bowing*
TinyDeeDee: What happened? (I don't think you should have more vodka, campari . . . whatever)

@TinyDeeDee: What happened? Casper took Her over to the bar. He bought Her a drink and They laughed. Cosy. I split (threw my drink at Her).
TinyDeeDee: I'm sure you'll get flowers, chocs, another apology.

@TinyDeeDee: Ha! I got a text. Quote: "OK Amy: as you can't trust me it's over. And a bit of advice: cut down on the cocktails."

@TinyDeeDee: And you know what! I saw them leaving together. Dee, I've had it. I knew it. I fucking knew it.

@TinyDeeDee: Yep. Pa gone. Casp gone. Nothing. I'm gone.
  TinyDeeDee: Oh Amy.

@Tooley14: So what do YOU suggest, huh? Bet you're listening.
  Tooley14: Yes, I am. Follow me. Give up and follow me.

@Tooley14: I do already.
  DM from Tooley14: Follow me.
  DM from Tooley14: Look out your window.

@Tooley14: Christ. Is that you on the bike? Is that a Harley?
  DM from Tooley14: I'm going on a fast ride to the mountains. You coming? I mean fast. I mean . . . there's nothing to lose, is there?

@Tooley14: How'd you know I lived here?

@Tooley14: You look like something out of a movie *laughing*
  DM from Tooley14: Okay . . . I'm dun waiting. See ya.

@Tooley14: Well I'm busy anyway *looking to see how much Campari I can get through before Mom gets home*

Oh god. Fuck *chucking empty bottle in shute* Closing down. Finito.

• • •

  TinyDeeDee: Oh Amy. Answer my DMs. Please. Please.

  TinyDeeDee: Where are you?

TinyDeeDee: Please, please, Amy. I'm worried about you.

Imbusyshopping: Honey, if you DM your address I'll send you a little pressie (floaty lilac skirt, so pretty—so your color).

Imbusyshopping: This book, too, says: "Run from any guy that strengthens a weakness in you!" So you did right with Casper honey! Okay luvvy?

Halibut4: I can send you some links about various detox recipes? If you want. Not that I'm saying you need them or anything.

Ramraidit: Hey! Where are you, Cutest-Little-Butt in the Twittersphere? Beach holiday? Tanning yourself up for me?

• • •

TinyDeeDee: Amy, it's been 2 weeks! PLEASE could you text me. I've just emailed my number.

Imbusyshopping: Please come back, sugar. We miss you.

Halibut4: I hate it when people disappear. Have you disappeared?

DM from Tooley14: Brave. You're brave. You realized what I said was true. Didn't you? You've escaped, haven't you? Where are you?

• • •

@Halibut4: No, Hal. I haven't disappeared. Not yet. But I am about to. Cheers! *sips a Bloody Mary you would be proud of*

@TinyDeeDee: Sorry, Dee. I've been coping with stuff. I had bullshit in my head about Casper.

@TinyDeeDee: Yeah, the blonde was an OLD friend from when they were Maddi's age. Seems he was telling the truth, apparently.

I won't get Casper back. But I'm not upset. Because I know now, I'm natural lonely. I like being lonely.

I'm lonely in my head. I have my cocktail friend. But thanks anyway to all of you. *big hugs*

@Ramraidit: Cheers! And bottoms up! *opens another mini Campari*

@Imbusyshopping: Cheers! Here's to the dollar stores *knocking back anti-sad medication*

> Tooley14: So where do you go from here, Amy? The bottom of the bottle?
> Tooley14: Is that the best escape?

DM to @Tooley14: Okay. Where can we meet? Do you "not care" enough to meet me? Do you?
> DM from Tooley14: You were scared of me before.
> When I had the bike.

DM to @Tooley14: Well maybe you're right. Maybe I don't care any more. Not now.

DM to @Tooley14: Anyway, a miserable saddo like you is my

last non-hope. *smiling a bit* Come up two flights and push open the door on the right.

    Tooley14: I don't have to smile at your mom, do I?

@Tooley14: She's taking Maddi to school. *laughing* I'll start scrambling us some eggs.

    Tooley14: Okay. I'm on my way.

Rules for Love and Death

BY ELLEN WITTLINGER

THE NEWS HIT the high school Monday morning before the end of first period. Danny Bommarito had been killed in a car wreck Sunday night on Route 55 on his way home from Nicole Nesbit's house. As soon as Mr. Simonson announced it over the P.A. system, somebody started screaming in the hallway outside my geometry class. Ms. West put her hand over her mouth and leaned against the chalkboard while Mr. S. said that any friends of Danny's who were upset could leave class to talk to a counselor or the school nurse.

I bet Danny didn't know how many friends he had. In about a minute there were throngs of kids moving through the hallway, holding on to each other, sobbing like mad. Since Danny was a senior and most of the kids in my geometry class are only sophomores, hardly any of us knew him that well, but there were a few girls crying, and Will Jasper, who was on the football team with Danny, put his head down on his desk. I had never spoken a word to Danny Bommarito—at least, not out loud—but I had intended to, eventually. As soon as I figured out what to say.

Danny was in my study hall last year. He sat with the other juniors and seniors who did things: Peer Leaders, International Relations Club, student government. He was not just a jock—he did everything. If I got there early enough to get a seat at the right table, I could spend most of the period watching him without anybody noticing. I especially loved watching him laugh at jokes. Sometimes I even snickered along with him, which made the kids at my table stare at me like I was possessed. He had a really happy laugh that kind of exploded out of him.

When the bell rang, Danny would lean back in his chair and stretch out before he got moving, like school didn't rule him the way it did the rest of us. One time I stayed sitting in my seat too while everybody else grabbed their books and stampeded out of there. Suddenly Danny turned his head and looked right at me, like he'd known I was there.

"Hey," he said, and gave me a wink. That's all. "Hey," and a wink. Then he pulled himself out of his chair and went to catch up with one of his friends. I couldn't believe it. He knew I was there. He saw me, he spoke to me—he winked.

I went over and over it in my mind—it seemed like we had a secret now, Danny and I. Isn't that what a wink means? Or maybe it meant, I know you watch me. That might be okay too . . . if he knew I was interested. But the year was almost over by then, and there wasn't really time for another wink.

At the beginning of this year I made my friend Violet go with me to a few Peer Leaders meetings, although I didn't tell her why. She had a boyfriend already, and I thought it might seem childish to her that I was following around some guy I barely knew. I didn't realize Danny's girlfriend, Nicole, was president of Peer Leaders. Ugh. They constantly found excuses to touch each other, like it was normal to give somebody a neck massage every time they blinked. I could never get up the nerve to speak to him, so I don't know if he remembered me from study hall or not. I was working on a question I could ask him, but Vi and I quit the group when we found out the freshmen and sophomores had to do fundraising.

"Not me," Violet said. "I'm in high school! I'm not selling candy bars door-to-door like some second grader!"

It's not like Danny Bommarito was the only good-looking upperclassman; he was just the one who seemed right to me. I don't know how to explain it, but when I heard him laugh I'd get chills down my back. He had dark wavy hair that was always a little too long in the front—not perfect, you know, but *perfect*. And he seemed like a guy who'd be nice to you, if you ever actually knew him.

So when Mr. Simonson said there was this car crash last night . . . Well, it couldn't be true because I never even had a chance to talk to Danny Bommarito . . . and I was in love with him.

In a few minutes Mr. Simonson was back on the air. "It's clear to me that it will be difficult to conduct regular classes today in light of the tragedy that has befallen us." That's the way he talks. "I am dismissing classes for the remainder of the day. However, I urge those of you who need comfort to seek out our excellent staff here at the school." He ended by begging us to drive carefully, but by that time we were halfway to our lockers and nobody was listening any more.

I stared into my locker, but I didn't know what to take out of it. Ms. West hadn't even given us any homework yet—there was nothing to do. A group of freshmen girls huddled together on the floor nearby, getting in everybody's way. They were consoling each other and trying to squeeze out a few tears. One of them kept ripping tissues out of a little plastic package and passing them to the others. God, they probably wouldn't be able to pick Danny out of a line-up.

"Casey! Can you believe this?" Violet came tearing around the corner. "It's not even nine o'clock yet and we're out of school! We should go someplace and do something!"

I shrugged half-heartedly. "Don't you want to hang with

Burt?" Vi has been my best friend since kindergarten, but last year she also began to be Burt Baldwin's girlfriend, and it definitely got in the way of our friendship. We could never make plans until she'd checked with Burt to see what he wanted to do. She said rule number one was: Never neglect a girlfriend for a guy, unless you're in love with the guy. Then, apparently, anything is permissible. And, of course, Violet is in love.

She gave me a little tap on the back. "Don't be like that. I don't always hang with Burt. Besides, I just saw him and he says he's going back home to sleep."

"Not a bad idea," I said.

"Casey, this is a free day! We have to do something. It's like a present!"

Is that what it was like? How thoughtful of Danny to give us all a present. Even before I slammed my locker and started hightailing it to an exit, the tears began to creep down my cheeks. Violet was behind me, so she didn't notice right away.

"Why are you running?" She caught up with me as I headed out the back cafeteria door and almost fell over a girl lying motionless face down on the bottom step. My God, had everybody been in love with Danny Bommarito?

There weren't many people coming out this way—it was the exit to the teachers' parking lot, and they were probably still inside, meeting in small groups, all their hands over all their mouths. They probably knew all the details by now: where exactly it had happened, whether anybody saw it, who else got hurt, whose fault it was. I kept imagining Danny's green Honda flipped over on its back like a turtle, wheels spinning. I tried not to think where that meant Danny had been. Trapped inside the car? Thrown out on to the highway? Had he known he was going to die? Thinking about it made me put my hand over my mouth.

I made it to the corner where the trees started before Violet caught sight of my face.

"Are you crying?"

I wasn't making a sound—no sniffing, no hiccuping, nothing. I just let the silly water leak out silently.

"I didn't even think you knew Danny Bommarito!" Violet said. "Did you?"

I shook my head. "No, but I might have someday."

"What, you mean, like, you had a thing for him?"

I sighed. "Sort of."

Violet put her arm around my shoulder. She actually is a good friend when she's available. "Why didn't you tell me? I didn't even know!"

I swiped at the tears with the sleeve of my jacket. "It wasn't like you and Burt. But I thought it might be someday."

"I can't believe you didn't tell me this!"

I shrugged and gave a mucusy sniff, wishing I didn't sound so pathetic. "You're always so busy with . . ."

"I wish you'd stop saying that, Casey. We're still best friends—we're supposed to tell each other everything." Rule number two.

"There wasn't anything to tell. I just thought . . . I thought I'd talk to Danny someday, and . . . I don't know. He winked at me once. I just thought I'd get to talk to him." I could feel another downpour building behind my eyes.

Violet sucked in her breath. "You really liked him, didn't you?" I nodded and she hugged my shoulder tighter. "Oh, poor Casey! He is really cute. Was, I mean. God, I'm glad I didn't know him very well. It would be awful to have a friend who died young like that. It gives me goosebumps to think of it."

We stopped at the corner of Edgewood and Harrison and shivered, even though it was a warm Indian-summer day. I found a half-used tissue in my pocket and blew my nose. "Where are we going? Home or downtown?"

"Well, if you feel like it we could go to the Pancake Palace and get some breakfast? I didn't have time to eat before I left home this morning. And there's something I want to talk to you about, too. If you're okay." She gave me a slippery little grin and I had an idea what the topic was going to be. The last thing I was in the mood for this morning was tales of weekend lust in Burt's family room while Burt's family was somewhere else. But what choice did I have? Violet is my best friend. There are rules, you know.

• • •

We got a booth in the back corner so we could have some privacy. It was amazing how many other kids from school showed up. I guess grief makes you hungry. I ordered the special—two scrambled eggs, bacon, home fries and a biscuit—while Violet, who had already eaten a bowl of cereal this morning, ordered a cup of coffee and an English muffin.

"I thought you were hungry," I said. "You aren't getting nuts about your weight again, are you?"

"Don't worry so much. It's just hard to eat when you feel like this."

"Like what?"

She sucked in her breath and fluttered her hands in front of her chest to indicate that they were ready for take-off, I guess. Vi can be a real drama queen. She likes to give you a big build-up before she tells you anything, which makes even ordinary stuff seem important. I don't have that talent, or maybe I just don't think anything that happens to me is that important.

"What?" I repeated.

Violet leaned across the table to whisper to me. "That's what

275

I wanted to talk to you about. I'm so excited."

"Why? Tell me, already."

The slippery grin returned. "We did it. Last night!" She spoke so quietly I had to read her lips, but then, the words were pretty simple to understand.

It's not like I was shocked or anything. I knew they'd been heading for it—Burt, especially, had been heading for it. Violet had been changing her mind practically every day: do it, don't do it, do it. I guess she'd finally made up her mind.

But on the other hand, I *was* shocked. This was Violet, who I'd known since forever, who took dancing lessons with me at Ms. Patty's, who slept in my bunk with me at Camp Nashatoga on the nights the camp staff told ghost stories, who went with me the first time I visited my father after he moved out, who never told her mother it was me who gave her that botched haircut in the seventh grade. It was bad enough she had a boyfriend and I didn't—but now she'd taken it one giant step further. Into the mysterious territory of sex: a faraway land to which I'd certainly never be able to follow her. I wasn't even sure I wanted to.

"Can you believe it?" she said. "I wasn't going to, but then, I don't know, nobody's ever home at Burt's, and all of a sudden there didn't seem to be a reason not to."

"You had a few hundred reasons last week," I reminded her. "Like whether you were in love or not, for one."

"I decided I am," she said firmly.

Just then the waitress brought big white plates, mine heaped with greasy food that didn't seem so appetizing any more. I wished I liked coffee so at least I'd have that in common with Violet.

"Are you mad at me? Do you think it was wrong?" Violet dumped two packets of Sweet'N Low into her cup.

I shrugged. "It's your decision." All of a sudden I had this vision of the two of them lying together naked on some scratchy old brown couch with squeaky springs. God, Violet had seen Burt Baldwin naked. Ugh! It was one thing to hang out with the guy, kiss him and stuff, but to actually sleep with him? He was so . . . lumpy. And he was trying to grow this skimpy little mustache. And he hardly ever even spoke to me. If I was going to sleep with somebody, he would have to be . . . well, Danny Bommarito. But when I thought that, a hot nausea swept over me. I had to say something to Violet, though, so I said, "You did use something, didn't you?"

Violet ducked her head—I guess my voice carries. "Casey! Keep it down! I'm not advertising it!"

"Sorry."

"Of course we used something. Burt had condoms."

Condoms. Plural.

All of a sudden I remembered the time Vi and I found some condoms in her older brother's room and filled them up like water balloons. We were only about ten at the time. They looked so funny we called them our hot-dog toys and laughed until we practically peed our pants.

Violet grabbed my hands and leaned over the table to get my attention back. "It was wonderful, Case. Now I really understand what love is. Burt was so sweet. He kept asking me if it felt good."

I swallowed. I did actually want to know about this—I wanted the information from someone who'd been there, just in case I was ever faced with a sudden journey myself. Still, it was embarrassing to have to ask. "*Did* it feel good?"

I could tell she was glad I wanted to know. "I wish I could explain it to you," she said, her face dreamy. I remembered one time she'd told me, "If you love somebody, it should show on your face." Violet's face looked more like somebody appreciating a hot-fudge sundae.

"Well, try," I said.

"It's not like anything else."

"Really? I thought it would be just like volleyball."

She ignored me. "It's like floating on clouds or something. It's just . . . wonderful!"

Floating on clouds? Like those babies in the toilet-paper commercial? I needed one or two details, just in case. "Did he get on top, like in movies?"

She nodded.

"And it didn't hurt or anything? When he . . . you know . . . put it in?"

Violet smiled. "You don't think about things like that, if it hurts or not. You're just thinking about how much you love him, and how you want to hold on to him and keep him warm inside you for ever!"

Sounded sort of like a broken toaster to me. Enough. These weren't details anyway. They were advertisements.

"Will you go to the funeral with me?" I asked.

"What?" Violet was far away, dreaming of her love. I guess you forget about death in the land of toast. "You want to go to Danny Bommarito's funeral? Why? Funerals are awful— besides, you didn't really know him."

Right then I came up with a rule of my own, but I didn't tell Violet: if you love somebody, you should show up at their funeral. "Well, I'm going," I said solemnly. Violet frowned.

"They'll probably let us out of school to go," I said. "Like they did in middle school when that girl died of leukemia."

"That's true." She thought about it as she snitched half a piece of my bacon. "Did he really wink at you?"

I nodded.

Violet returned from Loveland to earth. She looked deep into my eyes. "Well, you can't go by yourself, Casey. I'll go with you so you can just fall apart if you want to. I'll be there to hold you up."

. . .

But when Wednesday afternoon rolled around and we signed out of school with a throng of other, mostly older kids, I thought Violet might be the one who'd need holding up. I'd gone to look for her and found her standing in front of her locker having an argument with Burt. I waited in a doorway down the hall, but I could still hear them.

"Don't be like that, Burt," Violet said in a begging voice I hated.

"Hey, go if you want to. I don't care. But I'm not wasting my afternoon at some crying-fest funeral for some kid I don't even know."

"The point is, you know Casey. We'd be there to support her."

"I don't know Casey. She's your friend." Burt was scanning the passersby, giving big grins and thumbs-ups to kids he was willing to admit he knew.

Violet gave up. "Fine. Are you coming over tonight?"

"Why don't you come by my house? Everybody'll be out again." He was looking at her now, his arm creeping around her side to lie on her butt. I felt like knocking it off myself, but Vi let it stay.

"I have a paper to write," she said, but she didn't sound too sorry about it.

"So? Write it afterwards!"

"No! Burt! Just because . . ." And then her voice got too low for me to make out, but my imagination filled in the blanks.

Burt looked angry. "God, Vi, I didn't think you'd turn into such a priss afterwards. What's wrong with you! How about this? You call me when you don't have so much homework to do." He stalked off, shaking his head; Vi slammed her locker door and then slumped against it. Was this what happened after you floated on clouds together?

"Hey, Vi!" I called, like I'd just shown up. "The bus is here." She took a deep breath before she joined me.

The school had chartered a decrepit bus to take those of us who didn't have a car or a ride to the funeral. It was too old to have seat belts, which seemed pretty lousy considering where we were going and why. Violet and I chose a front seat as the bus filled up with the JV football team and a bunch of the younger cheerleaders.

"I don't even know any of these kids," Violet said. "I bet they think it's weird we're going."

"It's not weird. Anybody can go to a funeral."

"Yeah, but we didn't know this guy," Violet reminded me in a grouchy whisper.

"We could have known him," I said. Anyway, I felt sure that by watching him all those months I knew the real Danny a lot better than most of these second-stringers did.

Violet rolled her eyes at me, scratched the back of her head, then stuck her hand down her turtleneck jersey to rearrange her bra strap. She was so fidgety she was making me jumpy too.

"What's the matter with you?"

"I feel all itchy," Violet said. "I think I'm allergic to funerals."

"I've never even been to one before," I admitted.

"You haven't? God, my mother is always dragging me to say goodbye to every ancient relative who bites the dust."

"Violet!"

"I'm sorry, but I hate funerals. They're so fake. You stand there looking at this person you barely knew lying in a big silver bullet, all powdered and dressed up for the big trip to nowhere." She shivered. "People act like they're so upset, even when they aren't. It's a funeral rule. When my great-aunt died last year, everybody came up and shook her daughter's hand and said how terrible it was and how they'd all miss dear old Polly. *Nobody* liked this woman—she was the crab of the family. She had a cocker spaniel she trained to bite people. But as soon as she's out from underfoot, they're all crying about it. It gives me the creeps."

"This funeral won't be like that. Everybody will be upset."

Violet sighed. "Oh, yeah. That'll make it a lot better."

"You know what I've been thinking about?"

"God knows."

I wasn't sure I should actually mention this to Violet, but the coincidence of it kept occurring to me. "You slept with Burt Sunday night, right?"

"Shh!"

"Sunday?" I whispered.

"Yes!"

"I keep thinking, you and Burt were probably doing it when Danny had the accident. He probably died while you were making love for the first time. Isn't that weird?"

"Casey! God, you're freaking me out!"

"I don't mean it that way. I just mean, there was this terrible event happening at the same time that a good thing was beginning. In the same town. It just seems weird that I know about both things."

"It seems weird that you thought of it like that. Sex is nothing like death."

"They're both life-changing experiences. Especially death, I guess. But sex changes you too, doesn't it? You're not the same afterwards."

"That's the truth." Violet bent forward in the seat, her arms hugging her stomach. "Could we just not talk for a few minutes? This whole funeral thing is making me nauseous."

• • •

There was no room to sit down by the time the bus unloaded us at the church, so we stood at the back not far from the closed casket, which was on a wheeled cart surrounded by Danny's football teammates. They all had on dark suits and ties, so they were hardly recognizable as the same guys who shoved each other around in the halls at school. I had to look away from their faces as they wheeled the casket up the aisle to the front of the church. Some of them had tears rolling down their cheeks already. When I saw that, it hit me like a punch in the gut. This was real—Danny Bommarito was on the big trip to nowhere.

I couldn't actually hear too much of the service because there was a lot of crying going on. I cried too—it was almost impossible not to when everybody else was, but I wasn't feeling as heartbroken or cheated as I had on Monday when I first found out. I was actually having a hard time remembering exactly what Danny Bommarito looked like. Violet managed to stay dry by scowling at the bald head of the man in front of us.

When the minister was finished speaking, the organ music blasted out of the ceiling speakers and the pallbearer team started rolling the casket back down the aisle. Behind them came a couple who must have been Danny's parents, and a younger sister—the father was in the middle with an arm around both females. All of them had swollen faces and red eyes. And then I saw who was coming next: Nicole Nesbit, Danny's girlfriend, one parent on either side of her, holding her up.

I watched her come closer. The president of the Peer

Leaders couldn't seem to pick up her feet and kept stumbling on the carpet. Her mouth sagged open as if she didn't have the strength to keep it closed, and her eyes were swollen shut like two raw, red clamshells. Even her hair—Nicole Nesbit's beautiful dark hair—hung alongside her cheeks in damp, lanky hunks. When she passed me, I could hear how her breathing made a rasping noise in her chest; I could see she wasn't even inside herself. If you love somebody, it should show on your face.

"I have to sit down," I whispered to Violet, clutching her arm. She lurched to attention; this was the job she'd signed up for. Some of the people in the back rows had left through side doors, so Violet steered me to an empty pew and eased me into it like I was breakable. For a minute I had trouble breathing.

"It was too hard for you, wasn't it? God, Casey, I didn't know you loved him so much!" I looked up at her, my mouth open to explain, but nothing came out. Violet began to cry.

"I feel so stupid now," she said, slumping down next to me, holding my hand. "All that crap about being in love with Burt. That's how I wanted to feel, but it wasn't real, like . . . like this." Now she was really sobbing and everybody was respectfully averting their eyes. "It wasn't wonderful. It was weird and embarrassing and I don't care if we never do it again!"

Miraculously my voice returned. "Really? No clouds?" I asked, digging in my purse for tissues.

"I guess Burt made it to the clouds, but I sure didn't," she said, shuddering and mopping her face. "I slept with him to find out if I loved him or not. I guess I got my answer."

We sat there by ourselves until the church was almost empty. Violet, not in love with Burt Baldwin. Me, not in love with Danny Bommarito.

Cool Cats and Melted Kisses

by Luisa Plaja

Disappearing-Act Dad (D.A.D. for short) has lived up to his name and down to my expectations. Again. It doesn't matter, though. I am independent and perfectly able to cope.

I am also in a foreign country, alone and terrified.

I start by exploring the flat. This is my new home for the summer while my confident big sister, Sofia, "travels the world" (last heard from while boarding the Eurostar to Paris) and my mother "expands her horizons and finds herself" (currently on a residential "life skills" course on the Isle of Wight). And me? I run away from the humiliation of school and into the total abandonment of staying with my estranged D.A.D. I cannot believe that this seemed like a good idea when Mum suggested it.

The full self-guided tour doesn't take long. I find three bedrooms, and I don't think any of them can be Dad's. I know from Sofia that he has a New Woman and It's Serious. But these rooms all contain single beds and there are no signs in the flat of Wicked Stepmothers-to-be, or any of the ingredients for making poisoned apples. Or any food at all, in fact. There's also no perfume, no straighteners, no rail of designer clothing. No trace at all of Glamorous Woman, aka Dad's "type." (My hippie-chick mother was a two-kid-length blip in his trophy-wife life.)

The kitchenette has seen cleaner days and there's some suspicious black stuff on a pan in the sink, but I don't think it's relevant to my investigation so I don't obtain a sample for forensic analysis. I also find a bathroom (just as well, really). This features a titchy bath, a shower attachment, an antique toilet with a chain and a rusty-tapped bidet. Next, my super-sleuth skills locate a balcony that extends from the bedroom to just past the cooker. The view is pretty amazing—all rolling hills and churches and old-looking stone houses. Taking that and the bidet as evidence, this explorer concludes that she is definitely in Central Italy.

I knew that, though, of course. What I haven't worked out is who exactly I'm supposed to be living with, since it is clearly *not* Dad at all. I'm also not sure how my father can be capable of disappearing *again* so spectacularly when he hasn't seen me for nearly four years, and the last time ended in me telling him I didn't need him. In fact, I told him I didn't need *anyone*. I said I was independent, like a cat.

I was almost thirteen. I was also testing him. I've had a cat phobia since I was tiny and a neighbor's cat took a dislike to me and got his claws out to prove it. Dad was supposed to remember that. He was supposed to have replied, "How can you be *anything* like a cat when you're *terrified* of cats?" Then maybe he was supposed to laugh and give me a hug, or tickle my anger out of me with that annoying, oafish-dad technique my best friend Fazia is regularly subjected to.

But Fazia's dad is always around. My dad is just some stranger, and I'm just stopping by at his house for a saucer of milk.

Except he's not here and there's no food.

And I'm now fairly certain that he doesn't live here.

I go back for a deeper investigation of the bedrooms.

The first one has a 95 percent pink Hello Kitty throw-type

cover on the bed and several graphic novels covering Kitty's ears on the matching pillow case. Hello Kitty is not the kind of cat I'm scared of, but she's also not a cat I'd emblazon on any of my clothes or bedding. One reason is that I have my own style (big, low-cut, homemade dresses, combat boots). Another is that they probably don't put Hello Kitty on plus-sized clothes. My size is the main reason I have my own individual style. I need camouflage tents to go with my boots. Ha.

Looks like I'll be sharing a flat with a cutesy cartoon girl. So far so alarming. But Bedroom Number Two is at the other end of the scary spectrum. The bed has black sheets on it—*all* black—and it looks like it hasn't been made in several years. According to my dad's mumbling before he dumped me here, my housemates have only been here one night. They haven't even unpacked, as far as I can see. How can you rumple a bed that much in one night? Goth Sheet Girl must be a restless sleeper, or possibly an actual vampire who uses her bed for killing sprees.

I go to the third bedroom and dump my stuff on the non-vamp, non-cartoon-covered bed, as I conclude that this room has to be mine. It's the only one without an unpacked suitcase or duffle bag in it. It's also the only one with a neutral bedcover. I wonder if my dad chose it, though I suspect it was New Woman. If I remember one thing from Dad's eight years of living with me, it's that he doesn't really get involved in the house or the kids. Especially not the kids. I lie back.

It's another minute before I realize that the quilt features tiny embroidered animals, white on white. Slinky, long-tailed silhouettes.

Cats.

I leap off the bed and back to the balcony for gulps of air.

• • •

ELLIE AND DISAPPEARING-ACT DAD: SIXTEEN
MAGICAL YEARS IN SEVEN EASY STEPS

- Ellie aged naught to eight. Dad present at occasional family dinners but mostly working at work, working at home, working at working. Generally absent.
- Ellie aged eight to twelve. Occasional weekend visits at Dad's place in London after the divorce. Dad laughs a lot with Sofia, the fun-loving, perfect daughter. Ellie feels left out—imperfection embodied in girl form. Ellie goes to bed early every night and is pronounced a "good girl, but so serious."
- Ellie aged twelve to sixteen. Dad chats to Ellie weekly on the phone from Italy, the country of Dad's birth, which he has now moved back to, taking up a professorship at the university. Both stick to the following script:
  Disappearing-Act Dad: How are you?
  Ellie the Dutiful Daughter: Fine.
  D.A.D.: How's your mother?
  E. the D.D.: Fine.
  D.A.D.: Where's Sofia?
  E. the D. D.: Here. *(Hands phone to Sofia. Exits.)*
  The script stands a strong chance of winning an Oscar for Most Unoriginal Screenplay.
- Ellie is sixteen and escaping school-related humiliation. Dad meets Ellie off Cheapie Flight at the No-frill-o Airways terminal. Small talk is made, covering topics such as Knowledge of Italian (Dad's is native, Ellie's is basic) and Mobile Phones (Dad's is lost, Ellie's is expensive to use).
- In the car. Ellie and Dad now stretch to topics as diverse as The Weather (unsurprisingly hot—it's August) and The Traffic (surprisingly light—it's August).

- Ellie is brought to the apartment, assuming Dad will be living there too. Well, you do, don't you, when you go to stay with your dad for the summer? You expect that your dad will actually be staying with you. You have clearly forgotten the truth of D.A.D.

  Dad mentions two housemates—teenage girls he's renting to, sent by the letting agency, who moved in yesterday. He says he hopes they'll all get on. He hands Ellie a wodge of money. He says she should call if she needs him.

- D.A.D. disappears, his trademark move, and how he gets his name. Ellie remembers that Dad has lost his phone and she couldn't call him even if she wanted to.

• • •

When I'm breathing again, I grip the balcony railing and crane my neck slightly so that I can make out the main square with its fountain and grand medieval buildings. There's a United Nations of studenty people hanging around on the stone steps. They're all draped over each other and half of them have mobile phones pressed to their ears.

People. Connecting. Everywhere.

I want to go home. I want to hide in my bedroom, under my patterned duvet and total lack of cat insignia.

Let's face it: I am no intrepid explorer. I don't have the people skills, for a start. I mostly only ever do sociable stuff for Mo-related reasons, and look how that all turned out. (Fazia's the big exception to my "books are my only friends" rule because she's been my best friend forever, and *not* because I'm in love with her brother. And I so wish I wasn't in love with her brother.)

I feel achy and empty.

Maybe it's hunger. I thought the new Fancy Signora

Stepmum would be cooking me local delicacies. Now I'm thinking I might not even meet her. I'll have to survive on the Italian equivalent of Pot Noodle from the convenience store across the road. Potto Noodle-o. I bet it's more delicious because it's Italian. My stomach rumbles.

There's another sound too—metallic and hollow.

A key in the lock.

Disappearing-Act Dad, perhaps back already to say sorry for abandoning his youngest daughter? Or to tell me he's found his phone and/or he's giving me a new number?

No one calls my name, no one seems to know I'm here. So it has to be a housemate. I'm not ready to meet her. I don't think I will ever be ready to meet her. In fact, if I manage to go back into my room, I'm going to phone Mum and ask her to change my ticket home. My dad and I might be estranged, but these girls are *actual* strangers. Mum won't expect me to stay here. I know she doesn't have Dad's address either, because she "can't keep track of that man," and all these arrangements were made on the phone—the phone he's lost. Mum will call Dad a "useless, unreliable, irresponsible man." Again.

I wait. A door shuts inside the flat. And then silence. My new housemate must be in her black Goth-ness or pink Kitty-ness, and I should brave my white felines and ring Mum.

But when I do, there's no answer. I'm only supposed to use this phone to contact England in emergencies, but I think this counts, so I text Fazia and tell her my life is falling apart and it's all her brother's fault.

She texts back that she's out shopping with her mum and she's sorry—again—about her brother, but men are rats, except Hot Harry, and she'll write more later. She ends with, "Hang in there, Ellie Els! Xxx"

She has kinder nicknames for me than her brother does.

• • •

I'm used to it really. When you're my size and at my level of shy not-fitting-in-ness, and you're also called Elena Minghelli, you've got to expect it. I've been Ellie the Elephant since I was small. Though I was large even when I was small, of course. A baby elephant. It was a few years before I realized that "elephant" was not a good thing to be.

Just the other week, Mo managed to top that when he called me "Minger-Ellie."

Minger-Ellie, get it? Ellie *Minger*-Ellie. What took *that* nickname so long to emerge?

Ha.

Ha.

HA.

This is especially funny coming from the mouth of the boy you've fancied all your life, who also happens to be your best friend's brother. And, oh, perhaps on the night your best friend told you she's sure you're "in with a chance." Say the night of the Thank God The GCSEs Are Over Party—the one everyone calls The TGTGCSEAOP (also known as the "Big Sneeze").

Normally you wouldn't be seen dead at this sort of skinny-bodied-cloney, no-self-respecty snogfest of a phlegmy school-related disco. But tonight is different. Tonight you're officially "in with a chance" with Mo! And you've worshipped him for years! Since when you were five and he let you eat his last Christmas tree Santa chocolate! And when you were ten and he interrupted Space Monster Spewing Mutants II: The Revenge, Level 22: The Oozing Dungeon, to let you and Fazia play Pink Princesses Get Dressed! And when you were thirteen and you slept over at Fazia's and the smoke alarm went off and he held the door open for you! He practically scooped your

290

not-remotely frail, damsel-in-distress body up in his manly fifteen-year-old fireman arms and carried you through the raging flames of Casa Khareem. (Turned out there was no fire—Mrs. Khareem was up early and burned some toast and the Khareem smoke alarm is ultra-sensitive. But still. There was plenty of fire in me.)

So. I am In With a Chance at the Big Sneeze.

I arrive, wearing a new red dress I've spent a week making. And matching lipstick. And a smile. I stand near him, holding a bottle of beer I have no intention of drinking. Fazia raises her eyebrows at me and wanders off to find Hot Harry, the guy she always snogs at the end of any given social occasion. One day, one of them might actually ask the other out.

Tonight I'm in with a chance with Mo.

He's with his deep-giggly friends. They're going, "Haw-haw, haw-haw," like a pack of donkeys.

"Look, it's Smelly Ellie Minghelli. Haw-haw," Donkey Number One says.

"Ellie the Elephant. Haw-haw," adds Donkey Number Two.

Donkeys One and Two nudge Mo.

"She's made an effort tonight. Haw-haw," Donkey Number Three says, giving Mo a full shove, clearly far manlier than his puny nudging donkey friends.

There's a silence. The donkeys stare at me. This is the bit where Mo sweeps me up in a fireman's lift and rescues me from the burning, um, donkey barn.

Instead, he says something to his friends. They all bray madly. And then I hear something else. Fazia denies it for days afterwards, but I hear it. I hear him call me "Minger-Ellie." Minger. It's a few steps closer to loserville than "elephant." It's like "smelly" and "ugly" combined. I've been promoted.

The donkeys go wild—haw he haw he haw.

So I have a new nickname and it's coined by Mo. Fan-bloody-minger-tastic.

I stay put, because I am independent. I hold out until I see Mo snogging Holly.

Holly is the kind of fair maiden guys fought over in the olden days; duels at dawn. Holly is *perfect*. Holly is "in with a chance" with every single boy in the school. Guys are lucky to be "in with a chance" with Holly, not the other way around.

That's when I burst into loud, stupid, obvious tears and storm out of the party. Oh yeah, I really am that dignified. Minger-Ellie leaves the Big Sneeze in sniveling disgrace. It's a surefire way to make the new nickname stick. And stick it does.

Fat chance, the one Fazia said I was in with.

She apologizes for her brother, but of course it's not her fault. It's like if males aren't insulting females and/or leaving them, they cease to exist.

And I sort of wish that would happen, really. The world would be a more perfect place.

• • •

Fazia hasn't texted back yet and the sky is growing darker. I'm coping with the bedcover, at least. I change into pajamas, pull out a book and read on my bed for ages, carefully ignoring the cats. Eventually, though, I have to leave my room because I can't go forever without using the toilet. I may be Minger-Ellie and the laughing stock of my whole school but I'm still made of a human-related substance, deep down.

I open my bedroom door a crack and peer out. There's no sign of life so I dart quickly into the bathroom.

And that's when I walk in on a naked guy.

Yes, naked. And a guy.

Just when I've been wishing the whole male population of

the world away, one appears naked in my flat.

My pajamas are fluffy and have teddy bears on them. No one outside my family was supposed to see them. When I left my room, I dashed past the other bedroom doors just in case they were open and my new housemates saw something they shouldn't.

I now see almost everything I shouldn't.

I see a naked guy. Young. A bit older than me, I think. Fit. Buff, even.

He has one foot in the bath and his body half turned away from me.

I scream.

He yelps and gapes at me. "Oh Jesus, doesn't the lock work? Oh Jesus, I didn't realize!"

His accent is American. His body is . . . really interesting.

I gulp and tug at my pajamas (the bears! the bears!) but I can't seem to speak. I see chest. I see muscle definition. I see a small line of hair starting at his navel. I see more.

While I'm busy seeing all these things, he's grabbing the nearest towel, which seems to be a hand towel.

No, it's smaller than that. It's a titchy little bidet towel, designed to dry certain private parts of the body. It has a flowery pattern on it.

The boy covers one private part of himself in flowers. His, um, front part. I can still see the rest. I try not to look but my eyes are drawn there.

He finds a bigger towel. He doesn't look at me as he wraps it around himself and lets the bidet towel drop to the ground.

With the bottom part of him covered, my eyes travel north and I take in the dark tattoo on his shoulder. It is a girl's name—"Jen"—plus a heart. It dances as his arm muscles move, tying his towel tighter.

He has gorgeous arms.

I wonder what "Jen" would say if she knew I'd walked in on her boyfriend like this. And is Jen the Hello Kitty girl or the vamp? The boy has longish hair, but I'm still not sure which girlfriend is more likely, not until he puts some clothes on.

"It was locked!" The boy stares accusingly at the door. "I checked."

"Oh," I say. It's the first thing I've said. It occurs to me that I shouldn't still be standing here at all, but I'm kind of frozen.

"I'll ask my dad about the lock," I manage. Yay, my voice is back. And it seems to want some exercise, too. "It's just typical of my dad to put me in a flat with total strangers as housemates and not even check the bathroom door lock works and . . ." I hesitate. "Are you the boyfriend of one of my new housemates?"

"No," he says. His hand is all clenched where he's clutching the tied edges of the towel. "I live here. Since yesterday."

He *lives* here? "Wait—you're my actual housemate?"

"I guess," he shrugs. "There's me, and there's Yoshi. We moved in yesterday. Yoshi's something else—wait till you meet her."

I'm confused. It's none of my business, but I say it anyway. "So who's Jen?"

The boy looks shocked. Then he turns his head and frowns at the tattoo. "Oh. I'm not with Jenna anymore. That's why I'm here."

He tattooed her name on his shoulder, but he's already moved on. He already thinks Yoshi is "something else," and he met her yesterday.

Yeah, he's a guy, all right.

He holds out the hand that's not engaged in towel-clutching

duties. "Pleased to meet you. I'm Andy. So you're the landlord's daughter?"

I nod. "Ellie," I mumble. I shake his hand. And I'm now staring again.

I snap my eyes away.

"Okay, so . . . I'll just come back later," I say, suddenly swept up in a shyness I probably should have felt a lot earlier. "A lot later. And, I'll, um, knock first."

Andy looks relieved. "Thanks, Ellie," he says.

"That's okay. So I'll be going." I edge out of the door.

"Hey, Ellie?" Andy says.

I slink back, my eyes fixed carefully on the ceiling this time. "Yes?"

"Nice pajamas." He grins.

I pull at the hem of my pajama top. I wish I could bring myself to say something cheeky like "nice birthday suit," like Sofia or Fazia probably would in this situation.

I turn to leave, and that's when I meet my other housemate, who's just walked into the flat and is staring toward the bathroom, and me, in curiosity.

This one is definitely a girl. She has funky bright-pink and black hair that's spiked at the front and all different lengths. She's covered in bright makeup and her lipstick is the color of bubblegum. Her clothes are mismatched and clashy, with all shades of pink from pastel to electric. She looks like something off a high-fashion shoot.

She looks stunning.

Andy pokes his head out from behind the bathroom door, now covered in about three more towels. He beams at the style princess. "Hey, Yoshi! This is Ellie." He waves a hand between us. "Ellie, Yoshi. I'm about to have a shower and the lock's broken—don't come in!"

"I buy pizza?" Yoshi says. "For three?"

She looks at me and I nod. Well, I'm starving.

Andy shuts the door halfway through saying, "Yoshi, you're the best!" He couldn't have just said "yes"?

I'm almost relieved to go back to the cat-filled room and change out of my pajamas.

• • •

After Yoshi gets back, Andy emerges from his vamp cave dressed in head-to-toe black. The pizza smells delicious. We sit and eat and talk.

Well, Yoshi doesn't talk all that much. She's way too cool. Or maybe her English isn't that great. But Andy works hard to include her in the conversation and he laughs in her direction all the time and generally looks interested in her. Then he looks disappointed when she says something about "having exam" in the morning and she goes to her room to study.

He definitely likes her. A lot.

Tattoos are forever, but "Jen" is clearly forgotten.

When we're alone, Andy asks me about Dad, because he knows that the landlord's name is Armando Minghelli, a professor at the university.

"So you're Ellie Minghelli?" he asks, and I brace myself when I nod. But he doesn't laugh, or think of a nickname.

"My name's Elena really, but I don't like that either," I tell him. "I hate my name. I get teased about it at school." I don't tell him exactly how or by who.

"I hear you. I have issues with my name, too," he says. "Though I'm starting to forgive it now, if it's the reason I'm here with the world's coolest roomie." He grins. He has to mean Yoshi. He has seen my teddy-bear pajamas.

Andy continues, "I guess your dad wanted two girls to move in with you, huh? This mix-up probably happened because I'm called Andrea." He spells it for me. "I'm Italian-American, and it's a boy's name. But that didn't stop the stupid things they said in the locker room at high school back in the States. It was bad."

Oh, yeah? I'll bet my story beats his.

"The girly-boy stuff has mostly stopped now, and I'm in Italy." He runs a hand through his longish hair. "But it was Jenna who called the agency, and she said the girl there was Aussie. And Jenna called me her roommate, not her ex-boyfriend. They do so many sublets in this city of students, they don't really check stuff."

I stare at him. Apart from the hair, there's nothing remotely girly about him. Stubble. Large hands. Muscles. Sexy smile.

Extremely recent break-up with a live-in girlfriend whose name is tattooed on his arm and who made post-break-up arrangements for him. Obvious attraction to our other housemate.

Focus, Ellie, focus.

"So why did Jenna find you another place to live?" I don't know why I want to know, but I do.

His eyes shift downwards. "Well, she wanted me to leave."

"Yeah?" So she broke his heart?

Or *he* broke *hers*? And she issued him with an eviction notice? That's what Mum did with Dad in the end. "*I'm sick of hanging around waiting for you,*" Sofia and I heard her shout. "*Just get out of my life and stop even* pretending *you have any interest in me or the girls.*"

Andy says, "Yeah. She . . . she threw me out."

Good for Jenna. "My dad definitely said I'd be sharing with two girls," I tell Andy pointedly. Suddenly, I want him to worry.

He worries. "Do you think he'll let me stay?"

I feel instantly bad, so I tell the truth. "He probably won't even notice. He doesn't really pay much attention to me." That sounds a little pathetic so I add, "I think he thinks I'm all grown up, now I'm sixteen. Independent." Like a cat. That sounds less pathetic, but it's a lie because he didn't pay much attention to me when I was twelve, either. Or six, for that matter.

"You're sixteen? You going into junior year?"

"Um . . . I've just finished GCSEs. I'm starting A levels next year—like your high school leaving thingies. I think." Then I blurt, "I hate school. I can't wait to leave forever, but I like . . . I like studying." This is a terrible thing to admit. Social death. "I just don't like the people much." That is possibly worse.

Andy laughs and pulls up closer to me, settling in his chair like I've just given him a License to Talk About Yourself in Tiny Detail.

"I feel the same," he says. "I had the toughest time in school, mostly because I refused to be like everyone else."

"Oh. I don't refuse. I'm just . . . *not*. I can't help it." I have no idea why I'm saying that. Except that it's true.

He nods. "High school sucks," he says. "But it's over pretty quick, in the grand scheme of things, and I promise it gets better after that. All those haters? They kind of get over themselves. Or they're easier to avoid. Or override." He grins at me. "You know, with your superior intellect."

I'm not sure I have one of those, but I don't like to mention it.

Andy's still smiling at me. "I go to school in Chicago now and that's pretty cool."

Huh? "You're still at school?"

"I'm a JYA at the international university here," he says. "For college credit, you know?"

I must look really confused because he explains, "I'm nineteen. So is Yoshi, though she's from Japan. I know her from class. We take Italian culture and language together. The rest of the time, I study philosophy. It's my major back in the

States." He smiles, eyes shining with love for his subject. I feel myself relaxing about my earlier admission.

"This city's famous for its philosophical thought," I say, because Dad told me that once. But, bizarrely, all that springs to mind right now are the Italian chocolates Dad used to buy us for a taste of home. "Chocolate kisses," they were called, if you translated the Italian. Inside the wrapper of each one there was a little philosophical quote. Faz and I would stuff ourselves and giggle for hours at the messages. We'd take it in turns to read them out in silly voices.

"They even wrap their chocolates in philosophical thoughts," I say, which has to rate pretty highly on the Stupid Things to Say scale.

But Andy gives a huge belly laugh. Then he gets up. "Well, I have the same test as Yoshi so I'd better get studying too. See you tomorrow, Ellie Minghelli."

The vamp bedroom door shuts behind him.

I'm all alone again.

I decide to intrepidly venture downstairs and onto the street, where the shops still seem to be open even though it's getting late. I buy myself a small box of those famous chocolates and unwrap one.

"*In order to find perfect love, embrace imperfection,*" the flimsy paper reads.

"Embrace imperfection?"

Welcome to my life.

• • •

Surprise surprise, I don't see much of Dad for the next few days. He does come round a few times, and the first time he finds out about one of my new housemates being male. He asks whether I mind and when I say "no" he says, "Good. I trust that agency."

299

Yes, because they clearly try to meet their clients' needs . . . by sending the opposite of what they've asked for.

And aren't fathers supposed to worry about their daughters sharing bathrooms with strange men?

Not mine.

I ask him to fix the bathroom door lock and he does. He tells me to call if I need anything. I don't tell him I don't have his number. He doesn't ask what I've been doing all day.

What I've been doing all day is exploring. Mostly on my own but also with Andy, whenever he's not "in class," as he calls it. It just kind of happens, because he knows his way around. We've been thrown together. I'm enjoying myself, though. I've found we can talk about anything and everything, and we do.

When I finally get hold of Mum, she doesn't sound like herself. She's been out loads with the people from her course. She tells me about women called Tasha and Rose and Hannah, who she feels like she's known forever. Then she goes on about their tutor, Robert, and how much fun he is and how he's just one of them, really, and he's turned his life around with the power of positive thought and he's an inspiration.

She certainly sounds positive. She won't even join me in bad-mouthing Dad, which is a total first for her. She's not worried about Dad losing his phone and us not knowing where he lives. She says, "I'm sure he'll get a new phone soon, and anyway it sounds like he's popping round a lot." She adds, "Ellie, don't let this go to your head, but I trust you, and I know you'll be fine. And don't be afraid to ask Armando for help if you need it. He's not as useless as you think he is." She contradicts herself spectacularly in the next sentence, something only my mother can do with such style. "Anyway, you could probably look after him better than he could look after you. Honestly, Ellie, try to enjoy yourself. Think positively. Have fun. Robert says . . ."

"But, Mum," I burst in, because she doesn't seem to get it. "He's got me sharing with a boy! A nineteen-year-old *boy*!" I stop short of saying "with a tattoo." "And Dad doesn't even care!"

"Is he a nice boy?"

"Does such a specimen exist?"

"Ellie!" She doesn't know about Mo, but she's probably guessed. She has spooky powers like that, my mum. "Does he make you laugh? Does he listen to you? Is he kind?"

"Yes," I admit.

She uses her Mum powers to analyze that single word and the next thing she says is, "Okay, *now* I'm worried." Then she laughs.

"Mum!" Honestly, this isn't like her. Well, it's a bit like her, but with added sparkles and a feather boa. What are they teaching her on this course? "He's just come out of a big long-term relationship. And I'm pretty sure he likes someone else. Our other housemate, who's drop-dead stylish and gorgeous."

"Huh," says Mum, and I wait for her to reassure me about my own looks and style. She does, but it never helps. She has to say that stuff—she's my mother and it's in the contract. She adds, "You can still be his friend, you know. Men are human beings, like you and me." She sighs. "I think I'd forgotten that myself, until this week."

It occurs to me for the first time that while she's "finding herself," she might be looking for someone else.

• • •

A couple of days later, Andy and I are walking around town. Andy's chatting away as usual, telling me about this barmy professor who asks the students for cigars during lectures. He tells me all about the lectures, too. He's not ashamed of being passionate about academic stuff. He's so intense. He's not like Mo, who's always playing to his gang of donkey friends.

We pass a gorgeous little church with an inviting patch of green in front of it and he switches into telling me about its history and then, kind of out of the blue, he says, "Let's sit down?" and I answer, "Okay."

I settle on the grass next to him and watch as he digs into his messenger bag and brings out a tiny box of chocolate kisses. There are three in the pack and first we have one each. We laugh at the cheesy quotes. He insists I should have the third chocolate, and I remember that's how my crush on Mo started—with chocolate. But maybe it has extra power in this city—some kind of a force that radiates out from the factory and beams its rays over us all.

Maybe that's why I can't stop thinking about kissing Andy.

When I go quiet, he looks at me. He says, "I'm glad the agency thought I was a girl. It's worth the hell I went through in school about my name. If I'd been called Bob, I might never have met you, Ellie."

He laughs and I think, oh no. I am so falling for this guy. And I never feel like he's going to turn my name into a stupid nickname. In fact, I love it when he says my name. I could listen to it forever.

I shake myself. He is still a guy, and you never know with guys. I never thought Mo would turn on me either, or snog Holly in front of me immediately afterwards.

"And Yoshi, too, of course," Andy continues, giving me a jolt of reality. "Yoshi's great—she's one of a kind." He hesitates. "Hey, can I ask you something?" He touches my arm.

My heart does a little fluttery thing and I can't believe myself. I can't wait for my hormonal teen years to be over so that I can stop getting crushes. As soon as I'm twenty I'll dye my hair gray and get loads of cats. It will be hard for me, but I'll adjust, because cats are what women have when they don't want men. Anyway, cats are cooler than men, and when they leave you, you don't mind because you're expecting it. Cats have no loyalty but you still love them.

I'll just have to get over my phobia first.

Andy says, "So Yoshi . . . well, she told me about these tickets she got hold of for a concert on Friday. She says it will be really cool and she asked me to go with her . . ."

The fluttering turns to pounding. Oh no, oh no.

". . . and it's far away in this little town, kind of romantic." He sneaks a glance at me. "And I wondered . . ."

I tune him out and focus on the whooshing sound in my ears as he keeps talking.

He's finally going out with Yoshi. It had to happen. She's perfect.

"So what do you think?"

He's asking *me* what I think of him going out with Yoshi? Like he needs my blessing?

But Fazia asks me what I think of Hot Harry all the time. It's a friend thing. I think of Mum, telling me to be friends with Andy, and that boys are human.

I swallow hard. "Sure," I say.

"Yeah?"

"Yeah. Yoshi's great," I add.

"I know. She really is," he confirms. He smiles as if he has never smiled before. "Yoshi is the best!"

"The best," I echo.

We walk back in silence. Something's changed between us. My stomach lurches when he unlocks the door and sprints up four flights of stairs. I stagger behind him, out of puff and out of luck. He's probably dying to see Yoshi right now.

Andy goes to his room and I go to mine. I collapse on my bed and try to conjure some kind of anti-love spell to get rid of these feelings for him that are coursing through my body. I blame the chocolates.

I text Fazia and say, "Faz help, am in LOVE!" and she texts back with, "Me too! Hot Harry finally asked me out! Woo hoo!" and then, "Happy for you! Big bro missed his chance! Luv ya, tell me ALL! Xxx"

So I text back with "No, Faz. It's BAD. He loves sum1 ELSE," and she texts back, "Soz, hun. Luv sucks. Xxx"

Not when you're Fazia, though, it doesn't.

Or if you're Yoshi, and Andy is crazy about you.

• • •

I see Disappearing-Act Dad exactly twice in the next two days.

The first time, he turns up at the flat while Yoshi, Andy, and I are eating pizza. We do that every night. Yoshi still doesn't talk much, and she and Andy certainly don't act exclusive or anything around me. But the concert is on Friday and I guess that's their first date, and things will change after that.

When Dad arrives, he does something fiddly to the kitchen tap, which has been dripping for a while. I'm not sure how he could have known that, though, because I didn't tell him. He generally fusses around for a while longer, then he tells me to call him if I need anything—his new catchphrase—and he leaves.

The second time, I run into him in the street. Well, he's in the street and I'm sitting at a cafe table with Andy, talking about his Italian studies lecture that I gatecrashed. (We watched a film, and I even sort of imagined I was on a date at the cinema with Andy, until I managed to stop my evil thoughts.)

I've sat in lots of cafes with Andy by now, but today feels different. I'm distracted because, during a heated bit of discussion, his hand somehow landed on mine. He doesn't seem to have noticed, but it's all I can think about. It's making blood rush to my head.

Then I see Dad in the distance. I pull my hand away and Andy stops talking.

I call out to Dad and he comes over. He's with a tall woman who's wearing expensive-looking clothes, a scarf around her neck and a hairband of sunglasses. As Dad greets me and Andy, I find myself wondering whether she has an extra pair of eyes at the top of her head, like some kind of alien. She's certainly acting weird—glancing at me with her nose wrinkled up in an aloof sort of way. It occurs to me that this is my new Wicked Stepmother-to-be.

Dad talks to Andy about some house issue or other and she hangs back, all polite smiles. After a minute or so, she touches Dad's arm and asks him something, and I recognize my name and the Italian word for daughter. Dad nods and she tuts at him and holds out her hand to me.

"I am Adelina and I am pleased to meet you, Ellie."

I'm not quite sure what I mumble in response but she doesn't really listen anyway. She turns to Dad and says something in quick-fire, angry-sounding Italian. He replies and then he says to me, "Adelina would like you to have dinner with us."

She says something else, in the same annoyed tone, and he replies, defensive, and I think I hear the Italian for "sorry" and the word "independent." But then some professor-type calls out to them from across the street and Adelina smiles and says goodbye to us, and Dad tells me to give him a call. Then they both disappear.

• • •

The next night is the night of the concert.

Or "weirdest night ever," as I like to call it.

At first, I'm slightly surprised to be involved at all. I was planning on staying out of the way, trying not to pine in my room, but when Andy asks me to go with him to pick up the hire car, I think I might as well.

He doesn't say much—he seems nervous as he signs about a thousand documents and shows half of Italy his American driving license. It all takes ages because he doesn't have a proper credit card, just some pre-pay thing, and this means the staff have to huff a lot and make thousands of long, sharp phone calls.

Finally, Andy drives the car back and double-parks it illegally outside the flat, which seems to be okay since there are about ten other cars parked the same way, all at different angles.

He groans. "I'm sorry that took so long, Ellie! We pretty much have to leave right now. Is that okay?" So I offer to run up and get Yoshi and he looks surprised but before he can say anything, Yoshi appears at the door.

She's wearing tons of bright makeup and three-quarter-length pastel-pink trousers with sparkly bits that clash with her shocking-pink sequined top. But it looks great on her, and she's obviously made an effort for tonight. I remind myself that my heart shouldn't be sinking at that. It's good. Why wouldn't I want my friends to be happy?

The weirdness starts when Yoshi nods at Andy. "See you later," she says. Then she sweeps off down the road.

"Where's she going?" I ask, confused.

Andy looks at her disappearing pinkness. "I guess to meet her date. She's given me our tickets, but the seats are right next to hers so we'll see them there."

Her date?

Our tickets?

We'll see *them* there?

"Is something wrong, Ellie?"

"Wrong" isn't the word, not if I'm on a date. With Andy.

Wearing one of my oldest dresses and with no time to change.

"Ellie? We have to leave. I'm so sorry about the time thing . . ."

He looks nervous. He *is* nervous. He's going out on a date with *me* and he's nervous!

Maybe Mum is right about men being human. Though this one is clearly insane.

• • •

It takes two fist-clenching hours of Italian traffic but eventually we get there. Andy double-parks the car and we stagger up a hill with the sun setting dramatically in front of us. He takes my hand and I realize it wasn't an accident, that day in the cafe when his hand landed on top of mine.

And I am on a date with Andy.

The venue is an open-air opera house, amazingly grand. The spotlights light up the old building and cover us in a yellowy glow. It feels unreal, like a film set.

We meet Yoshi and her date, who is at least ten years older than us and has a wacky sense of style and a pink shirt on. Maybe that's what they see in each other. They are pink together.

Andy buys us each a drink, and we settle down in the half-light with the excited hum of a thousand concert-goers building around us.

The concert itself is fun but weird. A pepper-haired man croons away to folksy ballads, mostly in lyrical-sounding Italian and occasionally in heavily accented Eeengleesh, which doesn't spoil the exotic effect.

Andy catches my eye in those parts and we try not to laugh. He tightens his hold on my hand and my heart swells. I can't believe I'm here with him. Then I really do giggle and Yoshi gives us a bit of a look, but Andy doesn't seem to care.

The concert ends in a swirl of standing ovations. I swear Yoshi and her date have tears in their eyes as they applaud.

"It was so perfect, no?" Yoshi's man enthuses before Andy and I say goodbye and trudge back to the hire car.

I will never get tired of holding his hand.

• • •

The car isn't there.

Andy stares at the empty space.

"You sure this is where we parked?" I ask him.

He moves his head slowly like an owl. "Three trees to the right, overturned garbage can, small family of wild cats." He sighs. "It was here, Ellie."

One of the cats turns to look at us then, as if it knows we're talking about it. A lot of Italian cats are skinny and feral, but somehow when we parked here earlier, I managed to walk past them with ease. I thought, *I can cope*. I thought, *something about me is different. I'm no longer a mouse*.

The cat's scrawnier brother or sister wanders over and eyes me suspiciously.

I breathe.

"The cats might have moved," I say. I wouldn't put it past them to have followed me to the concert with the intention of waiting till my guard was down and clawing my legs off.

"No, Ellie, it was definitely here."

I can see exactly what's in his head—it ticker-tapes across his face. It goes something like: "Oh, no! Someone's stolen our car! We drove for two hours to get here! How will we get home? Oh no! Someone's . . ." etc. Ticker ticker ticker.

Oddly, I'm not panicking. "Should we try to find Yoshi?"

"She was going back to Enzo's; he lives near here. I don't have her number." His voice is flat. He's doing an impression of a stone pillar. I decide to take control.

"Let's hire another car. You can explain it to the hire company in the morning. I bet they're insured for this kind of thing."

"I can't use that credit card again, and I don't have any money left," Andy says. "Those drinks were expensive. I'm sorry, El."

I take out my wallet. I have Dad's money, which I've barely spent, with the way I've been living. Plus he keeps giving me more. Euros upon euros, in cash. "I've got money."

"Oh, Ellie. This date was supposed to be perfect." He sounds miserable. "And anyway, who's hiring cars here at this time of night?"

"This is Italy," I say. "The country that never sleeps."

Andy looks doubtful. "I've never heard that before. I mean, seriously, I've never seen any evidence of that at all."

"Leave it to me," I say.

I am not a mouse.

There's a group of men by a scruffy car on the other side of the road. The car looks like one of the junkyard ones from Pixar's *Cars* movie—the little yellow one called Luigi—but it will do.

I dart across the road, leaving Andy where he is. I force out my best Italian—which isn't very good—for the longest time, and punctuate my persuasive argument by waving wads of my Dad's euros around. Eventually I cross back to Andy, who's at one with a lamppost.

I'm triumphant.

But Andy looks more worried than before, if that's possible.

"Ellie, what was all that about? I shouldn't have let you go over there—"

"You couldn't have stopped me. Here. We have a car." I hand him the keys to Luigi. A skeletal cat prowls past me. I stare right at it, but it ignores me.

Andy drives Luigi through the moonlit darkness, phutt-phutt-phutt. "Your dad's so right about you," he says after a while. He smiles a tiny smile, like he's just allowing it to creep through.

I eye him suspiciously. "What do you mean?"

"At the cafe. When he told his girlfriend—"

"Adelina?"

"Adelina. He told her you were fiercely independent. So much so that he didn't know how to be your dad."

I nearly gasp. "He never said that! Are you sure? Your Italian isn't that good."

His smile broadens. "Oh, thanks," he says sarcastically. "Well, okay, I understood the word 'independent,' and I know he was talking about you, and he was trying to field Adelina's accusations. She said he should have invited you sooner." He gives me a quick, shy look. "And I know you probably terrify him, because you're a force to be reckoned with."

I doubt it, but I have to change the subject now because we seem to be approaching a wide stretch of beach.

"Um, Andy, are we going the right way?" I ask.

"It was signposted here," he says.

"Okay." I pause. "It's just . . . we live in *central* Italy, and if we go any further now we might fall right off the edge of the country. So it doesn't seem very, you know, central, right now."

Andy grips the steering wheel tightly and pulls over to the beachfront with the engine still running. He groans. "You're right!" He stares at the dashboard. "And there's worse. There's a red light on here."

"Let me see." I crane my neck.

"It's the gas!"

"The what?"

"We're out of gas."

"Okay." I'm still feeling capable, even though I'm kicking myself that I didn't think to ask those Italian men whether there was any petrol in the tank before I gave them all my money. "So we'll get more."

"In the country that never sleeps?" He gives me a sideways look.

I look around. The streets are deserted. Metal doors cover the nearby shopfronts—they don't just look closed, they look fortified against nuclear attack. I have to admit Andy has a point. "Well, possibly I was wrong about that."

Andy grimaces.

"Okay. So we'll find a hotel." Wow, a hotel. Me and Andy in a hotel. A thrill runs through me. I could do anything tonight.

"Do you have any money left?"

I could do anything that costs nothing. "Um, no."

He takes out his wallet. "I have two euros."

I think. We could sleep in the car. We could figure something out in the morning.

Luigi is tiny.

But Luigi's headlights show that there's a whole beach in front of us. Rows of empty black-and-white deckchairs on a stretch of black and empty sand. We have our windows open and the night is balmy.

"Andy?"

He taps his fingers on the steering wheel.

"When Sofia went to Ibiza last year, she slept on the beach."

He looks out. "Isn't there a law against that?"

"I think she got moved on a couple of times. But that was in Spain."

He turns off the engine.

"If we get arrested, I'll tell them I'm Professor Minghelli's daughter. That's got to be good for something."

"Maybe in Perugia. You're not in Perugia any more, Dorothy. This is a one-fish town."

We wait a while.

Neither of us have any other ideas.

"Come on," I say. We head for our free Sands resort hotel.

Andy and I walk past the deckchairs, listening to the sea churn and hiss. This sound, combined with the oddly pleasant smell of seaweed and fish, is the only signal of where we are. The rest is pure, deep darkness, with just a hint of moonlight.

We head for the roar of the sea and stop when we feel the texture of the sand change under our combat boots. Behind us is a cluster of tall rocks, blocking the beach and the road from view, so we're completely cut off from the man-made world. The air is warm and damp. I've adjusted to the darkness now so I shut my eyes to get it back. I hear the repetitive whoosh of the waves. I hear Andy breathing.

"So . . . you never wanted to date Yoshi?" I ask. The night sky and the car bribery have made me bold.

Andy laughs. "Did you think I *did*?"

"No . . . yes." I take a deep breath. "I thought tonight was your first date with her."

"You have to be kidding me, Ellie!" He plays with my hair, rubbing the ends between his fingers. "Why would you think I wanted to date Yoshi?"

"Um." Where do I start? "She's gorgeous? She has an amazing sense of style?"

"Okay," he says. "That's true."

My heart doesn't even sink. I mean, it *is* true. But now, Andy is stroking my face.

"She's great," he adds. "But you're . . . you."

Oh?

"I can't stop thinking about you, Ellie."

OHHHH.

I open my eyes. A sliver of moon shines on us as he reaches for me. He wraps an arm carefully across my shoulders. It's like that comfortable warmth I felt when he put his hand on mine at the cafe, but it's combined with something else. I feel strong. Better still, I realize this feeling isn't new. I've always felt strong like this; I've just been stifling it, letting other people get to me. Getting at myself.

I put my arm around his waist.

He says, "Ellie?"

Instead of answering, I pull him close. It makes his T-shirt ride up slightly and I reach under it, let my hand touch his skin.

"Ellie . . ." His voice is croaky now.

I wrap my other arm around him and turn so we're face-to-face in the dark.

I press my body against his. I find his mouth with my mouth, just for a second. He seems tentative. Nervous. I kiss him until he relaxes into me and we kiss and kiss and kiss until we fold back, grasping at each other on the sand.

We don't exactly stop, but we do slow down. Or rather he does, and I follow because I'm glued to him. We kiss as much as possible as we unravel. Then we sit on the sand, or rather *in* the sand—our clothes are filled with enough gritty stuff to make our own private beach. I lean my head on his shoulder and he strokes my hair. It makes me tingle all over again.

I kiss his neck. "What philosophical thoughts are you thinking now?" I joke.

His voice is low. "You make it kinda difficult for me to think at all." He leans his head on top of mine. "That day I first met you? In the bathroom?" A laugh creeps into his voice. "I thought you'd never leave."

"You wanted me to leave?"

"No, I wanted you to stay and I wanted to do this." He kisses my lips and my world spins. "I had to recite philosophical theory in my head to stop myself."

"Seriously? In my teddy-bear pajamas?"

"They were super-cute. And you're beautiful."

"This boy at school calls me Minger-Ellie." Even as I tell him, I realize the nickname has completely lost its power. It says more about Mo than it does about me. "Minger is British for 'ugly,'" I explain. "I had a crush on him. Before."

Andy sounds angry. "Sorry, but that guy's an idiot."

"Yeah," I say, and then I add, "What guy?" and I kiss him.

He pulls away and says, "Listen, about the tattoo, Ellie . . ."

"Oh," I say, but I'm just so sure of this—of him, of us, of me, that I add, "It doesn't matter."

"It really doesn't," he says. "But just in case. It's henna. It's fading. I got it done before we broke up. Last-ditch attempt to save the relationship. It didn't work, and it hadn't worked for the longest time. The relationship, I mean." He sits up. "Jenna was seeing other guys. Our feelings for each other faded a long time ago. She just needed to give me a final push."

"Oh, I'm sorry." I take his hand.

"What about?" he asks lightly.

"About your girlf—"

"What girl?" he laughs, and he kisses me.

• • •

The sun rises, an orange ball over a shimmering gray-blue, and wakes us up even though we didn't know we'd gone to sleep. I walk back to Luigi holding hands with Andy and floating on air. Well, crunching on it, really, seeing as my boots are filled with sand, but I don't care.

"So what's next, Ellie El-raiser?" Andy asks, and I think he can call me whatever he likes and it will be okay, coming from him. "What's your plan for getting us out of here alive?"

"I thought I'd call my dad," I say. I check my watch. "I'll get the number for the university from Directory Enquiries, or whatever. I'll call him there. It must be possible. Besides, he *wants* me to ask him for help, doesn't he?" I realize it's true the second I say it. "He's been waiting. That's why he didn't invite me over until Adelina suggested it. He was waiting for *me* to ask *him*."

"I wondered about that," says Andy. "But I knew you didn't want to talk about it. You mean you've never even been downstairs?"

What? "I've never been *where*?"

"Downstairs. To your dad's place, I mean. In our building."

"Wait a minute." I look at him. "My dad lives in our building? You *know* he lives there?" Maybe that's how Dad knew about the dripping tap. Maybe he heard it.

"Sure," says Andy. "Wait, you *don't*?" He sounds amazed.

I shake my head. "He didn't tell me." And actually, "How did *you* know?"

"I guess the real-estate agency mentioned it. I didn't think you didn't *know*, Ellie! He always says you should call him if you need him."

"Well, yeah, but he meant I should phone him." Even though I don't have his number. "Didn't he?"

"I always thought he meant yell. You know. Like shout, '*Dad!*' down the stairs. Like you would at home, if you lived in the same house."

I seem to remember he rarely answered, when we lived in the same house.

"Or at least call at his door. He lost his phone, didn't he? He's the very cliché of an absent-minded professor." Andy laughs.

"He's hopeless. He can't manage to be my dad without an instruction manual. Written by me."

"I think he's trying, Ellie. In his own, imperfect way."

So then I think about imperfection. The mess we all make, living our lives. The way we call each other hurtful names and put each other down and ignore each other and make each other feel bad, and it's all so stupid, because we're all human. We're all as bad as each other.

And as good.

And as attached and alone at the same time. Prowling around each other like cats.

Andy takes my other hand and I melt into our chocolate kisses and it feels perfect, but I know it's not, not really. It's awesome, but we're just two people powered by a delicious moment. Embracing imperfection and making it shine.

In our case, though?

For the longest time.

Orange Tootsie Pop

by Cecil Castellucci

I HAVE ONLY been at Mayflower Middle School for three weeks and I already know a few things: Shoshanna and Brooke are the twin princesses of seventh grade and I am lucky to be their friend; on Thursdays Mrs. Gabriel our seventh grade homeroom teacher gives us treats; and I am in love with Kenny Kamil.

Today is the first time one of Kenny's friends, Eddie, passes me a note in class. He's always smiled at me before and nodded in my direction, but we had never made contact. When the note comes my way I don't think that it could possibly be for me, so I pass it to the girl next to me.

"Uh, this note is for you," the girl next to me whispers.

"What?"

"It says *Donna* on it," she says, pointing to the very clear, underlined and in capital letters name on the folded piece of loose-leaf paper. "That's your name, not mine."

"Oh," I say and I take it from her, put it on my lap, and open it up.

Donna,

Kenny, Jonathan and I were wondering if you wore colored panties? Also, do you wear a bra?

Please tick what style you wear.

317

___ *Thong*
___ *Bikini*
___ *Grandma*
___ *I don't wear underwear*
We are perverts. Ha. Ha. Ha.

For a guy that gets a 99 percent on every algebra quiz, Eddie could sound pretty stupid sometimes.

Shoshanna and Brooke meet me outside after school by the gymnasium entrance.

Shoshanna always looks so pretty. Today she's wearing her pale pink shirt, the one I love, with a cool-looking fairy on it outlined in glitter. Her hair, a honey-golden blonde, is woven into tight little braids, and her skin is a coffee-with-milk shade of brown, like she's been in the sun all day. I wonder if her mother takes her to a salon to get the braids done so perfectly, or if her mother does it for her at home.

I love braids. I wish I had the kind of hair that stayed in braids. But I don't.

We have the sweets Mrs. Gabriel gave us in homeroom today in a brown paper bag Brooke saved from lunch. I notice her name in cursive in light-blue pen on the fold. *BROOKE*. It's not her handwriting, it's her mother's. I know it to be impossible to forge. All of us have tried to copy Mrs. Farley's handwriting. All of us have failed. Brooke can never be counted on for an authentic-looking, adult-like note. That's the one thing Shoshanna doesn't like about her.

Even though it's the end of October, it's hot outside, so I take off my sweater.

"Oh, look, Donna's finally at the button stage," Shoshanna says to Brooke, pointing at my non-existent boobs. Even Brooke has tits. They are small—speed tits, she calls them—but, she always points out, at least she can wear a bra.

"They are an A cup," she says.

I look down at my flat chest and see what Shoshanna's talking about. My nipples have kind of puffed out and they are poking through my T-shirt like two sewn-on buttons.

I'm embarrassed, so I put my sweater back on.

"You should get a training bra, even though they're for babies," Brooke says.

"Boys like boobs. They like big ones. Like mine," Shoshanna says. Then she thrusts out her chest a little more to show me her boobs. Like everything about Shoshanna, even her boobs seem perfect to me.

We are hanging out at the basketball courts after school with one thing on our minds: Kenny and the boys and when they will get here. We all know that they'll be here soon to play their pick-up game and that we'll watch them, because they are the cool boys and we are the cool girls, and that is what we do.

We hang out and watch them.

"I heard Eddie passed you a note today and you didn't respond," Shoshanna says.

"It was a stupid note," I say.

"No, Donna," Shoshanna says. "No note a boy passes you is ever stupid."

"Yeah," Brooke says. "They might want to be your boyfriend."

"I don't want Eddie to be my boyfriend," I say.

"Oh," Shoshanna says. "I know you like Kenny, but Kenny is out of your league, Donna. No offense."

I have a sneaking suspicion that she is right. Kenny *is* out of my league.

"Probably he's going to ask me to go to the Halloween dance," Shoshanna says.

"Probably Shoshanna is going to be his girlfriend," Brooke says.

"Probably I'm going to let him feel me up. Or finger me," Shoshanna says. "I haven't decided yet."

I think about Kenny's hand snaking up Shoshanna's shirt and cupping her breast. I bet it would fill his hand and then he would squeeze it a little. I wish I had a breast that he could squeeze, instead of a button. I think about him sticking his hand up my shirt and feeling my button nipple. Then I get depressed.

"You should maybe settle for Eddie," Shoshanna says. "He's a brain, like you."

"I don't want to date a brain," I say.

"Me, neither," Brooke says. "That's why I'm going to go for Jonathan."

"Look, here they come," Shoshanna says, poking Brooke with her elbow. "Pretend you don't care."

Shoshanna and Brooke start pretending that they are very interested in something on the ground by their feet. Maybe they are looking at something, like an anthill. Or a special rock. Or some fall leaves that are a pretty color. I don't know, because I'm not looking at the ground with them. I'm looking at the boys.

I'm not a good pretender.

"Donna's peeking," Brooke says.

"Look busy," Shoshanna commands.

I take out a hairband and put my hair up in a ponytail so that it doesn't fall in my face. That way I look busy and I can see the boys better.

Once I asked my mom to make me tight little braids like Shoshanna has but she didn't know how to do it very well and when I came to school they were already falling out. I knew that I had made a big mistake and that everyone was going to laugh at me, the new girl with the bad braids.

I tried to pretend that I didn't care that I looked terrible.

But I couldn't. Instead of going to homeroom, I went straight to the bathroom to try to save the day.

That's where I met Shoshanna. In the bathroom, right after she had taken a poop. I knew it was a poop because of the smell and the noise. She came out and was surprised that she wasn't alone. She gave me a look while she was washing her hands, trying to see if I would tell anyone that she had pooped.

I tried to look like I didn't smell anything, even though I did, and that I wouldn't say a word. It must have worked because the next thing I knew her face softened as she took in the mess of my hair.

"You know, the problem is your hair is too fine for braids," Shoshanna said, coming over to me and then helping me take them out. The bell rang and we were going to be late for third period but we both didn't care.

I was hiding, because most of the hair had already slipped out of the braids and I was crying from the pinching of the tiny rubber bands.

"You're the new girl, right?" she asked.

I nodded while her hands methodically unbraided my hair.

"You could come and get pizza with me and Brooke after school if you like," she said.

I could tell that she felt sorry for me, but I didn't really care. I was new and miserable and lonely for friends.

Brooke was Shoshanna's best friend. They had been best friends since fourth grade. Brooke was small, but she was quick and sporty. The boys always came and talked to her because she played little league with them. She played on the same team as Kenny.

Shoshanna and I went to every game.

After that day in the bathroom, Shoshanna pretty much

always asked me to hang out with them. Except when she and Brooke were hanging out alone, which sometimes still happened. But I didn't care about that or feel left out or anything. I was just happy to be one of their closest friends. Even if I knew I was just the hanger-on.

Kenny, Eddie and Jonathan started paying attention to me after that, because I was friends with the cool girls and I was new.

Eddie was in almost all of my classes. But he wasn't cute. I didn't like his nose. It was like a potato. We were in all the smart classes together, although we didn't make a big deal out of it. Because that would be bragging.

At least that's what Shoshanna always said.

The boys still haven't come out on the court. I can see them lingering at the sports locker checking out a ball. There must be a cute high school girl working today. Or at least an eighth grader.

"Hey," Kenny yells across at me, because he catches my eye. "Go save us a court."

Now that we have been spotted first, Shoshanna and Brooke are done pretending that the ground is interesting, because really, they wanted to be paying attention to the boys. We go over to the best court, the one in the corner, and take our places against the fence while we wait for the boys.

The boys don't even thank us for saving them the court, even though we had to chase away some younger kids. The boys just put their backpacks down next to us for us to keep watch over and they start their game.

We're sitting on the sidelines, with the sun in our faces and our backs up against the fence, which gives a little under our combined weight.

"I think it's treat time," Shoshanna says. "I think we deserve it."

"Here, take one." Brooke violently shakes the brown paper bag that holds our Tootsie Pops in front of my face.

I want to pick the cherry one, or the grape. I don't want the orange.

Earlier, after homeroom, Shoshanna had said, "It's only fair to put our pops in the bag and pick at random. One of us might get a better flavor than what was left on their desk."

Brooke made the agreeing face, the one that you can't protest against and just have to go along with. Like if you didn't, you'd be toast.

On Thursdays, when Mrs. Gabriel gives us treats, we all come into homeroom in the morning and find a sweet lying on our desk. She always gives us the candy but then tells us to put it away.

"All I hear is sucking," Mrs. Gabriel says. "You can't suck on things while I'm calling roll. I can't stand the sound of your lips smacking! It's worse than when you're talking."

Maybe it turns her on.

Or, maybe she's just a bitch.

Most kids wait till the bell rings and then pull the wrapper off their treats and shove it quickly into their mouths while walking down the too-crowded hall and try to hurriedly finish it before they get to their first class of the day. Usually, they enter the room with chipmunk cheeks and have to swallow it before the teacher gives them a black mark for eating in class. I've seen one or two of them gag a little.

Shoshanna, Brooke and I have *restraint*. We have *patience*. We always save our treat for after school.

We're just like that, we three. It makes me feel pretty good to hang around with girls as cool as Shoshanna and Brooke.

In homeroom today I found a cherry-flavor pop on my desk. Shoshanna got orange, and I think by making us all put our candy into the bag, she's just being selfish, hoping for a better color.

Shoshanna is not the kind of girl who gets orange.

Sometimes I feel as though Shoshanna and Brooke think I am not cool enough to hang out with them. And I suspect they agree. I'm sure that they also think I'm not cool enough to get cherry on my desk.

"Come on!" Brooke says, shaking the bag again.

I close my eyes and put my hand in, hoping that I'll get my cherry back, or maybe the grape. I want to be that kind of girl.

A cherry one.

Instead, I pull out orange.

"Oh, too bad," Shoshanna says insincerely. She and Brooke give each other a look. A look that says cherry and grape are good ones to get and it doesn't matter whose hand goes into the bag next.

I frown a bit. But just a little. I freeze my frown and I force myself to smile. I don't want to look like a sore loser. But I am not a good liar. I don't pretend well. So I look at the sun and don't blink, because everyone knows that looking at the sun makes your eyes water.

I'm disappointed.

The ball slaps the backboard and we watch the boys play. After a couple of warm-up shots, Kenny Kamil finally waves to us and my heart skips a beat.

Even though I know that Kenny is probably going to ask Shoshanna to be his girlfriend.

Even though I should settle for Eddie because he has a brain.

Even though I would not let Eddie stick his hand up my shirt to feel my buttons.

Swoosh. Dribble. Swoosh. Slap.

Kenny Kamil and his green eyes are always glancing over at us. Probably he is looking at Shoshanna and not at me, although sometimes I pretend that he is looking at me.

The first game is over and the boys are now coming over to us.

They are a little sweaty. They glisten. They glow.

Kenny comes over and it really looks like he is eyeballing me. Makes me feel hotter than this Indian-summer day. Makes me feel hot like I need to take off my sweater again, even though there is a slight breeze and he'll see my buttons.

Shoshanna must think that Kenny is looking at me, too, because she whispers to me through closed teeth. "Don't forget that Kenny is mine," she says.

Like I could even forget.

I decide that I should ignore him even though it will break my heart. I should ignore him because what Shoshanna really means is, *Don't forget that I will give you the silent treatment if you talk to Kenny.*

But I can't ignore Kenny. He's right here in front of me. His knees are right in front of my face.

"Donna, how about you give me a lick of your Tootsie Pop, okay?" he asks.

"Kenny, I'll give you a lick of mine," Shoshanna says.

The boys snicker.

"Nah," Kenny says.

"I've got cherry," Shoshanna says. Like that explains everything.

"What do you say, Donna?" Kenny says. "Give me a lick."

Shoshanna shoots me a look. An evil look. A person might actually die from a look like that, so I look away quickly.

"Why should I give you a lick?" I say to Kenny. But I say it to his knees because I can't look up at him.

I want to give Kenny a lick. If he licks my lollipop then it's

325

kind of like swapping spit. And swapping spit is just like kissing. And I want to kiss Kenny so badly.

"You should give me a lick 'cause I like orange best," Kenny says.

I can feel Shoshanna nearly losing it next to me.

"If you give him a lick, Donna, then we are no longer friends," Shoshanna warns me.

Now I am looking at Kenny right in the eyes and he's looking back at me. We are locked in a moment together that I don't ever want to end.

I give him my Tootsie Pop.

Kenny licks it a bunch of times and then hands it back to me.

Shoshanna gets up and puts her hands on her hips.

Eddie and Jonathan are trying not to laugh, but they are. They are laughing at Shoshanna.

Shoshanna knows it, too.

"Brooke, come on," she says.

I notice that Brooke is still sitting down next to me. She looks stunned. Like she doesn't know what's going on.

"BROOKE!" Shoshanna yells.

That gets her attention and Brooke stands up.

"Donna, don't ever talk to us again," Shoshanna says.

She turns her back on me and Brooke follows her, trailing behind a little, like she doesn't want to leave the courts but wants to stay with us. Brooke even looks back wistfully when they leave the school grounds.

I'm surprised that I'm not running after them begging for forgiveness.

I'm surprised that I'm still sitting by the fence.

It dawns on me that the price for one moment of being the center of Kenny Kamil's attention is losing my only friends.

Eddie, Jonathan, and Kenny are all laughing. I want to cry

because I think they are laughing at me. Because I figure that they know like I do, for sure, that I am the biggest loser in seventh grade.

"I heard she let Danny McGowan finger her this summer in the pool," Eddie says.

"She's a slut," Jonathan says.

"Hey, Donna," Kenny says. "You never said what kind of underwear you wear?"

I look up at him.

They're not laughing at me at all.

"Bikini," I say and then I stick my hand in my jeans and pull out a piece of my cotton pink underwear for him to see.

"Nice," he says. "Okay. I gotta roll. I've got karate." Then he makes his hand into a fist and knocks it with Eddie and Jonathan's.

Then he turns to me and gives me his fist to knock with.

"See you, tomorrow, *Pinky*," he says.

I make my hand a fist and knock knuckles with him.

"Right on," he says and then he leaves the playground and walks home.

Jonathan and Eddie go back to the court and keep playing basketball and they don't seem to mind at all that I am still hanging out with them.

I suck the rest of my lollipop and contemplate my fate.

I know one thing for sure.

Orange is definitely my new favourite flavor.

Team Men

BY EMMA DONOGHUE

THAT WAS THE kindest thing Saul could say about anyone, that he was a real team man. "Jonathan," he used to tell his son over their bacon, eggs, sausage, and beans, "a striker's not put up front for personal glory. You'll only end up a star player if you keep your mind on playing for the good of the team. Them as tries to be first shall be last and vice versa."

Jon just kept on eating his toast.

Saul King believed in fuel, first thing in the morning, when there was plenty of time ahead to burn it up. "Breakfast like a legend, dine like a journeyman, and sup like a sub." That made him cackle with laughter.

The boy was just sixteen and nearly six feet tall. Headers were his strong point. When the ball sailed down to him he could feel his neck tighten and every bit of force in his body surge toward the hard plate at the front of his skull. The crucial thing was to be ready for the ball, to meet all its force and slam it back into the sky. On good days Jon felt hard and shiny as a mirror. He knew that if the planet Mars came falling down, he could meet it head-on and rocket it into the next galaxy.

But by now he had learned to pay no attention to his dad before a game. If Jon let the warnings get through to him, he couldn't swallow. If he didn't eat enough, he found himself knackered at halftime. If he flagged, he missed passes, and the goalmouth seemed ten miles away. If the team lost, his dad took it personally and harder than a coach should. Once when Jon fluffed a penalty kick, Saul hadn't spoken a word to him for a week.

"Nerves of steel," the graying man had said finally, as they sat at opposite ends of the table waiting for Mum to bring a fresh pot of tea.

Jon's fork clinked against his plate. "What's that, Dad?"

"If a striker hasn't got nerves of steel when they're needed, he's no right to take a penalty kick at all."

His son listened and learned. As if he had a choice.

The lads were already having a kickabout on the pitch when the Kings drove up. Saul got out; the car door in his hand as he watched the lads over his shoulder. "Well, well," he said, "who have we here?"

One unfamiliar coppery head, breaking away from the pack.

"Oh, yeah, Shaq said he might bring someone from school," Jon mentioned, hauling his kit bag out of the back seat.

"Now there's a pair of legs," breathed Saul. He and his son stool a foot apart, watching the new boy run. He was runt-sized, but he moved as sleekly as cream.

"A winger?" hazarded Jon.

"We'll see," said Saul mysteriously.

The new boy, Davy, turned out to be seventeen. Up close he didn't look so short; his limbs were narrow but pure muscle. The youngest of eight—one of those big rackety Irish families. His face went red as strawberries when he ran, but he never seemed to get out of breath—his laugh got a bit hoarser, that was all. He was a cunning bastard on the pitch. Beside him Jon felt lumbering and huge.

In the dressing room after that first practice, Davy played his guitar as if it were electric. He sang along, confidently raucous.

"Best put a bit of meat on those bones," observed Saul, and

loaded Davy down with five bags of high-protein glucose supplement. It turned out Davy lived just down the road from the Kings, so Saul insisted on giving him a lift home.

After a fortnight Davy was pronounced a real team man. He was to be the new striker. Jon was switched to midfield. "It's not a demotion," his father repeated. "This is a team, not a bloody corporation."

Jon looked out the car window and thought about playing on a team where the coach wouldn't be his dad, wouldn't shove him from one position to another just to prove a point about not giving his son any special treatment. Jon visualized himself becoming a legend in some sport Saul King had never tried, could hardly spell, even—badminton, maybe, or curling, or luge.

The thing was, though, all he'd ever wanted to play was football.

Jon was over the worst of his sulks by the next training session. He had every reason to hate this Davy, but it didn't happen. The boy was a born striker, Jon had to admit. It would have been nonsense to put him anywhere else on the pitch. He wasn't a great header of the ball, but he was magic with his feet.

And midfield had its own satisfactions, Jon found. "You lot are the big cog in the team's engine," Saul told them solemnly. "You slack off for a second, the game will fall apart."

Pounding along with the ball at his feet, Jon saw Davy out of the corner of his eye. "With ya!" Jon passed the ball sideways, and Davy took it without even looking. Only after he'd scored did he spin round to give Jon his grin.

"Your dad's a laugh. I mean," Davy corrected himself in the shower, "he's all right. He knows a lot."

"Not half as much as he pretends," said Jon, soaping his armpits.

"Is it true what Shaq says about him, that he got to the semifinal of the 1979 FA cup?"

Jon nodded, sheepish.

Davy, under the stream of water, sprayed like a whale. "Fuck. What did he play?"

"Keeper." On impulse Jon stepped closer to Davy's ear. "Dad'd flay me if he knew I told you this. He's never forgiven himself."

"What? What?" The boy's eyes were green as scales.

"He flapped at it. The winning goal."

Davy sucked his breath in. It made a clean musical note.

• • •

In October the days shortened. One foul wet afternoon, Saul made them run fifteen laps of the field before they even started, and by the time he finally blew the whistle, they had mud to their waists and it was too dark to see the ball. Naz tripped over Jon's foot and landed on his elbow. "You big ape," moaned Naz. "You lanky fucking ape-man."

The other lads thought this was very funny.

"You can't let them get to you," Davy said casually, afterwards, while they were cooling down.

"Who?" said Jon, as if from a million miles away.

Davy shrugged. "Any of them. Anyone who calls you names."

Jon chewed his lip.

"I've got five big brothers," Davy added, when he and Jon were sitting in the back of the car, counting their bruises. "And my sisters are even worse. They've always taken the piss out of me. One of them called me the Little Stain till she got married."

A grin loosened Jon's jaw. He stared out the window at his father, who was collecting the training cones.

"Just ignore the lads and remember what a good player you are."

"Maybe I'm not," said Jon, looking down into Davy's red hair.

"Maybe you're what?" Davy let out a yelp of laughter. "Jon-boy, you're the best. You've got a perfect footballing brain, and you're a sweet crosser of the ball."

Jon was glad of the twilight then. Blood sang in his cheeks.

Davy came round every couple of days now. Mrs. King often asked him to stop for dinner. "That boy's not getting enough at home," she observed darkly. But Jon thought Davy looked all right as he was.

Jon's little sister, Michaela, sat beside Davy at the table whenever she got the chance, even if she did call him Shortarse. She was only fifteen, but she looked old enough. As she was always reminding Jon, girls mature two years faster.

Davy ended up bringing Michaela to the local Halloween Club Night and Jon brought her friend Tasmin. While the girls were queuing up for chips afterwards, Davy followed Jon into the loos. Afterward, Jon could never be sure who'd started messing round; it just happened. It was sort of a joke and sort of a dare. In a white stall with a long crack in the wall they unzipped their jeans. They kept looking down; they didn't meet each other's eyes.

It was over in two minutes. It took longer to stop laughing.

When they got back to the girls, the chips had gone cold and Michaela wanted to know what was so funny. Jon couldn't think of anything, but Davy said it was just an old Princess Diana joke. Tasmin said in that case they could keep it to themselves because she didn't think it was very nice to muck around with the dead.

After Halloween, some people said Davy was going out with Michaela. Jon didn't know what that meant exactly. He didn't think Davy and Michaela did stuff together, anyway. He didn't know what to think.

Saul King expressed no opinion on the matter. But he'd started laying into Davy at practice. "Mind your back! Mind your house!" he bawled, hoarse, "Keep them under pressure!"

Davy said nothing, just bounced around, grinning as usual.

"Where's your bleeding eyes?"

"Somebody's not the golden boy anymore," commented Peter to Naz under his breath.

Afterwards, Saul said he had errands to do in town, so Jon and Davy could walk home for once.

"Your dad's being a bit of a prick these days," commented Davy as they turned the first corner.

"Don't call him that," said Jon.

"But he is one."

Jon shook his heavy head. "Don't call him my dad, I mean."

"Oh."

The silence stretched between them. "It's like the honey jar," said Jon.

Davy glanced up. His lashes were like a cat's.

"I was about three, right, and I wanted a bit of honey from the jar, but he said no. He didn't put the jar away or anything—just said no and left it sitting there about six inches in front of me. So the minute he was out of the room I opened it up and stuck my spoon in, of course. And I swear he must have been waiting because he was in and had that spoon snatched out of my hand before it got near my face."

"What's wrong with honey?" asked Davy, bewildered.

"Nothing."

"I thought it was good for you."

"It wasn't anything to do with the honey," said Jon, dry-throated. "He just wanted to win."

Davy walked beside him, mulling it over.

They went the long way, through the park. When they passed a gigantic yew tree, Davy turned his head to Jon and grinned like a shark.

Without needing to say a word, they ducked and crawled underneath the tree. The branches hung down around them like curtains. Nobody could have seen what they were up to; a passerby wouldn't even have known they were there. Jon forgot to be embarrassed. He did a sliding tackle on Davy and toppled him on to the soft damp ground. "Man on!" yelped Davy, pretending to be afraid. They weren't cold any more. They moved with sleek grace this time. It was telepathic. It was perfect timing.

• • •

"For Christ's sake, stay onside," Saul bawled at his team.

Davy's trainers blurred like Maradona's, Jon thought. The boy darted round the pitch confusing the defenders, playing to the imaginary crowd.

"Don't bother trying to impress us with the fancy footwork, Irish," screamed Saul into the wintry wind, "just try kicking the ball. This is footie, not bloody Riverdance."

Afterwards in the showers, Jon watched the hard curve of Davy's shoulder. He wanted to touch it, but Naz was three feet away. He took a surreptitious glance at his friend's face, but it was shrouded in steam.

Saul never gave Jon and Davy a lift home from practice anymore. He said the walk was good exercise and Lord knew they could do with it.

"I don't know why, but your dad is out to shaft me," said Davy, on the long walk home.

"No, he's not," said Jon weakly.

"Is so. He said he thought I might make less of a fool of myself in defense."

"Defense?" repeated Jon, shrill. "That's bollocks. Last Saturday's match, you scored our only goal."

"You set it up for me. Saul said only a paraplegic could have missed it."

Jon tried to remember the shot. He couldn't tell who'd done what. On a good day, he and Davy moved like one player, thought the same thing at the same split second.

"I don't suppose there's any chance he knows about us?"

Jon was so shocked he stopped walking. He had to put his hand on the nearest wall or he'd have fallen. The pebble dash was cold against his fingers. *Us*, he thought. There was an *us*. An *us* his dad might know about. "No way," he said at last, hoarsely.

Jon knew there were rules, even if they'd never spelled them out. He and Davy were sort of mates and sort of something else. They didn't waste time talking about it. In one way it was like football—the sweaty tussle of it, the heart-pounding thrill—and in another way, it was like a game played on Mars, with unwritten rules and a different gravity.

The afternoons were getting colder. On Bonfire Night they took the risk and did it in Jon's room. The door had no lock. They kept the stereo turned up very loud so there wouldn't be any suspicious silences. Outside, the bangers went off at intervals like bombs. Jon's head pounded with noise and terror. It was the best time yet.

Afterwards, when they were slumped in opposite corners of the room, looking like two ordinary post-match players, Jon turned down the music. Davy said, out of nowhere, "I was thinking of telling the folks."

"Telling them what?" asked Jon before thinking. Then he understood, and his stomach furled into a knot.

"You know. What I'm like." Davy let out a mad chuckle.

"You're not . . ." Jon's voice trailed off.

"I am, you know." Davy still sounded as if he were talking

about the weather. "I've had my suspicions for years. I thought I'd give it a try with your sister, but *nada*, to be honest."

Jon thought he was going to throw up. "Would you tell them about us?"

"Only about me," Davy corrected him. "Name no names, and all that."

"You never would?"

"I'll have to sometime, won't I?"

"Why?" asked Jon, choking.

"Because it's making me nervous," explained Davy lightly, "and I don't play well when I'm nervous. I know my family is going to freak out of their tiny minds whenever I tell them, so I might as well get it over with."

He was brave, Jon thought. But he had to be stopped. "Listen, you mad bastard," said Jon fiercely, "you can't tell anyone."

Davy sat up and straightened his shoulders. He looked small, but not all that young; his face was an adult's. "Is that meant to be an order? You sound like your dad," he added, with a hint of mockery.

"He'll know," whispered Jon. "Your parents'll guess it's me. They'll tell my dad."

"They won't. They'll be too busy beating the tar out of me."

"My dad's going to find out."

"How will he?" said Davy reasonably.

"He just will," stuttered Jon. "He'll kill me. He'll get me by the throat and never let go."

"Bollocks," said Davy too lightly. "We're not kids anymore. The sky's not going to fall in on us. You're just shitting your shorts at the thought of anyone calling you a faggot, aren't you?"

"Don't say that."

"Touchy, aren't you? It's only a word."

"We're not, anyway," he told Davy coldly. "That's not what we are."

The boy's mouth crinkled with amusement. "Oh, so what are we then?"

"We're mates," said Jon through a clenched throat.

One coppery eyebrow went up.

"Mates who mess around a bit."

"Fag-got! Fag-got!" Davy sang the words quietly.

Jon's hand shot out to the stereo and turned it way up to drown him out.

Next door, Michaela started banging on the wall. "*Jonathan!*" she wailed.

He turned it down a little, but kept his hand on the knob. "Get out," he said.

Davy stared back at him blankly. Then he reached for his jacket and got up in one fluid movement. He looked like a scornful god. He looked like nothing could ever knock him down.

Jon avoided Davy all week. He walked home from training sessions while Davy was still in the shower. In the back of his mind, he was preparing a contingency plan. *Deny everything. Laugh. Say the sick pervert made it all up.*

Nobody else seemed to notice the two friends weren't on speaking terms. Everyone was preoccupied with the big match on Saturday.

At night Jon gripped himself like a drowning man clinging to a spar.

Saturday came at last. The pitch was muddy and badly cut up before they even started. The other team were thugs, especially an enormous winger with a mustache. From the kickoff, Saul's team played worse than they'd ever done before. The left-back crashed into his central defender, whose nose bled all down his shirt. Jon moved like he was shackled.

Whenever he had to pass the ball to Davy, it fell short or went wide by a mile. It was as if there was a shield around the red-haired boy and nothing could get through. Davy was caught offside three times in the first half. Then, when Jon pitched up a loose ball on the edge of his own penalty area, one of the other team's forwards big-toed a fluke shot into the top right-hand corner.

"You're running round like blind men," Saul told his team at half-time, with sorrow and contempt.

By the start of the second half, the rain was falling unremittingly. The fat winger stood on Peter's foot, and the ref never saw a thing. "Look," bawled Peter, trying to pull his shoe off to show the marks of the studs.

The other team found this hilarious. "Wankers! Faggots!" crowed the fat boy.

Rage fired up Jon's thudding heart, stoking his muscles. He would have liked to take the winger by the throat and press his thumbs in till they met vertebrae. What was it Saul always used to tell him? *No son of mine ever gets himself sent off for temper.* Jon made himself turn and jog away. *No son of mine,* said the voice in his head.

Naz chipped the ball high over the defense. Jon was there first, poising himself under the flight of the ball. It was going to be a beautiful header. It might even turn the match around.

"Davy's," barked Davy, jogging backwards toward Jon.

Jon kept his eyes glued to the falling ball. "Jon's."

"It's mine!" Davy repeated, at his elbow, crowding him.

"Fuck off!" He didn't look. He shouldered Davy away, harder than he meant to. Then all of a sudden Jon knew how it was going to go. He wasn't ready to meet the ball; he didn't believe he could do it. He lost his balance, and the ball came down on the side of his head and crushed him into the mud.

Jon had whiplash.

Saul came home from the next training session and said Davy was off the team.

"You cunt," said Jon.

His father stared, slack-jawed. Michaela's fork froze halfway to her mouth. "Jonathan!" appealed their mother.

Above his foam whiplash collar, Jon could feel his face burn. But he opened his mouth and it all spilled out. "You're not a coach, you're a drill sergeant. You picked Davy to bully because you know he's going to be a better player than you ever were. And now you've kicked him off the team just to prove you can. So much for team-fucking-spirit!"

"Jonathan." His father's face was dark, unreadable. "It was the lad who dropped out. He's quit the team and he's not coming back."

One afternoon at the end of a fortnight, Davy came round. Jon was on his own in the living room, watching an old France 1998 video of England versus Argentina. He thought Davy looked different—baggy-eyed, older somehow.

Davy stared at the television. "Has Owen scored yet?"

"Ages ago. They're nearly at penalties." Jon kept his eyes on the screen.

Davy dropped his bag by the sofa but didn't sit down, didn't take his jacket off. In silence they watched the agonizing shoot-out.

When it was over, Jon hit rewind. "If Beckham hadn't got himself sent off, we'd have demolished them," he remarked.

"In your dreams," said Davy. They watched the flickering figures. After a long minute he added, "I've been meaning to come round, actually, to say, you know, sorry and all that."

"It's nothing much, just a bit of whiplash," said Jon, deliberately obtuse. He put his hand to his neck, but his fingers were blocked by the foam collar.

"You'll get over it. No bother."

"Yeah," said Jon bleakly. "So," he added, not looking at Davy, "did you talk to your parents?"

"Yeah." The syllable was flat. "Don't worry, your name didn't come up."

"I didn't—"

"Forget it," interrupted Davy softly. He was staring at the video as it rewound; a green square covered in little frenzied figures who ran backwards, fleeing from the ball.

That subject seemed closed. "I hear you're not playing, these days," said Jon.

"That's right," said Davy, more briskly. "Thought I should get down to the books for a while, before my A-levels."

Jon stared at him.

"I'm off to college next September, touch wood." Davy rapped on the coffee table. "I've already got an offer of a place in Law at Lancaster but I'll need two Bs and an A."

Law? Jon nodded, then winced as his neck twinged. So much he'd never known about Davy, never thought to ask. "You could sign up again in the summer, though, after your exams, couldn't you?" he asked, as neutrally as he could.

There was a long second's pause before Davy shook his head. "I don't think so, Jon-boy."

So that was it, Jon registered. Not a proper ending. More like a match called off because of a hailstorm or because the star player just walked off the pitch.

"I mean, I'll miss it, but when it comes down to it, it's only a game, eh? . . . Win or lose," Davy added after a moment.

Jon couldn't speak. His eyes were wet, blinded.

Davy picked up his bag. Then he did something strange. He swung down and kissed Jon on the lips, for the first time, on his way out the door.

Pencils

BY SARA WILKINSON

"WHY D'YOU HAVE all those pencils anyway?" Trace demanded in her loud, playing-to-an-audience voice. "It's not like you even *use* them. Who in their right mind needs seven identical pencils?"

A titter ran round the room and all eyes watched for the inevitable action that would follow.

Trace jabbed at the pencils so that they scattered out of line and skidded across the desk.

"It makes me mad to just *look* at them!" she announced and swept them off the desk. They flew helter-skelter over the wooden floor and rolled under the desks. Trace glowered at me defiantly.

Like a trained monkey I did what was expected of me and collected them silently, sweating all down my back and trembling in case the lead had broken inside one of them. I sat down in front of the desk and pulled my chair in as far as possible and slowly wiggled each lead. Luckily none of them was seriously damaged, but I had to sharpen them again as one had lost the tip of its point—I needed them all to be the same length, exactly.

Pencil sharpening calms me down, although it obviously has the opposite effect on Trace. I get agitated easily and I'm not considered quite "normal" (although I think the definition of "normal' is often quite abnormal). For instance, I like to put everything in place and have routines to feel secure and I don't like people much. They don't understand me and I certainly don't understand them.

"Ergh!" Trace groaned in exasperation and flounced off with her little group of chosen friends. The drones—the useless males—just stand about looking on with bored, expressionless faces. Out of lesson time they stick to the wall day after day doing nothing and hoping that some desperate girl will fling herself at them, wanting to get laid. I have no contact at all with the drones.

Ed on the other hand is a different kind of male, the kind that all the girls fancy—big, blond, beautiful and brainless—and is geared up to becoming a professional footballer. And he is going out with Trace. Everyone wants to be in the alpha group with Ed and Trace. I am allowed on the very edge of the group "just for comedy value." I know this because I can hear them discussing it and laughing at me (for some reason, they think that because I wear glasses and keep to myself that my hearing's impaired). I know what "comedy value" means, of course, but I have never found anything funny or comic in my life. Why *do* people laugh?

"Oh, let him sit at our table," said Trace. "He's so—like—weird. Though he makes me mad, I like him 'cos he's different. I like to try and wind him up till he doesn't know what to do. Mostly I can't get a reaction but sometimes he explodes and then boing! He's off like a manic spring."

"Well, he just pisses me off," said Ed, "but we'll keep him just for comedy value. (There's that expression, you see.) He fancies you anyway; he'll do anything you tell him."

I'm known by many names at school: Saddo, Loser, Weirdo, Geek, Nerd, or Freak. I don't usually answer but if I do, I'll answer to any of these names—it's easier than making a fuss, and the teachers pretend they don't hear how everyone talks to me. In fact, the teachers are just as bad. If they want to ask me a question they just point at me, and say, "You!" No one ever asks me if I have a real name.

• • •

There's nothing odd about all of this. I'm completely used to it. It's pleasantly predictable, in fact.

Even when I was very young I didn't often speak, so my parents didn't speak to me much either. Whenever I *did* speak they looked at me as if they couldn't understand a word I was saying, or perhaps they couldn't be bothered to listen.

When I was about eight-years-old, my father decided to make a bit of an effort with me and see if he could interest me in making things out of wood, like him. He took me out to his shed in the garden. I loved it in there—the smell of paint and creosote and the oily steel tools. I was desperate to explore everything behind this usually locked door.

And this is more or less how the conversation in the shed went. I know it's correct because I wrote it down after it happened. I'm always writing things down so that I can try to work out what people mean and why they say what they do.

"Let's start with a toy boat," he'd said.

"What for?" I'd asked. (I had no interest in toys or boats.)

"Because it's a nice first project to make and you can make some funnels and paint it. It'll be fun and we can do it together."

"I don't understand why it will be 'fun'. What does fun mean? The funnels won't really work. I don't need a toy boat. What would I *do* with it?"

"You can launch it on the pond and see if it floats," Dad had said.

"But of course it will float, we know already that it will float because it'll be made of wood, and wood floats. I want to see what's in that box instead," I'd said, climbing on a stool and grabbing a large dusty cardboard box and at the same time knocking a full bottle of whiskey off the shelf, which smashed on to the floor. Alcohol vapours filled the shed. I'd ignored this new smell because I didn't like it. I was more interested in the box.

"Wow!" I'd said, opening the box to reveal a large quantity of brand-new, best-quality HB graphite pencils.

"You useless little freak, look what you've done!" my father had shouted, staring at his shattered whiskey bottle and suddenly losing it. "You're no son of mine, you're bloody abnormal. Why the hell don't you want to make things and play like normal kids? What is it with you and pencils? You can't bloody well have my genes, you little misfit, you're nothing to do with me—I always thought your mother was up to no good!"

I'd lined up all the pencils along the workbench and counted them. One hundred and forty-four!

He'd stormed into the house and upstairs. I could see him through the bedroom window taking clothes out of the wardrobe.

So you see it was nine years ago that I found out that I was a freak, abnormal, and a misfit. That's quite a lot to discover all at once.

When we next heard from my father, he was living at the bottom of the road with a new woman and two new children. One day I saw the children close-up and they were both wearing glasses like me and had my prominent nose and would have had my protruding teeth, only they wore braces, so I think my father was wrong about the genes. They were clearly only a year or two younger than me so I think it must have been him who'd been up to no good, not Mum. One was in the year below me at school and both were obviously drones so I had no interest in them.

I still share the house with my mother and we still only speak when necessary. I think, along with everyone else, she's probably forgotten my name by now. And from when Dad first left, I was capable of looking after myself. I could cook eggs, buy my clothes, put them in the washing machine, and get myself to school.

Now I keep the kitchen spotless, scrubbing the floor and work surfaces and cleaning the cooker once a week. I like to try out new recipes from my *Cooking for One* cookbook. My mother keeps the fridge and cupboards well stocked. One day, a noticeboard appeared on the wall with a pencil attached by a string so that I could write down anything I needed. Once a year, a wrapped-up, usually pointless-looking toy, book, or game has been left on the kitchen table for my birthday. The *Cooking for One* cookbook is the only really useful thing my mother has ever given me. Our routine hasn't changed in the last nine years, and the only other people who have entered the house are the meter man and the plumber.

The best thing about my father going to live with the new woman and my half-brothers is that I have his workshop to myself. When he moved out he left everything behind in the shed without a second thought. I have no more interest in making boxes and bowls than I had in making toy boats, but his tools and large box of pencils are another matter. The smell of cedar-wood pencils and the smell of the oily precision tools make me feel wild with desire and even give me exciting feelings in my trousers. I used to spend hours laying out the tools and measuring the length of everything in the workshop and writing the results down in my notebook.

When I was eleven, I noticed a little brown leather suitcase behind the shed door. It smelled musty and was scuffed and

had tarnished brass catches that snapped open and shut. I
can't think why I'd never noticed it before. From that day on
I have always carried the suitcase to school, and everywhere
else come to that. Every morning I pack my seven identical
pencils, my sharpener, steel rule and engineer's try square.
Recently I added a pair of callipers. My father used them to
check the diameter of bowls and candlesticks that he made on
his lathe, but I have other ideas.

• • •

At the beginning of every day when I arrive at school I
sharpen my seven pencils and lay them in a perfect line on my
desk, each one exactly the same length as the others and the
same distance apart, meticulously measuring with the steel
rule and making sure they are square with the edge of the
desk using the engineer's square. I keep the same seven
pencils until they are down to 75 mm long and then I replace
them with seven more pencils from the box in the shed. It's
not an obsession; it is just something I do.

   School is tedious but I work hard at math on my own at
home. Although there are a few other fairly bright kids at
school, I don't think there has ever been any as clever as me.
The drones make a point of not being clever on purpose. And
the girls are really only drone-fodder so I ignore them—
except, of course, for Trace.

   It takes a lot to distract me from my pencils, but it's a fact
that I'm nearly as interested in Trace's breasts as I am in them.
I desperately want to discover whether her breasts are perfect
or not. I have an awful suspicion that they might not be, and
that one might be bigger than the other. This worries me a
lot. I think about it so much that sometimes I can't even
concentrate on my math.

   Once when Ed went out of the room, Trace seized the

346

opportunity to tease me. First she slowly undid the buttons of her blouse, revealing a pale pink lacy bra with a deep-pink rosebud in the middle, then she snatched one of my lined-up pencils—and plunged it behind the rosebud and down her cleavage and danced around the room.

"Come and get it, Weirdo!" she taunted in a sing-song voice. "No hands allowed!"

Having only six pencils lined up on my desk brought me out in a cold sweat—I could feel it dripping down my back, down my bottom, and down my legs into my socks. On the one hand I wanted to get my pencil back as quickly as possible, but on the other hand I wanted to linger over Trace's breasts to try and gauge which breast, if either, was larger. I rushed toward her, tripping over a chair leg in my haste, and lunged at Trace's cleavage, with everyone (except the drones) shouting and whistling. I grabbed the pencil with my teeth and then went into a trance-like stare. Unfortunately I was so close to Trace's breasts that instead of the wonderful view I'd anticipated, all I could see were two large fuzzy pink blobs with what looked disconcertingly like one rose-colored nipple between them. I began to feel trembly and stirrings in my trousers.

"Hurry up, Perv!" (a new name to add to the others) Trace demanded.

"Errgh! Gross! How *could* you!" the girls squealed. The drones stayed stuck to their wall without a sound.

I slunk back to my desk and placed the pencil back safely with the others, after checking for damage (luckily there wasn't any). But I was none the wiser about Trace's breasts. Probably that is just as well, as the thought of any lack of symmetry about her—I shudder at the thought of the misplaced nipple—is too unsettling. However, I think it's only fair at this point to reveal a little secret of my own.

Imagine my horror when one day I noticed, while standing naked in front of the full-length bathroom mirror, that my left testicle hung a little lower than my right. I panicked and tried to prise it up but of course it just dropped down to its previous level again. I realized that I'd have to devise a plan to rectify the matter.

Every night I tape the testicle, or rather that side of my scrotum, up so that it is level with the right side in the hope that it will eventually cure itself. I read that, like uneven breast sizes (and feet, but I have no interest in feet other than for their normal use), a lower-hanging testicle, especially a left one, is entirely "normal". Eighty percent fall into this category. Why aren't the remaining twenty percent the "normal" ones? Why isn't perfection considered normal and imperfection abnormal? What reason can there possibly be for one testicle to be lower than the other? And why would one breast decide to grow larger than the other? I start applying the tape even more tightly, giving it an extra hard yank.

• • •

Our school is in the north of England on the edge of a small town surrounded by moorland with sheep and rocky outcrops and crags. The area is famous for its beauty, but most of the kids at the school think the town is boring, and the hills are even more boring, and so on Saturdays they head for the city. I like walking in the hills and sitting reading on the rocks. Sometimes I take my binoculars to look at the other people on the hills.

One day, during a study period, Trace and others were sitting squashed together on a metal table, kicking the table legs monotonously. I was doing calculus at another table, when Trace—looking out of the window—suddenly said,

"What's up them hills?" I couldn't help looking up at the window along with the others.

"They're just hills," said Ed.

"Anyone been up 'em?" asked Trace, after a pause.

(A longer pause.) "What for?" said Ed.

The drones looked round at me.

"Hey, what about you, Freako? You been up 'em?" demanded Trace, staring at me. I nodded my head and looked down. I hated being stared at, even by Trace.

"Why?" asked Trace. Here we go, I thought. Now she'd started on me I knew she wasn't going to let go.

"To walk," I mumbled, without meeting her stare.

"Along with all those other saddos who wear long woolly socks and hats and stupid clothes and *really* big unsexy boots and carry maps and smile at each other all the time like they're in one great big la-la club together?" asked Trace.

"There's no compulsory dress code," I said. "You can wear what you like."

"Good, 'cos *I* want to walk up them hills, too," said Trace. "And you'll have to come with me, Freako, so I don't get lost."

"What, hold on, you can't do that Trace. Not with *him*!" groaned Ed. "Say someone sees you?"

Trace ignored him and continued to stare at me. I naturally assumed that she was taunting me again, but my heart beat loudly as I hoped beyond all hope that she really meant it, that she really wanted to be with me—just me—up in the hills. I started fantasizing about making egg sandwiches. I'd never met anyone out of school on a Saturday before, let alone Trace, and I felt a stirring in my trousers again, which pulled at the taped-up testicle.

"Ten o'clock in the car park, at the sign to the moors—and don't be late," she added sharply. "And that goes for you too,"

349

she ordered Ed, bursting my bubble, virtual egg sandwiches flying out from my thoughts in an instant.

At ten to ten the next morning I was waiting with my case (containing three egg and cress sandwiches, among other things—yes, I did make them after all, even for Ed), near the signpost pointing the way to the moorland path.

It was a bright but slightly chilly day, and it had rained overnight so I had taken the precaution of wearing my walking boots and an anorak with my shorts, but left the woolly bobble-hat at home in case it offended Trace. At five to ten Ed appeared, wearing over-white squeaky trainers, jeans, and an Alpine fleece. He grunted to me. We shuffled from foot to foot in embarrassment, as we had nothing to say to each other and wished the other one wasn't there. The shuffling went on for some time with each of us looking at his watch at intervals but not saying anything. Ten o'clock arrived and went and then ten past and twenty past. Perhaps Trace had no intention of coming and was just winding us up for a laugh, I thought. At half past, Ed was hopping mad and his shuffling had turned into a primitive kicking dance with some added backward and forward steps and some grunts thrown in.

"Where the hell is she?" he muttered crossly, glaring and looking round. I think he was checking that no one he knew could see him with me. He jabbed out a message on his mobile but got no reply.

Two minutes later a four-wheel drive with darkened windows swerved into the car park and a back door opened. A long, shapely, tanned leg appeared, followed by another one. Trace jumped out, her high blonde ponytail swishing behind her. She was wearing the tiniest pair of white shorts, a low-cut black T-shirt showing a perfect cleavage, and a little pair of slip-on shoes. Ed and I both stared at the cleavage. "Hi!" she waved. In her hand was a pink cord that was attached from her hand to something in the back of the car. She gave a little pull and a small creature with four tiny legs, a sparkly collar, and a ridiculous pink waistcoat appeared on the other end. She scooped it up and slammed the door. The car roared off in a cloud of dust.

"Oh my God, what the hell is *that*?" asked Ed.

"I think it is a diminutive dog," I answered.

Trace skipped toward us. "Meet Froufrou," she said.

"What the hell d'you bring that thing with you for?" asked Ed.

"'Cos it's a dog and dogs are s'posed to go outside, right? So I'm taking her outside. Froufrou's never had a walk before, she's—like—delicate, so you'd better carry her. Right?" Trace thrust Froufrou into one of Ed's large hands.

"Weirdo, I like the sexy white knees!" she said to me, staring at my thin white legs. "D'you like my tan?"

"It's great," I stammered, looking at the evenly colored golden cleavage.

"Out of a bottle, of course," she laughed, and bounded off up the path like a mountain goat.

"It's really nice up here," sighed Trace. She danced around with the delight of a small child and effortlessly climbed higher up the rocky path toward the crag on her long tanned legs. "Aaah, I love those cute little sheep, they look really cuddly," she said, pointing to the woolly black-faced moorland sheep who were staring at us warily. "And look at all them teeny little purple flowers like bells!"

"That's heather," I said.

"Heather's lucky, isn't it? We must all have some of this, then we'll always be lucky!" She bent down and picked little bunches of heather and stuck one enticingly down her cleavage.

"For you, Freako, so you can have a long and weird life,"

351

she said solemnly, pushing another sprig through my buttonhole. Then she ran back to Ed and Froufrou who were lagging behind. Ed was sulking at being left with the dog. "Look what I got!" she sang. She stuck some in Froufrou's collar. "Who's my gorgeous? You're my gorgeous, of course, Froufrou! And now you're gonna live a long time too, 'cos you've got your very own lucky heather," she announced while stroking the little dog's head.

"Here, Eddie, babe, this is for you so we'll have a lucky life together, just you and me—and, of course, little Froufrou." Trace laughed and tickled Froufrou under the chin, then stuck a sprig of heather through Ed's zip pull. "Look a bit happier about it," she pouted at him, stroking his face.

Ed ripped the heather out and chucked it down on the ground, before grabbing hers from her chest and chucking that down too.

"That's not very nice," said Trace, putting on a whiny little girl's voice. "Don't you want us to be lucky together?"

"Bloody superstition! I don't need no stupid lucky heather and nor do you!" he said angrily and stomped along in his too-white trainers, which by now had gathered large splotches of mud.

Ed looked foolish and cross at having to carry Froufrou, who in turn looked up adoringly at him with saucer eyes. He scowled back at her. Passing walkers stared at Ed, said hello politely, and then laughed at him behind his back.

"Even the really weirdo ones are staring at me, damn them—no, especially the weirdo ones—the saddos with beards and woolly hats and compasses. It's humiliating. I'm a footballer, for God's sake, not an effing pansy!" he muttered through gritted teeth.

We plodded on in silence on a narrow path alongside the edge of the crag. I was just wondering when we should stop and have the egg and cress sandwiches from my suitcase, when Ed suddenly exploded with anger.

"This rat-thing is meant to be a dog, right? And dogs are meant to walk, right?" he announced, looking like a thundercloud. "Okay, so let's see if it *can* walk. Right!"

He threw Froufrou down on the path in front of him. Froufrou propelled herself forward in a frenzy of excitement at her first taste of freedom, racing at full speed on her ridiculous tiny legs. As she'd never walked anywhere before in her life, she was unaware that if a path goes round a bend you have to go round with it. So Froufrou carried straight on instead.

Then Froufrou disappeared.

"You idiot!" Trace shrieked at Ed. "What've you done to my little Froufrou?"

"You take a look for me, Freako, I caaan't," she wailed at me.

I put my case down and looked over the edge. Something was hanging from a sparkly collar hooked over a branch like a Christmas decoration. Its legs were whirring like a tin toy's. The branch was several feet below the edge of the cliff, growing from a gnarled tree clinging on to the almost sheer rock face. Apart from a thin ledge a few feet below that, there was nothing but a long drop down to the ground below.

I would have liked to measure the distances accurately but unfortunately I didn't have the correct measuring equipment in my suitcase. I thought, I must remember to carry a plumb line in future, or perhaps I could throw pebbles down and count the seconds.

"It's sort of okay, she's still alive. You can look," I called to Trace.

Trace rushed to my side and peered down. "Froufrou, my baby, my little one, don't go away, we'll get you, I promise, babes," she shouted. Froufrou clearly couldn't go away even if she wanted to and she looked up at Trace with bulgy eyes—her throat constricted by the collar—and set up an eerie howl.

Ed joined us to look over the edge and let out uncontrollable guffaws. "Oh, man! God, that's the funniest thing I've ever seen. I must get this or no one's gonna believe it!" he said, crying with laughter and getting out his mobile. He snapped photos wildly. The wind started blowing ,and Froufrou slowly revolved half a circle one way and then half a circle back again. Round and back, round and back.

"Wow, thanks for showing me every angle, rat-thing," Ed called down. "I'll make a video too."

"How DARE you! You're *sick*! That's my bloody dog, my little baby!" screeched Trace. "And it's all *your* fault. You go and get her *now*. You put her down and you're the one who's meant to have the muscles. Well, use them!"

Ed laughed. "Whoa! You crazy or what?" he said. "No way! I'm not risking my life for that! It's only some dumb rat-dog! Just leave it. It'll die soon, then I'll come back and take some pics of its skeleton and we can have a laugh over them. Oh, wow, I've got a really great idea! We can put before and after pics up on the net—maybe even make some money or get famous from it."

"I hate you," she shrieked. "We're finished, you're dumped, get it? I'd rather go out with Freako than you!"

I knew I was probably grasping at straws, but I thought I could see an opportunity.

"I'll get her for you, Trace," I said.

"How the hell are *you* going to do that, Mr. White-kneed, skinny, I-so-don't-think-so superman?" she demanded, a little unnecessarily I thought, but I made allowances for her agitated state.

I snapped opened my suitcase and produced a short piece of jute rope.

"What the hell? You some kinda bloody perv carrying a piece of rope round with you in that case?" asked Trace. We all stared at the rope and could see that it clearly wasn't long enough to do anything with—except perhaps throttle someone, which Trace clearly wanted to do.

"It's just in case," I said, not meaning to make a pun.

"That's good, that is. I like that. Just in case," said Ed, but he didn't sound as if he liked it. He eyed it suspiciously.

Froufrou's howl had gone up an octave.

"You stupid bloody useless ignorant males," said Trace looking exasperated, "I'm ringing nine-nine-nine."

But there was no signal.

Trace began to cry.

"Run down and get help, Ed, *please*! You can run the fastest," she pleaded.

"After what you said to me? *No way*," he said decisively. "Remember, you dumped me."

"You're a disgusting, heartless, weirdo-sicko coward!" screamed Trace.

Froufrou's howl turned into a thin wail.

"I'll go," I said, hoping to redeem myself in Trace's eyes. I moved toward my case to close it before setting off when suddenly Trace pounced at it and grabbed one of my seven super-sharp pencils.

She jabbed hard at Ed with it. Jab, jab, jab. "Coward, coward, coward," she chanted.

"No one calls me a coward!" shouted Ed, taking a step backward to avoid her and trying to grab the pencil at the same time, but Trace was quicker. I stood transfixed, staring at my pencil.

She took a step forward. "Oh (jab) yes (jab) you (jab) are," she jabbed. How dare she use my pencil like that? I thought. I could see where they were heading so I rushed to the rescue and lunged forward.

I was aware of two things as I sat up on the edge of the path where I'd slipped over. The first was that I had been successful in my rescue: the pencil was safely in my hand and it was still in one piece—only the outer bit of the lead was broken off so I would be able to sharpen it.

The second thing I noticed, apart from the crows cawing as they circled round like vultures overhead, was the silence. Froufrou's wailing had completely stopped.

I got up slowly and replaced my pencil and the rope in my case and snapped it shut. Perhaps I ought to peer over the edge, I thought. Trace was lying on the ledge, face up. Her eyes were wide open with an unblinking expression of surprise. One tiny leg belonging to Froufrou was visible from underneath Trace. One of Trace's hands held a bunch of leaves, as if she'd been picking them for us like the lucky heather, and there was a long red scratch up her forearm. Up above her the branch, where the tin toy Froufrou had hung, was snapped in two. She must've tried to grab it, or Froufrou, on the way down.

My eyes traveled further down the rock face to a gully way below. I could see a shape that could be Ed but I couldn't be sure so I went back to my suitcase and got out the binoculars. I wiped the lenses with a cleaning cloth and carefully adjusted them to focus on the ground below. I didn't dwell long on the shape that had been Ed, as he looked a mess, which wasn't very pleasant. I replaced the binoculars and took out all three egg and cress sandwiches—the walk had given me an appetite—and snapped the suitcase shut again. Then I strode briskly down the path, munching the sandwiches and enjoying the clean air and the freedom of the great British outside.

When I reached the bottom I called the mountain rescue service from the public call box, although it didn't escape my notice that there was a certain irony in calling the "rescue service." Does one "rescue" a corpse or simply pick it up? I mused.

• • •

The police officer looked at me and gave a long sigh.

"Well, it's not quite normal, is it? Most people don't go round carrying measuring equipment, callipers, an engineer's square, and a short length of rope and so many sharp pencils when they walk up hills, do they? They carry sandwiches, water, maps, a compass, and the like in a rucksack."

"I'd already eaten my sandwiches and I am not like most people, Officer. 'Most people' are not going to be famous mathematicians, Officer, like *I* am," I answered.

"Slightly odd one in here, but I think he's telling the truth. There were no other witnesses to the incident—but I don't think this one's capable of making anything up—just a bit weird. And I wish he'd stop calling me 'Officer.' It's not bloody natural in a teenager," I overheard him say to another policeman outside the room.

I bristled. Of *course* I had told the truth—more or less. I told him that Trace slipped while hysterically looking down at her unfortunate dog and Ed tried to grab her to pull her away, but they both slipped and went over, quick as a flash. Well, I could hardly say that I had pushed them over the edge, killing them both while rescuing my pencil, could I?

• • •

"I understand," said the young mortuary assistant. "Of course, a quiet little moment won't do any harm although I'm not sure it's strictly allowed. Close to her, were you?"

"I was very close once," I replied, thinking of the time I retrieved my pencil from Trace's cleavage.

"Well, I'll be just outside. Don't hesitate to call me if you need me. There you are, she looks perfect, doesn't she?" said the mortuary assistant as he gently pulled back the sheet, exposing Trace's head. He stroked her hair, patted my arm, and then left the room. I heard the door click shut after him. Luckily Trace's eyes were closed so she couldn't look at me with accusing eyes. I imagined her suddenly sitting up and saying, "So what're you going to do to me now, Perv? Not that I can do anything to stop you!"

I glanced at the closed door then folded the sheet down to Trace's waist, exposing her beasts. I surveyed them carefully, then I put my suitcase flat on the floor and opened the brass catches as quietly as I could and removed the pair of callipers. I carefully adjusted them and measured the left breast width-wise between the callipers' pincers and then I placed them over the right breast. It was a full 50 millimeters smaller. I smiled.

Then I covered Trace up to her neck again and put the callipers back into the suitcase. I had just snapped it shut when there was a light tap on the door.

The door opened and the mortuary assistant's head popped round.

"Said your goodbyes?" he asked.

"Oh, yes, this is closure for me," I answered.

"Would you like to say goodbye to your other friend?" the mortuary assistant asked.

"What other friend?" I asked, feeling a little puzzled.

"Edward, of course," he said.

"Oh, no, no!" I reply in horror. I'd already forgotten about Ed and the thought of seeing him again was very distasteful.

I mumbled my thanks and set off quickly for home.

So she was flawed, I thought. I was right all along. I no longer have to think of Trace's breasts—I can put them out of my mind for ever. Closure. I can put the callipers back in the shed and concentrate on my mathematics.

"Froufrou! I'm home!" I call as I walk through the front door. Froufrou runs yapping toward me. Yes, believe it or not, Froufrou had been dragged out alive but a bit squashed from beneath Trace. I thought it my duty to take her in and we get on very well together, even though she has a little problem and will have to sleep on incontinence pads indefinitely due to her trauma.

I go into the bathroom and stand in front of the full-length mirror. Two sprigs of lucky heather, Froufrou's and mine, are stuck with tape to the corner of it.

I drop my trousers and pants and carefully peel off the tape from around my left testicle.

"Perfect, it's worked!" I think, looking at the reflection of my symmetrically hanging scrotum.

Yours Truly

A. M. HOMES

I'M HIDING IN the linen closet writing letters to myself. This is the place where no one knows I am, where I can think without thinking about what anyone else would think, or at least, it's quiet. I don't want to scare anyone, but things can't go on like this.

Until today I could still go into the living room and talk to my mother's Saturday morning Fat Club. I could say, "Hi, how are you? That's a very nice dress. Magenta's such a good color, it hides the hips. Nice shoes, too. I would never have thought of bringing pink and green together like that." I could pretend to be okay, but that's part of the problem.

In here, pressed up against the towels, the sheets, the heating pad, it's clear that everything is not hunky-dory. I've got one of those Itty Bitty Book Lights and I'm making notes.

Today is Odessa's day. At any minute she might turn the knob and let the world, disguised as daylight, come flooding in. She might do that and never know what she's done. She'll open the door and her eyes will get wide. She'll look at me and say, "Lord." She'll say, "You could have given me a heart attack." And I'll think, *Yes, I could have, but I'm having one myself and there isn't room for two in the same place at the same time.* She'll look at my face and I'll have to look at the floor. She won't know that having someone look directly at me, having

360

someone expect me to look at her, causes a sharp pain that begins in my eyes, ricochets off my skull, and in the end makes my entire skeleton shake. She won't know that I can't look at anything except the towels without being overcome with emotion. She won't know that at the sight of another person I weep; I wish to embrace and be embraced, and then to kill. She won't get that I'm dangerous.

Odessa will open the door and see me standing with this tiny light, clipped to the middle shelf, with the pad of paper on top of some extra blankets, with two extra pencils sticking out of the space between the bath sheets and the Turkish towels. She'll see all this and ask, "Are you all right?" I won't be able to answer. I can't tell her why I'm standing in a closet filled with enough towels to take a small town to the beach. I won't say, *I'm not all right. God help me, I'm not.* I will simply stand here, resting my arm over my notepad like a child taking a test, trying to make it difficult for cheaters to get their work done.

Odessa will do the talking. She'll say, "Well, if you could excuse me, I need clean sheets for the beds." I'll move over a bit. I'll twist to the left so she can get to the twin and queen sizes. I'm willing to move for Odessa. I can put one foot on top of the other. I'll do anything for her as long as I don't have to put my feet on to the gray carpet in the hall. I can't. I'm not ready. If I put a foot out there too early, everything will be lost.

Odessa sometimes asks me, "Which sheets do you want on your bed?" She knows I'm particular about these things. She knows her color combinations—dots and stripes together— attack me in my sleep. Sometimes I get up in the middle of the night, pull the sheets off the bed, throw them into the hall, and return to sleep. She will ask me what I want and I'll point to the plain white ones, the ones that seem lighter, cleaner than all the others. Odessa reaches for the sheets and in the instance when they're in her hand, but still in the closet, I press my face into them. I press my face into the pile of sheets, into Odessa's hands underneath. I won't feel her skin—her fingers—only cool, clean fabric against my cheek. I inhale deeply as if there were a way to draw the sheets into my lungs, to hold the linen inside me. I breathe and take my head away. Odessa will pull her hands out of the closet and ask, "Do you want the door closed?" I nod. I turn away, draw in my breath, and make myself flat. She closes the door.

• • •

I'm hiding in the linen closet sending memos to myself. It's getting complicated. Odessa knows I'm here. She knows but she won't tell anybody. She won't go running into the living room and announce, "Jody's locked herself into the linen closet and she won't come out."

Odessa won't go outside and look for my father. She won't find him pulling weeds on the hill behind the house. Odessa won't tell him, "She's in there with paper, pencils, and that little light you gave her for Christmas." She won't say anything. Odessa understands that this is the way things sometimes are. She'll change the sheets on all the beds, serve the Fat Club ladies their cottage cheese and cantaloupe, and then she'll go downstairs into the bathroom and take a few sips from the bottle of Johnnie Walker she keeps there.

I'm hiding in the closet with my life suspended. I'm hiding and I'm scared to death. I want to come clean, to see myself clearly, in detail, like a hallucination, a deathbed vision, a Kodacolor photograph. I need to know if I'm alive or dead.

I'm hiding in the linen closet and I want to introduce myself to myself. I need to like what I see. If I am really as horrible as I feel, I will spontaneously combust, leaving a small heap of ashes that can be picked up with the Dustbuster. I will explode myself in a flash of fire, leaving a letter of most profuse apology.

Through the wall I hear my mother's Fat Club ladies laugh. I hear the rattle of the group and the gentle tinkling of the individual. It's as though I have more than one pair of ears. Each voice enters in a different place, with a different effect.

I hear them and realize they're laughing for me. They're celebrating the fact that I can no longer pretend. There are tears in my eyes. I'm saying thank you and goodbye. I'm writing it down because I can't simply go out there and stand at the edge of the dining room table until my mother looks up from her copy of the *Eat Yourself Slim Diet* and says, "Yes?"

I can't say that I'm leaving because she'll ask, "When will you be back?"

She'll be looking through the book, flipping through the menus, seeing how many ounces she can eat. If I tell the truth, if I say never, she'll look up at me, peering up higher than usual, above the frameless edges of her reading glasses. She'll say, "A comedian. Maybe Johnny Carson will hire you to guest host. When will you be back?"

If I go without answering, the other ladies will watch me leave. When I get to where they think I can't hear them, when I get to the kitchen door, they'll put a pause in their meeting and talk about their children.

They'll say they were always the best parents they knew how to be. They'll say they gave their children everything and it was never enough. They'll say they hope their children will grow up and have children exactly like themselves. They'll be thinking about how their children hate them and how they hate their children back because they don't understand what it was they did wrong.

"It has nothing to do with you," I'll have to say, "It's me, it's me, all mine. There is no blame."

"Selfish," the mothers will say.

• • •

I'm here in the linen closet, doing my spring cleaning. I'm confessing right and left and Odessa knocks on the door. She knocks and then opens the door. She's carrying a plate with a sandwich and a glass of milk. Only Odessa would serve milk and a sandwich. My mother would give me a Tab with a twist of lemon. My father would make something like club soda with a little bit of syrup in it. He would use maple syrup and spend all afternoon telling me he'd invented something new, something better than other sodas because it had no chemicals, less sugar, and no caffeine. Odessa brings me a sandwich and a glass of milk and it looks like a television commercial. The bread is white, the sandwich cut perfectly in half. There are no finger marks on it, no indentations on the white bread where Odessa put her fingers while she was cutting. The glass is full except for an inch at the top. There are no spots in that inch. The milk looks white and thick, with small bubbles near the top. It looks cool and refreshing. Odessa hands me the plate. I look at her for a moment. She is perfect. I drink the milk and know that I will have a mustache. I look at Odessa and want to say, "I love you." I want to tell her how no one else would bring me a glass of milk. I want to tell her everything, but she starts talking. Odessa says, "Make sure you don't leave that plate in the closet. I don't want your mother finding it and thinking I've lost my mind. I don't want bugs in there. Bring it out and put it in the dishwasher. Don't stay in there all day or you'll lose your color." I nod and she closes the door.

I'm hiding and I'm eating a cream cheese and cucumber

sandwich and having my head examined. I'm in the neighborhood of my soul and getting worried. I'm trying not to hate myself so much, trying not to hate my body, my mind, the thoughts I think. I'm hiding in the linen closet having a sex change. I'm in here with a pad of paper writing things I've thought and then unthought. Thoughts that seemed like incest, like they shouldn't be allowed.

I'm trying to find some piece of myself that is truly me, a part that I would be willing to wear like a jewel around my neck. My foot. I love my foot. If I had to send a part of myself to represent myself in some other country, or in some other way, I would amputate my foot and send it wrapped in white tissue on a silk-embroidered cushion. I would send my foot because it is me, more me than I'm willing to let on. There are other parts that are also good—hands, eyes, mouth—but after a few months I might look at them and not see the truth. After a few years I might look at them and think of someone else. But my foot is mine, all mine, the real thing. There is no mistaking it. I look at it; I take off my sock and it screams my name.

I could go on for hours demonstrating how well I know myself through my foot, but I won't. It's embarrassing. The foot, my foot, that I wish to wear on a ribbon around my neck is an example of grace twisted and trapped. Chunks of bone and flesh conforming to the dictum: form follows function. It's a wonder I'm not a cripple.

I'm hiding in the linen closet, writing a declaration of independence. I'm in the closet, but the worst is over. There is hope, trapped inside my foot; inside my soul there is possibility. I'm looking at myself and slowly I'm falling in love. I've figured out what it takes to live forever. I'm in love and I'm free.

I want to throw the door open and hear an orchestra swell.

I want to run out to the Fat Club ladies and tell them, "Life can go on, I'm in love."

I'll stand in the living room, facing the sofa. I'll stand with my arms spread wide, the violins reaching their pitch. I'll be sweating and shaking, unsteady on my feet, my wonderful, loving, lovable feet. At the end of my proclamation my mother will let her glasses fall from her face and dangle from the cord around her neck.

"Miss Dramatic," she'll say. "Why weren't you an actress?"

The fat ladies will look at each other. They'll look at me and think of other declarations of love. They'll look and one will ask, "Who's the lucky man?"

There will be silence while they wait for a name, preferably the right kind of name. If I tell them it isn't a man, their silence will grow and they'll expect what they think is the worst. No one except my mother will have nerve enough to say, "A girl then?"

I'll be forced to tell them, "It's not like that." One of the ladies, the one the others think isn't so smart, will ask, "What's it like?"

I'll smile, the orchestra will swell, and I'll look at the four ladies sitting on the sofa, the sofa covered with something modern and green, something that vaguely resembles the turf on a putting green.

"It's like falling in love with life itself," I'll say.

My mother will look around the room. She'll look anywhere except at me.

"Are you all right?" she'll ask when I stop to catch my breath. "You look a little flushed." I'll be singing and dancing.

"I'm fine, I'm wonderful, I'm better than before. I'm in love."

I'll sing, and on the end note cymbals will crash and the sound will hold in the air for a minute. And then swinging a top hat and cane, I'll dance away. I'll dance down the hall toward the den.

I want to find my father in the den, the family room, watching tennis on television. I want to catch him in the middle of a set and say that I can't wait for a break. I want to tell him, "Life must go on."

He'll say that it's match point. He'll say that he's been trying to tell me that all along.

"But why didn't you tell me what it really means?"

"It seems pretty obvious."

And then I'll tell him, "I'm in love." There will be a pause. Someone will have the advantage. My feet will go *clickety-clack* over the parquet floor and he'll say, "Yes, you sound very happy. You sound like you're not quite yourself."

"I'm more myself than I've ever been."

I want to find Odessa. "Life will go on," I'll tell her. "I'm in love." I'll take her by the hand and we'll dance in circles around the recreation room. We'll dance until we're dizzy and Odessa will ask me, "Are you all right?"

I'll only be able to mumble "Ummmm, hummm," because my grin will have set like cement. I'm hiding in the linen closet writing love letters to myself.

Acknowledgments

"Girl Jesus on the Inbound Subway" © 2011 by Matthue Roth. First publication, original to this anthology. Printed by permission of the author.

"The Young Stalker's Handbook" © 2011 by Sarah Rees Brennan. First publication, original to this anthology. Printed by permission of the author.

"Lost in Translation" © 2011 by Michael Lowenthal. Originally published in a slightly different form in *Queer 13: Lesbian and Gay Writers Recall Seventh Grade*, ed. Clifford Chase (New York: Rob Weisbach Books, 1998). Reprinted by permission of the author.

"Confessions and Chocolate Brains" © 2011 by Jennifer R. Hubbard. First publication, original to this anthology. Printed by permission of the author.

"Iris and Jim" © 2006 by Sherry Shahan. Originally published in *ZY22YUA*, 2006. Reprinted by permission of the author.

"The Last Will and Testament of Evan Todd" © 2011 by Saundra Mitchell. First publication, original to this anthology. Printed by permission of the author.

"Headgear Girl" © 2011 by Heidi R. Kling. First publication, original to this anthology. Printed by permission of the author.

"Never Have I Ever" © 2011 by Courtney Gillette. First publication, original to this anthology. Printed by permission of the author.

"Dirty Talk" © 2011 by Gary Soto. First publication, original to this anthology. Printed by permission of BookStop Literary Agency, LLC, and the author.

"Abstinence Makes the Heart Grow Fonder" © 2011 by Jennifer Knight. First publication, original to this anthology. Printed by permission of the author.

"Somebody's Daughter" © 2011 by Shelley Stoehr. First publication, original to this anthology. Printed by permission of the author.

"Margo Ferkel's Two-Hour Blitz of Badness" © 2011 by Jill Wolfson. First publication, original to this anthology. Printed by permission of BookStop Literary Agency, LLC, and the author.

"Nude Descending a Staircase" © 2011 by Jennifer Finney Boylan. Originally published in a slightly different form in *She's Not There: A Life in Two Genders* (New York: Broadway, 2003). Printed by permission of the author.

"Scrambled Eggs" © 2011 by Liz Miles. First publication, original to this anthology. Printed by permission of the author.

"Rules for Love and Death" © 2002 by Ellen Wittlinger. First published in *One Hot Second: Stories About Desire*, ed. Cathy Young (New York: Knopf, 2002). Printed by permission of the author.

"Cool Cats and Melted Kisses" © 2011 by Luisa Plaja. First publication, original to this anthology. Printed by permission of the author.

"Orange Tootsie Pop" © 2011 by Cecil Castellucci. First publication, original to this anthology. Printed by permission of the author.

"Team Men" © 2002 by Emma Donoghue. Originally published in *One Hot Second: Stories About Desire*, ed. Cathy Young (New York: Knopf, 2002). Printed by permission of the author.

"Pencils" © 2011 by Sara Wilkinson. First publication, original to this anthology. Printed by permission of the author.

"Yours Truly" by A. M. Homes. Originally published in *The Safety of Objects* by Amy M. Homes (New York: W. W. Norton & Company, 1990). Reprinted by permission of the publisher.

Author Biographies

Jennifer Finney Boylan is the author of numerous books, including the young adult series, "Falcon Quinn" as well as the bestselling memoir, *She's Not There*. She is a regular contributor to the *New York Times*, as well as an ongoing contributor to *Conde Nast Traveller* magazine. As well as being professor of English at Colby College in Waterville, Maine, Jenny is the Hoyer-Updike Distinguished Writer at Ursinus College in Collegeville, Pennsylvania. She serves on the judging committee of the Fulbright Scholars, administered by the U.S. Department of State. Jenny has been a frequent guest on a number of national television and radio programs, including *The Oprah Winfrey Show*. She lives in Belgrade Lakes, Maine, with her family.
www.jenniferboylan.net

Sarah Rees Brennan was born and raised by the sea in Ireland, where her teachers valiantly tried to make her fluent in Irish (she wants you to know it's not called Gaelic), but she chose to read books under her desk in class instead. After college she lived briefly in New York and somehow survived in spite of her habit of hitching lifts in fire engines. Since then she has returned to Ireland to write. Her Irish is still woeful, but she feels the books under the desk were worth it. *The*

Demon's Lexicon, her first novel, received three starred reviews and was a *Kirkus'* Best Books, an ALA Top Ten Best Books, and a Best British Fantasy Book. It was followed by *The Demon's Covenant*, and the trilogy will conclude with *The Demon's Surrender*.
www.sarahreesbrennan.com

Cecil Castellucci is the author of novels and graphic novels for young adults. Her short stories have appeared in numerous anthologies. Recent books include a YA novel, *Rose Sees Red*, and picture book, *Grandma's Gloves*. In addition to writing books, she writes plays, makes movies and occasionally rocks out.
www.misscecil.com

Emma Donoghue (who despises sport in all forms) is the least qualified person in the world to write a story about footie, but when she had a notion to retell the Bible story of David, Jonathan, and Saul it seemed to her as if a boys' soccer team (all hormones and bruises) would be the perfect setting. So she got a good friend to help her with the technical details for "Team Men," and apologizes for any errors. Born and raised in Dublin, Emma started coming out of the closet at fourteen, the scariest truth-or-dare period of her life. These days she lives in Canada with her girlfriend and their two small children, and is lucky enough to do nothing but write for a living. Her books of fiction include fairy tales (*Kissing the Witch*), historical novels (*Slammerkin*, *Life Mask* and *The Sealed Letter*), and contemporary ones (including *Stirfry*, *Hood* and *Landing*). Her bestselling novel *Room*, a horrifying tale told through the eyes of a five-year-old boy, was shortlisted for the Man Booker Prize and the Governor General's Awards.
www.emmadonoghue.com

Courtney Gillette is a writer, teacher, and lover of milkshakes. Her work has appeared in *Tom Tom Magazine*; *No, Dear*; *The Queerist*; and Spinner.com, among others, as well as the Lambda Award-winning anthology *The Full Spectrum: A New Generation of Writing About Gay, Lesbian, Bisexual, Transgender, Questioning and Other Identities*, edited by David Levithan and Billy Merrell. In 2009 she became a Literary Death Match Champion. Her most favorite thing in the world is Willie Mae Rock Camp for Girls, a non-profit organization whose mission is to teach and empower girls. She lives in Brooklyn, and rides a sweet blue bicycle.
courtneygillette.wordpress.com

A. M. Homes has received many awards for her writing, including Fellowships from the John Simon Guggenheim Foundation, the National Endowment for the Arts, NYFA, and The Cullman Center for Scholars and Writers at The New York Public Library, along with the Benjamin Franklin Award. She is the author of the novels, *This Book Will Save Your Life*, *Music for Torching*, *The End of Alice*, *In a Country of Mothers,* and *Jack*, as well as the short-story collections, *Things You Should Know* and *The Safety of Objects*, which was adapted into a film. She is also a Contributing Editor to *Vanity Fair, Bomb*, and *Blind Spot*. Homes was a writer/producer of the hit television show *The L Word* and wrote the television adaptation of her first novel, *Jack*, for Showtime.

Born in Washington, D.C., Homes now lives in New York City.
www.amhomesbooks.com

Jennifer R. Hubbard lives and writes near Philadelphia, Pennsylvania. She is a night person who believes that mornings are meant to be slept through, a chocolate lover, and a hiker. Her short fiction has appeared in literary magazines such as *Willow Review* and *North American Review*, and her short non-fiction has appeared in *AMC Outdoors*. Her first book was the contemporary YA novel *The Secret Year*. She blogs at writerjenn.livejournal.com. www.jenniferhubbard.com.

Heidi R. Kling is the author of *Sea*, a story of hope after tragedy set in the aftermath of the 2004 Indian Ocean tsunami, which was an IndieNext pick that sparked the popular #sealove campaign on Twitter. She contributed an essay to *A Visitor's Guide to Mystic Falls*, where she peers into the complicated relationship of the undead *Vampire Diaries* brothers. Getting paid to re-watch episodes of hot, shirtless bloodsuckers? Definitely a perk. She lives in Palo Alto, California, with her trauma-psychiatrist husband, two wildly entertaining children, and an old, tired dog. A former actress and children's theater director/playwright, she is writing a "*Romeo and Juliet* with magic" fantasy series, while remembering to be grateful, each and every day, that she didn't have to wear headgear to high school. heidirkling.com

Jennifer Knight has been an avid reader and writer since she was young, but never imagined herself as an author until her college days, when she stumbled upon an unfinished book idea amid her failed attempts at picking a major. That first idea was ultimately a bomb, but it got her going in the right direction—one that led to the publication of her debut novel, *Blood on the Moon*. Ever since, she has preferred to write for teens, claiming that they are the most enjoyable and challenging audience available—not to mention that it gives her the opportunity to relive (and redeem) her own disastrous high school experiences with good humor and a healthy smattering of sarcasm. Jennifer lives in South Florida with her family, where she spends every available moment lost in her head, dreaming about what comes next.

Michael Lowenthal grew up near Washington, D.C., where the truth often seems in short supply, and was inspired to tell stories as truthfully as possible, even—especially!—when the truth requires making things up. He is the author of the novels *Charity Girl*, *Avoidance*, and *The Same Embrace*, as well as stories and essays that have been widely anthologized. He lives in Boston, Massachusetts, and welcomes dares. www.MichaelLowenthal.com.

Liz Miles's first writing commission was to examine and report on the quality of the food, beer, and atmosphere in London pubs—a tough beginning! Since those heady, tortuous days, she has discovered yet more joy in writing a wide range of books, from comic-strip stories about cream-bun fights to biographies of Louis Pasteur and Will Smith. Her only distractions from writing and reading (books, blogs, and tweets) are watching movies and eating New York cheesecake.

Saundra Mitchell has been a phone psychic, a car salesperson, a denture-deliverer and a layout waxer. She has dodged trains, endured basic training, and hitchhiked from Montana to California. She teaches herself languages, raises children, and makes paper for fun. She is also a screenwriter for Fresh Films and the author of *Shadowed Summer* and *The Vespertine*. She always picks truth; dares are too easy. www.saundramitchell.com

Luisa Plaja was born in Glasgow and spent her earliest years in Sicily and her school years in the suburbs of London. As an Italian girl in England and an English girl in Italy, she was a mixed-up girl all over the place. She believes that school days might not be the happiest days of your life but they definitely have their uses as a writer's resource and well of fascinating characters and conflicts. She now lives in Devon and is the author of several novels for teenagers, including *Split by a Kiss*, *Swapped by a Kiss* and *Extreme Kissing*. www.luisaplaja.com

Matthue Roth is a novelist and performance poet. He has filmed for HBO's *Def Poetry Jam* and *Rock the Vote*, performed with Deepak Chopra and Carlos Santana, and completed three national tours with his own brand of poetry that isn't quite hip-hop and isn't quite storytelling, but still manages to be funny and sweet and brutal, and brutally honest.

Matthue's first novel was *Never Mind the Goldbergs*—a coming-of-age tale of a teenage Orthodox Jewish girl who stars on a television sitcom—and his second was the memoir *Yom Kippur a Go-Go*. He is also the author of the novels, *Candy in Action,* featuring supermodels who know kung fu, and *Losers*, which is about teenage Russian Jewish immigrants and geeks who want to take over the world. "Girl Jesus" is a sequel to *Losers*.

Matthue writes for the *Forward, Bitch Magazine*, and the *San Francisco Bay Guardian,* and he keeps a secret online journal. www.matthue.com.

Sherry Shahan has written over thirty books, including *Purple Daze*, a provocative free verse novel in which six high school students navigate war, riots, love, rock 'n' roll, school, and friendship. When she's not writing, she hits the dance floor, and even enters contests at dance conventions. She says, "It's fun to wear clothes that sparkle, and glue-on false eyelashes." Sherry lives in California in a funky beach town. www.sherryshahan.com

Gary Soto is a highly acclaimed poet, essayist, and fiction writer who was born and raised in Fresno, CA. His was a breakout voice in Latino literature. He is the author of many much-loved novels, short stories, plays, and poetry collections, including *Accidental Love*, *The Afterlife*, and the acclaimed *Baseball in April and Other Stories*. He has received numerous awards and recognition for his work, including the Literature Award from the Hispanic Heritage Foundation, PEN Center West Book Award, Author-Illustrator Civil Rights Award from the National Education Association, and a National Book Award nomination. www.garysoto.com.

Shelley Stoehr has authored four award-winning novels for young adults, including the popular, award-winning *Crosses*. Reviews have described her as "one of the new young breed of truth-telling, young-adult writers" (*The Horn Book*), and said her "narrative flow is a strength, as is her ability to capture the rhythms, attitudes, and feelings of teens" (*School Library Journal*). Shelley's weekly posting of short fiction can be found at outsidergirlswrite.blogspot.com. www.shelleystoehr.com.

Sara Wilkinson is new to fiction writing, but not new to teens. She was brought up on the cliffs of Cornwall but spent much of her life in London and Essex, teaching young people how to use mallets and chisels to attack pieces of wood rather than each other. She says that one of her happiest writing achievements was to feature both daughter and poodle in her book on how to carve bits of tree. As well as chiseling wood, she bashes stone into shapes and retreats into other worlds. She lives in Wivenhoe, Essex, with her partner and her two maladjusted dogs. Her daughter, along with a bad-tempered hedgehog, is her most frequent visitor.

Ellen Wittlinger began her writing career as a poet at the Iowa Writer's Workshop at University of Iowa while studying for her Master of Fine Arts degree. Her focus changed to writing for young adults after having two children and working as a children's librarian.

Ellen's first teen novel was *Lombardo's Law*. She has had numerous successes for teen readers since. Her Printz Honor Book, *Hard Love*, was highly acclaimed for its portrayal of an unlikely relationship based on "zines, alienation and dreams of escape." *Parrotfish* received praise for its humorous and authentic look at the person behind labels such as "gender dysphoria."
www.ellenwittlinger.com

Jill Wolfson worked as a journalist for newspapers and magazines around the country after attending Temple University. Her award-winning novels for young people include *What I Call Life; Home, and Other Big, Fat Lies*; and *Cold Hands, Warm Heart*. Jill has taught writing at several universities and is a long-time volunteer at a writing program for incarcerated youth. She lives in Santa Cruz, California, and has two college-aged children, Alex and Gwen.
www.jillwolfson.com